ROBINSON'S DREAM

MARK LAGES

authorHOUSE®

AuthorHouse™
1663 Liberty Drive
Bloomington, IN 47403
www.authorhouse.com
Phone: 1 (800) 839-8640

Published by AuthorHouse 01/23/2020

ISBN: 978-1-7283-4468-3 (sc)
ISBN: 978-1-7283-4469-0 (e)

Library of Congress Control Number: 2020901472

Print information available on the last page.

CHAPTER 1

A TOUGH DECISION

—•◦•—

I n one way or another, we all make plans. We envision our lives a certain way, and then we do what we think is necessary to make them that way. My wife and I have been relatively good at this. Her name is Martha, and my name is Robinson. Our last name is Cahill. My parents tagged me with the unusual name "Robinson" because they thought it would somehow help make me resourceful like Robinson Crusoe. Maroon me on a deserted island a thousand miles from civilization, and I would make do. I would find a way not just to survive but to lead a full and interesting life.

That's the personality my mom and dad foresaw for me. They planned for me to grow up fast and become a bright, resourceful, and admirable man, who would set healthy goals for himself and work like the devil to reach those goals. My dad was that kind of man. And my mom? She was the woman behind the man. That was how their generation operated. She watered and fertilized the soil, trimmed off the dead leaves, and sprayed for bugs, but Dad did all the growing, sprouting, and blooming. They were two very proud people, and they made a great team.

Martha and I have had a slightly different arrangement. We each have grown independently of the other. Neither of us is any more important than the other, yet we also tend to each other. We are individuals, yet we're also a team. And when it comes to making decisions, we're both part of the process, unlike my parents. Dad had the ultimate say, kind of like a dictator.

The story I'm about to tell you is about one of these decisions Martha and I had to make. It was a tough decision, and it was important that we didn't screw it up. This decision concerned our nineteen-year-old son, Robert, who had put us between a rock and that proverbial hard place. We had to decide in a hurry whether to get the police involved or to handle the situation on our own.

I'll explain in a moment, and I'll also ask what you would do if faced with the same circumstances. If you're anything at all like us, you won't find an obvious answer. Sometimes you can easily say, "Do it this way" or "Just do it that way," and the correct course of action is clear. But other times you just don't know what to do. You weigh everything and give it your best shot, but you're still baffled. That's the kind of situation we were facing with our son.

I should tell you a little about our boy. His name was Robert, and he was not an easy boy to raise. I think I realized we were going to have trouble with him when he was eight years old and got caught shoplifting a handful of candy bars from the grocery store on the way home from school. I explained to him that stealing was morally wrong and that if he got caught doing it again, he'd be punished. Instead of saying he would never steal again, he asked me what the exact punishment would be if he got caught. I think he wanted to know whether the benefits of stealing outweighed the risk. This question was troubling. He wasn't deterred from stealing—he was calculating whether it was worth it. For Robert, stealing wasn't a moral issue. It was economic, like he was calculating the potential profits of starting a business versus the associated risks.

I don't want to give you the impression that Robert was a young boor or a smart aleck, because he wasn't. In fact, he was always a very friendly and charming boy, and we received many compliments from other adults as to how polite and well behaved he was. It was one of the great mysteries of his personality that he could be such a fine and personable young man and at the same time be such an outright criminal. I hate to use the word *criminal* when I speak about my own son, but as I look back, that's exactly what he was. He'd smile at you, making you feel good about yourself. He'd make you feel at ease with him, and then at the same time, he'd have his hand in your back pocket, lifting your wallet like a common thief or a con man. Did this bother him at all? I don't really know. I talked to him about it, but the truth is that I didn't know whether he was being honest with me when he said he was sincerely trying to be better or whether he was just telling me what I wanted to hear to get me to leave him alone.

The situation was so strange. Neither Martha nor I was anything like Robert. Both of us had made it through our lives without lying to, stealing from, or twisting the arm of anyone. We were what you would call "good people." I was a writer, and Martha was an attorney. Whenever I told people I was a writer, they always asked, "What kind of books do you write?" It was a perfectly acceptable question, I suppose, but it was a difficult question to answer. I always wanted to be truthful, so I'd respond by saying something like, "I write novels that are about life." I usually got a weird look from the person, as if to say, *Doesn't every author write about life?* But I have yet to come up with a better description of my stories. They are not your run-of-the-mill mysteries, romance novels, crime dramas, action stories, or on-the-edge-of-your-seat disaster stuff. They are just about people. And they are pretty good, if I may say so myself. I actually have a small following of fans who like to read my books, and they think I'm very talented. But do I make any money at it? The truth is that I don't really make enough for a flea to live on, so I have a secondary job writing manuals for consumer products. When you buy an appliance and cuss like crazy at the indecipherable manual that came with it because it's nearly impossible to understand, I'm the guy to blame. I don't tell people what I do to earn a living when I first meet them. It tends to be a real conversation killer. That's why I just say I'm a writer, even though I know what their next question will be.

Martha is an attorney, true, but don't let that lead you to believe she is like most attorneys. Martha isn't out to sue and make tons of money. The firm she works for doesn't advertise on TV, promising million-dollar court awards. Martha is a contract specialist. It's her job to keep people out of court, to keep them from suing each other. We don't talk much about her work because, for the most part, it is rather dry and technical. I think the novels I write are a lot more interesting. But here's a funny aside. Martha has never read a single one of my books. Not ever. She says she spends so much time reading contracts all day that reading anything during her spare time isn't even slightly enticing. We talk about my stories often. She just doesn't read them.

Anyway, what I wanted to say is that we are decent people. We obey laws, behave ourselves, and stay out of trouble. We both work hard at our jobs and have always tried to set a good example for our son. Martha likes to refer to herself as a Girl Scout, which I guess would make me her Boy Scout—always helpful to others, always dedicated to doing the right things, always as honest as the day is long. So imagine how we felt about our son and the way he was behaving. We loved him like all parents love their children, but it was so painful to see how he was turning out. Why Robert? And why us? Martha and I asked these questions over and over, but there weren't any satisfactory answers. Had we done something wrong as parents? If we did, we had no idea what it was.

The situation I want to tell you about started when Martha decided to throw one of her dinner parties. She invited her boss and his wife as well as a couple of her friends from work along with their better halves. That made eight of us. Our dinner table seats ten people, so there was room for two more. Martha then had what turned out to be a really awful idea: to invite Robert and his girlfriend to join the rest of us. Robert was still living in our house at the time, and Martha thought it would be nice to include him and his girlfriend, treating them like adults.

"They're always hanging around with other kids," Martha said to me. "It would be good for them to join us, to sit down and socialize with some more mature people."

I saw the logic in this, and I agreed that it was an excellent idea. So Martha asked Robert if he wanted to join us, and he said yes. Now we had ten at the table.

Immediately following the dinner, Martha and I agreed that it had been a big success. We thought everyone had a great time, and nothing had gotten out of hand. Robert and his girlfriend looked like they fit right in. They dressed nicely and behaved themselves, acting like adults. The dinner was so promising, and I told Martha how impressed I was that our son seemed to be growing up. I mean, the boy was always polite, but now he seemed even more personable and mature.

Martha's boss's name was Jeremy Whitehouse. He did most of the talking during the dinner, which was appropriate since he was the boss and the senior member of our group. Jeremy was in an especially good mood that night. He talked about how nice our house was, and then he went on about the recent trip he and his wife had taken to Costa Rica. Then he talked a lot about work and mentioned what a great job my wife had been doing for his firm. "Everyone at our firm has to pull his or her own weight," he said. "But your wife is very special. I don't know what we'd do without her." He said this after his third glass of wine, and I figured he probably wouldn't have been so complimentary without the wine to loosen him up.

Then after his fourth glass of wine, he began talking about his coin collection. It was a collection he said he'd been working on since he was a small boy. He'd been buying, selling, and trading coins for nearly his entire life and had no idea what the collection was worth. He kept it in several safe deposit boxes at his bank, but he had brought the collection home to have an appraiser come over to the house and determine its current value.

"The appraiser is coming out this week," he said. "Then back to the bank it all goes. Our insurance company is requiring the appraisal. It's so they have an idea of how much they're saving if and when we ever turn in a claim and they turn it down." Everyone laughed at this.

I was so proud of Robert that evening. I was even proud of his girlfriend. They were very cordial to our guests, and they seemed to enjoy themselves. Maybe they were growing up. Maybe they weren't going to be kids forever. It's funny, isn't it? I was so happy that night and so encouraged. I asked myself later if it was true what some people said, that you couldn't trust anybody any further than you could throw him or her. I always cringed when I heard people say that. It was too cynical, and it wasn't really true. For example, I have always been able to trust my Martha. And I could always trust my parents. And I could even trust my brother, Ted, who was kind of a jerk. But Robert? My own flesh and blood? Sad to say, it turned out that my son would be a completely different story.

I learned about the burglary four nights after our dinner party. Martha came home from work and told us what had happened while we were eating. Robert was there, and he acted like he couldn't have cared less. I knew what he was thinking, as in, what did anyone care if some rich attorney had lost his precious coin collection? I liked Martha's boss, so I felt bad for the guy. I knew the collection meant a lot to him, not just in terms of its value but in terms of its sentimental meaning. Seriously, the poor guy had been collecting these coins his entire life, ever since he was a kid. Then in one fell swoop, just like that, they were gone, stolen, robbed from him by some asshole crook, who probably didn't even appreciate them, someone who would probably sell them for pennies on the dollar. To do what? To support a drug habit? To pay off some gambling debt? Who knew?

I don't ordinarily use cuss words, but my use of the word *asshole* to describe the thief was deliberate and appropriate. I truly don't like people who steal. They really bother me. I have had people steal from me, and I know what it's like. It's an awful experience. I remember in the eighties, when it was popular to steal radios from cars, someone broke into *my* car to take its radio. It was a very good radio. I had paid quite a bit for it, but the cost to repair the shattered window of my car and the damage done to the dashboard was surely greater than the cost of the radio itself. And how much did the thieves get for the radio when they sold it? Probably next to nothing. Maybe a couple of hundred dollars. It was a joke. I had to leave my car at the dealership for over a week for repairs, and I had to rent a car in the meantime. All that time and money wasted for a couple hundred dollars. As long as I am alive, I will never understand the mind-set of the thief. And yes, they are assholes.

Anyway, the day after Jeremy told Martha about the theft, she was in Robert's room, collecting his dirty clothes so she could do the laundry. Yes, she did Robert's laundry, even though I asked her not to and told her to make him wash his clothes himself. So yes, Robert was a little spoiled, but I don't think this accounted for what Martha found in Robert's room. She had opened his closet, where he often threw dirty clothes, and noticed a blanket that belonged on his bed. It was bunched up on the shelf over the hanging clothes. She thought it was odd and had no idea why the blanket was there. She pulled it down to put it back on the bed where it belonged, revealing a stash of wooden cases she didn't recognize. She told me her heart jumped.

She suddenly knew who the cases belonged to and what was in them. It was Jeremy's coin collection! She pulled one of the cases down and opened one of its drawers. In the drawer was an assortment of old and ostensibly valuable coins. Robert was the thief! Her own son. Her own flesh and blood. Martha put the case back up with the others and replaced the blanket where she had found it.

When Martha told me about what she had found in Robert's room, she was crying. I think more than anything, she was hurt, but she was also afraid. I was truly surprised. I didn't think Robert would do such a thing, even though I also knew this was exactly the sort of thing he *would* do.

I tried to calm my wife down because it made me feel bad to see her so upset. Then she spoke through her tears.

"Do you want to see them?" Martha asked.

"No," I said. "I don't need to see. I believe you."

"I can't believe he would do this to me."

"And to me."

"Yes, of course, to you too."

"We need to figure out what to do," I said.

"Oh God," Martha said, and she started crying again. "What *are* we going to do?"

"This time he's gone too far."

"Agreed."

"This is no handful of candy bars from a grocery store. This is a major act of theft."

"It's serious."

"I hate to say it, but we should probably call the police," I said. It was hard to believe I had said this, but I did.

"The police?"

"This is a crime."

"But Robert is our son."

"He's our son, but he also needs to learn a lesson, and he's not going to learn anything if we cover up for him and pretend like nothing happened."

"Jesus, Robinson, they'll put him in jail."

"Which is exactly where he belongs."

"There must be something else we can do."

"Like what?"

"Like make him return the coins to Jeremy."

I could hear the wheels in Martha's head spinning. Anything would be better than involving the police. "And we say what? That he was just borrowing the coins for a day or two?" I asked sarcastically.

"Maybe he could return them anonymously. That could be done somehow."

"And how would he learn from that?" I asked.

"We could punish him."

"Punish him how? He's not a little boy anymore. Christ, Martha, he's a grown man. It's not like we can take one of his favorite toys away or keep him from watching cartoons on the TV for a week."

"But he's only nineteen."

I thought about this and said, "I'm so fucking mad at him."

"I am too, but I don't want him to go to jail."

"How else is he going to learn?"

"He'll have a record."

"He deserves to have a record."

"Oh God," Martha said, and she started to cry again. "What is happening?"

"Whatever we do, we're going to have to act fast," I said. "We need to do what we decide to do before he sells the coins, before he gets rid of them. If we don't act right away, he'll just deny ever having them."

Martha stopped crying and looked at me. I knew she agreed with me about acting fast, but she still didn't know what we were going to do. And neither did I. "What do you think of us calling Dr. Gates?" she asked.

"To do what?"

"To get his opinion."

"I guess that's an idea," I said.

"He *knows* Robert. Maybe he even knows him better than we do. He'll know the right thing to do for Robert's sake."

"He might."

"I'm going to call him now."

Martha picked up her phone and called Dr. Gates. The doctor was Robert's psychiatrist. We had been taking Robert to see Dr. Gates for the past three years, hoping he could help Robert. We thought the doctor had made a lot of progress with their sessions since Robert hadn't been in any kind of trouble recently. He seemed to be growing up. He seemed to be more aware of the feelings of others. And he seemed to be lying to us less often. Or so it all seemed.

And it suddenly struck me like a brick to my forehead that we were now calling a man for advice to whom we had paid a small fortune and trusted to make our son a better person, a man who had totally failed to do his job. Seriously, why would we want this man's advice? Did he even know what he was doing? Robert was possibly worse now than he ever had been.

8

Anyway, this was what I was thinking when he took our call. Martha talked to him, not me. That was fine. I wanted him to hear about what Robert had done, and I wanted Martha to put him on the spot. Martha asked the doctor, "What do you think we should do?"

"Put him on speaker," I said. "I want to hear what he has to say."

Martha put the doctor on speaker.

"This all surprises me," the doctor said.

"How do you think we feel?" I asked.

"Not so great, I'm sure."

"I thought you told us that you were making progress with Robert," Martha said.

"I thought I was."

"Obviously, you thought wrong," I said. "Now we have a major problem on our hands. You haven't done anything. And what have we been paying you for?"

"It doesn't do us any good to point fingers," Martha said. "We need to figure out what to do."

"Yes, yes," the doctor said.

"Then what the hell do we do?" I asked.

"What are *your* thoughts?" the doctor asked. This was clever, putting the ball back in our court.

"The way we see it, we can do one of two things," Martha said. "We can call the police, or we can try to handle this ourselves."

"Ah, the police," the doctor said.

"Bad idea?" Martha asked. I think she was hoping he would say yes.

Now the doctor did what he was so good at. He talked and talked, basically saying nothing. He said, "Well, the police are one way for you to go. Of course, Robert will probably face a trial and some jail time. There's no telling how long he'll be locked up in jail, since this is his first offense. But your boss might ask the DA to go easy on him. I don't know him, and I don't know how angry he is. But I can tell you that if I was your boss, I would be pretty upset. But some people can be surprisingly forgiving. Who knows? Maybe your boss will be one of those people and encourage the DA to go easy on Robert, and maybe no jail time will result at all. If you do go the police, you'll probably want to get a good criminal defense lawyer to protect Robert's rights. Although that is kind of weird, isn't it?

9

You'd be turning him over to the justice system and then paying someone to defend him from it. Of course, your second alternative is to handle this on your own.

"I assume you'll have to figure out a way to return the coin collection to your boss without him knowing that it was Robert who took it. You'd be kind of skirting outside of the law, and Robert might not learn much from it. He might think his mommy and daddy are always going to save him from trouble whenever he misbehaves. On the other hand, jail is a horrific place. I've seen some good kids ruined by jail time. Not to mention the fact that jails are not safe. Your son could be hurt. And your son will also have a criminal record. Yet he *will* learn a lesson. He will probably think long and hard before he steals again. Then again, he might learn nothing at all and just hate you for calling the police on him. No telling exactly how Robert will react. If there's one thing I've learned about Robert over the years, it's that he can be unpredictable."

The doctor stopped talking, and I looked at Martha. Then I said to the doctor, "You haven't told us anything we don't already know. And somehow you've been able to talk quite a long time without giving us a single word of advice."

The doctor thought about this and said, "My advice is that you do what you think is right."

"In other words, you *have* no advice. Sorry if we bothered you," I said. I reached over and ended the call on Martha's phone.

"You just hung up on him," she said.

"I did," I said. "I can't believe we've been wasting money on that guy. And for how many years have we been writing that idiot checks?"

So, what did we decide to do? That is the question, isn't it? What would you have done if it was your son and you were in our shoes? We decided not to do anything that night. We wanted to sleep on the matter and choose our course of action when we woke up in the morning.

That night, as soon as my head hit the pillow, I fell sound asleep. I was exhausted. I was tired of thinking about Robert and being awake. For a while I slept calmly, and then after a few hours I began to fidget and sweat, and then I began to dream.

I was at home in this dream. It was late morning, and I was seated at my desk, writing a short story on my computer. Martha was at work, and

I'm not sure where Robert was, but he was also out. I had the house to myself, and I had turned my radio on to a classic station. The volume was down low. The station was playing a repetitive baroque string piece, but I wasn't sure who the composer was.

I heard a knocking sound, and I stopped my writing. Then I heard it again, louder this time. Someone was knocking on the front door, and I thought it was odd that he or she wasn't using the doorbell. We had a perfectly good doorbell. The knocking grew louder and more agitated, and I stood to answer the front door. Now it sounded like someone was pounding on the wood with all his or her might harder and harder, growing increasingly impatient.

"I'm coming, I'm coming," I said. "Just hold onto your horses. What in the hell?"

I walked to the front door and twisted the doorknob to pull the door open. Standing on the porch were two men. One man was a tall, fat Asian guy, bald and nicely dressed in a suit and tie. The other man was a shorter Hispanic fellow, who wore his long black hair in a ponytail. He was also dressed in a suit and tie. I'd guess both men were in their forties, and to tell you the truth, they were a little scary looking. I had no idea who they were or what they wanted.

Chapter 2

Search Warrant

———•◦•———

"Can I help you?" I asked.

"Are you Robinson Cahill?" the man with the ponytail asked.

"I am," I said.

"Do you have a wife named Martha?"

"Yes, I do."

"And a son named Robert?"

"Yes, and who are you?"

"Name is Rudy Gonzales. This is my partner, Eddie Yang. We're policemen. Can we come in?"

"Policemen?"

"We're detectives."

"Can I see your badges?" I don't know why I asked this. It just seemed like the right thing to ask.

"Badges?"

"You know, your policeman badges."

"Jesus," Rudy said. Then to Eddie he said, "Get out your badge." Both men reached into their pockets, and they pulled out badges and ID cards. "Satisfied?" Rudy asked me.

"I guess so."

"Now can we come in?"

"What's this all about anyway?"

"We'd like to tell you inside. Don't want to alarm your neighbors, you know. And we think you'll appreciate us keeping this matter private."

"Then come in," I said. I had no idea what matter the guy was talking about, but I couldn't see the harm in letting a couple of legitimate cops into the house. They stepped in, and Eddie closed the door.

"Nice house," Rudy said, looking around.

"Thanks," I said.

"Must've set you back a few bucks."

"We like living here."

"You're a writer?"

"I am," I said.

"Must have to sell a lot of books to afford a place like this."

"My wife is an attorney."

"Oh?" Rudy said. Then he turned and looked at Eddie. "The wife's an attorney," he said to him.

Eddie laughed.

"Where's the kid's room?"

"You mean Robert's room?"

"Do you have any other kids?"

"No," I said. "Just Robert."

"Can you take us to his room?"

"I suppose so. But you still haven't told me what's going on. Why do you want to see Robert's room?"

"We got a tip."

"A tip?"

"From a reliable source. The tip came in this morning. I took the call myself, and the caller was pretty specific. We're looking for something specific. That's what police work is all about. It's about specifics."

"I see," I said.

I led the detectives to Robert's bedroom. They stepped in and looked around, and Rudy asked, "Is that your boy's closet?"

"It is."

"Mind if we poke around?"

"Listen," I said. "Don't you need a search warrant to be doing this?"

"I thought you were okay with us looking around."

"I am, but don't you need a search warrant? Isn't that the way this works?"

Rudy looked over at Eddie and said, "Show him the search warrant."

"Sure," Eddie said. He reached into his pocket and removed a folded piece of paper. He flashed it in front of me and then put it back in his pocket.

"That didn't look a warrant," I said.

"Oh?" Rudy said. "What did it look like?"

"It looked like a take-out menu for a Chinese restaurant."

"A take-out menu?"

The two detectives laughed. Eddie looked at Rudy and said, "I don't think he trusts us."

"Are you calling us liars?" Rudy asked me.

"No, no, that's not what I meant."

"That's what it sounded like."

"I'm just telling you what I saw."

"And I'm telling you that you saw a search warrant. Signed by the judge this morning."

"Okay," I said.

"Do you have any coffee?" Rudy asked.

"Not made."

"I could really go for a cup of coffee." Rudy looked at Eddie and asked, "How about you?"

"Coffee sounds great," Eddie said.

"Do you happen to have a French press?"

"I don't," I said. "We have a regular drip coffee maker. But it makes decent coffee."

"Do you grind your own beans?"

"No, we buy them already ground."

"Which ground beans do you buy?"

"I don't know. My wife buys the coffee."

"Jesus," Rudy said. "You're obviously not used to having cops in your house. But make what you got. I'm dying for some kind of coffee."

"Okay," I said.

Rudy and Eddie put on latex gloves, and they opened Robert's closet doors. Rudy grabbed a chair, and he placed the chair in front of the closet. "Mind if I use this to stand on?" he asked. "You know, so we can reach the stuff on the top shelf?"

"Be my guest."

"Well?"

"Well what?" I asked.

"How about that coffee?"

"I'll be right back," I said, and I left the room. I went to the kitchen to make the coffee. I then grabbed my cell phone and called Martha's office. I got the receptionist, who told me Martha was in an important meeting and couldn't be interrupted. I asked her to have Martha call me as soon as she was done with the meeting. I called Robert, and his phone went straight to voice mail. I heard Rudy calling for me from down the hall.

"Is that coffee ready?" he asked.

"It's about done," I said. When the pot was full, I poured two cups and took them to Robert's room. "Cream or sugar?" I asked.

"Black is fine for us."

"What the hell?" I suddenly said. I couldn't believe my eyes. I looked around, and the room was crowded wall to wall with junk. Well, not exactly junk. Actually, there was some very valuable stuff. There were wide-screen TVs, computers, printers, cell phones, stereos, and speakers, all of them still packaged in their cardboard boxes. There was also a stack of car radios and a grocery bag full of candy bars.

Rudy stuck his hand into the bag of candy bars and said, "There must be over a hundred in here." He pulled out a Hershey bar and tore off the wrapper, taking a bite from it.

"Where did all this stuff come from?" I asked.

"The closet. Where do you think we found it? Under the bed? In the nightstand?"

"Aha!" Eddie said. He was standing on the chair, pulling an object out from the shelf. "I think this might be one of them."

"One of what?" I asked.

"Eureka!" Rudy said. "Specifics!"

"Specifics what?" I asked.

"Specifics as in specifically what we were looking for," he said. Then to Eddie he said, "Are there any more?"

"There's a few of them."

"Bring them all down. Let's see what we've got." Rudy set his half-eaten Hershey bar down on Robert's bed. Eddie handed the wood cases down to Rudy. There were five cases. They were now on the floor, and Rudy opened one up. "These must be worth a fortune."

"What are they?"

"Coins," Rudy said.

"Coins?"

"You know, those round and flat metal things you buy stuff with. Heads and tails. Drop it in the slot and pull on the handle. A penny saved is a penny earned."

"I know what a coin is."

"Some of them are worth a lot of money, and people collect them for fun. People like old Jeremy Whitehouse. Does the name ring a bell?"

"He's my wife's boss."

"He's been collecting coins since he was a little kid, and get a load of this. Someone ripped off his collection two days ago. And lo and behold, here it is, stashed in your son's bedroom closet."

"I knew nothing about this," I said.

"Oh, really?"

"Honest to God." The way I said this made it sound like I was lying, but I wasn't, or was I?

"Didn't you learn about the coins from your wife just last night? Didn't she find them here in this very closet, under a blanket? Didn't she tell you about them?"

I thought hard for a moment, and I could vaguely recall Martha saying something about them. But I couldn't remember knowing they were stolen by our son. And certainly not that they were hidden in his closet. I said, "You'd think if this had all happened like you're saying, I'd remember more about it."

"You're what we refer to as an accomplice."

"How could I be an accomplice to something I knew nothing about?"

"You didn't know about the collection?"

"Well, I knew about the collection."

"Didn't Jeremy go on and on about it during dinner at your house? Didn't he talk about bringing the collection home from the bank and getting it appraised?"

"Yes, he did. But how do you know that?"

"And wasn't Robert there?"

"He was there."

"Taking it all in like a sponge?"

"That doesn't prove he took the coins."

"Yet here they are, in his closet."

I tried to think of a reasonable explanation, and I said, "Maybe someone put them there."

"And why would someone do that?"

"I don't know," I said. "Maybe someone who was trying to get even with him."

"For what?"

"How would I know?"

"Did he have a lot of enemies?"

"All good men have enemies," a voice said. This deep man's voice was coming from across the street. Wait a minute, across the street? Where were we?

We were no longer in Robert's room. In my dream we were now standing on an unpaved street in old Dodge City, Kansas, and Matt Dillon was standing in front of a saloon, facing us. He was wearing a big cowboy hat, a leather gun belt, a red shirt and scarf, a vest, a clean pair of pants, and a dusty, old pair of cowboy boots. His marshal's badge was pinned to his vest, and it glistened in the sunlight. In his low voice, the marshal said, "I never met a good man in my life who didn't have his fair share of enemies."

"Yes," I said. "See?"

"That proves nothing," Rudy said.

"It proves that Robert could've been framed," I said.

"People are always trying to frame me," the marshal said. "For murders. For stealing. For horse thieving. You name it, and I've been accused of it."

"These cops are trying to frame my son."

"Are they?"

"I think they are."

"How much do you know about Robert?"

"I know everything. I'm his father. He's lived with me under the same roof for nineteen years. I ought to know if he's a thief or not."

"You ought to," the marshal said.

"What's that supposed to mean?"

"It means you ought to, but maybe you don't. Or maybe you *do* know your son, but you're not willing to believe what you know. What did Dr. Gates call it? Denial?"

"Dr. Gates?"

"Robert's psychiatrist."

"How did you know about him?"

"I'm the marshal in this town. There isn't much I don't know. Few things get past me. I make it my business to know what's going on."

"If you know so much, then tell me who tipped off the cops about the coins. If I know who turned Robert in, maybe I can tell you who's framing him."

"Should I tell him?" the marshal asked Rudy.

"Go ahead," Rudy said. "It's no skin off my nose."

"Brace yourself," the marshal said to me.

"Just tell me, for Christ's sake."

"It was your wife."

"Martha?" I said. "I don't believe that."

"Call and ask her," the marshal said.

"I tried calling her. She's in an important meeting, and she can't be interrupted."

"She's not in a meeting. She told the receptionist to tell you she was tied up so she wouldn't have to talk to you. She's deliberately avoiding you."

"I don't believe that."

"Believe what you want," the marshal said.

Now we were all suddenly back in Robert's room. The two detectives were sipping their coffee, and the marshal was going through the boxes on the floor. "I could use one of these big- screen TVs," he said.

"Then take one," Rudy said.

"And I wouldn't mind having a computer."

"Eddie and I are taking a couple of printers," Rudy said. "It's first-rate stuff. And Eddie has dibs on all the Three Musketeers in the paper bag, but if you see anything else that strikes your fancy, feel free to help yourself. We haven't taken an inventory yet."

"What's in the wooden cases?" the marshal asked. He had noticed the coin collection off to the side.

"Coins," Rudy said. "We can't give those away. We need to account for all of them. They're the reason we came out here in the first place, and their owner wants all of them returned. We hear the owner is a real anal guy."

"I have no interest in coins."

"What the heck is going on in here?" I asked. I couldn't believe what these guys were doing right in front of me, like I wasn't even there.

"Just finger-dipping a little icing off the cake," Rudy said. "No harm, no foul. No one will miss the things we're taking."

"But isn't it illegal?"

"Who's going to know?"

"Well for one, I know."

"And you're going to tell on us? I doubt it. You need us on your side, and you don't want to piss us off. That would be a real bad idea. Anyway, isn't there something you should be doing besides looking after us? What were you doing when we first got here?"

"I was in my study, writing a short story."

"Maybe you should go back to work on it."

"What page are you on?" the marshal asked.

"I was on page four."

"How many pages is it going to be?"

"I'm not sure yet."

"I always wanted to be a writer," the marshal said. "I've got some great stories I could tell about the Wild West. All of them are true. Stories you wouldn't believe. What's that they say, that truth is stranger than fiction?"

"It can be," I said.

"What's your story about?"

"Do you really want to know?" I asked.

"I do," the marshal said. "I think we all do." He then looked over at Rudy and Eddie and asked them, "How about you guys? Do you want to know what the story is about?"

"I'd like to know," Rudy said.

"Same here," Eddie said.

I looked at the three strange lawmen, trying to decide whether they were serious about this or whether they were just pulling my leg. "Come on," Rudy said. "Out with it. What's it about? Now you've made us all curious."

"Fine," I said. "I'll tell you. It's about my first job. Well, it's *based* on my first job. It isn't word-for-word true down to every detail, but it's more or less true to the events that occurred. I changed some minor things to make the story more interesting to the reader, but like I said, the story is basically true."

"And?"

"And it's about a boss I had when I was working in my early twenties. He wasn't the man who hired me, nor was he there when I first came aboard. He was brought in from another company to run our department about a month after I started my job. In the story I named this character Jim Caldwell. This company I had been working for was a commercial property management firm with about twenty employees. I was kind of a gopher, doing all the work no one else wanted to do. It was a summer job. I wasn't really serious about getting my foot in the door of the property management business. I just wanted to earn some extra cash for the summer while I was out of college. I had responded to an ad I found in the newspaper for a position that required no experience. Just a week or so after Mr. Caldwell took his place as our boss, he called us all into a staff meeting, and that's where the story begins."

"What was the meeting about?" the marshal asked. He was looking over one of the big-screen TV boxes and talking to me at the same time.

I told the marshal that the meeting had nothing to do with property management or any of our job responsibilities. Instead, it had to do with the company supply room. That was the whole subject of the meeting. And Mr. Caldwell said it was a very, very serious matter. "One or more of you may lose his or her job," he said.

CHAPTER 3

AH, BUT THE STRAWBERRIES

———•◉•———

M r. Caldwell was a jackass. That is the most succinct way I can think of to describe the man. I was much happier with my previous boss, Mr. Green, who was affable and a total joy to be around. When Mr. Green first hired me, I thought for sure I was going to get a kick out of my new summer job. Mr. Green was kind, energetic, and he liked people, a true team leader. By virtue of his great personality, he made his employees *want* to do a good job. Everyone he supervised loved working for him, and we all wanted to please him. And I think he wanted us to look forward to coming to work each day. Property management was not exactly a glamour-and-glitter sort of vocation, but Mr. Green made it fun.

But it was adios to Mr. Green and hello to Mr. Caldwell. I have no idea why Mr. Green was replaced. Some higher-up moron must have thought the employees were enjoying themselves too much, and work isn't supposed to be fun, right? Work is supposed to make you miserable, so I'm guessing this was it. Mr. Green was sent packing to who knew where, and Mr. Caldwell took his place as the new man in charge. Do you know who this guy reminded me of? Swear to God, he was the spitting image in every way of Humphrey Bogart playing that idiot Captain Philip Francis Queeg in *The Caine Mutiny*. "Ah, but the strawberries!" Have you seen that movie? If you have, then you know exactly what I'm talking about.

It didn't take long for Mr. Caldwell to call all hands on deck for a staff meeting, and regarding what? It was regarding the supply room. Apparently, Mr. Caldwell was convinced, or maybe even had some proof, that company employees were helping themselves to some of the supplies for personal use. In other words, they were stealing from the company, and Mr. Caldwell was going to put a stop to it. He told us he believed in running a tight ship and said, "Some heads may have to roll." He told us his intention was to call each and every one of us into his office to discuss the supply room and the theft he was sure was taking place.

"I'm going to give you the opportunity to come clean in private," he said. "You won't be embarrassed in front of your fellow workers, but you will be expected to tell me the truth. And keep in mind that *I happen know more than you think.*"

Well, that last line really had us all wondering just what it was Mr. Caldwell *did* know. Me? I was skeptical. I figured it was really more like a schoolteacher saying, "I have eyes in the back of my head," but a lot of the employees at the company were seriously concerned. What if he knew they had grabbed a ream of paper, a box of paper clips, or a handful of felt pens? What if he had proof? What if the old jackass did have eyes in the back of his head?

One by one Mr. Caldwell called us into his office for our private interrogations. I found the whole process fascinating, and I watched with great interest as my fellow workers ambled into the man's office and then came out. The first victim was Suzie McConnel, a sweet, young girl in her early twenties who had been working at the company for a couple of years. We weren't very close friends, but I was friendly with her, and sometimes we sat, ate, and talked during our lunch breaks. Like me, she brought her lunch with her and ate in her cubicle.

When she left Mr. Caldwell's office on the morning of her meeting, her eyes were red and bloodshot, and I figured the jackass had made her cry. I was empathetic but also nosy. I wanted to know exactly what the man had said to her to upset her to the point of tears, so I approached her during our lunch break to ask her what had happened.

"It was awful," she said.

"Why? What did he say?"

"It was what he knew."

"What did he know?"

"Everything," she said. She didn't seem to want to talk about it at first, but I pressed on.

"He knew everything about what?"

"Everything about the supply room. You know, the supplies. I'm embarrassed to tell you."

"I won't judge you," I said. "You can trust me. You can tell me what happened."

She looked at me and decided I was safe to talk to. She said, "I'm probably the cause of this whole mess."

"Mess?"

"The missing supplies."

"I didn't know any supplies were missing. And what makes them missing? Don't people just use them?"

"I've been taking things home with me."

"Like what, a few paper clips?"

"Like reams of copy paper, staples, brads, and a carton of presentation folders. And, yes, even some paper clips. I don't know. A bunch of stuff, I guess. But I don't know how he knew it was me."

"Why would you take office supplies?"

"For my boyfriend."

"He has a thing for office supplies?" I asked, smiling. I was trying to be humorous, but my little joke wasn't really all that funny.

"He's starting his own company, and he's short on capital. Every little bit helps, and I thought I could pitch in with some supplies. A little here and a little there. I didn't take a lot. Just what Tom needed."

"Tom is your boyfriend?"

"Yes," Suzie said.

"How did Mr. Caldwell know you were taking the supplies to Tom? Did someone rat you out?"

"I don't know."

"But he said he knew?"

"He said he was positive. What could I say? He was right, and I was guilty."

"Maybe he was just guessing."

"Oh, no. He knew."

"Maybe he was just pretending to know, counting on you to panic and admit to what you did. What exactly did he say to you?"

"He said there's been a shortage of supplies over the past several months. He said Mr. Green knew about it but that he didn't want to do anything. He said, 'I'm not going to let it continue, not under my watch.' Then he said he'd done a lot of investigating and that he now knew exactly

MARK LAGES

what I'd been doing. He told me there was no use denying it, that I would be better off telling the truth rather than lying. He said lying was the worst thing I could do. So, I told him everything. I admitted to all of it."

"Then what did he say?"

"He said it might cost me my job."

"He said he was going to fire you?"

"He said he was going to think about it, and that's when I started crying. You know, I can't lose this job. I can barely pay my bills *with* the job. And if he fires me, how would I get a new job? I'll have no references. What would Mr. Caldwell say to another employer when they called? Would he say, 'Yeah, she was great except she stole all our supplies'? Seriously, I'll be up a creek."

"I see what you mean," I said.

"I don't know what I'm going to do."

"Maybe he'll give you a second chance."

"Maybe he will. But the truth is that he just doesn't seem like the type to hand out second chances."

I tried to make Suzie feel better, but I don't know that I did much good. The poor girl was truly upset. And the story hardly ends there. There were other employees Mr. Caldwell raked over the coals, too. There was Walter Lindstrom, one of the associate managers. I also saw him coming out of Mr. Caldwell's office, and while his eyes weren't red from crying like Suzie's, he had a long face like his dog had just died. He didn't look at all happy.

Later that afternoon, I asked Walter how his meeting with Mr. Caldwell had gone, and he said, "Terrible."

"What happened?" I asked.

"He knew about the coffee."

"The coffee?"

"Listen," Walter said. "I know what I've been doing wasn't right. But I just got in a habit. I don't know why. I guess I wasn't thinking straight."

"What were you doing?"

"I've been stealing coffee from the supply room to use at home. My wife and I haven't had to buy coffee for years. Dumb is what it was. Dumb, dumb, dumb."

"How did Caldwell know?"

24

"That's the weird thing. I don't know how he knew. But trust me, he knew. Someone must've seen me doing it and told him about it."

"What exactly did he say?"

"He said now was the time to come clean. He said he knew what I'd been taking from the supply room and that fessing up was the right thing to do."

"But he didn't mention coffee specifically?"

"He didn't need to say anything about coffee. I'm telling you, he just knew. He knew, and I knew. We both knew exactly what he was talking about."

I was only a twenty-year-old kid, but I could see exactly what Mr. Caldwell had been doing. Why couldn't people who were years older than me see it? I didn't know. Maybe it was their guilt. Clearly, guilt makes some people susceptible to being tricked into making confessions. It was something the police probably knew all about.

The most surprising victim of Mr. Caldwell was Everette Hopkins, our senior property manager. Everette had been with the company for nine years. I'd guess he was in his fifties, surely an age when a man has plenty of gray hair and ought to know better than to steal from the supply room. But when he met with Mr. Caldwell, he wound up spilling his guts and admitting all his supply room crimes like a murder suspect coming clean before a judge. I knew about what had happened because he told all of us about his meeting with Mr. Caldwell.

Everette called us all into the conference room, and he confessed to us, trying to make things right, trying to set a good example, and trying to say to us, "I'm not perfect, but at least now I'm being honest. And so long as I live, I'll never steal from the supply room again." It was pathetic, seeing this senior, gray-haired marionette having his strings pulled by Mr. Caldwell. Dance, Everette, dance!

When my time came for Mr. Caldwell to interrogate me, I was ready for him. Although I didn't really need to be ready, since I had never taken anything from the supply room. He could try to make me feel guilty, but it wouldn't work.

"Now is the moment of truth," he said to me.

"About what?"

"About what you've been up to."

"And what do you think I've been up to?"

"I think we both know."

"Honestly," I said. "I don't know what you're talking about."

"The supply room," he said.

"I understand that some people here have been taking some things from the room, but I have nothing to fess up about. The only supplies I've taken were for work-related tasks for the company."

"I see," Mr. Caldwell said.

"I'm telling you the truth."

"I know more than you think I know."

"I don't know what you know. Honestly, I'm telling you the truth."

As if he hadn't heard a word I said, Mr. Caldwell said, "I know exactly what you've been up to. You may as well stand up and take responsibility for it."

"But I haven't been up to anything."

"Do you understand that your job is on the line?"

"I guess," I said. He was obviously trying to frighten me. "I didn't take anything from the supply room," I said, repeating myself. "I don't even have a use for anything that's in there. What am I going to do with any of that stuff? Start up my own property management company?"

Mr. Caldwell leaned back in his chair and drummed his fingers on his desk. "A smart guy, eh?" he said.

"I'm just trying to be honest with you."

"Okay then," Mr. Caldwell said. "I guess we're done here. You can leave."

"That's it?" I asked.

"That's it for now."

I stood up and left Mr. Caldwell's office. Suzie saw me leaving the office and took me aside in the hallway. "How did it go?" she asked.

"Okay, I guess."

"Did you admit to anything?"

"There wasn't anything to admit to."

"Oh," Suzie said. I think she was actually a little disappointed.

The next day Mr. Caldwell called me into his office again. He was busy working at his desk, writing something on a sheet of paper. He set his pen down and looked up at me. "Ah, yes, young Cahill," he said.

26

"Yes, sir?"

"So, you think you can pull the wool over my eyes."

"Sir?"

"I've been around, you know."

"I believe that," I said.

"Then you know that I know."

"I still don't understand what that means."

Mr. Caldwell was drumming his fingers on his desk again. "You're going to college, right?"

"Yes, I am."

"So, you're not an idiot."

"No, I don't think I am."

"So, if you're not an idiot, then I guess that makes you a liar." Mr. Caldwell was now staring at me, confident he'd made a point.

"I still don't get it," I said.

"Listen, everyone and their brother steals from the supply room," he said. "Don't you think I'm aware of that? What do you think the point of these meetings with you and your fellow employees has been? To discover if they've been stealing from the company? Hell, I already know that. They've been doing the same thing everyone here has been doing since this company first opened its doors. The point of the meetings hasn't been to discover things about our workers that I already know. It's been to see if they can be honest with me. And you know what? Everyone has come clean and told me the truth, every pathetic, sticky-fingered employee except you, Cahill. And I can't have someone working for me who waltzes in here and lies to my face. Thieves I can live with. Thieves are the lifeblood of the business world but not liars. There's nothing worse than a liar, especially a liar who has the audacity to lie to me. Now do you get it?"

"Sort of," I said.

"Then you'll understand why I'm firing you?"

"Firing me?"

"As of right now."

"You've got to be kidding." I knew he didn't care for me much, but I was surprised he'd actually have the nerve to fire me.

"Do I look like I'm kidding?"

I looked at Mr. Caldwell, and, no, he didn't look like he was kidding. The jackass was dead serious. He was giving me the boot.

"Is anyone else getting fired?" I asked.

"No, just you, kid."

So how about that? It was my first legitimate job with a legitimate company, and I'd been fired, first for not stealing, and second for telling the truth about it. It was crazy, and I was pretty darn angry about it. But little did I know Mr. Caldwell was doing me a huge favor. If he hadn't fired me, I would never have met Martha. I always wanted to go back to his office and thank him, maybe shake his hand. "It was the best thing you could've done for me," I would say.

I went home that evening and told my dad I'd been fired from my job, and he laughed. He then said, "Dumbbells like Mr. Caldwell are a dime a dozen. Don't let it bother you. It's water under the bridge, Son. Do you mind doing physical labor? What do you think of getting a little sun and exercise? An attorney friend of mine has been looking for a college kid your age to help him around the house and yard. He's got a lot of odd jobs he doesn't have time to do, and his wife is driving him crazy about them. He asked me a couple days ago if you'd be interested in doing some summer work, but I told him you had a job. But no longer, right? Do you want the guy's phone number? Give him a call, and he can probably put you to work right away. I'm sure he'll pay you the same as you were making. And he'll pay you in cash, no taxes taken out of your paycheck."

I said, "Why not?"

I got the man's phone number, and I called him up the next day. His name was Eric Weller, and he lived in a big house on a six-acre estate in the foothills. He had a whole list of things his wife wanted done to the property, and he said I could pick and choose which items I wanted to work on. He said, "I don't care if it all gets done or not, and I don't care which items you pick from this list. So long as progress is being made, my wife will leave me alone."

On my third day working for the Wellers, I discovered that they had a daughter. Her name, of course, was Martha, and she was a college student too but attending a different university. She would hang around and watch me work, bringing me lemonade, freshly squeezed from the lemons off their backyard tree. She also brought me cookies she had baked with her mom, and she talked. Man oh man, could this girl ever talk; there wasn't a subject on earth she didn't have an opinion on. But not in a bad way. I mean, she wasn't a know-it-all. She just happened to find life fascinating, and she was always trying to decipher the ins and outs of it. It became clear to me after about a week that Martha was very bright, probably even smarter than me, and I liked being around her. I was strongly attracted to her, not in an obsessive sexual way. It wasn't like that. I just really liked her a lot, and I wanted to get to know her better.

Finally, just a week before school was going to start, I got up the nerve to ask Martha out on a date. I invited her to come to the beach. I said I'd pick her up in the morning and have her home in the early evening, and she didn't even have to think about it. She immediately said yes to my proposition, and when I picked her up, she looked so different. She no longer looked like the daughter of a friend of my dad's. Instead, she looked like a girl who was going out with me on a date. I can't really explain the change, but there was one. Maybe it was her makeup or the way she was wearing her hair or the clothes she put on. Surely we would have a great time together. We might even kiss once or twice. Who knew? I tried to imagine exactly what it would be like to kiss her mouth, her soft lips, her wet teeth. There'd be lightning and thunder. The heavenly heavens would open up, and the earth would tremble.

I didn't kiss Martha on that date, but I did on our second time out when we went to the movies. Have you ever kissed someone and drifted off into another world? Do you know what I mean by this? The very first time I kissed Martha, I was transported. I imagined myself standing in a field of tall grass and wildflowers. It had just rained, and the air was fresh and cool. There was a rainbow painted in the sky. There were old oak trees here and there, and there was a brook that gurgled and sparkled in the sun.

I was knee deep in the flowers and grass, walking to nowhere in particular, when I felt a tap on my shoulder. I turned around and recognized the ancient man's face. So, who was he? It was the Greek philosopher Plato, a notebook in one hand and a ballpoint pen in the other. He looked at me and then wrote something down in the notebook. "Is it love?" he asked.

"Is what love?" I said.

"This thing you're feeling for Martha."

"We hardly know each other."

"But you've asked yourself the question, right? You've asked yourself, 'Is this love?'"

"I suppose I have."

"And what answer did you come up with?"

"I didn't have a good answer."

"I see."

"I like her a lot."

"That's obvious by the way you're kissing her."

"Ha, I suppose it is."

CHAPTER 4

SAYING GOOD NIGHT

———•———

I don't know if this is true, but I remember hearing that dreams that seem to last an hour really last only minutes and that dreams that last a few minutes occur in less time than the blink of an eye. Do you think this is true?

Plato laughed, and I asked him what was so funny. He said, "Love is amusing."

"Amusing?" I asked.

"The word *love*, I mean. It's got to be one of the most amusing words on earth."

"How so?" I asked. I wasn't disagreeing with him, but I wanted to hear his explanation.

"What do *you* love?"

"In what way?"

"Precisely. That's exactly what's so amusing. We throw the word *love* around like it has so much meaning, but we throw the word around so often that it almost has no meaning at all. I happen to love the movies, and I'm so glad you went to see one tonight with this girl. What do you think of the movies? We didn't have anything even approaching them in ancient Athens. We didn't have *Gone with the Wind* or *The Wizard of Oz* or *Star Wars*. I'm not even exaggerating when I say I absolutely *love* the movies. I love every little thing about them. I love that they're so much larger than life, that they can make you laugh, cry, or jump from your seat. I love that they cause you to fall head over heels in love, idolize, and adore. And I love the movie theaters. I love the buckets of hot buttered popcorn, great, big, ice-cold Cokes, and chewy Jujubes. I love it when the person you went to the movies with loved the movie you just saw as much as you did. How do you feel about the movies? Are we on the same page?"

"I guess so."

"What else do you love? You want to know what else I love? I love the first days of spring, how the air is so welcoming and warm, and there is the wonderful aroma of jasmine, gardenias, and citrus blossoms, and the buzzing of the honey bees, and all the hopping grasshoppers, fluttering butterflies, and cheerful birds singing up in the trees. And I love banana splits and hot fudge sundaes during the summer months. I love listening to Frank Sinatra on my record player, and I love my big La-Z-Boy chair, where I can kick off my shoes, recline, and read a good mystery while it's raining cats and dogs outside, flashing, and booming. Yes, and I love a little lightning and thunder with my rain. I love having nothing to do and looking up at airplanes on lazy afternoons as they fly high overhead with their pressurized cabins. I imagine all the people in them, traveling to who knows where, snoozing, reading magazines, and talking to their neighbors. I love hearing kids playing baseball in the park, and I love the satisfying sound of a wooden bat whacking the ball. And I love my two dogs, the way their toenails go clickety-clack on our hardwood floors, the way they devour their food, the way they romp around in the yard outside for hours on end, and how content and peaceful they are at the end of each day when they finally fall asleep. And I love all the sunsets, the way God ensured we would have a great red, yellow, and orange light show to mark the end of each day. I could go on and on. There are so many wonderful things in the world to love. Don't you agree?"

"I do," I said.

"Do you love your parents?"

"I do," I said.

"That's a different kind of love, isn't it?"

"I suppose so."

"The way you love your father is not the same way as you might love a hot fudge sundae."

"That's true."

"And you don't love your mother the same way you love watching a sunset."

"That's also true."

"Yet we use the same word."

"You're right, we do."

"Think of your parents," Plato said. "You love them more than anything, right? Think of how they've always made you feel safe and secure. Think of how they loved you. Think how proud they were of you and how it made them feel so good when you did good and how they patted you on the head to show their approval when you did something right. They have been your teachers, and you learned everything from them. You learned how to behave in the world, how to have manners, how to always do your best, and how to be brave. And you learned that bravery isn't being fearless but that it's dealing with fears. You learned how to ride a bicycle and catch a baseball and kick a soccer ball and throw a football. You learned how not to play with matches and how not to bully weaker kids and how not to cuss and how not to take things that don't belong to you. And you have always looked up to your parents. It was as if they knew it all; they knew everything there was to know about our mighty, whirling world. You have always adored them, because they loved you, cared so much about you, and gave you life. Am I striking a chord? Do you understand what I'm talking about?"

"I do," I said.

"They are not hot fudge sundaes."

"No, you're right."

"So, now that you're a little older, what will you do? My guess is that you'll do what we all do. You will seek out yet another kind of love. In your case, this will be a girlfriend, a mate, a wife. This will be a completely new kind of love, won't it?"

"Yes," I said.

"You'll be obsessed right up to your eyebrows. It will no longer be enough to love; now you'll want to fall *in* love. It might be with this girl you're kissing or maybe with someone else. But your love for this girl won't be anything at all like the love you feel for your parents. It will be an entirely new ball of wax. You'll put this girl on a pedestal. You'll want to be as close to her as possible, in every way imaginable. You'll want to touch her, to explore her body, and to make passionate love to her. Then you'll want to get married and share every square inch of your life with her. You'll promise your loyalty until the day you die. You'll agree to be faithful to her and to love and cherish her forever. They'll ring the church bells, announcing your love to the world. Is this what you see in your future?"

"I think so," I said.

"Not exactly the love you feel for your dad. Or for your mom. Or for a hot fudge sundae."

"No," I said.

"Yet it is called 'love.'"

"You're right."

"And there is more."

"There is?"

"Add in your good friends, neighbors, cousins, aunts, and uncles. Maybe there are a lot of them, or maybe there are just a handful. But you love some of them too, right? Isn't this fair to say?"

"I can think of a few good friends and relatives I can say I love," I said.

"It's another kind of love. It's nothing like the love you feel for your wife or for your parents or for a hot fudge sundae, right?"

"You're right," I said. "It's not like those."

"But it is still love?"

"Yes, I would call it 'love.'"

"Then comes one of the most important events of your life. You will learn that your wife is pregnant, that you're bringing a new life into the world. You'll soon have a daughter or son, and the baby will be yours to teach, care for, guide through the ins and outs of living. And most importantly, it will be yours to love. At first it will seem like a little alien, brand new to your household, gurgling, fidgeting, cooing, and sneezing at all hours of the night, tossing and turning in its crib. Then something remarkable will happen to you. You will fall madly in love with this little cricket of a human being, and there won't be anything in the world you wouldn't do for it. It will have you wrapped around its finger, and as the years pass, this love will grow in leaps and bounds. Then, as your child matures, so will you, and you'll come to realize how imperfect you are and how imperfect your child is. And now you'll be bedazzled by how important your love is. It becomes the one thing you must both hold onto like a lifeline. It is not the same kind of love you feel for your wife or parents or friends or a hot fudge sundae, is it? It is yet another kind of love."

"Yes," I said.

"Now do you see why I find love between people so amusing? It's absurd, isn't it? We use the same exact word to describe all these totally different kinds of affection. There is our love for things, for our parents, for our sweethearts, and for our friends and neighbors. And there is our deep love for our children. Love is virtually everywhere we go, but it's all so different. Saying that we love is like using the very same noun to put your finger on the concept of a candle, a dog, a cat, a lawnmower, a tree stump, a cumulus cloud, or a rocket. Am I right?"

"I suppose you are."

Plato was quiet for a moment, and then he asked, "Are you still kissing that girl?"

"Her name is Martha."

"Fine. Are you still kissing Martha?"

"I am," I said.

"How long do you think this kiss is going to last?"

"I have no idea."

"Keep it up. There's something else I want to talk to you about."

"I'm listening."

I was listening, but Martha was through kissing me, and she pulled her head back for air. "A girl has got to breathe," she said, laughing.

My eyes were now open. Plato had vanished, and so had the meadow we were standing in. The gurgling brook had run dry, and the wildflowers were gone.

Martha and I were now standing face-to-face in the soft yellow glow of the bug-repelling lightbulb that illuminated the front porch of Martha's house. The door swung open, and Martha's dad appeared in the doorway. "Ha, I thought I heard the two of you talking out here," he said. "How was the movie?"

"It was good," Martha said. "I was just about to come inside."

"We were just saying good night," I said.

"Ah, of course," her dad said. It was obvious we'd been kissing, but he pretended not to know.

"Good night," Martha said to me.

"Good night," I said.

"Call me tomorrow."

"I will," I said.

Martha then stepped into her house, and her father smiled at me as he shut the door. I walked back to my car. I climbed in and started up the engine, driving down the street toward my own home. When I arrived and came into the house, I found Mom and Dad in the family room, watching the TV. I said hi to them, and then I walked to the kitchen, pouring a tall glass of milk. I took the milk and a handful of chocolate chip cookies up to my room, turning on my FM radio and lying on my bed. I thought about Martha. I wasn't thinking about her and the movie but only about her. I was deep in thought, wondering, *Do I love her?*

How the heck would I know? I was only twenty, and what did I know about love?

All I'd ever learned about love I'd learned from watching and listening to my parents, and they must have loved each other a lot, right? Sure, they did. They got married, and they had me, the progeny of their affections. I was living and breathing proof that they couldn't keep their hands off each other. It had to be love. What else could it be?

As I lay on my back, listening to the radio, I thought of Mom and Dad. What was it ministers always said? 'To have and to hold? From this day forward, for better, for worse, for richer, for poorer? In sickness and in health? To love and to cherish, until death do us part'? I had always assumed that Mom and Dad had agreed to some lofty vows that were similar to this, if not exactly the same, word for word, and so far the old grim reaper hadn't done anyone part. Yes, my dear mom and dad, the two love birds, were quite alive, loving each other forever and ever.

It was funny. That evening my dad looked like a bum. He was barefoot, wearing a dirty white T-shirt and an old pair of sweatpants. Looking less bum like was my mom. She was wearing a cotton dress and fuzzy red slippers. My dad was seated at one end of the sofa, and mom was at the other. Mom was crocheting a little red sweater for my cousin's new baby, and dad was nursing a cold beer. It was late, and they were watching an episode of *Mary Hartman, Mary Hartman*. I could hear them laughing from all the way up the stairs. I never did understand that show, but Mom and Dad liked it. I grew curious, so I got up from my bed and stepped out of my room, leaving my milk and cookies behind and sneaking down to the base of the stairs to eavesdrop on my parents.

"Barbara and Ted Harris got home from their vacation yesterday," my mom said.

"Good for them," Dad replied.

"Two weeks in Peru."

"You don't say."

"Barbara told me they had the time of their lives."

"Barbara? She would have the time of her life watching paint dry."

"I don't know why you say that."

"Because the woman is an idiot."

"She's a friend of mine."

"She still thinks Nixon ended the war."

"He *did* end the war."

"If you think that, then—and I hate to say this—you're as dumb as she is. We didn't end the war. We lost the war, and Ho Chi Minh won. I don't know why Americans can't get that fact through their thick skulls."

"Anyway, I don't see what Vietnam has to do with traveling to Peru. I'd like to travel to Peru."

"To do what?"

"To see the ruins. They're supposed to be spectacular."

"If you really want to see them, check out a book from the library. There are lots of good photos."

"A picture of a place is hardly the same as being there in person."

"You're right. Photos are a lot better. You don't have to fly in a stuffy plane, get a passport or go through customs, stay in some crappy hotel, hike your tail off, or fight off all the local beggars. You can just sit and open a book in your living room."

"You're impossible."

"Just pragmatic."

"When is the last time we went anywhere?"

"You don't remember?" my dad asked. "We flew back east to see your niece get married. Oh, *that* was a lot of fun."

"Well, I had a good time."

"There were some highlights," Dad said sarcastically. "My favorite part of the trip was our hotel, sleeping with my head in a disgusting pillow that had been drooled on and coughed into by a thousand previous room occupants."

"They clean and change the pillowcases, you know."

"But they don't change the pillows."

"You liked the wedding, didn't you? You told me you always liked my niece."

"She's a sweet kid."

"Then see? You *do* like her."

"But that clown she married? Where in the world did she dig him up?"

"They met in college."

"Was he a janitor?"

"No, he was a philosophy major."

"I should've guessed by his hair."

There was a pause. Then Mom said, "You're way too critical of people."

"Just calling a spade a spade."

There was another pause. Mom and dad laughed at something on the TV. Then Mom said, "Do you think Robinson is going to be okay?"

"Why do you ask that?"

"He wants to be a writer."

"What's wrong with being a writer?"

"Aren't all writers miserable? Don't they lead miserable lives? Aren't they all unhappy? I don't want our son to be unhappy. I want him to enjoy his life."

"I guess some writers are miserable. Are you thinking of any in particular?"

"I don't read that much, and I don't know that many writers by name."

"So, you're just guessing?"

"It's just what I've heard. And it's the impression I get. And aren't a lot of them heavy drinkers? I would hate to see Robinson became an alcoholic."

Dad laughed at this and then said, "So, what's your plan? Do you think we should tell our boy not to write?"

"No, I don't think that."

"He loves his writing."

"I know he does."

"Would you prefer that he do something he doesn't love?"

"No, of course not."

"Then I still don't see what you're driving at."

"Maybe he could write, you know, more as a hobby, doing it in his spare time, but have a real nine-to-five job to support himself."

"A real job?"

"Something that pays well. And something that will keep his family chugging along without all that unhappiness hanging around him. A job working for a legitimate company. He could be working as a valued employee, as someone who's taking part in our society rather than as someone who's just writing about it. It seems to me that writing is kind of an outside-looking-in way of life. Wouldn't he be better off being in the mix, being a part of the world? You know, working hard and getting things done?"

"I never really thought of it that way."

"But do you understand?"

"I get what you're saying."

Mom and Dad thought for a moment, and then Mom said, "What do you think we did?"

"Did?" my dad asked.

"What did we do to make him want to become a writer?"

"I'm not sure we did anything."

"We must have done something."

"I think kids just turn out being what they turn out to be. Honestly, I don't think parents have as much to do with how their children turn out as they'd like to think."

"No?"

"You try to bake a cake. So you go to the grocery store and buy what you need. Then you line up all the ingredients. You spread them out, stir them up, and you put them all together exactly according to your recipe. You stick your pan in the oven and set the timer, but when the timer chimes, and you pull the pan out, voilà! It isn't a cake at all. It's a juicy hunk of beef Wellington or a Cobb salad or a baked Alaska, and you say, 'What the hell?' That's what I think that raising a child is like. You never know what you're going to get, even if you thought you knew."

"I never thought of it that way."

"Look at my sister's kids."

"What about them?"

"Born to the same parents and raised under the same roof, yet they're as different as night and day. Todd is a hippie, and Frank is a young businessman. Opposites, right? Who would've guessed? Certainly not my sister."

"I guess you're right."

Mom and Dad stopped talking again and watched the end of their show. This was the first time I realized they were concerned about me becoming a writer, and it made me wonder a little. Would I be miserable? Was writing really such a bad way to make a living? Would I become an alcoholic? I didn't feel that way now, but I suddenly wished I hadn't eavesdropped. These weren't things I needed to hear.

"I'm going to bed," Mom said.

"Good idea," Dad agreed.

"Are you coming with me, or are you going to stay up?"

"I'm coming with you."

"Lock all the doors before you come up."

"I will, but I don't know why we lock the doors every night. Honestly, there isn't really anything in this place that's worth stealing."

"You never know what thieves are thinking. Judy Ackerman's house was broken into last month, and they stole her husband's favorite blanket. It had a hundred holes in it, and the batting was coming out all over the place. That's all they took. They took it right off the couch. Ted was furious."

"Why on earth would they steal a blanket?"

"Maybe they needed one."

"That's just dumb. It's hard to believe someone would be dumb enough to risk going to jail just to steal a worn-out blanket."

"Like I said, you never know what thieves are thinking," Mom said. She was now at the foot of the stairs while Dad was locking the doors. I had already returned to my room.

I heard the stairs creaking as she made her way up. Then she was in the hallway. Her footfalls suddenly stopped outside my room, and she tapped on my door. "Are you still awake?" she asked. She was nearly whispering.

"I am," I said.

"Good night, dear."

"'Night, Mom."

She walked on. Dad came up the stairs, and after I heard him pass my room, I took off my clothes and climbed into bed. I was suddenly very sleepy, and I tumbled into the strangest dream as soon as my head hit my pillow.

In this dream, it was fifteen years into the future, and I was a married man. I was married to Martha. It was before we had Robert. We were childless, and we were vacationing in Peru. Mom and Dad's conversation about Peru must have triggered the dream, and it took me a while to get my bearings.

We were hiking in the mountains, headed toward the ruins. I'd never been to Peru before, so I have no idea how accurate my dream was regarding its depiction of the terrain. There were lots of cliffs and rocks and winding roads, and the place was as green as the wet side of a tropical island. It was raining lightly, and we were wearing plastic parkas to keep dry. There were twenty people in our group, and we were following a guide named Enrico, who talked to us as he walked. He was going on and on about the history of the ruins.

Right in front of Martha and me was a girl I had known from high school. She was no longer a girl. She was a woman now, and she was walking with her husband. I didn't recognize the husband, so she must have met him after graduating from high school. Her name was Gabriela Sachs, and I used to have quite a crush on her. It wasn't unusual for her to appear in my dreams now and then, and she was always very pretty, just as she had been back in school. Unlike Martha, she had long blonde hair and amazing blue eyes, but she wasn't your stereotypical dumb and self-absorbed blonde. She was as smart as a whip, articulate, and kind. I never did get up the nerve to ask her out on a date, so I didn't get to know her well. But I thought about her a lot, just the way a dumb boy would do.

"Fun, isn't it?" Gabriela said. She had turned around to talk to me.

"Yes," I agreed.

"And who are you?" Martha asked.

"Your husband used to have a crush on me."

"Oh, did he?" Martha glared at me.

"I didn't ask them to come," I said. "I don't know what they're doing here."

"We're here to see the ruins," Gabriela said.

"So are we."

CHAPTER 5

MACHU PICCHU

—•—

"Everyone, stop here," Enrico said. "This is the best overall view you'll have of the ruins. From here you can see it all. We're lucky today is a clear day. Everyone, please take a few steps forward. There's room here for all of you."

We were high on the mountain that overlooked the ruins, at the edge of a cliff. There was a guardrail around the flat dirt area to keep people from falling down to the rocks below. The view was spectacular. I'd never seen anything quite like it. There were a few wisps of clouds here and there, but like Enrico said, it was for all intents and purposes a clear day.

"Closest to us, at the base of the mountain, is Dionysus's Garden," Enrico said. "It was here that guests drank, ate, and danced day and night to music played by some of Greece's finest musicians. Imagine it in your mind's eye. Picture the famous statesmen, philosophers, artists, poets, and writers who reveled all hours of the day and night on vacation, rubbing elbows with the gods and each other in these lush Peruvian gardens, such a long way from home. And just past the gardens is The Heracles House, home away from home for the great Heracles, equipped with its own private gymnasium and sunning area. To the left of The Heracles House is the Plutus Complex, the forty-room guest tower where some of Greece's most illustrious of the illustrious were housed as guests. The two-thousand-plus-year-old guest book for the Plutus Complex, which has been restored and put on display in the lobby, reads like a who's who of ancient Greece and her allies. To the right of The Heracles House is the once-world-famous Priapus Ristorante, which served all the guests at Machu Picchu with culinary delights and delicacies shipped in from all over the world. Just behind the Priapus is the Ambrosia Bar & Grill for more casual dining. Beyond these structures is the Great Helios Park, where guests would sunbathe, write, and read. And beyond Helios Park are a number of other facilities, which include the famous Cerus Gymnasium, the Eros Museum of Sex and Love, and Zeus's Amphitheatre. All of these are open to the visiting public, and you'll be able to stroll at your leisure from one feature to the other once we hike down to the base of the mountain and enter the resort."

"Amazing, isn't it?" Gabriela said to me.

"It is," I said.

"Honestly," Martha said. "I think it's so interesting that the ancient Greeks discovered the Americas such a long time ago. You never read about this in any history books."

"I was thinking the same thing," Gabriela said.

"What I wouldn't give to go back in time and be here during Machu Picchu's glory days."

"Yes," Gabriela said. "Wouldn't that be amazing?"

I was glad to see Gabriela and Martha being civil. It could have been a problem having them in the same dream, but they seemed to be getting along.

We hiked down the mountain, and in no time, we were at the resort's entrance. Gabriela and Martha were now friends, and they wanted to go straight to the Eros Museum. This left me alone with Gabriela's husband, a man who was a few inches taller than me named Chet. We each ordered a glass of wine from a young male server in Dionysus's Garden and then sat at a granite bench and talked.

"So, what do you do for a living?" I asked.

"I'm a bank robber," Chet said.

"No," I said, laughing. "I mean, what do you really do?"

"I was serious. I rob banks for a living. Been at it for twelve years."

"And you've never been caught?"

"Not once."

I thought it was odd that Chet would tell me, a stranger, that he was a practicing bank robber, so I asked, "Do you usually tell people what you do for a living?"

"I have no problem with it."

"Aren't you afraid they'll blow the whistle on you? Call the police? Tell the banks?"

"I have nothing to be afraid of. The cops and the banks both know what I do for a living, but they haven't been able to figure out a way to stop me. It's all under control. I have a foolproof system."

"A system?"

"Yes, a system. You know, a method."

"Which is?"

"Which is confidential, my friend." Chet winked at me and smiled.

"I see," I said.

"I have a crew of five men. Even they don't know how it all works."

"How can that be?"

"Each man has his own specific responsibility. Each man does his job, completely unaware of what the other four men are doing. In fact, they don't even know each other. They're like little independent cogs in a machine. Only I know how the whole scheme works."

"But it works?"

"Like a charm. It's infallible."

"Interesting," I said.

"Impressive, isn't it?"

"I guess so."

"Like I said, I've been doing it for twelve years, and I make a good living at it. I'm not rich, because I'm not greedy. I'm very careful. I only steal what I need in order to live a comfortable life."

"Does it ever bother you?"

"Bother me?"

"It's immoral to steal, isn't it?"

"Not really. It's more just a fact of life. Stealing has been going on since the beginning of time. It's something that always has been and just is and always will be. That's the way one has to look at it. It's like gravity. Or energy. Or light. There will always be men stealing from other men, and there just isn't much point in making a big moral issue of it. It rains because it rains, and we build roofs to keep dry and protect ourselves. Men steal because men steal, and we try to keep our possessions and protect ourselves from that too. But we don't call rain immoral, do we? There would be no point to it."

Just then, a young man brought our wine. He handed each of us a glass, and I thanked him. "Here's to hoping you don't get caught," I said, and I softly clinked my wine glass against Chet's.

"Yes, that's a good toast."

"I hear prison is pretty bad."

"Bad, yes. Of course, if we locked up everyone who truly belonged in prison, we'd all be living in one, and we wouldn't need to build them. It would save a lot of money." This seemed like an odd thing to say, but I ignored it. "So, what do *you* do for a living?" Chet asked me.

"I'm a writer."

"Oh? What do you write?"

"For money or for free?"

"For both."

"For money I write instruction manuals for products. For free I write novels and short stories."

Chet laughed. "Be careful of those novels," he said. "You think robbing banks is dangerous?"

"Meaning?"

"I had a friend who wrote novels. They're the worst. They destroyed his marriage and landed him in jail."

"Oh?" I said. "How did that happen?"

"I'll tell you. He was a great writer. I mean, he was really quite good, and his career was taking off. People liked his books a lot, and they were beginning to sell. But he also had a small problem, which turned out to be a big problem. His problem was that he got so deeply involved in his work that he didn't know if he was coming or going. What I mean to say is that he *was* the characters while he was writing about them. He was no longer just him, the author, but he became the character he was writing about, not just while he was writing but in real life. Anyway, he was writing a story about a man who cheated on his wife and stole from his father, and the next thing he knew, he was cheating on his own wife and stealing from his own dad. His wife left him, and he got five years in jail when his dad pressed charges. It was a tough break for someone who was just trying to write a story."

"I'll say."

"So, watch yourself."

45

"I'll be sure to do that," I said.

Chet set his wineglass down on the bench and said, "I've got to go pee. Can you excuse me?"

"Sure," I said.

"I had to go when we were up on the mountain, but there weren't any restrooms. So I held it. Then I forgot that I had to go. Now suddenly it just hit me, and I feel like my bladder is going to burst. I've really got to go."

"Have at it," I said.

"Any idea where the restrooms are?"

"No idea."

"I'll find them," Chet said, and off he went to relieve himself. He was dancing while he walked, trying to keep from peeing on himself.

I stood up and stretched. I took my glass of wine over to the edge of the garden, to a path that meandered through the ruins. I felt like exploring. I didn't plan to go too far. I wanted Chet to be able to find me when he returned, but just as I stepped onto the path, a person took hold of my elbow. I turned to see who it was, and it was Plato, smiling and releasing me.

"I thought I might find you here," he said.

"You were looking for me?"

"We didn't finish our conversation. Our talk about love. While you were kissing that girl."

"Her name is Martha."

"Yes, I remember."

"I married her."

"I can see that. I had a feeling you were going to marry her. She was the one."

"Yes," I said.

"And perhaps now *is* the best time for us to resume our dialogue. Now that Martha is here. And now that Gabriela is also here."

"What does Gabriela have to do with this?"

"Quite a lot, actually. You used to be quite fond of her, no? You had a crush on her?"

"I suppose I did."

"I want to talk to you about the most powerful love a man or woman can feel. Mind you, it's not one's love of a thing. It's not one's love for a parent, a relative, a friend, or a child. It's the love one has that never was. It's a love unfulfilled. It's a love that never had a chance, and it has a specific name."

"A name?"

"They call it unrequited love."

"Sure," I said. "I've heard of it."

"It is *the* most powerful manifestation of love in all of Zeus's universe. It can drop the strongest men to their knees, and it can make weaklings of the most steadfast women. And do you want to know why? It's because our desire for what we can't have always burns a thousand times hotter than the satisfaction of having what we have. It is a problem that is never resolved, a wet, sweet kiss never tasted, a fleshy hand never held, a warm embrace never embraced. It is lonely, devastating, crippling, painful, and debilitating, and it never, ever lessens. It's an all-consuming, raging conflagration that cannot be doused with an entire sea of water. It is like gravity itself, yet the further you get away from it, the stronger its pull. It is a heart-wrenching memory that never disappears into the distance. Believe me when I say I know what I'm talking about. I have felt this love, and I still feel it. I know exactly what it's like."

"You still feel it? For whom?"

Plato ignored my question and said, "She is here. She is here with you."

"Who is here?"

"Your unrequited love."

"You mean Gabriela?"

"Yes, Gabriela. She is here. You have brought her here to the ancient ruins with you. You have let her into your night's dream."

"My dream?" I said. I turned to look at Plato, but he was gone. "My dream?" I said again. I was alone on the path, deep in the recesses of the ruins. I suddenly broke out in a sweat, and my knees felt weak.

Gabriela.

I remembered her. Having her in my biology class made high school tolerable. I remembered what she looked like, her golden blonde hair and morning glory-blue eyes and her young girl's slender body. She was not tall. She was a little shorter than me. I remembered her clothes. She was the only girl in high school whose clothes I paid attention to: her thick sweaters, soft Levi jeans, and the knit scarves she wore on cool winter days to keep her gentle throat warm. Christ, this girl had a smile that could melt an Alaskan glacier, teeth so perfect, and skin so clear and healthy that you could mistake her for a young goddess. No, she *was* a young goddess. And I had no idea what she was doing, hanging out and talking and eating lunch and laughing among the rest of us zit-riddled and greasy-cheeked pubescent mortals who made up the pathetic balance of our school's student body.

To me she was perfection. Too perfect to approach. Too perfect to talk to, to smile at, to—God forbid—touch. I remembered the closest I ever came to her. She was in line for the school bus, standing a few kids ahead of me. Her hair was in a shimmering golden braid, and the afternoon sunlight made her shoulders sparkle. There were sparkles woven into her sweater, like tiny stars, like the Milky Way.

She was talking to the girl behind her, who was standing right in front of me. They were talking about the football game coming up on Friday night. They were both going to the game. Me? I didn't go to the games, mostly because I didn't like football players. Most of them were jerks, and speaking of those jerks, Stanley Richardson and three of his friends were walking by us on the way to Stanley's car. They didn't take the bus. Stanley had his own car, a Plymouth Roadrunner his parents had bought for him on his sixteenth birthday. It was a hot rod. A very cool car for a boy his age to own. Stanley eyes met with Gabriela's as he was walking past, and I guess they knew each other. Gabriela stood on her toes so she could see Stanley over the crowd. "Hey Gabriela," Stanley said. "Why don't you let me drive you home this afternoon? You can sit on my lap and tell me the first thing that pops up."

It was crude, right? I couldn't believe what a jerk this guy actually was, but Gabriela? What did she do? She just blushed a little, and then she laughed aloud. I think she actually liked Stanley's joke, and this hurt my feelings. So why should my feelings have been hurt? I didn't know, but they were. The boy had been rude and disrespectful to the girl I adored. She was *my* girl, not his. By insulting her, he had insulted me, but I was too weak and cowardly to do anything about it. Besides, she seemed to like Stanley. The situation was very confusing, painful, hurtful, and humiliating. And the funny thing was, I'm not sure Gabriela even knew my name. Maybe this was what hurt more than anything.

And now? Here she was, twenty years later and in my dream at Machu Picchu, strolling with my wife through the Eros Museum. Was Plato right? Was this a burning conflagration that couldn't be doused with a sea of water? Honestly, what would I do? I mean, what would I do if I had the girl all to myself? What if Martha walked off to see something else, and what if Gabriela and I found ourselves alone together? Would I have the gumption to approach her? Or maybe she would approach me. Maybe she would tell me that she'd loved me for all these years and missed me. Maybe she had a crush on me. Maybe she would say something to me like, "I had such a thing for you in high school. I didn't think you liked me the same way that I liked you. But here we are now, together. Just the two of us, alone."

What would I do? Would I step forward and take her in my arms? Would I hold her tight? Would I kiss her on the mouth? The answer was yes, yes, yes. It was definitely a yes. I would hold her and kiss her trembling lips. I would pick her up in my arms and carry her off with me to the nearest bedroom so we could make love. Jesus, it would be a dream come true, kissing her, touching her, holding her tight, and feeling her heartbeat against my chest.

Then I woke up. So the truth was out. The cat was out of the bag, at least as far as I was concerned. I looked at Martha sleeping beside me, totally unaware of my imagined infidelity, and I suddenly felt so guilty. What the heck was wrong with me? Cheating on Martha in my dreams? I looked at the clock sitting on the nightstand, and it was a little after three.

I was wide awake, so I climbed out of bed and walked to the kitchen, where I made a cup of coffee. I took the coffee into my study, and I turned on my computer. I'd been working on a short story about a man in Southern California who was sucked into a religious cult. I started to type but was interrupted. It was Martha. She'd noticed I wasn't in bed and came looking for me.

"What are you doing up?" she asked.

"I guess I just woke up," I said.

"Why didn't you go back to sleep?"

"I didn't feel tired."

"Do you know what time it is?"

"It's a little after three."

"It's too early to be up. You should go back to bed. You're going to be tired all day."

"I'll be fine. If I get tired, I'll take a nap."

"It isn't good for you."

"What isn't good for me?"

"Missing sleep. It's bad for your body, and it messes with your thinking."

"Like I said, I'll be fine."

"What are you working on?"

"The religious cult story."

"I thought you weren't going to write that one."

"I guess I changed my mind."

"I think you ought to write a story about a dog. People love dog stories. You should be writing things people want to read. Upbeat things. Happy things. Things that make people feel good. Dogs make people feel good."

"Yeah, *Old Yeller* is a real mood lifter."

"You know what I mean."

I thought Gabriela would have appreciated my writing, no matter the subject matter. It was a terrible thing for me to be thinking, but that's what went through my mind. And the way I was now remembering Gabriela, you'd think she was real with her blonde hair, morning glory-blue eyes, and trembling lips. But in a way she *was* real. I mean, she was a real reflection of my restless soul when I had no cause to be restless. She was a reflection of my loneliness when I had no right to be lonely. Yes, she was a figment of my imagination, but she was real. She was as real as I was, as real as my aversion to writing a short story or novel about a dog.

"Give up on the dogs already," I said to Martha.

"I'm going back to bed."

"Okay," I said.

"You sure you don't want to come with me?"

"I'm sure."

"I'll rub your back."

"Thanks but no."

Martha turned to leave, but then she stopped. Instead she stepped toward me and put her hand on my shoulder. "There's something I should tell you."

"What is it?"

"Stop typing for a moment and look at me," she said, and I stopped typing. I looked into her brown eyes, which were now beginning to well with tears. Something important was on her mind.

"What's wrong?" I asked.

"Nothing is wrong."

"Then what is it?"

"I think it's happened."

"You think what has happened?"

"I missed my, you know. I made a doctor's appointment for tomorrow if you want to come with me."

"You think you're pregnant?"

"It's possible, right?"

"Jesus," I said. "That's wonderful."

"It is, isn't it?"

"Did you do one of those pregnancy tests?"

"No, I want the doctor to tell me. I want to know for sure."

"Yes," I said. "We should know for sure."

"Maybe the doctor can tell us if it's a boy or a girl. Do you want to know?"

"I already know," I said.

"What do you mean?"

"It's a boy, Martha. I know it's a boy. Don't ask me how I know, but I know. We're going to have a boy, and we're going to name him Robert."

And I was sure. Like I said, I don't know how I knew, but I just knew for sure. A boy named Robert. We had already both agreed to name the baby Robert if it was a boy. I stood up and gave Martha a long hug, and then I walked her back to our room. She climbed into bed, and I kissed her on the forehead. "I wish you'd come back to bed," she said.

"Now? After getting news like this? There's no way I'd be able to sleep."

"You're happy?"

"Christ, yes, I'm happy."

"So am I," Martha said. Then she closed her eyes, and I kissed her again.

I went back to my study, and I wrote. I closed the file on the religious cult story and opened a new file. I knew exactly what I wanted to write. It would be a long letter to Robert. It would be a letter he could open and read on his eighteenth birthday, a letter that told him how I felt about becoming a father, a letter that told him everything I was thinking, a letter that expressed how much I loved him and how I looked forward to being his father. And I would give him some great advice, the kind of well-meaning and wise advice a good father gives to his son.

I spoke the words aloud as I typed. The letter was coming out exactly as I had hoped. "Dear Robert," I started off, "by the time you are reading this letter, you and I will have spent eighteen years together."

CHAPTER 6

DEAR ROBERT

———— •◦• ————

There was so much I wanted to say. I began my letter to Robert by telling him about my experiences with my own father. I could sum up my relationship with Dad by a single word: complicated. Things probably didn't have to be this way, but they were. I was never exactly sure what my father thought, and I didn't want my relationship with Robert to be harmed as mine had been. I wanted my intentions to be clear, open, and honest. I wanted to put all my cards on the table.

I wrote to Robert that when I was young, my father scared the hell out of me. Sure, he was nice to me, and he told me he loved me, but he also loomed over me many times like a horrid, frowning, floor-pounded "Jack and the Beanstalk" giant. He could be my pal and best friend on one day, yet on the next he could be extraordinarily mean and demanding. It's hard to explain why this was. Maybe his manner was supposed to be hard to explain. Maybe that was just his generation versus mine. Maybe that's the way things between fathers and sons were supposed to be during those days. I can give an example if you don't know what I'm talking about.

When I was nine, I had a good friend named Bobby Ericson, whose parents bought him everything he asked for. He always had a ton of stuff I wished my parents would have bought for me. He had a new ten-speed bike, a Daisy BB rifle, a shiny Briggs & Stratton powered go-cart, a pricey down-filled sleeping bag, and a state-of-the-art nylon camping tent and backpack. Jesus, there was no end to things his mom and dad would get for him. My dad told me his parents were trying to buy Bobby's love, and I remember not feeling sorry for him but thinking how lucky he was and how I wouldn't mind someone buying my love.

Anyway, one day Bobby's mom bought him a new Hohner Marine Band harmonica. The thing was absolutely amazing, and now I had to have one too. I asked my mom whether she'd buy one for me, and she said I'd have to ask my dad. So I asked him, and at first, he didn't seem too excited about spending money on another of my attempts to keep up with Bobby. But a few weeks after I first asked, he took me completely by surprise and drove us to the local music store. He actually bought me one of the little silver harmonicas, and I was thrilled. Dad was smiling, and he told me that he'd had a harmonica when he was a kid. "It's a great little musical instrument," he said. "I hope you enjoy yours as much as I enjoyed mine."

And I did enjoy it. I learned to play "Oh! Susanna," and I played the song over and over until my parents were close to going out of their minds. Then one afternoon, a month or so after dad bought me the harmonica, I was looking for it but couldn't find it anywhere. I mean, I looked high and low, and all over the place. I used to take it with me wherever I went, so it could have been left just about anywhere. After a couple of days of looking, I realized I had lost it, and I felt terrible about this.

Then a week passed, and Dad asked me why I was no longer playing "Oh! Susanna." I told him I was tired of it, and then he asked to see the harmonica. "Maybe I can teach you a couple new songs," he said. "I might still be able to remember how to play them." And that's when I had to fess up and tell him the harmonica was lost. "Lost?" my dad said. "What the fuck? You mean, you lost it already?" And that's when the old, frowning "Jack and the Beanstalk" giant reared his ugly, angry head. "What the hell? Do you think that money grows on trees? How could you lose it already? This is exactly why I didn't want to buy you the damn thing in the first place!"

Mom tried to calm my dad down, but the old guy was really angry. He had turned from my best pal into my worst nightmare. Now his big question was, "How am I going to punish this little shit so he learns a lesson?" So what did he do? I was too old for a spanking, and my allowance had already been cut off for several weeks because of a small incident where I had talked smart to my mom. So he grounded me. For two weeks I had to come straight home after school and spend my afternoons holed up in my room. I could come out to eat dinner, but that was it. After dinner, I was back in my room. I suffered two full weeks of this, all because I had done something all kids did. I lost something. And you know what? The truth is that I lost something more than my Marine Band harmonica. I lost my pal. I lost the nice guy I had thought was my best friend and buddy. Yes, I lost my buddy. During the two weeks I was being punished, Dad barely said a word to me.

"I've tried not to be that guy," I wrote to Robert in the letter. I stopped writing for a moment, and I wondered. What kind of dad would I be for the eighteen years before Robert got this letter? I would certainly be a lot more understanding than my dad. Then I gave Robert my first piece of advice: be understanding. That was so darned important, wasn't it? It meant to put yourself in the shoes of others and try to understand their sides, to feel what they were feeling, to get their unique sets of problems and challenges.

I think this is important advice for everyone. There is way too much selfishness in the world these days. We are too concerned with ourselves and our immediate perceived needs, and not as aware as we should be of the plights of others. I wrote, "The world would be a thousand percent better place to live if only people were more in tune with others. So, you take the first step. You be the first to do it. You can set the example for others, and I think you'll be rewarded with riches beyond your wildest dreams. Not riches like gold and silver but the kind of riches that nourish your heart."

Yes, this was good. But being understanding was only one thing. Tolerance was another. I wrote to Robert that I hoped I had raised him to be tolerant. It was so important. People are all different, and they all have different needs, and they come from different directions, and they strive for different hopes, desires, and goals. They all worship God in different ways, and sometimes they worship different gods, or sometimes they have no god or gods at all. Like I said, it's important that we try our best to be understanding, but it's equally important that we all allow each other to be different. What kind of dreary, lousy world would we live in if everyone was exactly the same? Too many people hate others because they're a little different. Or they laugh at them, ridicule them, ignore them, or write them off as jerks or nutcases. Or we go out of their way to make them conform to the rest of us. We shouldn't be doing any of these things to one another. We should hail our differences because all the differences are what make us so extraordinary. They make up the land beneath our feet, the food in our bellies, and the oxygen in our lungs. *Vive la différence, n'est ce pas?* And not just between the sexes but regarding it all.

I was pleased with what I was writing, and the next thing I wanted to discuss was forgiveness. I wrote to my son, "There's no way anyone can go through his life without hurting others, or without being hurt by them. It's just the way things have been arranged by God, by nature, or by whatever or whoever you believe created us. What's that they say? That you can't make an omelet without breaking a few eggs?"

I wrote that the key to living a great life wasn't steering clear of hurting others, nor was it preventing others from hurting you. Rather, it was found in the magic of forgiveness. When we forgive, we acknowledge that the world is a sticky place to live, and likewise, when a person forgives us, he or she is acknowledging the same. When we forgive, we are all cutting each other a little slack, which is only fair, right? After all, who in the world is perfect? We all make mistakes, and we all suffer because of them. In other words, we're all in the same leaky lifeboat. Forgiveness allows us to stay afloat and bail out the sea water, to live together as we should live together. It allows us to be friends rather than combatants and archenemies. I can think of no act that is any more compassionate, constructive, appropriate, and righteous than the act of forgiving.

I also wrote to Robert, "Forgiveness can be tricky. Some people are way too generous with it, letting other people walk all over them. And some people are way too stingy with it, living unnecessarily angry and lonely lives. But the positive power of forgiveness in a pair of deliberate and careful hands is undeniable. Be wise with it, keeping in mind that too much or too little of anything is never a very good idea."

All this talk about forgiveness brought me to love. Good, old tried-and-true love. I probably should've begun the letter with it. For what is life without love? In my letter I then told Robert that I loved him and that I would always love him no matter what. By no matter what, I truly meant just that. A parent's love for his or her child has to be unconditional. And why is this? It's because if you bring a life into the world, you owe it your love always. You are totally responsible for it. It is a literal extension of yourself, and as such, you are called on to love it, care for it, and guide it for as long as you are able. I can think of nothing more personal than a child, a child who was made from a part of you and a part of your lover.

This child *is* your flesh and blood. I wrote to Robert, "I will love you with all my heart until the day I die, and if there is such a thing as life after death, I promise to love you for the duration of that eternal time as well. For you are a piece of me, and together, we are as one. It may not feel like this at times, but this is the truth. And the same exact thing holds true with your mom, for you are as much an extension of her as you are of me, and we will both love you forever. It's the one thing you can always count on."

I told Robert there were things Martha and I expected from him in return for our love. It wasn't like we were agreeing to a deal, trading this for that. It's just that we were owed. We were, for example, owed his honesty. I wrote, "Tell the world all the lies you want, but stay on the level with your mom and dad, and we will be able to do right by you. But only if you're honest with us." I also told Robert that he owed us his best efforts not just for things he might be doing for us but for everything he did.

"A man who does not always do his best is not really a man," I wrote. "Anyone can cruise through life by doing only what is necessary to get by, but real men and real women give it all their best shot. You will be respected for it. People will look up to you. And you will almost always be rewarded for it." I also told Robert that he owed us his best attempt to be moral. I wrote, "Sometimes it may seem unclear what morality is, but usually it isn't really all that hard to figure out. Use your head and your heart, and you're almost certain to be able to discern the difference between right and wrong. Then do what is right."

"There is something else I want from you," I wrote in Robert's letter. "You don't owe this to me, but maybe you'll owe it to yourself. Stay on your toes. Keep a vigilant watch. Keep your eyes and ears open, and beware. Beware of what? Beware of the status quo. It is the silent killer. 'The killer of what?' you ask. It's the knife-wielding, cold-blooded murderer of all that is right and magnificent about you. It sucks the life out of your soul. It steals your breath and stops your heart. Forget violence, hatred, greed, lust, vengeance, corruption, vice, and racism. The status quo trumps them all. It is mankind's most vicious enemy, panting and drooling in the wings, just waiting for you to let your guard down. I don't think there's anything more tragic in the whole wide world than a man who has lost his individuality, lost his essence, lost all the things that help him stand apart from his peers. Stand up for yourself and be you. Don't fear ridicule and jeering from idiots. Be true to yourself and take your own unique bull by the horns. You may find that this is difficult at times, but trust me, in the long run, you'll thank me for warning you and encouraging you. This might be the most valuable advice I'm giving you."

I was now looking at my computer monitor. I was scratching my head, trying to think of what else to add to the letter. And it hit me. It had to be said. I wrote, "Don't ever expect to be a perfect anything. Knowing what you should do and actually doing it can be two utterly different things. I've never been a perfect son to my own father, and so I don't expect you to be the perfect son to me, no matter how hard you try. You may give it your best shot and fall miles short. That's life, kid. Welcome to the club. What I'm trying to say is that you should cut yourself some slack and give yourself a break when one is due. Always be demanding of yourself, but don't be impossibly hard on yourself. Do your best while realizing that your best is only a human effort and that human beings are often by nature clumsy, imperfect, infallible, weak, misguided, and prone to error. I will never expect you to be perfect. I ask only that you do your best. That will make me proud."

I stared at my computer monitor again. I could've racked my brain and come up with more, but I decided that I'd touched on the major points I wanted to make. I then printed out the letter and signed it. I put it in an envelope and sealed it, writing Robert's name on it. I looked at the clock, and it was now seven, time for Martha to be getting out of bed. A couple of seconds later, she appeared in my doorway, holding a cup of coffee and yawning.

"How's the story coming?" she asked. She still thought I had been writing the story about the man who joined the religious cult.

"Good," I said.

"I still think you should write a story about dogs."

"I know."

"Did you finish the story?"

"I did," I said. "Do you want to read it?" I knew she'd say no. She never read anything I wrote.

"No, thanks," Martha said.

"I think it has a happy ending."

"You think?"

"I guess it all depends."

"On what?"

"On how things turn out."

"You're not making any sense. Does the story have an ending or not?"

"It will have an ending eventually."

"Well, whatever that means," Martha said, and she rolled her eyes.

I laughed. Then, changing the subject, I said, "Can I ask you a question?"

"Of course," Martha said.

"Let's say you decided to write Robert a letter."

"Robert?"

"Our son."

"You're sure he's going to be a boy?"

"Yes, I'm sure."

"Okay, go on," Martha said, laughing. "Let's say I decide to write him a letter."

"You're writing the letter this morning, to be opened and read by him in the future when he turns eighteen. You want to tell him in this letter how you feel about him and give advice for his future."

"Shouldn't I have already done those things before he turned eighteen?"

"Just say it works out this way," I said. "Never mind what you should have already said and done. Say you decide to write this letter for him to open and read when he turns eighteen."

"Okay," Martha said.

"What would you say?"

"I guess I could say a lot of things."

"Such as?"

"Well, the first thing I'd tell him is that I love him."

"Good, good. So would I."

"I'd tell him there was no love stronger than a mother has for her son."

"Then after that?"

Martha thought for a moment. Then she said, "I'd tell him to be happy."

"Be happy by doing what?"

"Just by being happy."

"I mean, how would he achieve that?"

59

"Two things I can think of," Martha said. "First, he needs to find a job he loves. He's going to spend most of his adult life working, so it ought to be at something he loves. When you meet people who are happy, they are usually people who are happy with their work. There's nothing worse than spending day in and day out laboring at something you can't stand."

"I would agree with that."

"There are a lot of miserable people in the world."

"I would agree with that too."

"Some are just miserable people by their nature, but I'll bet most of them hate their jobs. So, if you're asking me what will make our son happy, that's my first suggestion—for him to find a job he loves."

"And the second thing?"

"Second, he'll need to find the right person to share his life with, someone he truly gets along with, someone he loves more than anything. Someone who makes him happy to be alive. Someone who makes him want to get up in the morning."

"Have you found that in me?"

"Of course I have."

"Seriously?"

Martha gave me a look. "Now you're being insecure. You know I don't like that."

"Sorry," I said.

"If I didn't love you, would I have married you?"

"I suppose not." I thought for a moment, and then I asked, "Do you really like your job?"

"I think I do."

"Only *think* you do?"

"I mean, it's work, isn't it? Sure, I like it, but there's a reason they call it work. It's because it is work, and it can be a pain. But yes, on the whole, I enjoy doing what I do. It is what I chose. No one twisted my arm, and the truth is that it can be a lot of fun. It requires a lot of skill and brains and experience. It keeps me on my toes. I find it's a very good fit for me."

"Didn't you become an attorney because your dad wanted you to be an attorney?"

"At first that was part of it."

"But?"

"I actually do enjoy it. And it pays well."

"The money makes you happy?"

"Of course the money makes me happy. Money is always nice to have."

"Would you do your job for less money?"

"I don't know. I've never really thought about it."

"That would be a good test, wouldn't it? To do the job for less money and see how much you like it then."

Martha stared at me for a moment and then said, "That's kind of silly."

"Is it?"

"You know, in high school I thought it would be fun to be a florist. But I was just a kid. A florist, really? I would've been bored out of my mind, a grown woman doing the same things day after day, stuffing cut flowers into cheap vases, pretending I was being creative. And doing it for so little money. What does a florist make anyway? I don't even know. Probably not a whole heck of a lot. Anyway, it was just a casual daydream. I was never really serious about it. How about you? You always wanted to be a writer, didn't you? Or did you ever want to be something else?"

"Honestly? I thought it would be fun to drive a truck, to travel all over the country, cruising the interstates and listening to country music on my radio."

"I have a hard time picturing you as a truck driver."

"Yeah, me too."

Martha thought for a moment and said, "You really wanted to do that?"

"I did for a while."

"That's funny."

"The florist and the truck driver," I said, and Martha laughed at this.

"Sounds like the title of your next short story."

"Yeah," I said.

"I'm going to get another cup of coffee," Martha said, and she turned to leave.

Yeah, a truck driver. Hauling goods. Keeping a lookout for cops. Trying to stay awake.

After Martha was gone, I imagined myself sitting behind the big steering wheel of my own eighteen-wheeler. I was listening to George Jones on the radio, watching America pass by, keeping my rig in my lane. Yes,

I was there in my imagination. I was actually there, and I set the scene. Lots of asphalt. Endless vistas. Up ahead there was a car pulled over to the side of the highway. There was a young man standing behind the car, and he was trying to flag me down. I figured he was having some kind of trouble, so I pulled the rig over just ahead of him. He came up to my window, and I rolled it down.

"Having trouble?" I asked.

"Yes, sir," the young man said. "I'm out of gas."

"That's tough," I said. "The nearest gas station is twenty miles up the road."

"Damn," the kid said.

"Let me give you a lift."

"Are you sure?"

"It's no problem," I said.

"Thanks, mister," he said. "I'll be right back." He ran back to his car and grabbed a leather satchel. He locked the doors and ran back to me. He opened the side door and got into the passenger seat. "Man, I really appreciate this. I can't believe I ran out of gas. I usually watch the gas gauge. It was pretty stupid of me."

"It happens," I said. "I've run out of gas before. More times than I care to admit."

"It was nice of you to stop."

"My name is Robinson," I said, and I reached over for a handshake.

"I'm Robert," the kid said, shaking my hand.

CHAPTER 7

ONE WILD RIDE

⸺•⸺

W as it him? One minute he looked exactly like my son. Then the next moment he looked like someone else. It was weird how I couldn't get his face to hold still.

"Where are you headed?" I asked.

"Vegas," Robert said. "How about you?"

"Salt Lake," I said.

"Sorry if I slowed you down."

"Don't worry about it. I'm just glad I could help. What's in Las Vegas. Do you have family there?"

"No family. I'm just moving there. My mom and dad live in California, but I'm leaving the state. It's a lot cheaper to live in Vegas."

"I see," I said.

"Mom and Dad pushed me out of the nest. That's what they called it. In other words, they asked me to leave the house and fend for myself."

"How old are you?"

"Twenty-one."

"Are you mad at your parents for asking you to leave?"

"What's to be mad at? I'm a big boy. They wanted me out of the house, so I'm out of the house."

"Do you have a girlfriend?"

"No," Robert said.

"Maybe you'll meet a nice girl in Vegas."

"Maybe. But if I don't, that's fine. I'll be fine living by myself. In fact, I look forward to being alone. There will be no one telling me what to do every minute of the day and no one breathing down my neck."

"Sometimes it's nice to have a companion."

"Maybe," Robert said. "Or maybe not. Not to be rude, but do you mind if I turn off the radio?"

"Go ahead," I said.

"No offense, but I can't stand country music."

I laughed. "I felt the same way about country music when I was your age. I used to wonder who in the heck listened to that stuff. Certainly not anyone I knew."

Robert smiled and reached to turn off the music. He leaned back in his seat, trying to get comfortable.

I asked, "Do you think you're going to miss your parents?"

"Miss them?" Robert said. He laughed at this. He didn't answer my question, and I figured his laugh was meant to tell me how he felt. I thought about this, and at his age, I probably wouldn't have missed my parents much either.

"What does your dad do for a living?" I asked.

"He's a writer."

"That sounds interesting."

"You think so? I guess if you think sitting on your butt all day in front of a computer sounds like fun, then yes, it's interesting. But it's not anything I'd ever want to do for the rest of my life. I like action, if you know what I mean. I like to do things."

"What does your dad write about?"

"Well, that's a good question. He gets paid to write up instruction manuals for products. I don't know how much they pay him, but I'm guessing it's not very much. Seriously, how much could you possibly make doing that? I guess he's good at it, because he always has work. Or maybe he's always busy just because he doesn't charge a lot. There's always some project he's working on, but I don't think he really likes any of the assignments. What he really likes is to write his fiction. He's published a bunch of short stories in magazines. As for novels, he's published six or seven of them, but he's had no best sellers. He's not very well known. It's not like anyone would ever ask him for an autograph."

"Does your mom work?"

"My mom is the one who makes all the money."

"What does she do?"

"She's a lawyer."

"Ah," I said.

"Dad calls her his Queen of Fine Print. She does a lot of stuff with contracts."

"Do you love your parents?"

Robert had to think about this a moment. Finally, he said, "Yes, I love my parents. I mean, they're my parents, right? I have to love them."

"But?"

"But I wish they understood me."

"They don't understand you?"

Robert gazed out the side window and said, "I'd rather talk about something else, if you don't mind."

"That's fine," I said.

We were quiet for a while longer. Robert asked, "How long have you been a truck driver?"

"Since I was your age."

"Wow, that's a lot of miles. How old are you?"

"Fifty-eight."

"Do you like driving a truck for a living?"

"I do."

"Do you ever get bored?"

"No," I said. "My mind is always busy while I'm driving. I'm always thinking about things."

"About things?"

"Yeah, you know."

"I think I'd get bored to death," Robert said. He was looking out the window again.

"What are you going to do for money when you get to Vegas?" I asked. "I mean, how will you earn a living?"

"I'm going into the restaurant business."

"As a waiter?"

"No, not as a waiter."

"As a cook?"

"No, neither. As an owner. I'm going to open up my own place."

"That requires a lot of capital."

"Oh, I have plenty of cash."

"Are your parents backing you?"

"No, they'll have nothing to do with this. They don't even know what I'm planning. I've never talked to them about it."

"Then where are you getting the cash?"

"That's a good question," Robert said. He stared at me, sizing me up. Then he said, "I don't know if I should tell you."

"You don't have to."

"But I think I will."

"It's up to you."

"You seem trustworthy enough," Robert said. He unzipped the top of his leather bag and tilted it toward me so I could see its contents. It was stuffed full of hundred-dollar bills. He said, "It's ransom money."

"How much is in there?"

"One million."

"Jesus," I said. "You're telling me that you're walking around with a million dollars on you?"

"Yep."

"And what did you mean that it's ransom money?"

"Exactly what I said."

"You're a kidnapper?" I asked, laughing.

"No joke."

He actually seemed serious, so I asked, "Mind if I ask who you kidnapped?"

"Not at all. But this stays between you and me. Do I have your word to keep this quiet?"

"My lips are sealed."

"It was the six-year-old son of Malcom Banks."

"The state senator?"

"He's also the owner of Banks International, the giant pharmaceutical company. The guy is loaded."

"Jesus," I said.

"I figured that to him a million was pocket change. And I was right. The dude paid me faster than a slot machine takes a fat woman's money. There was no hassle at all. No bullshit and no police."

"How do you know he didn't call the police?"

"I didn't give him time."

"What do you mean?"

"I snatched the kid at nine in the morning, and then I gave the senator an hour to pay. He didn't have time to do anything about it. I told him he had to pay in one hour, or the kid was as good as dead. Of course, I would never kill the boy. I just said that to make the senator cooperate. By ten o'clock I had the cash in my hands, and I was on the road."

"People think they can get away with kidnapping, yet they always get caught."

"Not always."

"Well then, usually."

"I don't even know about that. Most kidnappings are dealt with quietly and without the police. The ransom is paid, and the hostage is set free, no questions asked. The police usually never hear anything about it."

"Is that really true?"

"I think it is."

"You *think* it is?"

"I have no way of proving it. But look at me. Do you see the police after me? Do you see me in jail? Do you see me in a room being interrogated? No, I'll tell you exactly what you see. You see me free as a bird on my way to Vegas with a bag full of cash. And no one was hurt. It was pocket change for Senator Banks. I got my cash, and the kid was let go safely. Everyone got what they wanted."

"I guess that's true," I said. I didn't know what to say to the kid. What a warped view of the world he had. But I let it slide.

"You haven't asked me anything about my restaurant," Robert said. "Aren't you curious about it?"

"I suppose I am."

"Then ask me about it. Ask me what kind of restaurant I am going to open."

"Okay, what kind of restaurant will you open?"

"I'm going to call it The Outlaw's Hideout. It will be a theme restaurant, and the theme will be thirties bank robbers. You know, like Pretty Boy Floyd, John 'Red' Hamilton, Baby Face Nelson, Bonnie and Clyde, and John Dillinger. The restaurant will be a shrine to the whole lot of them. America's forgotten heroes. I'll have all sorts of memorabilia, photos, and copies of news clippings. The food we'll serve will be the sort of food that was popular in the thirties. I'm thinking Salisbury steaks, meat loaf, chicken-fried steak, chicken and dumplings, and all the rest of the old favorites. Every day, we'll have a blue plate special for the cheapskates. We'll play old thirties music from an authentic Wurlitzer jukebox. Can you picture it? I think it would be a smash hit. There will be people lined up at the door to get in, and there won't be an empty seat in the place."

"Sounds exciting," I said.

"I've been planning this restaurant in my head for years. It was just a matter of getting my hands on the money."

"And now you have it?"

"A million bucks."

"And you'll be legit?"

"That was always the goal. I never had any intention of being a career criminal. Once the restaurant is up and running, I'll invite my parents to come see what I've done. They won't believe their eyes, and they'll see that I wasn't such a screwup after all."

I suddenly heard something, and I turned and looked at Robert. "Do you hear that?" I asked.

"Hear what?"

"I thought I heard a police siren."

I looked in the big rearview mirror attached to the side of my truck, and sure enough, there was a black-and-white highway patrol car following right behind us, its lights whirling and flashing.

"Shit," Robert said.

"I'm going to have to pull over."

"You can't."

"What do you mean, I can't?"

"I mean, you *can't*. They're probably after me."

"How would they even know you're in here?"

"They'd just know. Were you speeding?"

"No, I was going the speed limit."

"Then why would they be pulling you over? Don't you get it? They know I'm in here. Somehow they figured out you picked me up."

"I thought you said no one had called the police."

"Well, maybe I was wrong."

"I can't just keep driving. Failure to pull over for a cop is against the law."

"So is kidnapping."

I thought about this. I said, "I say we pull over and see what they want. It might be nothing."

"Now there are *three* cop cars," Robert said, still looking in the mirror. "Keep moving."

"And do what? They're going to keep following us."

"Do you have a cell phone?"

"I do," I said.

"Hand it to me."

"Who are you going to call?"

"I'm going to call the highway patrol."

"How are you going to call them?"

"Just hand over the phone."

I pulled my cell phone out from my pocket and handed it to Robert. He dialed 9-1-1 and waited for an operator. He said, "Put me through to the main office of the highway patrol. We're being followed by two of their cars, and I need to speak to whoever is in charge. This is an emergency, a life or death situation. No, don't ask me any questions. Just put me through."

Robert stopped talking. He was holding the phone to his ear. "Are they putting you through?" I asked.

"She said she would."

"What are you going to tell them?"

"I'm going to tell them to back the hell off."

"And why would they agree to that?"

"Because I'm telling them that if they don't, I'm going to kill you."

"*Kill* me?"

"That's what I'm going to tell them. I'm not really going to kill you. You don't have anything to worry about. But I want them to worry about what I'll do, and I don't think they'll have the nerve to call my bluff."

An officer spoke to Robert on my cell phone. I could hear the muffled sound of his voice, but I couldn't hear what he was saying. When he was done speaking, Robert said, "I've got my gun aimed right at the son of a bitch's head. If you don't tell your men to back off, I'll pull the trigger. I swear to God I will. I've got nothing to lose. It'll be on you, not me. I'm giving you a choice. Back your cars off, or I pull the fucking trigger."

I could hear the officer talking again but still couldn't understand him. "What's he saying?" I asked.

"He's telling me to calm down. And now he's telling me he just told his men to stop following us."

"Seriously?"

"Look in your mirror."

I looked in the rearview mirror, and sure enough, the patrol cars were slowing down. "They're going away."

"That takes care of that."

"But they still know where we are."

"Be quiet a minute," Robert said. "I need to think of what we're going to do next."

I stopped talking so Robert could think. The officer was still talking on the cell phone. Robert ended the call so he wouldn't have to hear the man talking, and he handed the phone back to me. "What should I do?" I asked.

"Pull over up ahead and come to a complete stop."

"What for?"

"Just do it."

I slowed down the truck and pulled over to the side of the highway, coming to a stop. We were literally out in the middle of nowhere. "Now what?" I asked.

"Now drive again. Get back on the highway. Then pull over and do the same thing in a mile. We're going to pull off the highway and stop every mile."

"I don't get it."

"They're going to think I'm getting out of the truck. And I will eventually. But they won't know where. They won't know which of the stops is the one I'm choosing."

"I guess that makes sense."

"Of course it makes sense. Do you see any cops in your mirror? I don't see any in mine."

"They still seem to be gone."

"They're crafty, you know. We have to be very careful how we do this. They probably have unmarked cars watching what we do. Any of these cars passing us on the highway could be a cop. And any of the cars coming the other direction. I don't hear a helicopter, so that's a good sign. Apparently, they don't want you to die. They've decided that catching me is not worth you losing your life."

"I'm pulling over again."

"Good."

"Are you getting out here?"

"Nope, not yet."

"When are you getting out?"

"I haven't decided yet. Just keep driving."

As I drove, making my stops every mile, I thought back to when Robert had been a child, the time he got caught swiping candy bars from the grocery store. The store manager called me and said I could come pick Robert up. He said he wasn't going to call the police so long as I came. When I got to the store, the manager was very friendly. He was calm about the whole thing, and he spoke to me for about fifteen minutes. He said he'd been caught doing the very same thing when he was Robert's age. "My dad beat the snot out of me," he said.

"I don't beat my kid," I said.

"No, no, I don't expect you to. But I do hope you'll take this seriously. I realize they were only a few candy bars, but first it's candy bars, then it's a bike. Then the next thing you know, it's grand theft auto."

"Agreed," I said.

"I know exactly what I'm talking about," the manager said. "I got in some serious trouble as a kid. Candy bars were just the beginning. I know how these things snowball."

"Yes, of course," I said.

"Robert seems like a nice kid."

"We like him," I said, smiling.

"I'd like to see him learn from this."

"Don't worry, he will. You can be sure that his mom and I will see to it."

Well, a fine job we did.

Finally, Robert jumped out of my truck. It was the sixth time I had pulled over to the side of the highway. By now we probably had the police thoroughly confused. As he was about to run off, Robert said, "Keep stopping every mile. I know you don't have to, but I'd really appreciate it. Otherwise they're going to guess that I got out here."

"Okay," I said.

"And thanks for the lift."

"Are you going to be okay?"

"I'll be fine. I'm a survivor. I always land on my feet. You know, like a cat."

Robert slammed the truck door shut, and he ran off into the scenery. I put the truck in gear, and I drove forward, pulling back onto the highway. I began to cry. I couldn't help it. I was sobbing as I drove. I felt a gut-wrenching sorrow such as I have never felt in all my life. It was horrible, losing my only son. I sped up, and soon I was passing cars, going faster and faster, and crying even harder, I barreled down the highway at well over a hundred miles per hour.

And then the highway began to twist and turn like it was a river of molten glass, and the tires screeched around each death-defying turn. I stomped down on the brake pedal, but nothing happened. I was now completely out of control, and the scenery out the side windows was nothing but a gray wash, and the engine was whining and rattling like it was about to explode. And then everything went black. My eyes were closed, so I opened them.

I was on my back in a hospital room. There was a TV and a whiteboard on the wall before me. There was a window off to my left and an IV stuck in my arm. A cheerful nurse walked into the room, and she spoke to me as she began to fiddle with my IV bags. "Are you awake?" she asked.

"I think so," I said.

"How are you feeling?"

"A little confused."

"Do you know why you're here?"

"I think so. I was in an accident. I think I lost control of my truck."

"Your truck?"

"Yes, I lost control. I was driving too fast."

The nurse laughed, then said, "Sorry, I know I shouldn't be laughing. But you're not a truck driver, and you weren't in an accident. You had a massive heart attack in your home, and your wife found you on the floor in your study. She called 9-1-1, and you were brought to the hospital. You've been in the hospital for the past six days. We had you in an ICU for a while until we got you stabilized. But you made it. We think you're going to be okay. In fact, you're going home this morning."

"There was no truck?" I asked.

"No truck."

"And no police?"

"The police weren't involved."

"Where's my wife?"

"She should be here soon to take you home. She should be here with your son."

"With Robert?"

"Yes, with Robert. Such a sweet boy. He's been very worried about you."

"Jesus," I said, rubbing my eyes. "Are you sure it's okay to go home? I feel so strange and confused. I feel like I just got here."

"The doctor signed the papers an hour ago. Your wife will be here in a couple of hours. In the meantime, let's get you ready to go. I need to take your vitals one last time. Then you can use the bathroom before you leave."

"I don't need to use the bathroom."

"That's fine, but I still need to check your vitals." The nurse put the blood pressure sleeve on my arm and said, "Be sure to take it easy and eat some breakfast when you get home. You haven't had anything at all to eat this morning. You need some food in your stomach."

"Okay," I said.

CHAPTER 8

SHOVE AND GRAB

———————— ◦●◦ ————————

The car ride was a blur, but it was wonderful to be back at the house. It's always great to get home when you've been away for a while. I looked around, and everything was nestled nicely in its proper place. I walked into my study and looked at my desk, where my computer was still on, and there was a stack of unopened mail Martha had been bringing in while I was gone.

I sat down and pushed the mail aside, looking at my computer monitor. It was frozen on the short story I'd been writing just prior to the heart attack. Just as I started to read it, Martha appeared in the doorway with a fresh cup of coffee and asked whether I wanted breakfast.

"Robert and I have already eaten," she said. "But I can make you something. You can eat in here or at the kitchen table. It's up to you."

"I'm not that hungry," I said.

"The nurse told me to be sure you ate."

"Then make me a slice of toast."

"With an egg?"

"Fine, with an egg."

"Here or in the kitchen?"

"I guess I'll eat it here."

"I'm glad you're back home," Martha said. She set my cup of coffee down in front of me, kissed the top of my head, and left to make my breakfast.

I got back to my reading. The title of the short story I had been writing was "Shove and Grab." On its surface the story was about my true-to-life experience as a thirteen-year-old boy in junior high, playing flag football, but in a deeper sense, it was about my lifelong and somewhat painful relationship with my father.

When I was in the eighth grade, I was obsessed with becoming a great writer. I think I may have already mentioned this. True, the truck driver fantasy appealed to me for a while, but writing was always my primary passion. It's funny. If I ever had been a truck driver, I probably would've become one so I could write about it, not so I could move freight from one city to another. Writing was really all that mattered to me, and my parents knew this. I shared all the stories I wrote with my mom and dad, and they were supportive. Well, Mom was anyway. I think Dad had other plans for me. He imagined me being a *real* boy, doing real boy-type things, such as scuffing my knees and elbows, killing things, climbing up hills, catching lizards and snakes, winning races, and always being fearless. Life was confusing. I get what he wanted now, but I didn't get it back then. Back then I just wanted to write.

Anyway, in a not-so-subtle spirit of saving me from myself and molding me into a real boy, Dad signed me up for the school flag football team. The coach was Mr. Backlund, a tall, blond Swede with a military crew cut and a ridiculous silver referee's whistle always dangling from his over-exercised neck. The guy was a joke. No kidding. I didn't understand it then because I looked up to him like I looked up to the rest of my teachers. He had this low, loud, and authoritative voice that said to us kids, "You will do what I say or else!" You didn't dare cross him. You did what he said.

Mr. Backlund knew us from our daily PE class, and he knew who was weak, and who was strong. He also knew who could throw a ball the farthest, run the fastest, and catch. The first thing he did as our football coach was to assign us to our positions. The more talented boys took their places, and the rest of us were put on the offensive and defensive lines. Me? I was to play defense. I was told my job was to shove the kid in front of me and try to grab the flag of whoever had the ball. It was simple enough for an imbecile to understand. I just had to shove and grab. Shove the blocker out of the way and grab the flag.

When the season began, we practiced for a couple of hours each day after school, preparing for the first big game. We'd spend the first hour performing all kinds of dreadful exercises and running laps around the field until our legs ached and felt like they were falling off. Then we'd split up into sides and scrimmage for an hour. Shove and grab. Shove and grab.

Jesus, it was probably the most idiotic routine I'd ever been subjected to. But the other boys loved it, so I pretended to love it too.

The truth? I was terrible at this game. I was neither big nor strong, and I was about as tough and aggressive as a tea leaf. It was so bad that the offensive linemen on our team argued with each other over about who'd be awarded the easy task of blocking me during the scrimmages, since I made them look so good at their jobs. I was pathetic. I really was, and I had about as much business playing football with these boys as any of them had playing violins and cellos for the Los Angeles Philharmonic Orchestra.

Finally came the day of the first game. Like I said, I was put on the offensive line. I'm going to describe the kid I was up against, the kid I was supposed to shove. I had no idea what his name was. It was probably something like Butch, Buster, or Mack, or maybe just Ape. I'm kidding about Ape, of course, but the name would've suited him. He was an imposing, muscular ape of a thirteen-year-old. I swear to God this kid's jaw already had a five o'clock shadow, and his voice was lower than our coach's. His shoulders were broad, and his legs were thick, and he had forearms like a pair of wrecking balls. He glared at me right before the first play of the game, and then he crouched in a set position. He said, "I'm going to knock your faggot head off." Those were the last words I heard before the football was hiked, before Ape's giant Popeye forearm crashed violently into my face, knocking me backward on my butt. When the play was over, I reached to my nose and felt the warm blood gushing from my nostrils. Christ, it hurt like holy hell. And I began to cry like a baby.

"Look, look," I heard one of the kids say, "Robinson got his nose broken. Come and check it out! Look at this!"

Yes, I was crying. I felt like I'd been run over by a car. But I was also making a complete fool of myself, and the kids were having the time of their lives. There's nothing like a lot of blood and some tears to get thirteen-year-olds excited. "He broke his nose! He broke his nose!" I heard them saying this over and over, but my nose wasn't broken. It just hurt and was very bloody. It was bloody enough to get my mom to run out on the field to rescue me. It was the most humiliating day of my life. Mom got on her knees, cradled my head in her arms and lap, and wiped the warm blood from my nose using the fabric of her dress. That incident marked the end of my flag football career.

During the ride home from the game, Mom was furious with my dad for having signed me up for the sport, and Dad was mad with my mom for having taken me off the field.

"It's just a bloody nose," my dad said. "Jesus, you'd think he'd broke an arm or a leg."

Anyway, Mom got her way, and Dad took me off the football team. Dad never did say this was okay with him. He never did say anything about that game at all. And let me tell you this: I think silence can be a lot more hurtful than words. Honestly, it would've been so nice if Dad had said *something*. But he chose to give me the silent treatment, and his silence said it all. I was a disappointment to him. On future Sundays when Dad watched football on TV, I saw something when he watched his games, when he watched his favorite pro players in action. There were admiration, respect, and awe, things he would never feel for me. When he saw me or read one of my stupid short stories, I think he now saw only a mama's boy with a bloody nose. He saw *"Mommy"* holding his boy's injured head, tears squirting from his eyes in front of the rest of the team. Gad!

You probably think I'm oversimplifying my life when I say that this little story about my flag football experience is a conclusive representation of all that ever happened between my father and me. Surely, a relationship between a father and son is more complex. But is it? I thought I'd put my finger right on the heart and soul of our father-son bond, or lack thereof, however you want to look at it. It no longer makes me angry, and I don't resent my father for his ways. I don't dislike him, despise him, or hate his guts. If anything, I feel sorry for the guy. I was angry with him when I was younger, but the anger has morphed into pity.

Earlier, I believe I said my relationship with my father was complicated. But I take that back. It was actually quite simple. So long as you played by his man rules, you were gold. Veer off course, and you were shit. There wasn't much more to it than that.

Martha brought in my toast and egg, and she set the plate on my desk. "Reading your story?" she asked.

"I am," I said.

"Are you happy with it?"

"I think it's good."

"What's it called?"

"I've titled it 'Shove and Grab.'"

"Sounds like a Black Friday at Walmart."

"Yeah," I said, laughing. "It does at that. But it's not about shopping. It's about football."

"You wrote a story about football?"

"It's about my brief experience with it when I was in junior high."

"You played football?"

"Flag football in the eighth grade. My dad signed me up for the team, and my mom made me quit."

Martha thought about this and said, "I once dated a football player in high school."

"I never knew that," I said. I was surprised to hear this. She'd never mentioned it before.

"His name was Brad Mason. He was a wide receiver, one of the star players. He was a senior, and I was a sophomore. He was so handsome. Mom always said I was so lucky to have such a good-looking kid interested in me. And my dad? He adored that boy."

"Your dad liked him?"

"My dad liked him because he was everything he had imagined for me. He was tall, smart, built like a young Greek god. And best of all, he was a star football player. And his dad was an attorney."

"Aha," I said.

"My dad told me several times what a great son-in-law Brad would make. Seriously, I think my dad liked him even more than I did."

I laughed. "So, who broke up the relationship?"

"Brad did surprisingly."

"Why was that surprising?"

"Because I was the one who should've pulled the plug. He turned out to be a rat."

"A rat? Did he cheat on you?"

"It wasn't that."

"Then what was it?" I asked. I was being a little nosy, but I was very curious.

"Brad and I were close. I don't mean just as in being very good friends, but we were also close sexually. I was doing some things with him that I'd never done with a boy. No, we weren't having sexual intercourse, but we did a lot of things. Then one day my parents went out of town, and I invited Brad to come over to our house. It was just the two of us, and we were having fun at first. Then Brad said we should go to my bedroom. Now that I look back, I should've said no, but I didn't think Brad would want me to do anything I was uncomfortable with. I thought we'd just do some touching and kissing, and a little undressing, and I figured it might be fun.

"Well, one thing led to another, and we had removed most of our clothes. Honestly, it was kind of a thrill, and I liked it at first. But then Brad was increasingly more aggressive than usual, and the next thing I knew, he had removed my panties and he had pinned me down on my bed. I said no to him, but he wouldn't listen. I'm sure I tried to push him off, but before I knew what was happening, he was inside of me. I couldn't scream. He put his hand over my mouth with one hand and held me down with the other, having his way with me. God, I didn't know what to do. I mean, I liked him, but I didn't want to have sex. Not like that."

"He raped you?"

"I guess by today's standards, yes. But back then I don't think anyone would've called it rape. And there was no way I'd ever tell anyone what had happened. I was too embarrassed and too racked with guilt. I felt like I had caused the whole thing to happen. After all, what the heck was I doing inviting him over to the house while my parents were gone, agreeing to go to my bedroom? And he never hit me or threatened me. It all just sort of happened. We were out of control. I didn't want it to happen, but it did."

"Still, what you've described was a rape."

"Yes, it was. But can you imagine what would have happened if my father had found out? How would he have reacted? Would he have been mad at Brad for raping his daughter? Or would he have been angry with me for leading the poor kid on? He would probably have said something like, 'What the heck were you even thinking?' I was the girl who had invited this fine young man over to my house while my parents were away to do what? What the heck did I *think* was going to happen?"

"Wow," I said.

"And that's not the worst of it."

"There's more?"

"The next day Brad told all his friends about us. It made me feel that to him I was more of a conquest than a young girl he cared about. I was a trophy to put in his glass trophy case. I was a touchdown, a game won. And now every time I saw one of his friends, I could see it in their eyes. They knew! They knew the most intimate details about me. It was awful. I can't describe how violated and betrayed I felt. And you know what? Even after all of this happened, I still didn't have the self-respect I needed to drop Brad from my life. Nor did I ever tell my parents about anything that had happened.

"Then finally, thank God, Brad broke up with me. He told me he wanted to date other girls, and he said he hoped I would understand. Can you imagine that? Nowadays, I would've kicked the rotten boy right between the legs, but back then things were different. He was Brad Mason. He was a good kid from a respectable family. And he was a great football player, so don't even get me started about football."

"I had no idea," I said. This story was disturbing, but I was glad Martha had told it to me.

"You're the first person I've ever recalled any of this to. Even after all these years."

"I'm glad you told me."

"It took me such a long time to forgive my dad."

"Forgive your dad?"

"If he'd been a better father, I would've been able to talk to him. Instead, I held everything in, and the guilt was awful. I needed someone to listen to my story and then tell me I wasn't a bad girl, that I wasn't to blame, and that everything was going to be okay. I needed a father."

"How about your mom? Couldn't you tell her? Where was she during all of this?"

"She was even worse than Dad. When Brad broke up with me, she said I'd never be able to hang onto a boy. Then she said boys as good as Brad didn't just grow on trees. Can you imagine that? She had no woman's intuition at all. She was as blind as a bat."

I'd been eating my toast and egg while Martha talked, and I was now done. And so was she. She grabbed the plate and fork, and took them to the kitchen. I thought about what she had told me, and I also thought about the story I had written. We were both talking about football and football players. Yet we were also both talking more about our fathers.

"You're not being fair," a familiar voice said. I turned to look. It was my father, now in the study with me, sitting in a chair and smoking a pipe.

"Dad?" I said. "Are you real?"

"I'm quite real."

I blinked and looked at the man. "I don't remember you ever smoking a pipe."

"I just took it up."

"You look like Fred MacMurray."

"That's just the look I was going for." Dad chuckled, and I had to laugh a little. I laughed even though he made me feel uncomfortable.

"What are you doing here?" I asked.

"I came to tell you a joke."

"A joke?"

"Don't tell me you're so serious these days that you can't enjoy a little joke."

"I can enjoy a joke," I said defensively.

"Good, good. Glad to hear it."

"Well, tell it then."

"Okay, there's a man who is extremely self-conscious about the size of his penis. He gets married, and his sex life with his new wife is great. But he has a secret. Every time they have sex, he turns out the lights so that it's totally dark. This goes on for many years. Well, eventually the wife grows curious about this, and one night she decides to find out what the deal is. So, right in the middle of having sex with her husband, she reaches over and turns on the nightstand light. She is shocked to discover her husband has been satisfying her with a plastic dildo. She says, 'So, is this what you've been doing all these years? Explain yourself!' The husband looks at her and says, 'I'll explain the dildo as soon as you explain how we have five kids!'"

I laughed. "That's pretty good," I said.

"Heard it at the country club. Not the sort of joke I can tell your mom, but I thought you might like it."

I thought for a moment. Then I said, "Things could've been so much better."

"Better?"

"Better between us."

"If what?"

"If you'd told me some jokes when I was growing up."

"You honestly don't remember?"

"Remember what?"

Dad puffed on his pipe and said, "I told jokes all the time."

"You did?"

"At the dinner table. In the family room. In the car. On the way home from your football practices. Listen, kid, I was a regular Milton Berle."

"I honestly don't remember that."

Dad puffed a little more on his pipe and smiled. He said, "That's the thing about memory, Son. It can be very selective. I don't care who you are or who your parents were or where you were born—your memory is selective. You remember what you want to remember or what you believe happened or what you're forced to remember. But seldom do you remember all you *should* remember."

Ouch!

He was right, of course. The man who had driven me crazy all my life was right.

And this suddenly said a lot about my writing. Why? I'd been writing and drawing from my personal recollections, which were what? Flawed? Incomplete? Warped? Had everything I'd been writing about been only a small and biased fraction of a truer and more accurate whole?

I turned to ask my dad, but he was gone. The chair he had been sitting in was empty. There wasn't even a wisp of pipe smoke remaining. I suddenly knew where I had to go. I knew exactly what I had to do. I walked out of my study to the kitchen. I couldn't find Martha or Robert, so I left a note saying I had to leave but that I'd be back.

I grabbed my keys and walked into the garage, climbing into my car. I started the engine and opened the garage door. Then, backing out into the street, I took off toward my parents' house across town. When I got there, it was evening. I parked along the curb of the dark street. The property was exactly as I had remembered it. There was the big mulberry tree in the front yard, the lawn was neatly mowed and edged, and there were a ton of flowers in the flowerbeds. My dad's old blue Ford Granada was parked in the driveway, and my red Schwinn ten-speed bike was lying on its side near the bushes. The lights in the house were burning. When I came to the front porch, I could hear my mom talking to my dad from behind the door. I couldn't tell what they were saying, but it probably had something to do with Dad's day at work. I opened the door, walked into the house, and Mom spotted me. She and my dad were seated at the kitchen table.

"There you are," she said.

"Just in time for dinner," Dad said.

"I made tuna casserole."

"It's your favorite, isn't it?"

"It's one of my favorites."

"He likes your meatloaf too."

"The meatloaf is my mother's recipe."

I took a seat at the table and said, "Can someone pass me the milk?"

CHAPTER 9

DICED MUSHROOMS

───•●•───

"Go easy on the milk, dear. This is the last of it. I need to go to the store tomorrow."

"Okay, Mom."

"How much milk do we go through anyway?" Dad asked.

"A lot."

"You'd think we had eight kids. That carton was full when I had breakfast this morning. I only had half a glass."

"I had a couple after school," I confessed.

"We ought to just invest in a cow."

"Don't be silly," Mom said, laughing.

"I'm dead serious," Dad said. "We could keep old Elsie at the side of the house."

"Can you please pass the casserole?"

Mom handed the casserole dish to me and said, "I used those little diced mushrooms you like."

"Thanks."

"Can you please pass the butter?"

"Go easy on the butter, dear. We're running low on that too."

"What *aren't* we running low on?"

I scooped up a couple of big servings of the casserole and plopped them on my plate. Then Mom said, "Your dad and I read the story you gave us yesterday. We both liked it."

"It was a good one," Dad said.

"Thanks," I said.

"You're a good writer."

"Maybe we have another Hemingway living with us. Wouldn't that be something."

"Did you get that other story back from your teacher yet?"

"Not yet."

"She probably gave you an A," Dad said. "I can't imagine she wouldn't have loved it. We both liked that one too."

"What's your next story going to be about?"

"I haven't decided."

"You must have something in mind."

"Well, I was thinking of two ideas. One story would be about some kids cheating on a school test."

"Aha," Dad said.

"That could be interesting."

"I cheated in school once," Dad said.

"You did?" I asked. This surprised me. It was hard to imagine.

"Only once. It cured me once and for all."

"Why? Did you get caught?"

"No, I got away with it. But I never did it again."

"Why not?"

"It was our first test in US History. I was sitting next to a kid named Ernie Parks. The kid looked like a brain. He was new to the school, so I didn't know much about him. But I figured he was a brain by the way he looked. He wore a tie to school every day, and he wore these thick Coke-bottle glasses. He always sat up straight and paid attention to every word that came out of the teacher's mouth. For sure I had him pegged for a straight-A student, a real teacher's pet. Anyway, we were all taking our test, and all the questions were true or false. From where I was sitting, I could see every answer Ernie wrote down, every T and F. I didn't even have to crane my neck or squint my eyes—the answers were right there for the taking. So I did it. I copied all his answers down on my test sheet, and when I turned it into the teacher and the end of the class, I was sure I had an A."

"So, what happened?"

"I got the test back the next day."

"And?"

"There was a big red D on the top of the paper. I had gotten a D! Hell, if I'd answered the questions myself, I figured I would at least have earned a C."

"What grade did Ernie get?"

"He got a D too, of course."

"I thought you said he was a brain."

"It turned out the kid was even stupider than I was. Can you imagine that? He looked like he belonged in an advanced calculus class, but he was as dumb as my big toe."

"Served you right," Mom said.

"That was the first and last time I ever cheated. It just goes to show that you can't trust anyone."

"Good grief," Mom said.

"I saw a kid get caught in my English class," I said.

"What'd the teacher do?"

"He came over and tore the kid's test up and then sent him to the principal's office. I heard some of the kid's friends talking about it. The teacher gave him an automatic F on his test. Sucked for him, since he was already failing the class. I think he had to take the class over in summer school. That was probably the last time *he* cheated."

"Cheaters never prosper," Mom said, summing the lesson up for us.

"Cheaters beware," Dad said. "Take Richard M. Nixon. Now there's a perfect example. Look at all the trouble that idiot found himself in."

"And to think I voted for him," Mom said.

"Don't feel bad. So did I. We both did."

"Susan Willis thinks he's going to be impeached."

"That'll be rich," Dad said.

"Why do you say that?" I asked.

"A bunch of crooks getting together and calling a man a crook. I think it's rich."

We stopped talking for a moment. Then Mom looked at me and asked, "What's the second story you were thinking about?"

"The second story?"

"You said you had two stories in mind."

"Oh, yeah. Well, I was thinking of writing about a girl in school who gets pregnant. She decides not to get an abortion, and just when she begins to show, she leaves school and stays with her aunt in another town. She doesn't want anyone in the school to know she's going to have a baby. The plan is for her to stay with her aunt and have the baby, and then the aunt will care for the child until the girl graduates. As for the father of the child, well, that's what this story will be about. The story is told from the baby's father's point of view and how the pregnancy and baby affect *him*."

"Interesting," my mom said.

"There are stories that have been written from the girl's point of view, but I've never read a story written solely from the boy's point of view."

"Hopefully you're not writing this story from your own experience," my dad said.

"No," I said, laughing.

Dad thought for a moment and said, "Whatever happened to that girl you were dating? You know, the hippie. What was her name?"

"Samantha," I said. "And she wasn't really a hippie. I don't know why you always call her a hippie."

"She seemed like a hippie."

"No, she wasn't a hippie," Mom said.

"Well, she *was* a Democrat."

"Her parents were Democrats," I pointed out. "She was too young to vote."

"Didn't she have a McGovern bumper sticker on her car."

"Who was she supposed to be for? Nixon? Even you don't like Nixon."

Dad laughed. "You got me there," he said. He stuffed a big spoonful of casserole into his mouth and said, "Now Ike—there was a great president."

"I liked him a lot," Mom said.

"Think of the interstates. I mean, seriously think about them. Jesus, Son, do you even know what it was like driving across country before Ike took office? We were living in the dark ages until Ike built the interstates. Those were the dark ages. All those poorly maintained, haphazard highways. One speed trap town after the other. Wrecks, broken-down cars, and overheated engines as far as the eye could see. Now it's smooth sailing. Forty-one thousand miles of slick, nonstop, modern landscaping and pavement. Now there's a story you can write about. What a great book *that* would make, the story of the interstate system. You ought to think about it. It's a terrific idea."

I realized something when I heard Dad suggest this, that he really was from a different generation. I mean, an entire book about the interstates? Really? Why in the world would I want to write a book about a bunch of roads? That's what I thought about while he was talking, and I wondered whether I would seem this out of touch with the world when I talked to my son. What ridiculous notion would I have about the world that would cause my son to scratch his head and say, "What the heck is wrong with this old fool, and what did I ever do to get saddled with this birdbrain as my father?" Did different generations really have to see the world so differently? It seemed that they did. And what would I do as a father when my dear son, my own flesh and blood, my acorn off the tree, looked at me as if I were from another planet whenever I spoke from the heart about the things *I* cared about?

"Does that interest you?" my dad asked.

"Does what interest me?"

"Writing a book about the interstates."

I didn't want to hurt my dad's feelings, so I said, "Maybe. It could be interesting."

"It's best-seller material, for sure."

"It might be," I said.

Dad took another big mouthful of casserole, satisfied that he'd given me some great advice. Meanwhile, Mom was now off in a different world. "I've always thought someone should write a book about homosexuality," she said.

"A book about fairies?" Dad asked.

"You want me to write a book about queers?" I asked. Now I was laughing.

"My cousin, Harv, is a homosexual. You both know that."

"So?" Dad said.

"Well, what about *him*?" Mom asked.

"What do you mean?" I asked.

"Do you think he's funny? Do you laugh at him?"

"Sometimes," Dad said.

I laughed at this. "It's not like we're twisting his arm to be a queer," I said.

"You both have a lot to learn."

"About what?"

"Homosexuals don't choose to be what they are."

"Sure they do," Dad said. "You can either choose to poke your little hot dog in another man's bun, or you can choose not to. It's all about choice."

"It isn't like that."

"Then what's it like?"

"Some people are just born to fall in love with people of the same sex. They don't have a choice. They simply are what they are. They can't wish themselves to be heterosexuals any more than a black person can wish himself to be white."

"That's such a load of crap," Dad said.

"Why do you say that?" Mom asked.

"I think it's offensive as hell when these queers compare their cause to the cause of colored people in America. There's no comparison at all. They cry about their civil rights. Give me a break. It's like saying that all bank robbers have civil rights because they can't help themselves from robbing banks. It's like defending check forgers, kidnappers, arsonists, and pickpockets. We all make choices in our lives, and we should act like adults and live with our choices."

"You are so ignorant sometimes."

"Just calling a spade a spade."

"Comparing homosexuals to criminals is ridiculous."

"Is it?"

"I agree with Dad," I said.

And I did agree with my dad. So, how old was I? Sixteen or seventeen, a junior or senior in high school. It was one of the few things my dad and I agreed on fully. "They ought to round them all up and put them on their own island," Dad said.

"Homo Island," I said.

"Come one, come all."

"Lots of florists, interior decorators, and antique store freaks."

"And hair stylists. Don't forget the hair stylists."

"One big happy family."

"Both of you are ridiculous," Mom said.

We all stopped talking for a minute and focused on eating our dinner. Dad said, "Have either of you heard the one about the Irishman and the Mormon?"

"I don't think I have," I said. Mom didn't say anything. But she did roll her eyes.

"There was an Irishman and a Mormon sitting next to each other on an airplane, and a stewardess stopped in the aisle with her refreshment cart to ask if they wanted something to drink. The Irishman asked her for a glass of whiskey, and the stewardess gave it to him. Then to the Mormon, she said, 'How about you? Would you like a drink too?' The Mormon frowned and said with disgust, 'I'd rather be stripped nude and raped by a dozen sinful whores than let liquor touch my lips.' Then the Irishman handed his drink back to the stewardess and said, 'Me too. I didn't know we had a choice.'"

I laughed at this, but my mom frowned. "You know I don't like those kinds of jokes," she said.

"You shouldn't say that," Dad said. "It makes the joke even funnier."

Dad and I were now laughing together.

He was right. He *did* like to tell us jokes. How could I have forgotten? When we were done eating dinner, Mom cleared the table while Dad and I went to the family room to watch TV. Dad turned on *Rowan & Martin's Laugh-In*, and the two of us watched the show, cracking up at all the dumb jokes and skits. "Here comes the judge. Here comes the judge," Dad said. "Jesus, I don't know why that's so funny, but it is, right, kid? Doesn't it make you laugh? How would you like a Walnetto? *Whack!* Ha, ha, ha. Too much, am I right?"

Then Dad stopped laughing and said, "You know what, Robinson? If we can't laugh at ourselves, we're all dead ducks. If we can't laugh at ourselves, we're going to wind up like those communist bastards in Russia. We'll be standing in line for toilet paper and crying into our vodka. And who wants to be a Goddamn communist?"

"Not me," I said.

"Have you heard the one about the Russian who wants to buy a car?"

"No," I said.

"Good, pay attention. This is pretty funny. There is a Soviet citizen who wants to buy a car. He has finally saved up enough money, and he goes to the appropriate car ministry. The minister informs the man that there are current shortages and that it will be three years before his car is ready. He says they will drop the car off to the man. 'Three years?' the man says. 'What month will it be dropped off?' The minister tells him it will be in August. The man asks, 'What day in August?' The minister says it will be on the second day of the month, and the man asks, 'Morning or afternoon?' The exasperated minister asks, 'Why do you need to know?' The man says, 'Because I have the plumber coming in the morning.'"

"That's pretty good," I said.

"That's Russia for you."

"Why do people even live like that?"

"Because people are idiots."

Mom was done cleaning up after dinner, and she joined us in the family room. She grabbed the remote from the coffee table and changed channels, turning on a made-for-TV movie about a housewife in Los Angeles, whose husband was a doctor and whose three children were in high school.

Mom said, "I've been waiting for months to see this movie. It's based on a best-selling novel. I don't recall the name of the book, but I read it last year on the beach while we were vacationing in Hawaii."

Dad listened while Mom talked, and when she was done speaking, he shrugged and said, "Fine with me."

"What's it about?" I asked.

"Just watch," Mom said.

So I watched, and as best as I could figure out, the doc husband had been diagnosed with cancer, but he couldn't get up the nerve to tell his wife or kids about it. He was just going on with his daily routine as if nothing was wrong with him. In the meantime, his wife was having an affair with another doctor at the hospital, and the two of them were trying to figure out how to spring the news of their affair on the husband and the kids. Then the wife learned of her husband's cancer from one of the nurses at the hospital, who it turned out was simultaneously having an affair with the husband. The nurse knew of the affair the wife was having with the other doctor, and she decided to tell her about her husband's cancer, hoping she would let loose of him. She wanted to be with him during his last days, and she didn't want him to be doted upon by the unappreciative wife, who obviously didn't love him anyway.

So in the scene we watched, the wife was confronting her husband about the cancer, and he denied it. But once the wife began to cry, the husband broke down and confessed. Then the children came into the room during this confession, and they heard everything. They too began to cry, and the next thing you knew, the whole family was in each other's arms and crying.

"I love you," the wife said. "I love all of you."

The husband said to his wife, "I love you too. I have always loved you."

"Where did we go wrong?" the wife asked.

"I don't know," the husband said.

"We're a family, right?"

"We are," the husband said.

"Oh, Daddy," one of the kids said. "We don't want you to leave us."

"Don't die," another kid said.

"We need you in our lives," the third kid said.

Well, my mom was now sobbing. It was quite a sight. She was wiping the tears from her cheeks with her hands and crying her eyes out. Dad went to the bathroom and returned with a box of tissues, handing it to her. "My God," Mom said. "This is awful."

"I don't know how you can watch this crap," my dad said.

"What if *you* were going to die?"

"I'm not going to die."

"Everyone dies. It just isn't fair."

"If everyone dies, then why get upset about it?"

"Because it's so sad."

"Jesus," Dad said.

"Don't you have any feelings at all?"

"Of course I have feelings. But this is a TV show. These people aren't even real."

"Damn you," Mom said. And she started crying even harder. It was kind of weird how hard she was crying. It looked like she was actually in pain."

"Jesus," Dad said. "Now you're making me cry." And Dad started sobbing, at first gently and then a little harder.

"It's so sad."

"It is," Dad agreed.

"What's wrong with you guys?" I said.

"There's nothing wrong with us," Mom said.

"The world is such a sad place," Dad said. "What's wrong with *you*?"

"This seems kind of stupid to me," I said.

"Stupid?"

"Getting this upset over a TV show."

Now both of my parents were literally bawling. They were so distraught that they could barely talk. "You should talk to Dr. Bell about this," Mom said.

"Dr. Bell?"

"About your aversion to emotion."

"That's an excellent idea," Dad said.

"Come with me," a voice said. I turned to look, and it was Dr. Bell. She was in the room with us. What the hell? Where did she come from?

"What are you doing here?" I asked.

"You need help."

"Help with what?"

"That's what we're going to find out."

"Dad, give me a hand here," I said. I was hoping my dad would interfere.

"You made your bed," Dad said. "Now you're going to have to lie in it."

"He's become so callous," Mom said, still crying.

"Follow me," the doctor said.

I stood up from the sofa, and I followed Dr. Bell out of the family room. I'm not sure exactly how it happened, but we were suddenly in her office. It all looked so familiar, like I'd been there a hundred times—maybe for real or maybe just in my dreams. I was now seated in front of the doctor's desk, and she was in her big leather chair. I looked around. There were diplomas on the walls, bookshelves full of books, and an oil painting of a city scene in Paris.

"I feel like I've been here before," I said.

"Not likely," the doctor said.

"I'm sure of it. I recognize the painting."

"Probably déjà vu."

"I guess that's possible."

"I'd like to play a little game with you."

"A game?"

"It's a game we psychiatrists play. It's called 'word association.'"

93

"Yes, I'm familiar with it," I said. "I learned about it in college."

"Are you up to it?"

"Why not?" I said.

"I'm going to say a word, and you're to tell me the first thing that comes into your mind."

"Yes, I know how it's done."

"Maybe we'll learn something."

"Okay," I said.

"The first word is *rabbit*."

"You want to know the very first thing I think of? That's easy. It's the cartoon character Bullwinkle. He says, 'Watch me pull a rabbit out of my hat.' Then he pulls out a roaring lion and says, 'Oops, wrong hat!' That's the first thing that comes to my mind. Does that help?"

"We need to do a lot more words. Not just one. I need to get a comprehensive picture of your psyche."

"Okay, go on."

"How about the word *beer*?"

"*Beer, beer*," I said. "I think right away of Billy Beer. Do you remember Billy Beer? They made it when Jimmy Carter was our president. Do you remember his crazy brother, Billy? They came out with a beer named after him, and I remember thinking, *Wow, what a bizarre country we live in*."

"How interesting," the doctor said. She was writing down some notes on a sheet of paper. "How about *tire*?"

"Like a car tire?"

"Whatever comes to your mind."

"I think of the movie *The Misfits*. Have you seen it?"

"No," the doctor said.

"It starred Marilyn Monroe and Clark Gable. Gable was an aging cowboy, and Monroe was a showgirl. They were out in the Nevada desert, trying to catch wild mustangs, and Gable and his cohorts, played by Eli Wallach and Montgomery Clift, chased the mustangs with their truck. They would rope the poor horses and tie them down with old car tires attached to the ropes. It was very disturbing to see these free animals roped and captured, to be sold to make dog food. It was such a great movie. I liked it a lot. It was in black and white and made back in the sixties."

"So, the movie disturbed you?"

"Yes, it did. I remember it bothered me a lot."

The doctor wrote down more notes and then asked, "How about the word *scissors*?"

"I think of cutting snowflakes from folded paper when we were kids. Did you do that? I got a big kick out of it. The bigger and more ornate the snowflake was, the better."

"How about the word *water*?"

CHAPTER 10

A FEW WORDS

——◦•◦——

"Well, *water* is an interesting word," I said. "And I'll tell you exactly what comes to mind. The first thing I think is, *Jesus, since when did this become such a thing?* I can't stand water. I really don't like it. Drinking it, that is. I don't see how people drink so much of the awful stuff. I mean, everywhere you go these days someone has a bottle of water that either they are drinking or they are offering to you. 'Would you like a water?' they ask. A water? They've got to be kidding. Who in the hell wants to drink water? Give me a Coke or a ginger ale or a cup of coffee or an ice-cold beer. But water? It's just so slippery and disgusting, and it has no flavor at all. It's like drinking stale, liquid air. It has no sugar. And it has no substance. I guess it's okay to swim in, shower in, bathe in, and even pee in. And it's useful for washing clothes and dishes, for cleaning the car, and for watering the lawn. But for drinking? No thanks. I'd rather chew on a cotton ball than drink a glass of water."

"I've never met anyone who didn't like water," the doctor said.

"I vote no on water."

"Very well," the doctor said. She wrote several sentences on her sheet of paper and looked up at me. "Let's move onto the next word. How about *father*?"

"Well, that's a loaded one," I said.

"What's the first thing that comes to your mind?"

"A *New York Times* crossword puzzle," I said.

"How interesting."

"I am speaking from experience. I've tried to solve these puzzles many times. I can get a few of the words right, but I can never get them all. Not even close. I know there are people who can do these puzzles, but I don't happen to be one of them. And I'm guessing most people are like me. We look at the list of clues, and we rack our brains for the correct words. It should be easy, right? I mean, the clues all make perfect sense once you know the answers, but coming up with the right answers is difficult and often impossible. The way I see it, this is a lot like being a father. You want to do the best job possible, but no matter how hard you try to do the right things, these right things always seem just beyond your reach. It should all make sense and be easy as pie, but it isn't. The clues should help you, but usually they don't help at all. Once all is said and done, all that's left for you to do is ask for forgiveness, apologize for biting off more than you could chew, and count on the power of your child's love to pull you through. Yes, you'll need that love. Like I said, there are probably lots of people who are very good at these puzzles, but I don't happen to be one of them. At least, that's the way I feel."

"You don't think you were a good father?"

"I don't know. And I think if I was a good father, I would know it. I would know in my heart that I had succeeded, that each and every one of those crisscrossed boxes had been filled with the correct letters of the alphabet and that all the clues would be checked off. But no, that's not how I feel."

"But you love your son?"

"Yes, of course, I love him. And I believe he loves me. But our love feels more like a consolation prize than a first-place medal."

"Maybe you're being too hard on yourself."

"That's possible."

The doctor wrote on her sheet of paper and looked up at me. "How about the word *planet*? What does that bring to mind for you?"

"*Planet*? As in Jupiter or Saturn?"

"Yes, or as in Earth."

"I think of absurdity."

"Absurdity?"

"I think of what happened to me a few weeks ago. Or maybe I'm what happened to it. I guess it depends on how you look at it. Martha was cooking lamb chops for dinner, and she realized she had no mint jelly to go with the chops. I was watching a movie on TV, and she came in and asked if I would go to the grocery store to pick up some jelly. Well, hell, I really didn't want to go. It seemed like such a hassle, my having to get up off the couch and drive all the way to the store during the middle of my movie. The store was about ten miles away from our house, and factoring in everything I would have to do, it would probably take half an hour or more to run the stupid errand. And me? I didn't care if we had mint jelly or not, but Martha couldn't eat lamb without her mint jelly."

"And this has what to do with the word *planet*?"

"I'm getting there."

"Okay, go on."

"How much do you know about planets? About stars? About outer space?"

"I know a little."

"Did you know that people standing on Earth's equator are spinning around the axis of the earth at a thousand miles per hour? Did you know people on the poles aren't spinning at all? Did you know that not only is the Earth spinning but that it's flying around the sun at sixty-seven thousand miles per hour? Just think of it. And did you know that you weigh most at the equator and less and less as you move toward the poles? Did you also know that Earth's core is nine thousand eight hundred degrees? And do you have any idea how big the sun is? It might surprise you. No doubt you'd never guess by looking at it, but a million Earths can fit inside the sun. Did you know the next closest stars to Earth are in the Alpha Centauri system, over four light-years away? Do you have any idea how far a light-year is? It's the distance it takes for light to travel a year, nearly six trillion miles. Six trillion miles? Imagine this distance and then put yourself in my shoes. Martha was asking me to drive ten miles to get her mint jelly, and I felt imposed upon. It seemed like such a hassle for a jar of jelly. It's absurd, isn't it? It's all absurd."

"I see what you mean," the doctor said.

"When Martha asked me to run to the store, I said, 'Jesus, Martha, seriously? You really want me to go all the way to the grocery store?'"

"Did you go?"

"I did," I said. "I got in my car and drove. I went into the store and found the mint jelly. I purchased it. I then drove the jelly home and gave it to Martha. What a royal pain it was. 'I hope you're satisfied,' I said, and Martha thanked me and smiled. Meanwhile, the Earth we were both on continued to whirl around the sun at sixty-seven thousand miles per hour. I'd call that absurd."

Again, the doctor wrote something down on her sheet of paper, and when she was done, she looked up at me. How about the word *good*?"

"I think of something that is cooperative."

"Cooperative?"

"Isn't that what *good* means?"

"Is that what *good* means to you?"

"It is," I said. "When I think of something being good, I think of that thing being cooperative. In other words, I think of it cooperating with the way I would like things to be. Same thing with people. When I think of a person being good, I think of that person behaving in a way that cooperates with how I'd like to see them behave. A good child is one who does as he is told, who treats others the way I would like to see him treat them, who conducts himself the way I would like to see the kid conduct himself. And a bad child? Well, a bad child does not do this. A bad child is uncooperative. And it's the same thing with everything else in the world. A good day, for example, is one that cooperates with how I would like to see a day play itself out. A good meal at a restaurant is one that tastes the way I want the meal to taste. A good politician? He is one who behaves the way I want him to behave. And a good country is one that treats its people the way I think they ought to be treated. And on and on, so that in essence, being good is all about being cooperative."

"So, what is bad? Is it the opposite of good?"

"Yes, but don't misunderstand this. Bad is *not* evil. Bad never has been evil. Bad is being uncooperative. A bad person, for example, doesn't necessarily have to do anything evil. He just doesn't cooperate with us. Look around. There are lots of bad people locked up in our jails and prisons, and they aren't there because they're evil. They are there because they refused to cooperate with the rest of us. They failed to obey the rules we made up and agreed to live by. And there are bad things and other people besides criminals. You can have a bad day, one of those rotten days that refuses to turn out as you would like it to. And there are bad leaders, those bad men who refuse to lead their people the way we'd like to see them lead. No, they won't cooperate with us, so we call them 'bad.' All kinds of things and people in the world won't cooperate with us. And one man's bad can be another man's good. While most of us would say a white supremacist group is bad, the members of that group call their cause 'good.' Republicans and Democrats argue until they're blue in the face and call each other 'bad' and 'good.' One man's art is often another man's garbage. One group's right is often another group's wrong. One country's system of government is another's tyranny. This is everywhere. All you have to do is look around at the world. The point being that good is not inherently good. Good is not a pure bar of gold. Good is entirely relative to the goals, desires, and opinions of those who are trying to make the world cooperate. In other words, good is just that. It is cooperation."

"You said that bad is not evil. What exactly do you mean by this?"

"No, bad is not evil at all. And contrary to conventional wisdom, the opposite of good is not evil. Evil is a dear and close friend to good and bad alike. When we want to make this or that good, we try to make it cooperate, and in order to make it cooperate, we often employ evil to get our way. Do you know how evil is defined in the dictionary? It is 'behavior that is profoundly immoral or wicked.' Profoundly immoral and wicked means are employed every day to make the world cooperate with us. In other words, we readily employ evil to make the world good. You want an example? Take our criminal justice system. We shackle those who won't cooperate and confine them to prison cells for years. Sometimes we even kill them. You might call it 'justice,' but I call it 'wicked' and 'immoral.' This is *not* how man should treat his fellows. And this is done on much larger scales. We obliterate cities, maiming and murdering thousands of people, and what are wars but struggles to make the rest of the world cooperate? No, the opposite of good is not evil. In fact, evil is often good's best and closest friend."

The doctor was writing all this down on her sheet of paper, trying to keep up with me. When I was done talking and when she was done writing, she looked up and said, "What about the word *arrow*?"

"Where are you coming up with these words?" I asked, laughing.

"Off the top of my head."

"*Arrow*, eh?"

"Go on."

"*Arrow* as in bow and arrow, as in the Indians who lived in America before the rest of the world swarmed in to make the land theirs? That kind of arrow?"

"Whatever kind of arrow comes to mind."

"America," I said. "It's my home. It's an amazing place. I love this country for so many reasons. And I have no desire to live anywhere else on the planet. It is 'good,' if you will, to a reasonable degree. But it is also one of the greatest, if not *the* greatest, tragedies of our times. A great land and people were obliterated by greedy immigrants so that what? So that we could cover the soil from sea to shining sea with pizza restaurants, grocery stores, gas stations, nail salons, parking lots, dry cleaners, city halls, shopping malls, office supply outlets, and vape stores? Listen, I know the transformation was inevitable, but it doesn't mean it wasn't a tragedy. When I think of what this country could've been without all the hard work, greed, and industriousness the settlers brought with them, it makes me sort of sick to my stomach. So, when you say *arrow*, it kind of makes me feel ill. Or maybe you were referring to a green left-turn arrow at a traffic signal cluster, in which case I would have to say, 'Good job.' Can you imagine having to wait for all the oncoming cars to clear at a busy intersection just so you could make a needed left turn?"

The doctor laughed at this. I was glad I could make her laugh. "You're an unusual patient," she said.

"You've been asking me questions, and I've answered them for you. Can I ask you a question?"

"I don't see why not."

"Where did you go to school?"

She had no difficulty answering my question. In fact, I think she was proud of her answer. "I went to UCLA," she said. "The whole way through."

"A good school."

"Yes, it is."

"Do you have any objection to turning this game around?"

"Meaning what?"

"I'll give *you* the words, and *you* tell *me* what they make you think of."

The doctor stared at me for a moment. Then she said, "Why not? You've been forthcoming to me, so I ought to do the same for you." I had a feeling she was just saying this to make me feel comfortable, but I played along.

"*Wife*," I said.

"*Wife?*"

"That's the word. What comes to your mind?"

"Oh my," the doctor said. "So many things. I used to be a wife, you know."

"You're not married now?"

"I'm divorced. My husband and I divorced eight years ago. We'd been married for thirty-two years. Up until the last few years, I thought we had a good marriage. I never in a million years thought we'd split up, but we did. I guess it just goes to show that nothing lasts forever."

"What was your husband like?"

"When I first met Todd, we were in the same psychology class at UCLA. Both of us had plans to become psychiatrists. Those were such great years. We had our futures ahead of us, and we were so in love. Seriously, I can't imagine two people any more in love with each other than we were. You asked me what Todd was like? He was handsome and brilliant. He had a wonderful sense of humor. He was kind, thoughtful, and always considerate. My parents adored him, and his parents liked me. We got married when we were each twenty-two, and our wedding was magnificent. I still can't believe how much money my parents spent on it: the flowers, the string quartet, the food, the open bar, and the rest of it. The whole nine yards. I think all of our parents were disappointed when we told them we didn't plan to have children. But our work meant the world to us, and we knew we wouldn't make good parents. In retrospect, I think we did the right thing. Kids are a lot of work."

"Tell me about it," I said.

"We eventually opened a practice together. Our lives could not have been any more perfect. Then about ten years ago, it happened."

"What happened?"

"Todd was becoming interested in his female patients."

"Interested?"

"Yes, interested. As in interested in dating them. At first, I didn't believe it. I told myself that I was just being overly suspicious and unduly jealous. I figured this was being brought on by my aging. After all, I was getting older, and I was not as alluring as I had been when I was younger. I knew this. I wasn't going to fool myself into thinking I would always be young. And at the same time, Todd was getting better looking. You know, the way some men do. He was more distinguished and mature, and it was no wonder I was getting suspicious. I did everything I could to keep myself grounded. I told myself over and over that Todd loved me and that he would always love me. That was, after all, what we had promised to each other when we said our vows. But finally, I couldn't ignore the signs any longer."

"The signs?"

"I mean, the changes in Todd. He was changing right before my eyes. He had joined a gym and stopped there every evening after work to exercise. If you knew Todd, you'd know that this was not him. And it wasn't just all the time he spent at the gym. Now Todd was very careful about what he ate, not so that he could be healthier but so that he could keep his physique in shape. And he was buying new clothes. He also bought a new car, a red sports car. And he was now wearing tighter underwear. I mean, why would he care about his underwear? Every weekend I had to wash them, wondering. And the cologne. Good God, the poor man reeked of cologne.

"So, no, this wasn't my Todd. This was *not* the man I fell in love with and married. He was turning into some sort of a cross between a psychiatrist and a wannabe Las Vegas gigolo. At first, I wrote this behavior off as a midlife crisis. Then I began to hear things."

"Hear things?"

"From other people. Certain things from my friends. Todd had been seen by them in restaurants, having dinner with some of his female patients, or in bars, or even once in a dark movie theater. Here I had always thought Todd was staying late in our office or visiting hospitals or having meetings with other doctors. This was all too much. I had heard it from several people, and there had to be some truth to it.

"I hired a private investigator to follow Todd around for a couple weeks, and when I got the report back, I couldn't believe my ears or eyes. I was told exactly what Todd had been doing, and I was shown photographs. There was now no denying it. The man was cheating on me, not just a little but all over town. At first, I was devastated, and I cried. Then I was furious. I sucked it up and confronted Todd, and you know what he said to me? He said, 'I'm really sorry, babe, but I think we ought to get a divorce.' There was no explanation for his behavior at all. I don't know. Maybe no explanation was needed. Six months later we were signing divorce papers, and now here I am, with no children and no husband. Nothing to show for myself except for this lame psychiatric practice. So welcome to my world. 'Wife?' you ask. I hope you're satisfied."

"Sorry," I said.

The doctor suddenly burst out crying. I reached for a box of tissue on her desk, and I tried to hand it to her. She just cried even louder and swatted it away. She said, "Get out of here. Just get out of here!"

"Maybe I can help," I said.

"Just leave!"

I suddenly felt a sharp pain in my chest. It really hurt, and I brought my hands up to hold my chest. "Shit," I said. I didn't know what else to say.

"What's wrong?" the doctor asked. Suddenly she had stopped crying.

"My chest," I said. "It feels like a darn cement truck is parked on it."

"It hurts?"

"It hurts like hell." I fell from my chair to the floor and went into a fetal position, still holding my chest with my hands. "Jesus, what's wrong with me?"

"I think you're having a heart attack."

"A heart attack?"

"How old are you?"

"I don't know," I said. And this was strange. I honestly didn't know my own age.

"I'm calling 9-1-1."

I must have passed out, because the next thing I knew I was in the back of an ambulance, which was racing through the streets. There was an EMT with me, and I reached and grabbed his forearm. "Where are we going?" I asked.

"To the hospital," he said.

"What's wrong with me?"

"You're having a heart attack."

"Is the doctor coming along?"

"What doctor?" the EMT asked. He didn't understand my question. He said, "There will be a doctor at the hospital."

"No, no, I mean my psychiatrist. Dr. Bell. You know, the woman who called you guys."

"I don't know any Dr. Bell."

"I was in her office."

"We picked you up at your home."

"At my home?"

"Your wife called 9-1-1. Good thing she did. Good thing she found you when she did."

"Where was I?"

"On the floor of your study."

On the floor, yes. But in my study? No, this was all very confusing, and I wondered if I *was* at home, and if so, what was I doing? Dozing off in my study and dreaming about Dr. Bell, or was I writing a story about her? Or was I just daydreaming. No, the visit to her office had seemed so real.

Dr. Bell, Dr. Bell. Who the hell even was she? Was she a real person, or did I just make her up?

The next thing I knew, I was being wheeled through the maze of hospital hallways. The EMTs stopped for a moment to talk to a doctor I guessed was telling them what to do. I must have been very ill, because I couldn't understand anything they were saying. I could hear their voices, but I couldn't make out the words. All of a sudden, I was moving again down this hall and down that hall and up an elevator and down another hall, left and right, through a pair of doors, until finally we stopped in a room. There a nurse worked quickly but methodically to set me up, attaching me to the equipment, taking my temperature, and checking my blood pressure. A machine was beeping, and that was a good sign. It was probably my heartbeat. Then I could hear a conversation from outside of the room, muffled voices, but there was no laughter.

"Am I going to be okay?" I asked the nurse, who was still in my room.

"We're doing everything we can," she said.

"Is my wife here? I'd like to see my wife."

"You'll be able to see her soon."

"And my son, Robert? Is he here too?"

"They're both here. Just be patient. There are a few more things we need to do."

CHAPTER 11

BEEP, BEEP, BEEP

───── ◦•◦ ─────

I was in an intensive care unit. I knew this because the nurse had finally told me where the hell I was. She also told me the doctor would be talking to me soon. I was new to this, having never been a patient in a hospital before. It was like being in a science fiction movie.

Beep, beep, beep. My heart was still beating, and that was a good sign, right?

"Well, hello there," a man's voice said. It was my doctor. He was dressed in a white cotton coat, gray slacks, and black shoes. And there was a stethoscope around his neck. "I'm Dr. Prout," he said. "I'll be your physician. Looks like you had a little incident with your ticker, eh?"

"I guess so," I said.

"We're going to take good care of you. If everything goes according to plan, and barring any serious inconveniences, we should have you back on your feet and throwing jabs at the real world in several days."

"That's good to know."

"We just need to run some tests and keep an eye on you for a short while." The doctor looked at the readout on the machine to which I was attached. "Nurse?" he said.

"Yes, Doctor," the nurse said.

"Let's give him some of that stuff in the yellow bottle."

"The yellow bottle?"

"Yes, I'm pretty sure it's yellow."

"There are three yellow bottles, Doctor."

"Use the one that starts with a *Z*." The doctor looked over at me and said, "I can never remember the exact names of all these confounded medications. They all sound the same after a while."

"This one?" the nurse asked. She was holding up a small bottle.

"That's the one," the doctor said.

I didn't say anything. I figured these people knew what they were doing, or they wouldn't be there. "My chest still feels a little tight," I said.

"We'll take care of that in a minute," the doctor said. Then to the nurse he said, "And give him some of that brown stuff."

"Yes, Doctor."

The doctor had a metal clipboard, and he was reading something from it. "Says here that your wife found you in your study."

"That's what I understand."

"What were you doing?"

"That's the weird thing, Doc. I don't remember being in my study. I thought I was sitting in my psychiatrist's office. I don't remember anything about my study."

"I see."

"But if my wife says she found me in my study, then I'm sure that's where she found me."

"What were you doing with your psychiatrist?"

"Word association."

"Ah, I see."

"We were actually talking about her divorce."

"You were talking about her divorce? Why *her* divorce? Who was examining whom?"

"Well, she was examining me, but we got on the subject of her divorce. She became very upset."

"I see."

"But I must have imagined it."

"Yes, yes, probably so."

"In fact, I don't even have a psychiatrist."

Beep, beep, beep. The doctor was now writing something down in the clipboard. When I said I didn't have a psychiatrist, it caused him to raise his eyebrows. But he didn't make a big deal out of it. He just said, "Sometimes heart attack victims will imagine they are somewhere else. It's nothing for you to worry about. We had a patient in here last week who was sure he had been climbing Mount Everest. The truth? His boss found him in a stall in the men's room at their office building, sitting on one of the toilets. He was in the middle of wiping himself. A wad of toilet paper was still in his hand."

"Weird," I said.

"Isn't it?"

"Should I give the patient a foot massage?" the nurse asked the doctor.

"Good idea."

"A foot massage?" I asked.

"It helps to relax the heart. Your heart is still a little stressed from the attack."

"Okay," I said.

The nurse lifted the blanket off my feet and began to rub my toes. Honestly, the massage felt good, and I could immediately feel the stiffness in my chest relaxing.

"Is his wife here?" the doctor asked the nurse.

"She's here with their son."

"Good, good. Having the family present always helps. Well, given that the family gets along." The doctor then looked at me and said, "Sometimes we get families who don't get along at all. I don't even know why these people come to visit. Last week we had a female patient whose husband showed up and sent her right back into a heart attack. Took us all by surprise. He seemed like a nice guy, but apparently the two of them didn't get along at all. Sad case. We lost her."

"You lost her?"

"She died. Kaput. Over and done with. Cold as a witch's tit in a brass bra."

"Jeez," I said.

"But I take it that you and your wife get along?"

"Oh, yes."

"And the kid?"

"I get along fine with my son."

"Good, good, then we'll let them in."

"Can I see them now?"

"As soon as your foot massage is done."

"Okay," I said.

The doctor was looking at me, smiling. "Do you know how to whistle?" he asked.

"I know how," I said. "But I'm not very good at it. Why do you ask?"

"A recent published study shows that if you can whistle 'On the Sunny Side of the Street' while your feet are being massaged, the calming effect of the foot massage is enhanced by twenty to thirty percent."

"I can try," I said. I tried to whistle the old song, but not only was my whistling awful; I also realized I didn't know the whole tune.

"It was just a thought," the doctor said. He looked like he wanted to put his hands over his ears.

"I guess I'm not much of a whistler after all."

"No, but you'll be fine," the doctor said. "Just try to relax. Seriously, you've got to relax. Concentrate on your feet and let the nurse do her job."

"I must admit this does feel good."

"I learned from the best," the nurse said.

"We had Sarah Rosenblatt come to the hospital to train our staff," the doctor said. "Maybe you've heard of her?"

"No," I said.

"Foot massager extraordinaire. A legitimate pioneer in her field. Wrote an entire book on it."

"She autographed my copy," the nurse said.

Beep, beep, beep. The doctor was writing on his clipboard, and the nurse was slowly working her way up from the tops of my feet to my ankles.

"Hey," the doctor said suddenly. "Do you want to hear a good heart joke?"

I thought it was kind of weird for a doctor to be telling his patients jokes about hearts, but I said, "Sure, why not? Let's hear your joke."

The doctor said, "A patient needed a heart transplant, and he was discussing the options with his doctor. The doctor told him there were three hearts available and that the man could choose one of them. The first heart was from a healthy young male athlete, who ate all the right foods and exercised every day. He died when he was hit by a car while riding his bike. The second heart was from a middle-aged pilot, who never drank or smoked a day in his life, but he died when his plane crashed into the side of a mountain. The third heart was removed from a seventy-year-old attorney, who diligently practiced law for over forty years. The man said, 'Heck, I don't even have to think about it. Give me the old attorney's heart.' The doctor asked why he picked this heart, and the man laughed and said, 'I want a heart that has never been used.'"

I laughed, but you know what? I thought I might have heard the joke before. Yes, for sure. In fact, I remember telling it to a few people.

"Jokes are always helpful," the doctor said.

"He knows a bunch of them," the nurse said to me.

The doctor was looking at his clipboard again. "It says here that you're a writer," he said.

"I am," I replied.

"What do you write?"

"Just stories."

"Stories? Like about what?"

"All kinds of things."

"Give me an example. Tell me about one of your favorite stories."

"Like a synopsis?"

"Something like that."

"Well, I wrote a novel about a guy who was bad luck. He didn't just have bad luck; he *was* bad luck. The title of the book was *Carrier*, and the idea was that this guy carried bad luck around with him and gave it to the people he had contact with. The story starts with a few incidents where strange misfortunes befall the man's close friends. Then his doctor gets in a car accident, and his accountant breaks his leg falling off a ladder. The mishaps increase in frequency, and the man figures out what's going on, realizing that the more contact he has with people, the more likely they are to have trouble. Slowly but surely, the calamities suffered by his victims become more serious and tragic so that people are eventually dying. He tries to keep away from others, but he finds contact with them to be unavoidable. So he moves out to the desert where he'll be alone, where he won't come into contact with anyone. He has his food and drink delivered to his driveway, but soon even the delivery boy dies in a horrible car accident. He finds himself trapped in this desert house, unable to contact anyone, unable to obtain food or drink, unwilling to even pick up the phone. A year goes by, and his brother, who hasn't heard from him for months, goes to the house to see if he's okay. He finds his brother's emaciated body on a couch, starved to death. The story ends as his brother kneels at the couch and holds his dead brother's hand in his. 'If only you had called me,' he says. He lets go of his brother's hand and stands up. He then steps outside to get some fresh air, and he removes his cell phone from his pocket to make a call to the coroner. Just as he's pressing in the number, there is a rattling sound, and the next thing he knows a diamondback snake bites his ankle. He kicks his foot to shake the snake loose, but as he kicks, he loses his balance and falls, hitting his head on the concrete steps to the house. He is now unconscious, and blood is oozing from the back of his head. A couple hours later, a group of vultures have surrounded his dead body."

"That's the end?"

"Yes," I said.

"Wow, that's quite an ending. It doesn't exactly make you feel warm and fuzzy."

"I suppose not."

"Me? I go for books that have happy endings. Maybe it's because I see so much tragedy here at the hospital that I *need* the happy endings. A guy has to feel there's always a ray of hope. There has to be light at the end of the tunnel. *You* know what I'm trying to say."

"Sure," I said.

"Are all your books like this?"

"No, not all of them."

"That's good." The doctor stared at me a moment. Then he said, "You should think about writing a book about a man and his dog. People love dog stories."

"So I've heard."

The doctor looked over at the nurse and said, "Give him more of the brown stuff."

"Already?"

"He needs it."

"Yes, Doctor."

"What does the brown stuff do?" I asked.

The doctor ignored my question. He said, "You know, you're not the first writer we've had in here."

"I didn't think I was," I said.

"Ever hear of an author named Ernie Hemingway?"

"Of course," I said. "Everyone in the country has heard of Ernest Hemingway."

"Not Ernest," the doctor said. "Not Ernest but Ernie. You know Ernie, like the kid in *My Three Sons*."

"Ah," I said. "Then no, I haven't heard of anyone named Ernie Hemingway."

"He was a patient here last year. He had a heart attack just like you. Except his wife didn't find him. His girlfriend is the one who called 9-1-1. Actually, we think she's the one who caused the heart attack. He was having sex with her and— *wham!* Next thing he knew, he was in the back of a speeding ambulance on his way here to see yours truly. Have you read any of his books?"

"Like I said, I haven't even heard of him."

"Ernie, not Ernest."

"Yes, you said that."

"He wrote some real crazy novels. He gave me one of them to read. I don't usually read novels, but the guy intrigued me, so I gave it a shot. It was some really weird stuff. The story I read made your tale about the bad luck guy seem like a Norman Rockwell painting."

"Did his story have a happy ending?"

"Well, at least he got that part right. Yes, it did have a happy ending. Everyone in the story lived happily ever after. Everyone except for the villain. Things didn't work out so well for him. He died a horrible death."

"What was the story about?"

"I forget, actually."

"You forgot the story?"

"The only thing I remember is the damsel in distress."

"The damsel in distress?" I said, laughing. I hadn't heard anyone use that term for years.

"Isn't that what they call it?"

"I'm not sure."

"I'm talking about the female character in the story, whose life is being threatened by the evil villain. You know, the lovely girl who the dastardly villain has tied to the railroad tracks. Often she's the hero's sweetheart. In this book the girl's name was Wendy."

"Okay," I said.

"She reminded me of a girl I knew in high school. Her name was Cindy. I had a terrible crush on her but never had the nerve to approach her. I would daydream about her constantly, but I never spoke to her once. Did you have a crush on a girl like that when you were in high school? It drove me crazy. I remember I used to sit alone in my bedroom and think of her for hours, and I would cry my eyes out. She terrified me, and yet I was head over heels in love with her. Yet the truth was that I didn't know her at all. Everything I believed I knew about her I had just manufactured in my imagination. She was a real person, and yet she wasn't. I mean, she was real all right, but I didn't have a clue what she was actually like. Then can you guess what happened? Her parents moved to Arizona and took my dream girl with them. Just like that, she was gone forever. I don't think she ever even knew my name. To her I was then, and always will be, just a nobody."

"That's kind of sad," I said.

"I guess it is."

"Were you shy around all girls?"

"No, just Cindy."

I thought for a moment and said, "I did have sort of a crush like that in high school."

"What was the girl's name?"

"It was Gabriela."

"That's a nice name."

"It's weird, but I still dream about her."

"Ha," the doctor laughed. "I dream about Cindy too."

"Sometimes I dream that she shows up somewhere with my wife and me, and my wife becomes friends with her."

"That's weird, but same thing happens to me," the doctor said. He looked over at the nurse and asked, "How's that foot massage coming?"

"I'm back on the heels," the nurse said.

"How long is this going to take?" I asked.

"Until we get you good and relaxed. I'd like to see your heartbeat slow down a little more."

"How fast is it now?"

The doctor looked at the machine and said, "You're still over a hundred. We need to get you in the seventies."

A second nurse came into the room. She put her hand on the doctor's shoulder and said, "The wife and kid are asking when they can come in to visit with the patient. What should I tell them?"

"It'll be soon."

"The kid keeps crying."

"See?" the doctor said to me.

"See what?"

"The boy really does love you. You've got him worried to death with this heart-attack business."

"He's such a sweet boy," the first nurse said.

"You're going to have to keep an eye on him," the doctor said to me.

"An eye on him?"

"It isn't uncommon for the children of heart-attack victims to act out as they get older. There was a study published."

"Act out how?"

"Most commonly they will steal from others."

"Steal?"

"They have suddenly been put in a situation where they are in jeopardy of losing a parent. It's shocking and traumatic for them, and subconsciously they are inclined to make an attempt to even the score by becoming thieves. We see many of these kids wind up in prison down the road. Like I said, there was a study published. It's a real thing, and I've seen it happen. I had a male patient in here six years ago, and now his kid is serving ten years for armed robbery up in San Quentin. I warned the dad when he was here, but he didn't believe me."

"Jeez," I said. "I've never heard about any of this."

"Well, now you know. How old is your boy?"

"I don't know," I said. "To tell you the truth, I don't even know how old I am."

The doctor looked at the nurse who was still massaging my feet. "More of the brown stuff," he said to her.

"Yes, Doctor," she said.

"You, fluff his pillow," the doctor said to the second nurse, who was still in the room. "Are you cold?" the doctor asked me. "They keep it pretty chilly in here."

"I'm okay," I said.

"We can get you a warm blanket."

"No, I'm fine."

"How about the plumbing?"

"The plumbing?"

"Do you need to urinate? Or have a bowel movement?"

"No," I said.

"Let the nurse know when you're ready."

"Why would she need to know?"

"She can help you out."

"Oh," I said. I hadn't even thought about this. What were they going to have me do? Did I have to relieve myself in front of the nurse? Would I have to use a bedpan? I didn't even want to think about it.

"I'll be right back," the doctor said.

"Okay," I said.

The doctor and the second nurse walked out of the little room while the first nurse continued to rub my feet.

Beep, beep, beep. My heart was still beating.

I closed my eyes. The room was quiet for several minutes, and then there were the strangest sounds. Had I fallen asleep? I certainly didn't feel the same. The air was thick, and my chest no longer felt tight. Instead, there was a throbbing pain in my left leg. And this is going to sound unbelievable, but I could hear gunshots.

The shooting was taking place not in the hospital but outdoors. There was a lot of shouting out there and in the hospital halls. I opened my eyes, but I wasn't sure what I was seeing. Bamboo? Yes, lots of bamboo. There was no one massaging my feet. The nurse was gone, and I was now alone in the room.

Then the doctor burst in. Strange, but he was now at least thirty years younger. I mean, he looked like a kid fresh out of medical school. "We've got to get out of here," he said. His voice was strained, and he was out of breath.

"What's the problem?" I asked.

"It's over."

"What's over?"

"The war is over. Everyone is leaving."

Again, I heard gunshots from outside. "What's the shooting all about?"

"It's a mess out there. It's every man for himself!"

"Jesus," I said.

"We've got to get out *now*."

The doctor removed the IV needle from my arm. "What about my clothes?" I asked.

"No time. Just follow me."

"Where are we going?"

"To the helicopters. Here, take this." He handed me an M-16. An M-16? How ridiculous I must have now looked, wearing a hospital gown and carrying a military rifle. But off we went. And now I was running like mad to keep up with the young doctor. Down the hall we ran. We ran out the side doors and into the parking lot. Bullets were whizzing past our heads, and grenades were exploding in the near distance. We ran across the lot and stumbled into the dank Vietnamese jungle.

CHAPTER 12

THE MALINGERER

———•———

"Are you sure you know where you're going?"

"I'm positive," the doctor said. "Stay right behind me and stop asking questions."

We made our way deep into the steamy jungle. We followed the muddy trail; it wound like a slithering snake through the thick tropical vegetation. Insects were buzzing and clicking, and I could hear loud, agitated birds—or were they monkeys? They were screeching, squawking, and chittering, making such a fuss over us, the human invaders. It was strange how these sounds seemed to echo. The jungle was saturated with wet life, yet it also smelled of death, of gunpowder, blood, and rotting human flesh.

We came across killed bodies everywhere, men and women who were still hopelessly holding guns or machetes, lying flat on their backs, on their sides, or on their fat bellies. They were soaked to the bone, stuck to the cold, slick mud with their eyes fixated—but on what exactly? They were staring at nothing at all. They were just stiff and frozen in place, into their awkward positions, some of them gripping their wounds and some looking as though they were trying to crawl away to safety.

"How far to the helicopters?" I asked.

"It's a ways," the doctor said.

"How far is a ways?"

"Keep the barrel of your rifle up, and be ready to use it." The doctor was still ahead of me, and I was ready to shoot the first thing that moved. Suddenly there was gunfire nearby, and the doctor fell to the jungle floor. "Down, down, down," he said to me, so I dropped.

"Where's it coming from?" I asked.

"That tree. It's a sniper. We've got to take him out."

"I can't see him," I said.

"He's right up there," the doctor said, pointing. "You keep him busy. I'm going to circle around." The doctor then took off into the jungle, and I shot at the sniper to keep his attention on me. He shot back. His bullets were splashing into the muddy path just ahead. I continued to shoot, and finally, after a couple of minutes, I heard a loud thud. The sniper was no longer shooting. He had fallen from the tree, and he was dead. The doctor had crept into the branches and sliced the sniper's throat with his knife. "I got him!" the doctor yelled from the tree. "All clear. Come on. Let's get moving."

We proceeded forward. The vegetation was getting thicker, the trail was getting much muddier, and the chatter of the birds or monkeys or whatever they were grew louder, angrier, and more agitated. I had the definite impression that we were not welcome in this jungle. The doctor was still ahead of me, and I followed.

"What did you think of this war?" the doctor asked.

"What do you mean?" I asked.

"Now that it's over."

"I guess I'm glad it's over."

"I mean, do you think it was all worth it?"

"I don't know."

"What do you think was accomplished?"

"I'm not really sure."

"Then what are you doing here?"

"I'm not really sure *how* I got here. I don't think I was drafted. If I remember right, the war was over before I turned eighteen. I think I missed it by a few months."

"And yet here you are."

"Maybe I'm dreaming."

"Pinch yourself. See if it wakes you up."

I pinched my arm, but nothing happened. "It hurts, but I'm not waking up. Maybe I didn't pinch myself hard enough."

"Here," the doctor said. He stopped walking and grabbed my hand. He then cut the back of it with his knife.

"Ouch!" I said.

"Blood," the doctor said. "That's your blood. And that was your pain. Now do you think this is a dream?"

"No," I said.

"You're here," he said. "We're both here in this God-awful place." The doctor turned and started walking again, and I followed. "Just as sure as the sticky, red blood is dripping off the back of your hand, the both of us are here. This is no dream."

"I wasn't going to come."

"What do you mean?"

"I mean, before they brought me over here, I wasn't going to come. I was going to refuse to go. I was thinking of moving to Canada. I remember now. Yes, I was strongly opposed to the war."

"Yet here you are."

"My dad must've talked me into it."

"Was he for the war?"

"No, but he was against dodging the draft."

"Ah, a hypocrite."

"Well, what have *you* been doing here?"

"Saving lives." Suddenly the doctor grabbed my M-16 out of my hands, and he began firing ahead of us. I hadn't seen them, but three Vietcong soldiers were running toward us, brandishing machetes. The doctor filled them with holes before they got to us. They fell in a heap about six feet away, bleeding, moaning, slowly dying. The doctor walked up to the wounded men and put bullets in each of their heads to put them out of their misery. "Vietcong," he said. He handed my rifle back to me. "Keep on your toes."

"I will."

"It's like they come out of nowhere."

"No kidding," I said.

We began to walk again, and the doctor said, "I'll tell you something funny. I mean, funny as in weird. Did you ever stop to think what would happen to you if you broke a law back home? Say you stole something valuable. Say you broke into someone's house and took something that didn't belong to you. There was no violence, mind you, just a simple run-of-the-mill involuntary change of ownership, moving an item from some poor slob's asset column to yours."

"Like stealing someone's coin collection?"

"Yes, exactly. I wasn't going to bring that up, but yes, that's what I'm talking about."

"What about it?"

"What happens to you when you're caught?"

"You're arrested."

"And then?" the doctor asked.

"You're prosecuted."

"And after you're found guilty?"

"You're probably thrown in jail."

"They take away a chunk of your life. A piece of your life that you'll never get back."

"True enough."

"And you're branded as a criminal. A minor instance of bad judgment like this can ruin your time on earth. But let me ask you this. What if, on the other hand, you grab a rifle and some bullets, join the mobilization of thousands of soldiers and bazillions of dollars' worth of lethal artillery and weapons, and turn a small and innocent country into a tragic, blood-and-guts parade of war? What if you willingly participate in the cold-blooded murder of a million of its citizens? What if you lie to the world and claim you're doing all this in the name of securing their freedom? What if you're also responsible for the deaths of thousands of your own citizens while perpetuating this nightmare farce? Are you arrested? Are you prosecuted by a DA? Do you serve any hard jail or prison time? Are you branded as a scoundrel and a criminal?"

"I think it's fair to say that most Americans were very unhappy with this war."

"Buy *why* were they unhappy? Was it because the war was horribly wrong, or was it simply because we lost?"

"You'd have to ask them."

"I don't need to ask them. I know the answer. *To your left!*"

"To my what?"

"To your left. The girl. Shoot her!"

I looked to my left, and a Vietnamese girl was walking up to us. She looked like she was about ten or maybe eleven or twelve. She was smiling at me, which led me to believe she was being friendly. She was holding something tightly in her hands. "Why should I shoot?" I asked the doctor.

"Jesus Christ," he exclaimed, and he jerked the rifle from my hands. He took aim and fired three loud rounds, all of them hitting the poor girl—one bullet in the center of her forehead and the other two in her chest. "Now, hit the deck!" the doctor suddenly shouted, and I dropped down with him. Then there was a violent explosion near the girl's body.

"What the hell?" I said.

"A hand grenade."

"I thought she was bringing us a gift."

The doctor laughed and said, "Oh, it was a gift all right. Courtesy of Ho Chi Minh. That grenade would've finished off both of us."

"Jesus," I said.

The doctor shook his head in disbelief. "How long have you been over here?"

"I'm not sure."

"You sure are naïve." The doctor handed the rifle back to me, thrusting it into my chest.

I was looking at the girl's bloody body. The blast had blown her hands and forearms off and made a mess of the rest of her upper body. "Damn, how old do you think she was?" I asked.

"Who gives a shit?"

"I thought you cared about these people."

"You don't seem to understand. I just want to get out of here alive."

We continued to walk. It wasn't sounding good. There was gunfire up ahead in the jungle, and it was difficult to tell how far away it was. "Sounds bad," I said.

"Someone needs to tell these zipperheads that the war is over."

"What are we going to do?"

"We're going to go around them."

"Off the trail?"

"Yes, off the trail. You have a better idea?"

"Not really."

"How's the leg holding up?"

"The leg?"

"The one I repaired in the hospital."

"Was there something wrong with my leg?"

"You took a few pieces of shrapnel in your thigh. Missed your femoral artery by a half inch."

"I don't remember that."

The doctor looked at me impatiently. I thought I was beginning to annoy him. He asked, "Well, how is the leg?"

"It feels fine."

"Good, then keep up with me. We've got to move fast. These bastards will kill us in a heartbeat."

We moved quickly through the vegetation. I fell several times in the process, but I got right back up. I was able to keep up with the doctor. It wasn't long until we had caught up to the gunfire. It was off to our right. It was difficult to see through the foliage, but the doctor guessed there were ten to twenty Vietcong soldiers causing the trouble. "What do we do?" I asked.

"We keep moving," the doctor said. "Hopefully they won't notice us. Try to walk quietly unless they start shooting at us. If they come after us, run like hell."

"Got it," I said.

The next thing I knew we were in a grassy open field, and there were hundreds of soldiers and South Vietnamese villagers. There were also several choppers, loud motors idling; they were there to pick up passengers. They were evacuating the soldiers and citizens, but they could take only so many at a time. There was a general feeling of panic in the air. I got the impression that if one didn't get on one of these helicopters soon, he or she would be captured by the Vietcong. And I knew the Vietcong were nearby, judging by our encounters with them. They were right there in the jungle. "We've got to get on one of these helicopters now," the doctor said into my ear. "There are too many people and not enough choppers."

A group of soldiers came running out of the jungle and into the grassy field. One soldier was carrying another on his back, and all the men stopped in the clearing, shouting, "Is there a doctor here? We need a doctor!"

"I'm needed," the doctor said to me.

"Have at it," I said.

"Get us a place in line. We've got to get out of here."

"I can do that," I said.

The doctor ran to the soldiers, and the one carrying his comrade dropped the man on the grass. The doctor stepped to the wounded man and fell to his knees. "You've got to save him," one soldier said.

"He took a round to his neck," another man said.

"He's bleeding bad."

"We tried to slow down the bleeding."

"We couldn't get it to stop."

"I need a T-shirt," the doctor said. "Someone take off his shirt and give it to me. Now!"

One of the soldiers took off his shirt. Then they all circled around the doctor and the wounded man as the doctor went to work on the bleeding neck. A soldier stepped up to me and grabbed my arm. "You can move to the head of the line," he said. "They're taking our wounded first." He had noticed my hospital gown and assumed I needed medical attention. "Come with me," he said.

Holding onto my arm and pushing his way through the crowd, the man got us toward the head of the line. "I'm not sure you should be doing this," I said.

"Don't try to be a hero."

"I'm not sure how bad my injuries are."

"We'll get you on the next chopper," the man said, ignoring me. "Keep up with me. They'll take you ahead of the others. Just keep quiet and stay with me." Then loudly he said, "Move aside, move aside. I have an injured soldier. Move aside!" The people in the crowd looked at us. They saw my hospital gown and immediately cooperated. It was so strange the way they all made room for us to move ahead. A Vietnamese man put his hand on my shoulder briefly.

"God bless you, son," the man said.

"Thanks," I said.

"Make room!" the man shouted.

In no time, we were at the head of the line, where they were boarding passengers for one of the helicopters. "Here," the soldier said. "I have a hospital patient. Make room for him." The two men in charge of letting people aboard the helicopter looked me over before letting me come aboard. One of them grabbed my elbow and pulled me forward, but the other stopped us.

"Let's see your injury," he said.

"My injury?"

"Why were you in the hospital?"

"Well, to tell you the truth, I thought I had a heart attack, but the doctor said I took several pieces of shrapnel to my thigh."

"You don't even know what you were doing there?"

"I'm not sure."

"Lift up your gown. Let's see your thigh."

I stared at the man a moment. Then I lifted my gown so he could check out my leg. "I'm not sure where the shrapnel hit me," I said.

"I don't see anything," the man said.

"I don't either," the other man said.

"Where is it?"

"I don't know," I said.

"He isn't even injured," a third man said.

"What are you trying to pull?"

"Pull?"

"Show us your injury."

"But I don't know where it is."

"He's a malingerer!" a soldier nearby shouted.

"A malingerer?"

"Listen, I didn't put myself in the hospital," I said. "I was just there. I just assumed there was something wrong with me."

"Do you have any idea of the hell the rest of us have been going through?"

"While you've been sitting in a hospital."

"The hell and the horror," a soldier said, and he started to cry.

"Get him out of here."

"Traitor!"

"Malingerer!"

Now the men began to shove me around from one pair of hands to the other. "Hippie!"

"I'm not a hippie."

"Do you have any idea what these men have been through?" another said to me. "Do you have any idea of the sacrifices they've made, the tragedies they've endured?"

"Malingerer!"

It was a nightmare. The men continued to shove me. Then one of them ripped off my hospital gown so I was naked. "There's not a scar on his body!" he exclaimed.

"Faggot!"

"Malingerer!"

"No, no," I said. There was more pushing and shoving. And then suddenly I woke up. I woke up!

Jesus, it *was* a nightmare. I had been dreaming. I opened my eyes and sat up. It was very, very strange. At first, I wasn't sure where I was, and then I recognized my surroundings. I was in my grandpa's house, and I was in his front room. I was lying on my back on his couch. I must have fallen asleep there, taking a nap.

It was night but not very late. It was dark outside, and the lights in the house were on. I could see the bald back of Grandpa's head. He was sitting in his favorite chair, watching a baseball game on the TV and smoking a cigar. He turned around and saw I was now sitting up.

"You're awake," he observed.

"I am," I replied.

"You fell asleep. I decided to just let you sleep."

"Wow," I said.

"You were tired?"

"I had the strangest dream."

"Ha," he laughed.

"It was awful."

"A nightmare?"

"You could call it that."

"Are you still up for a game of chess?"

"I suppose so." I looked at the coffee table. The board and pieces were set up. Now I remembered. We were going to play a game right before I fell asleep.

"Coffee?"

"That sounds good."

"I'll make a fresh pot."

"How long was I sleeping?"

"About an hour."

Grandpa stood up and walked to the kitchen to make a pot of coffee for us. I looked across the room at the old TV, and the game was in the third inning. "I'm confused," I said. "How old are we?"

Grandpa laughed. "How *old* are we?"

"Yeah," I said.

"Well, you just turned eighteen. You're almost done with high school. And I'm seventy-nine, almost done with my life."

"You've got a long way to go," I said.

"Well, I hope so."

"I know so. Take my word for it."

"I forget. Do you take cream or sugar with your coffee? I have sugar, but I don't keep cream."

"Black is fine."

"Then black it'll be."

I looked at the TV. "It's funny," I said. "I don't remember you being a baseball fan."

"I've always liked baseball."

"And football?"

"Not a big football fan."

"You're watching the Dodgers?"

"Big-time Dodgers fan. I've been a Dodgers fan ever since they moved to LA."

I thought for a moment, then said, "There are probably so many things I don't know about you."

"Don't feel bad," Grandpa said. "I never knew diddly-squat about my own grandfather. He was just a guy who drank a lot of Irish whiskey and smoked a big pipe. He worked with his hands a lot. He had rough calluses on his palms, and I remember those. But I have no idea what exactly he did for a living. Died when I was twelve. But like I said, I didn't know much about him. It was like he lived on another planet."

CHAPTER 13

A GAME OF CHESS

───────◆───────

G randpa brought over the coffee, and he pulled a chair up to the coffee table so we could play chess. Once he was seated, he told me to make the first move, so I slid a pawn forward. "Are you sure you want to make that move?" he asked, and I laughed. It was his way of making me doubt my strategy. He always said the same thing, no matter how I moved. I'd learned not to pay attention to it.

"Your move," I said.

"What were you dreaming about?" he asked.

"Vietnam."

"What about Vietnam?"

"I dreamed I was over there."

"Ah, a war dream."

"Something like that."

"I still have dreams about World War I."

"Do you?" I said, acting as though I was interested. But I wasn't really into hearing about his war dreams. Today I would probably want to hear more, but back then the very last thing I cared about was anything having to do with World War I. I don't know why this was. It just didn't interest me.

"What did you dream?" he asked.

"I dreamed I was over there when the war ended."

"That sounds like a good dream."

"It wasn't. Things were a mess. People were still killing each other, and I was trying to get out of there."

"You and thousands of others."

"Yes," I said.

"It *was* a mess."

"They weren't going to let me on the helicopter. They kept saying I was a malingerer."

"Oh, that's bad."

"Tell me about it."

"So, were you a malingerer?"

"I don't know. It was very confusing. You know how some dreams are. They don't make any sense. You're not sure of others, and you're not even sure of yourself."

"Sometimes I dream I was a coward," Grandpa said. "This wasn't true, so don't get me wrong. But I think I was afraid I might be one, so I dreamed that I was one—if that makes any sense."

"Supposedly I was staying in a hospital because I took some shrapnel in my leg, but when my leg was exposed by a man who was in charge of letting people into the helicopter, there were no scars at all. They all thought I was lying."

"Were you lying?"

"Honestly, I don't know."

My grandpa laughed. "Sounds like a dream. They never make any sense." Grandpa then stared at the chessboard, moved one of his pawns, and said, "Your move."

"What did you think of the war?" I asked.

"The Vietnam War?"

"Yes," I said. "Do you think it was a good war? Did you think it was right or wrong?"

"Well, I'll tell you. I think the very same thing of the Vietnam War as I think of Korea, as I think of World War II, and as I think of World War I."

"Which is?"

"Despite what people say, no wars are right or wrong. They are not moral or immoral. They all just are, and they prove my theory."

"Your theory?" I asked, and I moved my knight out.

Grandpa stared at the chessboard and sighed. Then he said, "Life is simple, Robinson. Much simpler than people imagine. It all boils down to just two basic lines. Two spectrums, if you will."

"Spectrums?"

"The first spectrum is from hate to love, and the second is from chaos to control. Every large and small variation of man's behaviors, endeavors, goals, accomplishments, and failures falls somewhere along the graduated lines of these two spectrums."

"Including wars?"

"Especially wars."

I looked over the chessboard. I then moved my bishop out. "How's that?" I asked.

"Are you sure you want to move that there?" Grandpa asked, and I smiled.

I ignored my grandpa's comment and said, "I don't really understand your spectrums."

"No? They're very simple."

"Can you give me an example?"

"Okay, let's take the Vietnam War. Very simple. What was the war about? It was all about stopping communism, right?"

"Yes, that's what they said."

"But why?"

"I guess because communism is no good. It's a lousy form of government."

"According to us."

"Yes, well, obviously not according to them."

"According to us. And on our spectrum of hate to love, communism is at the hate end of the line, no? All of us good Americans hate communism."

"I guess that's true."

"And what about the chaos-to-control line when it came to Vietnam?"

"I don't know what that means."

"We wanted to control their country's government."

"We did," I said.

"So, it's simple. We hated communism, and we also wanted to control Vietnam's government, so we went to war. It's as simple as that. Most wars are just that simple, people liking one form of government over the other and people wanting to take control of others. It's purely mechanical. There is no right or wrong."

"Your move," I said. I had just moved my bishop again. Grandpa stared at the chessboard.

"So, ask me anything," he said.

"What do you mean?"

"Ask me about any circumstance you can think of, and I'll show you how it's a result of the two spectrums."

"Okay," I said. That was my grandpa for you. Or perhaps it was just his generation, always oversimplifying complicated things. I thought about this for a moment, and I also watched grandpa make his chess move.

"Well?" he said.

"Okay, how about the baseball game you've been watching on the TV?"

"Too easy. Both teams love to win. Both teams therefore try to control the ball. The resulting conflict is a baseball game, and the team who is best at controlling the ball wins the conflict. There is no right or wrong."

"Why do you keep saying there is no right or wrong?"

"Because there is none."

"A lot of people say the Vietnam War was wrong. A lot of people called it 'immoral.'"

"That's because they don't understand the two spectrums as I've explained them to you. There is no right or wrong. There is only hate to love and chaos to control. You may love the hell out of communism, or you may despise it. Or you may feel totally indifferent. Further, you may feel it is necessary to control Vietnam's government, or you may feel that such control isn't important at all. But there is no right or wrong. There are only differences in viewpoints, opinions, feelings, desires, and goals."

"So, it isn't wrong to kill people?"

"Do you think it's wrong?"

"I think I do."

"Did you think it was wrong for the US to help defeat Nazi Germany?"

"Well, no."

"Do you know how many Nazis were killed in the war?"

"No, I don't."

"Millions of dead bodies. Literally."

"Okay."

"So, right or wrong?"

"I don't know," I said.

"I say neither. I say, we hated their government and their idiotic führer, and we didn't want them controlling us or our allies. It was pretty simple stuff. It was all about hate and control. It had nothing to do with right or wrong."

"What they did to the Jews was wrong."

"What we did to Native Americans was equally wrong, if you want to go there."

I looked at the chessboard. Grandpa was throwing me off my game. I suddenly saw what he was doing. If I didn't sacrifice my rook, in three moves it would be checkmate. So I moved the rook and let him take it. "You can have it," I said.

"Are you sure you want to do that?"

"Positive," I said.

There was a knock at the front door. I looked over at my grandpa. "There's someone at the door," I said.

"Are you expecting someone?" he asked.

"No," I said. "How about you?"

"No, not this evening."

"Who do you think it is?"

"I have no idea. Why don't you answer it? It's probably someone for you."

"Why would it be for me? I don't live here."

"Just a hunch," Grandpa said.

I got up and walked to the door. I turned the doorknob and pulled the door open, and I was I ever surprised. It was Rudy Gonzales and Eddie Yang, the detectives who had come to my house earlier. "What do you want?" I asked.

"We thought we might find you here," Rudy said.

"Can I help you with something?"

"Is Robert here?"

"No, my son isn't here."

"Well, who *is* here?"

"Just my grandpa and me."

Rudy turned to look at his partner. "Likely story," he said.

"It's the truth," I said.

"We heard otherwise."

"I'm telling you the truth."

"Mind if we come in and look around?"

"Do you have a search warrant?"

"Always with the search warrant," Rudy said to his partner. "Show him the warrant."

Eddie reached into his pocket and removed a folded paper. He waved the paper in front of me and then stuffed it back in his pocket.

"That wasn't a warrant," I said.

"Oh," Rudy said. "Then what was it?"

"It was a brochure for a vacation on an ocean liner to Alaska."

"The hell, you say," Rudy said, laughing. Eddie was laughing too. "He still doesn't trust us," Rudy said to his partner.

"But you can come in," I said. "We've got nothing to hide."

"Good decision."

"What are you looking for?"

"It's a *who*."

"A who?"

"Your question should be, *Who* are we looking for? And the answer is, Robert. We're looking for your son."

"I told you he isn't here."

"We heard otherwise."

"From who?"

"We just heard. That's all you need to know."

"Well, come in and look. You're not going to find him here."

I stepped aside, and the detectives entered the house. I shut the door behind them. Grandpa was gone, and I had no idea where. The first thing the detectives noticed was the chess game on the coffee table.

"Playing chess with Robert?"

"No, I was playing with my grandpa."

"Your grandpa?" Rudy laughed, and then so did Eddie.

"Where is he?" Eddie asked.

"My grandpa?"

"No, wise guy, your son."

"How should I know?"

"I have a question for you."

"Shoot," I said.

"How does it feel to be the father of a thief?"

"You haven't really proved anything."

"Sure we have." Rudy turned to Eddie and said, "Haven't we proved plenty?"

"You bet we have," Eddie said.

"What kind of father were you? Where were you during all of this?"

"Where was I?"

"Just letting it go on? Letting your son steal? Standing on the sidelines? Not saying anything?"

"Honestly, I had no idea," I said. "Parents don't always know what their children are up to."

"But you knew."

"I didn't," I said. This was a lie, but I said it anyway. What was I supposed to say?

"What about the CDs?"

"The CDs?"

"All those CDs your boy was coming home with. Did you think he was buying them? Where'd you think he was getting the money for them?"

"Playing video games."

"Are you serious?"

"He told me he was winning armor and weapons on his video games and then selling the items to his friends. He's pretty good at the games. I mean, he must be. He spends so much time playing them, and he does come home with a lot of CDs."

"He wasn't winning and selling anything. Open your eyes, man. He was shoplifting. We have proof of this too." Then to his partner, Rudy said, "Don't we have proof?"

"Ironclad," Eddie said.

"You hear that? Ironclad proof."

"I don't believe it," I said.

"What don't you believe? That we have proof? Or that your son is a thief?"

"I don't believe either. Well, maybe I knew he was taking some things but no more than any other kid his age, and how would you have proof?"

"Video surveillance cameras."

"Oh?" I said.

"And clerks at the stores. What do you think? That these proprietors just let these sticky-fingered kids waltz in and out of their stores, taking whatever they want? They've been watching Robert for quite some time."

"Why didn't they say anything earlier?"

"They were building their case."

"An ironclad case," Eddie said.

"And now the coins. Sort of like the straw that broke the camel's back."

"Snap," Eddie said. He broke an invisible stick in half with his hands.

"We come across parents like you all the time," Rudy said. "They think their kids are little angels who would never do any wrong. Or maybe they know that they're not, but they pretend they are. I don't know. You tell me. What kind of parent are you?"

"I'm a good parent."

"Are you?"

"I've tried to be."

Rudy sighed. Then he sat down in Grandpa's chair and said, "Eddie's going to look around the house for Robert. And me? I'm going to finish this game you were playing. Whose move is it?"

I sat down on the couch, looking at the chess game. "It was my grandpa's move."

"You mean Robert's."

"No, I mean my grandpa's."

"Ah, I can see what he was planning."

"You can?"

"You're not a very good chess player, are you?"

"I'm not that bad."

"Here," Rudy said. He moved his queen three spaces forward and said, "How will you respond to this?"

I looked at the chessboard. It was different. It was not how my grandpa and I had left it. "You've changed things around," I said.

"I haven't changed anything."

"It's not the same."

"It's exactly the same, except for my move."

"You're lying."

"But so are you. Do you really expect me to be honest with you when an honest word hasn't spilled from your lips since we got here?"

There was a knock at the door again. I had no idea who it was, and I said, "I guess I should answer that."

"Go ahead," Rudy said.

I went to the door and opened it. Jesus, this was not what I needed. Not at all. It was Robert, standing on the porch as if nothing at all was wrong. He was smiling, and he said, "Hey, Pop, I didn't expect you to be here."

"Quiet," I said. I stepped outside with him and closed the door behind me. "You shouldn't be here," I whispered.

"Why not?"

"The cops are here."

"What cops?"

"The ones who are looking for you. You know, about the coins."

"Coins?"

Sometimes my son could be very frustrating. "Why are you playing dumb with me?"

"I'm not playing dumb. I honestly have no idea what you're talking about."

"I think you should leave."

"But I just got here."

"Seriously, you need to get the hell out of here. These detectives mean business."

"I have nothing to be afraid of."

"Just stop it, okay? Stop pretending like there's nothing wrong."

"Calm down, Dad."

"I'll calm down when you're gone."

"Who is it?" I heard Rudy ask from inside the house, from behind the closed door. He was curious as to why I had stepped out on the porch and closed the door.

I opened the door a crack and said through the space, "It's a neighbor looking for my grandpa."

"Again, with the grandpa story?"

I turned my head. "Go, go, go," I said to Robert.

"Let me see who's there for myself," Rudy said. I could tell he was walking toward the door.

"Who is it?" I heard Eddie ask.

135

"I'm going to find out," Rudy said.

"Go!" I said to Robert. "Get out of here *now*."

I was finally able to convince Robert he had to leave, and he turned and walked away. "I'll call you," he said.

"Just get out of here. Run!"

Robert took off running just as Rudy pulled open the door. "It's him!" he exclaimed. He pushed me out of the way and took off after my son.

"What's going on?" Eddie asked. He was now at the door, wondering what was happening.

"Nothing," I said.

"Shit, it's him, isn't it?" Eddie said, and he took off too. Then I ran after Eddie, who was running after Rudy, who was running after Robert.

I had absolutely no idea what I would do if I caught up with them. Was there anything I *could* do? Robert was young. He should've been able to outrun the two detectives, but who knew? I suddenly felt like I was running under water, getting nowhere fast, and I lost track of the three of them. I stopped, leaned over, and placed my hands on my knees as I tried to catch my breath.

"What's all the commotion?" a voice said. I recognized the voice immediately. It was my dad, who was standing four feet away from me.

"It's Robert," I said, panting.

"What about him?"

"They're after him."

"Who's after him?"

"The cops," I said.

"The cops? What are you even talking about?"

"The CDs. The coins. The whole thing."

"You're not making any sense," Dad said. "Slow down and start from the beginning."

But no, I wouldn't start from the beginning. In fact, I wouldn't start anywhere. I realized I had already said way too much. "Let's talk about something else," I said.

"Like what?"

"I heard you're taking Robert to a USC game."

"Is that all right with you?"

"Yes, it's all right."

"I probably should've asked you first. I know how you feel about football."

"Honestly, it's fine with me."

"I did tell Martha."

"I know. That's how I know. She told me about it last night."

"Robert seems to get a kick out of the games."

"Yes, I think he likes them."

"He does," Dad said.

"And he likes doing things with you. It's important to him to be close to his grandpa."

"You and my dad had your chess games. Robert and I have our football."

"Right up to the day you die," I said. And as soon as I said this, I remembered the last week my father was alive. It had been a tough week for all of us but especially hard on Robert. No more football games and no more Grandpa. No more sitting on my dad's knee. No more of Grandpa reading stories aloud from his dog-eared book of *Aesop's Fables*. My dad loved reading those stories. He never read them to me, but he read them to Robert all the time. It was his way of passing down some wisdom to his grandchild.

"You look left out," Dad said.

"Left out?"

"You look like you've been overlooked. You know, like the kids are choosing teams, and no one has picked you. I hate to see you feeling this way."

"I'm fine."

"No, no, no, you're not fine. Remember who I am? I'm your father, and you're my son. I know you. I know you better than you know yourself. I watched you grow up from an infant into a man, and I have a real feel for this."

"A feel for what?"

"For what I just said. For knowing you. Aren't you paying attention?"

"Yes, I'm listening."

"Sit down. I'll tell you a story."

"Seriously?"

"Yes, sit down."

We were no longer in my grandpa's neighborhood. Instead we were in my parents' home, standing in their family room. I sat down on the couch, and Dad sat beside me. He put his hand on my knee and said, "Now, you just listen and let me talk."

CHAPTER 14

MOM'S ADVICE

———•◆•———

Fables. My dad loved them to death, especially those from good old Aesop. Uncle Remus was also okay, but Aesop's fables were his favorites.

My father leaned back and proceeded. "Once upon a time," he said, "there was a small community of mice in a house. They called a meeting to decide how to protect themselves from their archenemy, the cat. At the very least, they needed a way to know if the cat was approaching so they could run. It was a very important meeting, for the mice lived in constant fear of the cat's sharp claws and teeth. Many plans were discussed at the meeting, but none was satisfactory. Finally, a young mouse stood up and said, 'I have a simple plan that I'm sure will be successful. All we have to do is hang a noisy bell around the cat's neck so that whenever we hear the bell, we will know that the cat is coming.' All the mice were thrilled with this great idea, but as they were rejoicing, an old mouse stood up from the back of the room and said, 'This is a great idea, but I have one question. Who will bell the cat?'"

"So, who will do it?" I asked.

"That's the question, isn't it? The moral of the fable is that it's one thing to say what should be done and wholly another thing to actually do it."

"Yes," I said. "That's good."

"Want to hear another one?"

"I do," I said.

"I'll tell you about the fox and the grapes."

"Okay," I said. Seriously, I think my dad knew a hundred of these.

"One day a fox saw a beautiful bunch of grapes hanging from a vine that was trained up the trunk and branches of a tall tree. The bunch of grapes hung from one of the high branches so that the fox would have to jump up to get them. The fox readied himself and jumped. His first attempt failed. The grapes were too high for him to reach them, so he backed up and then took a running leap at them. Still he was unable to reach the grapes. He did this over and over until finally he gave up and said to himself, 'What a dumb fool I am. Here I am wearing myself out to get a bunch of sour grapes that aren't even worth the effort.' He walked away scornfully."

"And the moral of that one is?"

"That there are many people who despise and belittle that which is beyond their reach."

"How true that is," I said.

"Isn't it?"

"I love hearing these stories."

"I'm glad."

"But I've always wondered why you told them to Robert and not to me."

"That's a good question."

"Is there an answer?"

"Not a good one. Not an answer that will make you feel any better. I have been a much better grandfather than I was a father. I think if they're honest, a lot of men will have to admit the same thing. We learn as we get older, and most importantly, we learn how to treat those we love. I don't know what else to say. I'm sorry."

"I believe you," I said.

"It's the shits."

I laughed and asked, "Do you think I've been a good father to Robert?"

"Of course you have."

"Then why?"

"Then why what?" Dad asked. I suddenly realized whom I was talking to. I was talking to my dear, old dad. To the best of my knowledge, he knew nothing about Robert's kleptomania. He had no idea Robert was a common thief. If he knew, it would've turned him upside down and broken his heart. As far as Dad knew, Robert was a good kid who behaved himself, obeyed the laws, and loved his immediate family. His parents loved him, guided him, and looked after him. And his grandparents adored him. He had everything.

"Never mind," I said.

"Is there something you're not telling me?"

"No, there's nothing."

Dad stared at me for a moment, then said, "There's something I want you to see."

"Oh?" I said.

"It's a video your mom recorded several months before she passed away. I never told you about it. I was waiting for the right time to spring it on you."

"And now is the right time?"

"It is," Dad said. He picked up the TV remote and turned on the TV. The picture flickered, and then there was my mom's face, filling the screen. Dad turned up the volume so I could hear her.

"Hello, Robinson," she said. "I am fifty-seven years old, and I'm about to die. I hate to leave you, and I hate to leave your father. I hate to leave this world period, but my breast cancer is getting the best of me. There's not anything I can do about it, and there's no sense in crying over it. Life deals you your hands, and you do the best you can with them. Complaining about the cards you get is immature and pointless. It'd be like whining about the weather, and I've always hated it when people complained about the weather. There's no point to it, and it's a big waste of time and energy. It's better for us all to be grateful for whatever we get in life. No doubt you've heard the old cliché 'Count your blessings.' Yes, it's a cliché, but it's probably the best advice you can give another ever. Count your blessings, and you'll live an awesome, sun-drenched, rosy-red life in spite of every dark cloud overhead. You'll be smiling in the face of adversity. You'll be laughing at your sorrows, and you'll never regret it."

"That's good advice," I said to my dad.

"Keep listening," Dad said.

"Robinson," Mom continued, "you are me. You are of me, by me, and made out of me. Can you imagine? It is the most unreal and astonishing miracle in the world, the creation of a human life in the body of another. There are no words sufficient to express what it was like carrying you, having you grow in my belly. You were a part of me, and yet you were you. My food and water nourished you, and yet you also had your own personal blood, DNA, and tiny beating heart. For sure there is nothing in the world like being a mother. And that's how I'm speaking to you now in this video, as your dear mother, as the woman who carried you, as the woman who pushed you into the world, and as the woman who took such a true and intimate role in giving you life. Do you feel alive? Are you living, Robinson?"

"What does that mean?" I asked my dad.

"Just listen," Dad said.

"But of course I'm living."

"I said to listen."

"Being a mother is a curse and a blessing," my mom went on. "Do you have any idea what I mean by this? I will try to help you understand. The blessing aspect is obvious, right? But perhaps the curse is not so clear to those who have not been a mom. But God, what a total blessing to watch you grow up from an infant to a boy, to an adolescent, and to a thriving man. There is nothing in the world like it. Sure, raising children is a major hassle and a huge financial drain, and sometimes it's as hard as hell, but there's no experience in life that even comes close to it. If you were to ask me, What's the one thing in life you ought to do? I would answer that you should be a father. In the long run, if you're any kind of man, you will never regret it. I certainly have never regretted being a mom. It's a lot like climbing Mount Everest. The view and sense of accomplishment are unparalleled. Your legs hurt, and you are out of breath, and you feel like you're going to faint, but you wouldn't trade places with anyone. That's the blessing. That's one side of the coin."

"The coin?" I said.

"Keep listening," Dad said.

"On the other side of the coin is the curse," my mom said. "It's not an evil curse. It's nothing like that. It's just a curse. And maybe it's just because I had a son. Maybe it would be different with a daughter. Yes, if I had a daughter, things might be quite different. But I didn't have a girl. I had you, my son, my boy, and my handsome young man. There were so many things I wanted to tell you when you were growing up, but the curse kept me quiet. Was the silence of my own making? I don't think so. It's natural for a boy to listen to his father. His father leads by example. His father knows what it's like to be a boy, to catch frogs, play baseball, and see who can spit the farthest. His father is like a god, while his mom is what? A comforting reassurance? A warm hug? A tissue to wipe away the tears?

A lap to lie on? A healing salve, if you will. She is someone there to put a Band-Aid on a scuffed knee or remove a splinter or cook a favorite dinner. But a source of serious advice or direction, she is not, and she never will be. You said to me, in so many words, 'You wouldn't understand, Mom. Stick to sewing on buttons. Stick to doing the laundry. Stick to the things you know something about.'"

"Is she angry?" I asked.

"She's not angry," my dad said. "Keep listening. I think you'll understand."

"I don't blame anyone," Mom continued. "It would be like complaining about the weather, and I've already told you how I feel about that. It's a waste of time. It's pointless. No, I'm not even angry. So, what am I? I'll tell you exactly what I am. I'm a woman with a big untapped reservoir of good advice for my only child. So, I made this video. When I filmed it, I felt you were too young to understand. But now, given the years you've lived and given that your father has followed my wishes, you are at a place in your life where the things I have to say will have meaning. How old are you? Are you thirty? Or forty? Or fifty? Or older? I don't know. I left your age up to your father. Your dad has good judgment more or less, and I trust him. And more importantly, he loves you. As do I."

"You waited all these years?" I asked my dad.

"I did," he replied. "You weren't ready before now. You were still too stupid."

"Stupid?"

"Keep watching."

"Here's the first piece of advice I want to give you," Mom said. "You won't hear this from your father. I don't think he agrees with me on this. I'd like to see you go easy on people. Cut them some slack. Don't hold their feet over the fire if you can help it. Be kind to them and tolerant of their faults. The thing is this: We are all human beings, and humans are by their very nature flawed, misshapen, imperfect, and discolored. This is the way God made us, in his image, and contrary to what you will be told, God is a mess, and his children are a mess. They are greedy, lazy, lustful, violent, petty, and a hundred other distasteful things. When someone lies to you or steals from you or undermines you or even hurts you, keep in mind that the person is just a human being. Don't hold terrible grudges or seek revenge or foster hate. Instead, be that person's friend. Abraham Lincoln said it best when he said in so many words that 'the best way in the world to destroy an enemy is to make him your friend.'"

Mom paused for a moment, and I said to Dad, "Do you agree with Mom?"

"Not really," he said.

In the back of my mind, I had a feeling we were missing the entire point. Mom continued and said, "The second piece of advice I have for you is to cut yourself some slack. For all the reasons I just listed for others, you are not perfect, and you are going to make mistakes. Don't be too hard on yourself. You will be flying an airplane with a broken propeller, driving a car with a flat tire, sailing a boat with a hole in its hull the size of a fist, running a race with two left shoes. This is what life is all about. It isn't about always having the right tools and materials for the right job. It's more about making do with all the crummy tools and shoddy materials you've been given, finding ways to make them work for you. Don't be mad at yourself when everything doesn't work out right. Instead, you should be proud of yourself for being resourceful and diligent. Pin your own blue ribbon on your haphazard product and ignore the belittling jibes of others."

"Just the opposite of what you taught me," I said to my dad.

"Kind of," he said.

"You taught me to always be the best."

"I might have said something like that."

"Now for the third piece of advice I want to give you," Mom continued. "I want you to be a man. I want you to be a real man, not a John Wayne man or a Clint Eastwood man. I don't care if you cry when you get hurt or if you don't like sports or if you drink milk instead of whiskey or if you think handguns and rifles are ridiculous or if you think the military is for goons or if you don't drive a pickup truck or if you like cats or if you don't like shooting and killing wild animals. What I care about, and what every mother should care about, is that you're truly a man. I would like you to be someone who isn't afraid to say what he thinks. I want you to stand up for the weak, to have empathy for victims, to love living things, to be kind, helpful, sweet, generous, and thoughtful. I want you to love your family and be faithful to your wife. I want you to be moral and set a good example for your children. There's nothing more misunderstood than the goal to be a man. I see hordes of males in the world striving to be just the opposite. Show them they're wrong. You can show them the way."

"I like John Wayne," I said.

"So do I," Dad said.

"And I like Clint Eastwood."

"Dirty Harry was the best."

"Agreed," I said.

"Okay, okay, I get it," Mom said. "You boys have to have your heroes, but at least do me a favor and try to be the best you can be. At the end of the day, you should be able to look at yourself in the mirror and say, 'I'm far from perfect, but I did my best.'"

"I can do that," I said.

"It's good advice," Dad said.

"I thought you'd like it a little better if I put that way," Mom said.

Dad looked at me, and we both laughed. "It's like she's right here in the room with us," he said.

"Yes," I said. "But is she?"

"Maybe she is."

"You might want to grab a sheet of paper and write the rest of these ideas down," Mom said.

"Don't worry about the paper," Dad said to me.

"Why?" I asked.

"You'll see. You know how Mom could be. She goes a little overboard."

"Overboard?"

"Just listen."

"I can't tell you how many of my women friends have asked me about my tuna casserole. Of course, they want to know what kind of wine they should serve. I say always red. Red wine goes with tuna casserole. You might think white wine because tuna is a fish, but it's definitely red. Red wine goes with tuna casserole."

"What the heck?" I said.

"See what I mean?" Dad said.

"As for fashion, I advise against wearing dark blue with black," Mom said. "Your dad always wore the two together. A bad idea. Just the sort of thing a man would do. Did your dad listen to me? No, he thought he knew better, but take it from me. Dark blue and black do *not* go together.

I'll tell you one more thing your dad used to do that drove me crazy. He used to belch. Not just softly and into his hand but obnoxiously like some fat-assed sultan finishing off a ten-course meal. The air would come from way down deep in his belly and throat, and out of his mouth, especially after drinking a can of Coke or a Dr. Pepper. Oh, he thought it was funny, and he actually expected me to laugh at it, but it wasn't funny at all. I hated it. If you get hitched to a girl and you really do want to make her wish she hadn't married you, then belch. Otherwise, I suggest you keep your abdomen's air to yourself."

"I knew a kid in elementary school who could belch at will," Dad said. "Can't remember his name."

"I knew a kid like that," I said.

"Here's another way to get under your wife's skin," my mom said. "Observe how she installs rolls of toilet paper. What is she? Is she an 'over' or an 'under'? In other words, does she like the toilet paper hanging over the top of the roll or coming out from beneath it? Once you've established her preference, do the opposite whenever it comes time to install a new roll. It's the little things that drive people crazy, and with any luck at all, you'll have your wife pulling her hair out and cursing the very ground you walk on. On the other hand, if you wish to have a nice and harmonious marriage, check yourself."

"There's some truth to this advice," Dad said.

"Yes, there is. Except in our house, I'm the one who's picky, and Martha is the one who keeps installing the paper the wrong way."

My dad laughed at this. "Maybe Martha should be listening to this recording."

"Maybe," I said.

"Finally, I have some advice about your writing," Mom said. "Even at your young age as I'm making this video, it is clear to me that you will become a writer. A writer of what? Who knows? There are so many directions you can go. You can write novels, biographies, historical dramas, comedies, screenplays, self-help books, reference books, manuals, science fiction or nonfiction, thick or thin, inspiring or disillusioned, matter of fact and atheist or deeply religious tales. I've given a great deal of thought to this, and I think that, knowing you as I know you, your best bet is to write a book about dogs. Everyone in the world loves their dogs, and there's nothing quite like a great dog story to generate book sales. And that will be the point of it all, won't it? To make people happy? To sell lots of books? It would break my heart if you fell into the trap that so many writers find themselves in, wallowing in the morose recesses of life and death that writers for centuries have found themselves stuck in. And for what? To say you're deep? Who wants to be deep? No, you need a gimmick like a dog. Yes, dogs are your ticket. I may be telling you this late in your career, but it's like they say. It's never too late. Write that dog book. You won't be sorry."

"This is ridiculous," I said.

"Ridiculous?"

"Mom would never have said that."

"Oh, I think she would have. In fact, I think she just did. She said it loud and clear."

"This isn't real."

"Then what is it?"

I looked at the TV. Mom continued, "Listen, Son, this is a dangerous mission. And as always, should you or any member of your team be caught or killed, we will disavow any knowledge of your actions. This videotape is going to self-destruct in five seconds."

What?

Suddenly the room filled with smoke.

"Mom?" I said.

"She's gone," a voice said.

I immediately recognized the voice. It belonged to one of the people on our team. We were a team, right? Highly trained and handpicked by me. The best of the best. We were finally on our way to the house. All of us were coughing, and Barney rolled down his side window, and the smoke quickly blew out of the van. "Now, that's what I call a smoke bomb," Rollin said, smiling.

"I thought you'd like it," Barney said.

"How many will it take?" Cinnamon asked. Ah, the magazine cover girl, Cinnamon. She was as lovely as ever. She said, "I mean, given that they're even needed."

"Five, total."

"They won't be able to see their own belt buckles," Willy said, laughing. "They'll be running around like chickens with their heads cut off."

"That's the general idea. But if everything goes right, we won't even have to use them."

"Does everyone on the team understand what they have to do?" I asked.

"We've got it," Rollin said. "We went over it last night in the hotel room. Over and over."

"How about the coins? Who has the coins?"

"They're in the back of the van."

"And the boxes are wiped clean?"

"Clean as a whistle."

"Good, good. We should arrive at the party in about thirty minutes, then at the house fifteen minutes after that."

Then it's showtime, folks.

CHAPTER 15

WILLY DROVE THE VAN

———•◦•———

We parked the van a block down the dark, tree-lined street from Jeremy Whitehouse's estate. The plan I had come up with was simple compared to other plans we had executed. We knew Jeremy and his wife were at a cocktail party that evening at the home of one of Jeremy's clients. We had dropped Rollin off at the party, and his job was to ensure that Jeremy and his wife stayed at the party long enough for us to do what we had to do.

Rollin was disguised as Tom Anderson, the founder and owner of Anderson Electronics. Jeremy had been trying to sign on the company as a client for the past year, so all Rollin had to do was engage Jeremy in a conversation. There was no way Jeremy would pass up the opportunity to socialize with Rollin for as long as Rollin was willing to talk. If Rollin could keep Jeremy at the party for at least two hours, that would give us plenty of time.

When we parked on Jeremy's street, the first person out of the van was Cinnamon. She was dressed like a professional babysitter, because that's what she was supposed to be. Her job was to go to the house and take over for the teenage sitter Jeremy and his wife had hired to watch their seven-year-old kid. The sitter at the house was a girl from the neighborhood named Anna Harris. Fooling her would be easy. Cinnamon would tell her Jeremy had called her to take over since it turned out they were going to be gone all night, not to return until the morning of the following day. Cinnamon would pay the girl a nice bonus to keep her from questioning the switch. This part of the scheme proceeded without a hitch. Cinnamon was now in the house, watching the Whitehouse boy.

We needed to keep the kid upstairs while we went about our business, so Cinnamon told him she would play a long game of Monopoly with him. We knew the kid was crazy about Monopoly, and he jumped at her offer. They went to the boy's bedroom to play, and while they were there, Barney and I snuck into the house. We left Willy in the van. Willy was to be our getaway driver.

Barney and I went straight to the safe, which was next to Jeremy's study. It was no ordinary safe. It was an entire ten-by-ten vault made of eight-inch-thick concrete and steel reinforcement, and there was a steel security door to the room that could be unlocked electronically only by punching the correct code into a keypad. The keypad was on the wall to the right of the door.

"This shouldn't be a problem," Barney said. He unscrewed the cover from the keypad, exposing its electronic insides. He then began to fiddle with the wires and the circuit boards, attaching a device to the wires. He turned a dial until his device lit up. Then presto! The door was unlocked, and we were in. We had carried the coins in with us in a large burlap sack, and we removed the cases from the sack and put them into the vault on a shelf.

"Good as new," I said. "Let's close this bad boy up."

Barney shut the vault door and put the cover back on the keypad.

I said, "Let's get the heck out of here."

As we walked quickly toward the front door, I called Willy on his cell phone and told him to pull up to the house to pick us up. Then I called Cinnamon. "Hello?" she said.

"We're ready," I said.

"I'll stop by tomorrow," she said. That was our code for *I'll be right down*. Of course, we didn't want to tip the boy off that Cinnamon was leaving the house. To the boy she said, "I've got to go to the bathroom. Don't steal any of my money while I'm gone."

"Okay," the kid said, smiling.

The boy stayed in his room while Cinnamon made her way down the stairs to join Barney and me. Everything was going so well. The three of us opened the front door and stepped out to the porch. But just as I was about to close the front door behind us, a police car pulled up to the curb in the street. "Cops," Barney said.

"I see them," I said.

"The keypad must have been wired to a silent alarm."

"I was afraid of that," I said.

"I've got the smoke bombs."

"Throw them when I tell you to."

"Got it," Barney said.

"Timing will be everything."

"Agreed," Barney said.

"Hey, folks," one of the cops said. "Can I talk to you, please?"

"Us?" I asked.

"Yes, you. Do you folks live here?"

"We were visiting," I said.

"Ah, well, I'm going to have to ask you all for some identification."

"Identification?"

"An alarm was triggered in the house. Probably just an innocent mistake. You don't look like burglars, but I have to check you out."

"We don't know anything about an alarm."

"Your IDs, please."

"Now!" I shouted, and before the cop had any idea what we were doing, Barney set off the smoke bombs and tossed them strategically between us and the cops. Instantly, the front yard was clouded with thick, white smoke, and we ran to the van, in which Willy was waiting.

"Stop!" the cop shouted, but he couldn't see. There was no way he could chase us.

Once we were all in the van, Willy shoved it in drive and stomped on the accelerator. Off we went like a bat out of hell. By the time the cops got back into their car, we were long gone. Willy was one hell of a driver.

Away from the cops, we drove to the cocktail party to pick up Rollin. He was laughing when he got in the van. "The dude is a first-class schmuck," he said. "He seriously thinks he just signed up Anderson Electronics as a new client. I told him to come by my office in the morning to sign a contract. Ha, he's going to feel like an idiot."

"Well, at least he got his stupid coin collection back," I said. "That will soften the blow."

"Back to the hotel?" Willy asked.

"Back to the hotel," I said. "Our mission has been accomplished."

I was sitting next to Cinnamon in the van, and she put her hand on my knee. She gave my leg a gentle squeeze. "Are you coming up to my room tonight?" she asked.

"To your room?"

"I thought we could, you know, celebrate."

"We won't tell," Barney said, smiling.

"Our lips are sealed," Rollin said.

"I thought you two were married," I said to Rollin.

"Only in real life."

"Go with her," Willy said. "I would if I was you. You'd be crazy to turn her down."

"All right, all right," I said. "But only for an hour or so. Martha is expecting me home. She doesn't like it when I go on these missions. She worries, you know."

This made Cinnamon smile. The next thing I knew we were at the hotel, and a valet was taking the van. The others all went into the lobby while Cinnamon and I were standing outside. She looked up at me with her big, wet eyes. "Are you having second thoughts?" she asked.

"It's just kind of weird," I said.

"Relax. No one here knows who you are."

"I guess that's true," I said, and I followed Cinnamon in through the open glass doors. We walked across the lobby and to the elevator. We had the elevator car to ourselves, and it let us out on the fifteenth floor. We walked down the hall, where Cinnamon opened her room with her card key so we could enter.

"Nice digs," I said. "Have you got anything to drink in this place?"

"Champagne," she said.

"To celebrate?"

"Yes, dummy, to celebrate. Just relax. Take your shoes off and get comfortable." I sat down on the edge of the bed and removed my shoes. It felt good to be in my stocking feet. "You can do the honors," Cinnamon said, and she handed me the cold champagne bottle so I could open it.

As I undid the wire and foil, I looked at Cinnamon, and I had the strangest realization. She was Gabriela! And she was more beautiful than ever.

"You're Gabriela!" I said. "From high school. You're really her! I mean, right here in the flesh."

"Who did you think I was?"

"Cinnamon."

She laughed. "Cinnamon is my stage name. My code name. You knew that."

"I did?"

I popped off the cork top of the champagne bottle, and she laughed aloud. "Fill us up," she said, holding our glasses, and I poured the champagne into her glass, then into mine. I set down the bottle, and she took a seat next to me, handing me my glass. God, those beautiful eyes—they were driving me crazy.

"Here's to a successful mission," I said, and I raised my glass for a toast.

"Here's to it," she said. "And here's to us."

"To us," I said.

To us? What was I thinking? I suddenly felt as guilty as hell, and I didn't want to drink any of my champagne. I wasn't thinking of Martha, which would've made sense since I was on the verge of cheating on her. Instead, I was thinking about my son, Robert. Yes, I was about to betray the poor kid in the worst way possible, because when you betray your wife or husband, you also betray your children. A lot of people don't realize this, but it's true. I had to stop what I was doing with Cinnamon or Gabriela or whatever you want to call her before it was too late, before I succumbed and did something in the hotel room I would deeply regret. Oh, but the power! The power of the moment was upon us. The longing, the wish, and the desire!

Like a fool, I took off my shirt. Cinnamon, or Gabriela if you will, grabbed my shirt and tossed it on a chair, giggling. "You've gained a little weight since high school," she said while looking me over.

"Haven't we all?"

Gabriela laughed. She then undid the buttons on her blouse, exposing her milky white chest, and I reached my hands in so I could feel her warm body. God, she was now seriously driving me out of my mind. I leaned into her so my nose was deep in her thick hair. The smell of her hair! Have you ever noticed how a woman's hair smells? It's nothing short of amazing. I'd describe the smell to you, but it defies words. I inhaled, and my head suddenly felt dizzy. I was sure I was going to faint. Her hands were on my back, squeezing.

"I love you," I said.

"I love you too."

"I've always loved you."

"Ditto," she said.

"I can't believe we weren't better friends when we were in high school."

"I loved you then."

"Yes," I said. "I remember."

"Do you?"

"I think I do."

"We should've married."

"Yes," I said.

I was losing control of myself. The talk was all nonsense, but the feelings were so real. And this was all happening so quickly, I wasn't being careful or rational. I knew I needed help, and I knew also there was no way I could handle this alone. You know, it's like they say. The flesh is weak. It's so vulnerable and weak.

God, help me!

Now, I'm not a particularly religious man, but I do believe in God. Well, most likely not the kind of God you believe in, but I believe there is someone in charge of our big, whirling planet, someone we can go to for help when we are about to really fuck things up. And that's what I was about to do. I was about to make a real mess of things, having sex with this beautiful girl.

"I've got to leave," I said suddenly. I was surprised that I found the strength to say this.

"You're going to leave?"

"Like right now."

"Did I do something to bother you?"

"On the contrary. This is all wonderful, but I shouldn't be up here." I leaned over and put my shoes back on. Then I reached for my shirt.

"I really wish you'd stay."

"I know," I said.

"Did I say something inappropriate?"

"No," I said.

"The champagne was too much? Too expensive? I should've just got us a six-pack of beer."

"The champagne was fine."

Then Gabriela squinted and glared at me. "What did you think I had in mind?"

"I don't know. Maybe it's not what *you* had in mind. Maybe it's what *I* was thinking. I just know that I've got to get out of here. I need help."

"Help with what?"

"I know who I need to see."

"You're not making any sense."

I stood up from the bed and walked quickly to the door.

"Will I see you again?" Gabriela asked. She now seemed so sad. She looked like she might cry.

"Will I see you again?" I asked. "I don't know. I kind of hope not. No offense."

And now she did cry. "Please, don't go," she said.

"I have to."

I went out the door and rushed down the narrow hall to the elevator. I took the elevator to the hotel lobby, and then I walked through the lobby to the glass entrance doors, where I stepped outside. A car valet was standing at his podium, and I asked him to please get my car. "You didn't come here in your car," he said. "Your friends brought you in their van."

"You're right," I said.

"Do you want me to call you a cab?"

"No, I'll walk."

"It's a long way."

"I could use the fresh air and exercise," I said, and I wondered how the valet knew it was a long way for me to walk. Did he know where I lived?

I started walking and found myself downtown. What town was it exactly? I wasn't sure of the name of the town because I although it all seemed familiar; I also didn't recognize any of it. It was made of images and memories. There were many other pedestrians walking on the sidewalk, and I decided to ask one of them for directions.

I had no idea where I was. But I was sure of where I wanted to be. I wanted to find a church. That made the most sense to me, but what kind of church? Who knew? Any church would do. Any house of God. Any holy place of worship.

A man was suddenly coming toward me from the opposite direction, and I grabbed his elbow. "Excuse me, sir," I said. "Can you please help me? I'm looking for a church. Any church will do. Do you know if there's a church around here?"

"A church?"

"Yes, sir, any church. The closest one."

"I think there's a United Methodist church down the street and to the right at the second signal."

"That's great," I said.

"Just keep walking the way you were going and then make a right. I think the name of the street is Washington, but I'm not sure. I'm pretty sure it's the second signal. Yes, it is the second signal."

"Thanks," I said.

I followed the man's directions. I walked one block, two blocks, and I made a right turn at the signal and walked for a while. Sure enough, the church was ahead on the right-hand side of the road. I walked up the steps and opened its heavy wooden doors. The place was nearly empty. There were a few people in the pews, on their knees and praying quietly. A reverend soon approached me, a friendly-looking fellow dressed in black with his hair combed neat. He smelled a lot like a wet bar of soap, and he had a soft and melodious voice.

"Hello, son," he said. "Can I help you with something?"

"Maybe you can," I said. I stared at the man.

"With what?"

"I need to speak to God."

"Well, you've come to the right place."

"I mean, I need to speak to him, and I need him to speak back to me. We need to have an actual conversation."

"God speaks back to us in many ways."

"Not that kind of speaking," I said. I was getting a little frustrated. "I need him to speak to me with his mouth."

"I see."

"Can you help me?"

"I'm not sure anyone can."

"I think you can," I said. "You should know that I know the password."

"You do?"

Don't ask me how I knew this, but I did know. I said to the reverend, "Watermelon."

"My, my," the reverend said. He was scratching his head and smiling.

"Now can you put me in touch with him?"

"Yes, I can," he said. "Yes, I suppose I can. Come with me. I'll give you his address."

I followed the reverend down a hall and into his private office. He opened a drawer at his big wooden desk and removed a small rectangle of paper. It was a business card. The word *GOD* was printed in capital letters at the top of the card, and below it was an address.

"This is it?" I asked.

"This is where you'll find him."

"And he'll talk to me?"

"I'm not promising you anything. I'm just telling you where he lives. The rest is up to you."

"Okay," I said.

"When you step out of the church, turn left. Walk about a mile, and the complex will be on your right-hand side. You can't miss it. It has a big neon sign."

"Thank you," I said.

"Good luck," the reverend said, and I walked out of his office. I stepped out of the church and turned left as he'd instructed. It was very dark outside, and there were only a few streetlights in sight. The farther I got toward the address, the darker it got.

I passed a little café, which was closed. I passed a small bookstore and a second-hand clothing store. They were also closed. Then I passed an automobile body shop. The lights were on in the body shop, so I figured they were working late.

Then I finally arrived at the address on the card. I double-checked it just to be sure I was at the right place. It was a mobile home park called "The Oasis," and it had a huge sign on a pole featuring neon palm trees and a neon setting sun. I stepped up to the gate and opened it. I was looking for space forty-six, and the space numbers were on short posts in front of each mobile home. Walking down the unpaved drive, I heard my footsteps crunching on the gravel. Except for the yellow light spilling into front yards here and there from the small mobile home windows, it was very dark.

"Can I help you?" a voice asked. I turned to look, and it was a woman in curlers. I said to myself, "Why are women in curlers always living in mobile home parks?"

"Pardon me?" the woman said.

"Hi," I said.

"Who are you looking for?"

"I'm looking for space forty-six," I said.

"Oh, so you're here to see the Lord?"

"Yes, ma'am."

"Keep on walking. His place is the last home on your left. You can't miss it. It has the weeds in the front yard. We've been complaining to the management for years. You know, he really should hire someone to tend his yard. The rest of us are proud of our homes, and we take care of our yards."

"I see," I said.

"You might have to knock more than once."

"Why is that?"

"He's always got his TV on too loud. I think he's going deaf. We've complained to the management about that too. They talked to him, but he still has the volume up too high. But then, he is God. I mean, what can we really do?"

"Nothing, I guess."

"Well, I'll leave you be."

"Thanks," I said.

The woman walked away, and I continued to walk toward God's place. Soon I reach the home. I walked up the side path to the door, and I knocked several times. I could hear the TV blaring from inside.

There was no answer, so I knocked again. I knocked harder this time.

The door opened.

CHAPTER 16

THE BIG GUY IN THE SKY

———— •◦• ————

I figured the man who'd answered the door to be in his eighties. He was dressed in an old terry cloth bathrobe, and he had several days of gray stubble on his face. His hair was a mess, like he'd just gotten out of bed. When he smiled at me, I noticed that his teeth were dull and badly discolored, probably from smoking cigars; there was a lit cigar in his fingers, and he raised it to his lips to puff it.

"Can I help you?" he asked. As he spoke, swirls of cigar smoke came out of his mouth and nostrils.

"I hope you can," I said.

"Are you looking for someone?"

"Actually, I'm looking for God."

"Ah, well, how about that? You've come to the right place."

"He lives here?"

"Indeed, he does. What's your name?"

"Robinson," I said.

"Pleased to meet you, Robinson. Not to alarm you by my appearance, but I'm the guy you're looking for."

"You're God?"

"The one and only. The Great Almighty. The Creator. The Everlasting King. The Big Guy in the Sky." The man flashed a big, brown smile and outstretched his arms as if to say, *Here I am!*

"Oh, my," I said.

"Come on in, Robinson. I was expecting you tonight. Yes, I've been waiting and wondering. I was beginning to think you might not show."

"Are you sure it's okay?"

"It's all good, son. Please come in."

I stepped into the man's mobile home, and he shut the door behind me. The place stank of cigar smoke, mildew, and musty body odor. The TV was on loud, tuned to an episode of *America's Got Talent*, and there was a contortionist on the screen touching her nose with the heel of her foot.

"I watch this show with my wife," I said.

"I know you do."

"You know what we watch on TV?"

"I know everything."

"Then you know why I'm here?"

"Indeed, I do. I know exactly why you're here. You've come here troubled by some uncertainties. You're looking for answers."

"I am," I said.

"Easy enough. Why don't you take a seat so we can talk? You can sit on the sofa or the recliner. Take your pick from the two. I can sit anywhere. I'm not at all picky. But I'll tell you, while the couch is more comfortable, the recliner has a better view of the TV, you know, in case you want to watch the show while we talk."

"I didn't come here to watch TV."

"No, of course not."

I sat down on the sofa, on the end closest to the front door in case I needed, for some reason, to bolt and make a sudden exit from this strange, very un-godlike place. The lumpy sofa was surprisingly comfortable, like sitting on a big fluffy cloud. The man plopped down in his recliner so he would face both me and his TV set, and he dropped his old cigar butt in an overflowing ashtray.

"How do I know you're really God?" I asked.

"Ah, a little suspicious, are we?"

"Not suspicious. Just curious. You're not exactly what I expected God to look like."

"No?"

"Well, not exactly."

The man laughed and said, "But you're wrong about that."

"I am?"

"I'm exactly what you expected me to look like. From my messy hair down to my bare feet. If I looked any different, I would be someone else's God."

"What does that mean?"

"Am I real?"

"I suppose you are. I mean, I can see you, and we're here talking to each other."

"But am I real?"

"I don't know. Are you?"

"The answer is yes, that I am real. But I am real for you in a way you imagine me to be real. Maybe not as real as I am for some people but maybe more real than I am for others. Do you know how real I am to you?"

"I'm not even sure I know what you're talking about."

"Let me put it this way. I am real, but I also happen to be invented."

"Invented?"

"I am dreamt up, and I am imagined. So, I am only as real as you want me to be real. But for you, that is quite real and maybe more real than you care to admit. This is all new to you, isn't it? I happen to know there have been times in your life when you were a devout atheist, so talking to God makes you feel a little strange. Am I right?"

"I've questioned your existence."

"And why?"

"The idea of a God seemed preposterous."

"But now that your older, it's not so preposterous, is it? It's sensible. It's even rational."

"I guess."

"Funny how the mind works, isn't it? One day you're a rock- solid atheist, and the next day you're a believer? And now here I am, talking to you just as big as life. Nothing has changed in this picture other than you. *You* have changed. You've made a deliberate decision to say to yourself, in so many words, 'Hey, the God thing isn't such a bad idea after all. I could use a God to talk to. I have a lot of questions, and I would like to have some answers. I need advice. I need someone to point me in the right direction. Living without a God is a lot more difficult than I ever thought it would be.' And so, my once-unsure friend, here I am, exactly as you have imagined me, exactly as you want me. Am I just a hallucination? No, that's not it at all. I am real because you made me real. You blew life into my lungs, and I am consequently as real as this old bathrobe I'm wearing and as real as the cigar I was smoking. I am as real as all the aluminum-clad trailers in this mobile home park and as real as the gravel drive that takes you from one to the other. I *am* real."

"Okay," I said.

"You're not convinced?"

"Not entirely."

"Then let's talk about something else. Let's talk about something you do understand. Let's talk about love. You've been thinking about love recently, no?"

"I have."

"And it's real, isn't it?"

"Yes, it is."

"And powerful?"

"Yes, it's very powerful."

"Launch-a-thousand-ships powerful?"

"Yes, there's that."

"But ask yourself now, Can you see it? I mean, can you see it with your eyes like you can see a tree? Or a cow? Or the sun?"

"No, you can't see it."

"Can you hold it in your hands? Can you squeeze it? Or pet it? Or can you smell it?"

"No," I said.

"Can you cut it with a saw?"

"No."

"Can you measure it with a tape measure? Can you weigh it with a scale? Can you mold it with your hands like a lump of clay? Can you fire it in a kiln?"

"No, none of the above."

"And isn't it the same thing with hate? And isn't it also the same with envy, lust, desire, hope, longing, and all those other invisible machinations of the human mind?"

"Yes," I said. "I suppose that's true."

"Yet there's no denying their existence, is there?"

"There's no denying it."

"And so here I am. Maybe I am just invented. Maybe I am a figment of your imagination. Maybe I'm not the same for all who make me up. Yet I am real, just as if you could hold me in your hands."

"I think I understand."

"And I'm all powerful?"

"Yes," I said.

"Omniscient?"

"That too."

"The ultimate embodiment of love?"

"Yes, there's that."

"And wise?"

"Very wise," I said.

"So, you'll listen to what I have to say?"

"Yes, I'll listen."

"Good, good. Now we're getting somewhere. So, shall we get on with it? What questions did you have for me? What did you want to ask?"

"It's going to sound kind of silly."

"Do you remember Mrs. Brinkley in your fourth-grade class? What did she always like to say? Didn't she say that the only dumb question was the question not asked?"

"She did use to say that."

"Then ask me your questions."

"Okay," I said. I tried to think of my questions, but my mind was drawing a blank. It was as if my brain had turned to bread.

"I'll help you with this," God said, laughing. "You want to know if, when you dream of loving other women, that makes you unfaithful to your wife. You want to know whether you're effectively cheating on Martha."

"Yes," I said.

"Especially regarding the strange dreams you've had about Gabriela?"

"Yes, her."

"You dream that you love her."

"I do it often. Why do I do that? I have to say that the dreams are very pleasant, but when I wake up, I feel awfully guilty. And I barely knew the girl."

"And there's more to it."

"There is?"

"You want to know that, if you're unfaithful to Martha in your dreams, what gives you the right to teach morality to your son? Are you just another hypocrite? Are you talking out of both sides of your mouth? Should Robert even bother to listen to you? Well, should he?"

"I don't know."

"Has anyone ever told you the story about the man, the boy, and the crocodile?"

I thought about the story but couldn't recall it. "I don't think I've heard it," I said.

"I thought your dad told fables."

"He did, but he didn't tell them to me. He told them to Robert."

"Okay, fair enough" God said. "I'm going to tell you the story." God removed a fresh cigar from his pocket and lit it with his lighter. A cloud of cigar smoke went up and over the top of his head. He said, "In a jungle deep in Africa, there was a large pond outside of a village. A father would take his son to the pond on hot days, and the father would go swimming in the cool water. But he wouldn't allow his son to jump in. He told him, 'It's far too dangerous for you. A large, hungry crocodile lives in this pond, and there's no telling what he'll do.' So, the son would sit on the bank and watch his father swim. Every time they came to the pond, the father would jump in the water, and he'd tell his son the exact same thing. Then one afternoon, while the father was swimming, a large crocodile appeared and attacked the father while the son watched. He got a hold of the father's leg and began chomping away. Then it had the father in its jaws right up to his waist. As the man was being devoured, he called out to his son, 'See what I mean! I told you there was a crocodile in this pond. Son, whatever you do, stay out of this water, no matter what.' It wasn't long before the vicious crocodile had eaten the poor man whole. Several days later the boy returned to the pond with his mother. It was another hot day, and the boy wanted to go swimming, so he jumped into the pond. The mother gasped and said, 'Didn't your father tell you not to go into the pond?' The boy said, 'That old hypocrite? I'm glad Dad died. Now he can't tell me what to do!'"

"Jeez," I said.

"It's a good story, no?"

"It's an awful story."

"But it's so true, isn't it?"

"I guess so."

"The moral to the story is twofold, right? One, don't let your own wrong behavior keep you from teaching others to do the right things. And two, don't let the hypocrisy of others prevent you from listening to their good advice."

"Where did you hear that story?"

"I made it up."

I scratched my head, thinking. Then I said, "So, I made it up, since I made you up?"

God laughed and said, "Right you are. Wait a minute. Did you see that? That was amazing."

"What was amazing?"

God was now watching the TV. A blindfolded man had just shot an arrow through a balloon held in a woman's mouth. "How did he do that?"

"I don't know," I said.

"This show is great."

"Martha and I enjoy it."

"Where the heck do they find these people?"

"I don't know," I said. But I guess they hold auditions all over the place.

"And where do these people find the time to develop these queer talents? Don't they need to work for a living?"

"That's a good question."

"This is the way I see it," God said, now rubbing his chin and changing the subject. "You want to know if it's been your own foibles that have somehow caused Robert to become a thief, to steal Mr. Whitehouse's prize coin collection. Isn't that the issue here? Isn't that what's on your mind?"

"I suppose so." I thought for a moment and then said, "Yes, as a matter of fact, that's exactly what I was thinking about."

"I thought so."

"Listen," I said, "Robert didn't just acquire the urge to steal out of the blue. It had to come from somewhere, and it certainly didn't come from Martha. And it didn't come from his grandparents or from anyone else I know in our family. You know what I think of kids? I think they often come across as being naïve, yet I also believe they have an uncanny ability to detect lies. They have a special built-in radar. They know when they're being misled. They know when adults are phonies, and they can smell hypocrites a mile away. And I think Robert's antennae have been tuned in to me for years. I can't prove it, but it's a feeling I have. It's a feeling I get whenever I talk to him and especially when I give him advice. I can tell he's looking at me and saying to himself, 'Who the heck are you to tell me what's right and wrong? Look at yourself in the mirror, pal, and give yourself all this crazy advice. And then leave me be.'"

"Is he really saying that?"

"That's how it feels."

"I'll tell you another story."

"Okay," I said.

"Have you heard the one about the police officer and the man who was driving home from work?"

"No, I haven't."

God blew a cloud of cigar smoke up toward the ceiling and said, "There's a man, see, and he's driving home from work. He had to work late in the office, and he's in a hurry to get home. He's driving through the thick traffic, and a police car pulls up behind him and turns on his flashing lights. The man sees the lights and pulls over to the side of the street, and the police car pulls up behind him. The officer gets out of the car and steps to the man's open window. Before the officer can say a single word, the man says, 'Okay, okay, I know why you pulled me over, and I'm sorry, sir. I suppose you've been following me for a few miles now. I guess I'm in an awful hurry to get home. And yes, that pedestrian back there was in the crosswalk before I ran through it, but if I'd stopped for him, I would've had to slam on the brakes. I was going a little over the speed limit. Okay, okay, maybe a lot over. But like I said, I was in a rush to get home. And yes, I was probably weaving in and out of the traffic, and I suppose I should've used my turn signal when I was changing lanes. And there's no doubt about it. I did follow that one car way too close. But the guy was going way too slow. All this traffic can be so frustrating when you're in a hurry to get somewhere, and the other drivers aren't exactly cooperative. So, go ahead and give me a ticket. What's it going to be for? Take your pick, I guess.'

"When the man was done talking, the officer just stared at him. The man said impatiently, 'Well, what's it going to be?' The cop said, 'I just pulled you over as a courtesy to tell you your taillight was out. Until you started talking, I hadn't planned on writing you up for any of those things.'"

"Another good story," I said.

"Thanks," God said.

"I suppose you made that one up too?"

"*We* made it up."

"Yes, of course, we."

"And you get the point?"

"I do," I said.

"You know, we're all a bunch of idiots. We're also all *not* a bunch of idiots. We're wise and stupid, innocent and guilty, all at the same time. The Bible has a lot of things wrong, but there is one thing that it does have right; man was made in my image. Make no mistake about it. If I'd been using my head, I would've aimed a little higher. But I didn't. And what's done is done."

"Tell me what it's like."

"What what's like?"

"To be God."

"Like, how do you mean?"

"Like, how does it make you feel to know you've created the planet earth and all its inhabitants. Do you feel proud? Sad?" Embarrassed? Humbled? Mortified?"

"The truth? I feel imposed upon. I feel like an exhausted father whose needy children never grew up. Do you know what I'd like to see? Honest to me, this would make me the happiest guy on earth. I'd like to see everyone just take responsibility for themselves. Stop seeking my favor with your expensive churches, synagogues, mosques, and temples. And quit wasting your time expecting me to solve all your problems. Am I the numbskull who created all your stupid problems? No, all I ever did was plant a handful of seeds. I'm not the one who cheats, lies, plunders, steals, hoodwinks, bribes, and scratches and claws his backward way through life. I'm not the one who showers all that abuse on his children or who is unfaithful to his loving spouse or who is disrespectful to his parents. And I'm not the one who rapes and pollutes oceans, mountains, valleys, rivers, lakes, deserts, and mesas. I'm not the one who's slaughtering all the whales in the seas, and I'm certainly not the one who's spreading AIDS, shooting innocent people with handguns and assault rifles, or overpopulating the planet. I'm not even responsible for acts of God. So, what of the forest fires, earthquakes, hurricanes, and tornados? You can thank dear Mother Nature for these so-called acts of me. All these disasters are completely out of my hands. Don't you see? I'm just me, God, and no more or less. Yes, I'm willing to give advice here and there, but even then, you will discover that my advice is no better than the advice you'd give to yourself. And why? Because I am you. I never was anything else. I never claimed to be anything else. So, you get down on your knees and say you have faith in me? Try having some faith in yourself and leave me the hell out of it. I'm a busy man. There are books I would like to read, music I'd like to listen to, art I would like to see, and some good shows on TV I really don't want to miss."

I laughed and said, "I think I can understand how you must feel."

"Of course you understand," God said, laughing it up. "Everything I just said came out of your mouth."

"Which means I have to rethink everything."

"Everything?"

"I expected you to provide me with answers."

"But I did."

"No, as you have pointed out, I provided them. I listened to you, but I answered my own questions. And I am nothing but a human being. As a human being, I am flawed, corrupted, and untrustworthy."

God laughed and said, "Now you're catching on. Yes, now you're catching on."

"So, what's the solution?"

"There isn't one."

"So, we're all screwed?" I asked. "Is that what you're saying? That there is no hope?"

"I'm saying you're alive. So be alive. There is plenty of hope, and life is a marvelous experience." Just then there was a flash of lightning and a very loud thunderclap. It shook the mobile home to its core, and for a second the lights flickered on and off. "Mother Nature," God scoffed, and he shook his fist at the ceiling. "Now the power is probably going to go out. I hate it when that happens. And right in the middle of my TV show. It never fails."

Then there was another flash of lightning, and this time the thunder was even louder. It was so loud you'd swear it had crashed into the mobile home. And then the rain began to pour in buckets, and power went out completely. God was fumbling noisily through the kitchen drawers, looking for a flashlight.

"I can never remember where I put the thing," he said. "I was sure I left it in one of these drawers. Aha! At least there are some candles in here. Hand me the lighter on the coffee table, will you?"

I grabbed the lighter from the coffee table and walked in the darkness toward the kitchen. "Here," I said, handing the lighter to God. He took it out of my hand and lit one of his candles. It provided some light but not much.

"I should probably leave," I said. "It's getting late, and Martha is going to be wondering where I am."

"Let me get you an umbrella," God said.

"That would be great."

"I only have one, and it's falling apart. But it should last until you get home. Without an umbrella, you're going to get drenched."

God found the umbrella in the coat closet and handed it to me.

"Thanks," I said. I then stepped to the front door and opened it. I said goodbye, and God shook my hand.

"Take care of yourself," he said.

"I will. You take care of yourself too."

The next thing I knew I was on the sidewalk at the side of the street, alongside the neon mobile home park sign and gated entry. The rain was coming down even harder now, splashing at my feet, beating down on the sidewalk. The street was puddling up with water, and the cars were driving through the puddles. You could see the falling rain in the beams of their headlights and steam rising from the street.

Then, without any warning, the umbrella collapsed, and it was of no use at all. I tossed it aside and walked unprotected. I was on the sidewalk, headed home, when a car pulled over and stopped ahead of me. I walked up to the car. The driver had rolled down the passenger window, and she was calling me over. When I got there, the driver said, "Do you need a lift?"

"That would be great," I said.

"Climb in."

"I will," I said, and I opened the passenger door. Then I climbed inside. "Jesus," I said without looking at the driver. "It's really coming down."

"Robinson?" the driver said. I turned to look at her, and I couldn't believe my eyes.

"Mom?" I said. "Is that you?"

"It is," she said.

"What are you doing out here?"

"I was going to ask you the same question. I'm coming home. What are you doing out here?"

"I was seeing a friend."

"You're going to catch pneumonia, walking around in the rain like this."

"I had an umbrella."

"Then where is it?"

"I tossed it. It was broken."

"We'll get you dried off."

"Where are we going?" I asked.

"To my motel room."

"Your motel room?"

"There should be some towels you can use in the room. And we'll be out of this awful rain." I watched Mom as she talked. She looked so different. She was my mom, and yet she wasn't. The blue dashboard lighting illuminated her face, and, swear to God, she looked like a total stranger.

CHAPTER 17

THE HAPPY HOOKER

———•◦•———

She was wrapped in a one-size-too-small red sequined dress that barely contained her body, riding up high at her hips and cut low at her chest. What was most noticeable about this sparkly dress wasn't the dress itself but the amount of my mom's body the dress didn't cover. I'd never seen my mom show off so much flesh, especially so much cleavage, and I couldn't remember her ever having such a large and fleshy chest. Jesus, it was the kind of ample chest a man could happily lose himself in, cry himself to sleep in, smile like a bandit in, or suffocate in without even knowing what happened.

And her hips and legs! The dress rode up nearly to that magical area where her legs joined her body. I didn't realize Mom had such nice legs, the kind of legs a dancer has, yet my mom was no dancer. And you could see where Mom's stockings ended and where a garter belt contraption began, hinting at her undergarments. On the seat of the car was her red purse, sequined like her dress with a long golden chain. That was it. All she had on her was the skimpy dress and the small purse. What I didn't know was that she had her change of clothes in the trunk in a paper shopping bag. That was why we were headed to the motel room, so she could change.

"I'm sorry you had to see me like this," she said. She seemed embarrassed by her appearance.

"I think you're pretty," I replied, trying to be nice about it. And in a way, I meant it. Her face was amazing. She wore bright-red lipstick that matched the color of her dress, lots of rouge, and a pair of stunningly fake, jet-black, fluttering eyelashes.

"Do you really think I'm pretty?"

"I meant it. You kind of look like a movie star on her way to the Academy Awards."

Mom laughed and said, "I'm not exactly a movie star."

"No?" I said. I had to ask her this, so I did. "Then what are you?"

"I'm a prostitute."

"You mean like a hooker?"

"Yes, like a hooker."

"Like the happy hooker in that book?"

"Just like Xaviera."

"Does Dad know?"

"He knows nothing about it. And I'd appreciate it if you would keep this between you and me. Let's have this be a mother-and-son thing. You weren't even supposed to know in the first place. But I couldn't very well leave you out in that dreadful rainstorm, getting drenched to the bone."

"No," I said.

"I guess it was kismet."

"What is kismet?" Of course, I know what the word means now, but in this dream I was a teenager, and the word was new to me.

"Kismet," Mom said. "As in fate."

"Oh," I said.

"I guess someone was bound to find out sooner or later. Fate, you know. I guess it's better that it's you than your father."

"He wouldn't like it?"

"Are you kidding? He'd throw a fit. I'd never hear the end of it. And the money."

"And the money what?"

"It would have to stop. We would have to survive on your dad's salary, scrimping and saving, cutting corners, living like paupers."

"What's a pauper?"

"A pauper is someone who hasn't got the brains or gumption to do what it takes to earn enough money to eat decent meals and live a decent life." I had the distinct feeling that Mom was interjecting her own opinions into the definition, but I didn't pursue it any further. "We're going to stop at the motel," Mom said. "I'm going to take a shower, wash this makeup off my face, and change clothes. And you're going to get dried off. Then we're going home to wait for your dad to return from work. He's working late tonight. He'll be happy to see us. The poor clod works his tail off. It's too bad that he never learned how to earn decent money."

"They pay him, don't they?"

"Oh, they pay him."

"But not enough?"

"You catch on fast."

"How much do you get paid?"

"Some nights, quite a bit."

"More than Dad?"

"Much more. Being a prostitute can be a very lucrative endeavor."

I thought about this. Then I asked, "So, what do you do exactly?"

Mom sighed. I could tell from the nature of her sigh that she didn't want to discuss any details, but I was very curious. And to tell you the truth, I felt I had a right to know. She was, after all, my mother, so I stared at her until she finally gave in. "I do certain stuff with certain men," she said vaguely.

"Like what? Do you kiss them?"

"I try not to kiss them."

"Then what exactly do you do? Do you really have sexual intercourse with them?"

Mom smiled. I think my question surprised her. "With some of them I do," she said.

"Only with some of them? What else is there to do? What exactly do you do with them?"

"You really want to know, don't you?"

"I do," I said.

"Well, they're all very nice men. So, as I tell you about them, don't make the mistake of thinking they're bad. They just have certain idiosyncrasies."

"What's an idiosyncrasy?"

"It's something that makes a person special."

"Do I have an idiosyncrasy?"

"We all have them."

I had to think about this a moment. Then I said, "So, tell me what you do? You still haven't told me anything."

"Well, I have one client named Ned. He's about the nicest man you'd ever want to meet. He's in his late fifties. Don't laugh, but Ned likes to pretend he's a baby. He has me take off my dress, and he takes off all his clothes. Then he lies in my lap, and I nurse him. I mean, I don't actually nurse him, since I have no milk. But he keeps my nipple in his mouth and acts like a little child. And he always brings along a children's book, and he has me read to him from the book while he lays in my lap. His favorite is *The Little Engine That Could*. I'll bet I've read that story to him a hundred times. We do this for about an hour, because he says that's all he can afford. I'm not a cheap date, you know. I don't want to give you the wrong impression that I'm one of those cheap broads who'll do anything for a few measly bucks. I provide my clients with a first-rate service, and I'm not shy about getting paid a lot for it."

"That's weird," I said. "Why would a grown man want to pretend he's a baby?"

"It's an idiosyncrasy."

"Tell me another one."

Mom sighed again, and again I stared at her. "Well," she said. "There's Walt, the insurance salesman. He's about in his midthirties. He's married and has three children. Walt likes to watch me use the bathroom. I sit on the toilet and go, and he just stands there and watches. And when I'm done, he pays me. I get a hundred to pee and a fifty-dollar bonus if I'm able to have a bowel movement. I never know when he's going to see me, so I'm not usually ready for him. I often have to drink several glasses of water, and we sit at the edge of the bed and talk while my body processes the water. We talk about his wife and kids. I know everything there is to know about his family, all about their routines, their hobbies, their hopes and dreams, the vacations they go on, the friends they've made, and, yes, *their* idiosyncrasies. When I finally feel the urge to go, we head to the john together, and I sit down on the toilet to carry on with my business. It seems like a lot of money to pay for something that's over so quickly, but he really likes it. He told me that, of all the women he's seen pee, I'm his favorite."

"What a weirdo," I said.

"He's just a little different."

"I wonder what's wrong with him."

"There's nothing wrong with him. He just gets a kick out of seeing women go to the bathroom. It's not like he's a serial killer or a rapist or a thief. Trust me, he's as harmless as a bug."

"Tell me about another one."

"You *are* curious, aren't you?"

174

"You're my mom. I should know what you're doing with your time."

Mom smiled and said, "It isn't really any of your business. I don't even know why I'm telling you all this."

"Are you going to tell me more or not?"

"Okay, okay," Mom said. She looked ahead through the heavy rain. She was now looking for her motel. "There's always the night I spent with Aaron," she said.

"What does he do?"

"He's a CEO at a large food-processing company. But it's more what he is than what he does."

"Then what *is* he?"

"He's a homosexual."

"And he came to see you?"

"No one knows he's gay. He's still in the closet. When his thirty-year high school anniversary came up, he wanted to bring a date with him to prove he was straight. I tried to talk him out of this, but he insisted that I come. He paid me a lot of money to do this. He took me to the mall to pick out just the right dress and shoes. He bought me a blonde wig. For some reason I had to be a blonde. On the night of the big reunion, he picked me up and took me to the event in his car. Nice car. A brand-new Porsche. It was a lot of fun being all dressed up and driven in such a nice car. I felt like I was on an actual date. It made me feel very attractive.

"When we arrived at the reunion, there were more people than I expected. All of them were dressed so nice, and all of them had partners. I could see why Aaron wanted to bring me along. We walked around together, socializing with Aaron's old schoolmates, and he introduced me to them as his current girlfriend. We had decided in advance that I would be palmed off as a successful attorney. Aaron wanted his classmates to think not only that he was straight and successful in business but also that he was dating attractive and successful women."

"So, you had to pretend to be an attorney?" I asked. "What do you know about being an attorney?"

"Nothing," Mom said. "Whenever anyone asked me anything specific about my job, I would just change the subject. This was easier to do than you probably realize. This went along fine until I got engaged in a conversation with an idiot named Arnold Hardy. Arnold was one of

Aaron's classmates who was, as luck would have it, a real attorney. He wanted to talk shop in the worst way, and I had no idea what he was talking about. The guy just went on and on, talking about motions, objections, and rules of discovery until I was ready to unzip his pants and put an end to the conversation. *That* would've shut him up. There's no man in the world that can concentrate while he's getting his manhood serviced, if you know what I mean. I probably shouldn't be telling you this, but it's true. Boy, is it ever true. Men are so predictable."

"So, what did you do?"

"I finally got him to change the subject."

"So, what did you end up talking about?"

"Football."

"That was it?"

"It worked like a charm. It was either football or sex, and honestly, I would've looked pretty silly down on my knees while everyone else at the party was busy talking and eating hors d'oeuvres."

"Jeez, Mom," I said.

"You know, at first I thought this class reunion idea with Aaron was going to be a real drag. You know what I mean, right? Pretending I was someone I wasn't and being dragged around from one stupid, ancient classmate to the next. But you know what? It turned out that I had a pretty good time. Aaron was a very nice man, and all night he treated me like an actual princess.

"After the event was over, he took me out for dessert and coffee. We had such a good time talking and laughing, you'd swear this guy wasn't gay at all. You'd swear we were on a real date, a date that was going very well, a pairing of two people who had a possibility of a future together. I was actually kind of sad when the evening was over and he paid me what he owed and said goodbye. It seemed so abrupt. And so shallow." I looked at Mom's face. She now looked a little sad, like she might begin to cry.

When we arrived at Mom's motel, she pulled her car up to the building. It was still raining like crazy. We opened the car doors, and Mom went to the trunk to get her clothes while I ran to the room. When Mom arrived beside me, she unlocked and opened the door. Once inside, she rushed to the bathroom to pee. She didn't even bother closing the door. While she was still wiping herself, she told me to come in. "There are some towels over by the shower that you can use to dry yourself off," she said.

"Okay," I said.

"It'll take me a little while to get ready. You can watch TV. The TV here is supposed to get all kinds of channels."

"Sound good," I said.

Mom climbed out of her red-sequined dress, so she was in her bra, panties, and stockings. It was a little weird, but she obviously didn't mind if I saw her undressed. It was no big deal to her. I took a couple of towels from the rack by the shower. I then went to the other room to watch the TV and dry off.

"What's on?" Mom asked.

"I'm watching *Mannix*," I said.

"I'm going to jump in the shower. I need to clean all those men off of me."

"Okay," I said.

"Cologne and Certs. What a combination. My chest smells like a drugstore."

"Sounds bad," I said. Mom was giving me a little too much information.

I could hear her stepping into the water, and she talked to me from the shower stall. "What ever happened to that little girl you were going to ask to the school dance? What was her name? The little redhead?"

"Jennifer?"

"Yes, that's the one."

"I still haven't asked her."

"Why not?"

"I'm not sure what she'll say."

"There's only one way to find out."

"I know," I said. "That's what Dad says."

"Well then?"

"What if she says no?"

"Why would she say no? You're a good-looking boy. You have a good sense of humor, and you're smart. Truly, you have everything going for you."

"She might have a boyfriend."

"Well, does she have one, or doesn't she?"

"I'm not sure. It's just something I heard."

"Well, ask her if she has one."

"I can't do that."

"Why not?" Mom asked.

"I don't know."

"You're not going to get anywhere with girls if you're afraid to talk to them."

"I know, I know," I said.

"You know what they say. God helps those who help themselves."

"I didn't know God had anything to do with this."

"God has everything to do with everything."

"I suppose that's true."

"Do you know how your father and I met?"

"No, I don't," I said. Dad had told me, but I didn't want to say it.

"He asked me out on a date. Right out of the blue. You know, I didn't even know him. In fact, I didn't even know his name."

"But he obviously knew who you were?"

"He did. He saw me and said to himself, 'Now, there's a girl I think I could like,' and he mustered up the nerve to ask me out on a date, just like that.

"And you said yes."

"No, not the first time. The first time he asked me out, I said no. I told him I didn't know him from Adam, and you know what he said?"

"What?"

"He said, 'Then let's get to know each other. *Then* let me ask you out on a date again.'"

"And what did you say?"

"I said, 'Okay,' and we got to know each other."

"I heard the first time Dad talked to you that you were so drunk that you couldn't start your car, that he took you home from a party."

"Where'd you hear that?"

"From Dad."

"Well, maybe that's his version. I like my version a lot better."

I could now hear Mom climbing out of the shower and turning off the water. Then she was drying herself off and putting her normal clothes on. "You guys should get your stories straight," I said, laughing.

"I guess we should. I'll have a talk with your dad. But I still think you should ask Jennifer to the dance. Am I right? Nothing ventured, nothing gained."

"Maybe I will."

"When is the dance?"

"I think it's this weekend."

"Time's running out."

"It is," I said.

Suddenly Mom appeared in the room. She was done getting ready, and she looked like my mom again. The makeup and false eyelashes were gone, and the sequined dress, high heels, and little red purse were in the paper shopping bag. I turned off the TV, and we left the room.

It was still raining outside, and we had to run to the car. Once we were in, Mom started the engine and backed out of the parking space. She turned on the radio and tuned in to a popular song by Petula Clark. Then she proceeded to drive, and I leaned my head against the hard side window. This position wasn't particularly comfortable, but I was exhausted and could barely keep my eyes open. The next thing I knew, I was sound asleep and dreaming as Mom drove through the rain while the wipers swatted the water off the windshield.

"The storm should pass soon," a man's voice said in the dream.

"I hope so," I replied.

"More olives?"

"Sure," I said. The man held out a bowl full of olives, and I grabbed several of them. I popped one of them into my mouth and chewed. We were in a small wooden gazebo, protected from the rain.

"More grapes?"

"No grapes."

"More wine?"

"Why not?" I said. The man poured me half a glass, and I reached for it. I took a sip of the wine to wash down the olives.

Then I looked at the man. Yes, it was Plato again. Funny how a certain man or idea can get stuck in your head and also in your dreams.

The sun was high but gone, hiding behind the rain clouds, waiting patiently to make an appearance. Plato and I had been talking for hours, but I had no idea what we had been talking about. All I knew was what I was presently hearing, saying, and thinking. And what was I thinking? I was thinking that the olives tasted good, that the wine was just right, and that the humidity from the rain was making my shirt stick to the skin of my back.

Then Plato dropped a new thought log on the fire, and the flames ignited. An idea! A new query! My ancient Greek friend was always good for this. He began to ask me questions as he always did.

"Innocence," he said. "Tell me, Robinson, what is left when you take it away?"

"Guilt?" I guessed.

"A common misconception."

"Is it?"

"The idea that you are either innocent or guilty is so easy to understand. It's like day and night. Like hot and cold. Like rough or smooth. But no, innocence is different."

"How so?" I asked.

"First, ask yourself, What exactly *is* innocence?"

"Will a dictionary definition do?" I asked.

"That will be fine for now."

I reached for my cell phone and looked up the word. Then I said, "*Innocence* means that one is not guilty of a crime or an offense."

"Keep going to the next definition."

"It also means lack of guile or corruption."

"And also? Is there a third definition listed?"

"It's a euphemism for a person's virginity."

"Ha, I especially like that one."

"Yes," I said.

"Let's think about this. We get a good idea from all three definitions as to what innocence actually is. But let's forget about the crime and forget about the guile and forget about the sexual intercourse. How would you define innocence without alluding to these specifics?"

"I don't know."

"I would define it this way. I would say that innocence is a state of being too inexperienced in life to have been exposed to, or corrupted by, its vices."

I thought about this for a moment. "That's very good," I said.

"It's a good definition?"

"It's excellent."

"Then I ask you my questions again. What is left when you take it away? Or what is its opposite?"

"I don't know."

"That's a good answer."

"It is?"

"Well, it's a good answer in that it's an honest answer. I have my own answer. Consider what I have to say. Maybe we'll land on the same page."

CHAPTER 18

THE ROTHCHILDS

———•◦•———

The thunder and lightning had all but stopped, but it was still raining like crazy. I took another sip from my glass of wine, and so did Plato. I could feel the wine heating up my heart and going gently to my head. Plato then laughed happily and mashed a handful of olives past his lips, speaking to me with his mouth full. "Guilt is not the absence of innocence," he said. "Take away innocence, and what do you really have? It's not guilt at all. I say you have knowledge."

"Knowledge?"

"Innocence is the state of not knowing. Take a little of your innocence away, and you suddenly know a few things. Take all of it away, and you suddenly you feel like you know it all. You suddenly *know*. You can't help it, Robinson. Whether you like it or not, you have knowledge."

"I guess that makes sense."

"Most people don't see it this way. Most people think the opposite of innocence is guilt, and no one wants to be guilty. So they value their innocence, and they treasure the innocence they see in others, especially children. But this is a rather big mistake they're making. If the opposite of innocence is truly knowledge, then innocence is stupidity. And who in their right mind wants to be stupid? I certainly don't want to be stupid. Do you want to be stupid?"

"No," I said. "Just about the last thing I would ever want to be is stupid."

"Precisely. Yet knowledge, especially as it is described in the Bible, represents the ultimate downfall of man. It is not a good thing, yet—and get this—without knowledge we are doomed to be innocent, and we've already agreed that innocence is stupidity. So where does that leave us? We are up a creek without a paddle. Plain and simple. We're damned if we do and damned if we don't."

"Yes," I said. "I can see that now."

"Which brings me to your son, Robert."

"To Robert?"

"Think about knowledge and all it means to us. Just think about it deeply and think about your son. And maybe that's all you'll need to know."

So I did try to think. I closed my eyes and concentrated, but I didn't think of knowledge per se. Instead, I let my head wander, and I thought back to when Robert was a small boy. It's strange how the mind works, isn't it? It doesn't always do what it's told. I thought back to a sunny summer day when Robert was seven years old. We were walking down the sidewalk on the way home. We had been at the neighborhood park, playing catch with a Frisbee, and it was now early in the afternoon. As we walked, Robert spotted a shiny object in the gutter, and he stopped to pick it up.

"Look at this," he said. He showed me what he had found. It was a pocketknife, about three inches long. It looked like it was brand new. It had five sparkling diamonds embedded in its silver handle. At least I assumed they were diamonds. They certainly looked like real diamonds due to the way they twinkled in the sun. Robert opened up the knife, and on the surface of the blade were etched the initials JPR. Robert touched the edge of the blade with the tip of his finger, and it immediately drew a red bead of blood.

"Wow, it's pretty sharp," he said. "Check it out. This must be a good knife."

Was I dreaming or remembering? The memory seemed so true to life and accurate in every detail, yet I wasn't sure whether any of this memory had ever happened. I recalled saying to Robert, "I wonder if the diamonds are real."

Robert closed the knife and looked it over. "How can we find out?" he asked.

"We could take it to a jeweler."

"They could tell us?"

"Sure, they could. They could tell us right away. They'd know the difference."

"I want to do that."

There was a jeweler in a nearby shopping center, and Robert and I hopped into the car when we got home. I drove us to the shopping center, and we stepped into the jewelry store. The man who owned the store was a short, rotund man named Abe Richards. I handed the knife to Abe and said, "We'd like to know if the diamonds in this pocketknife are real." Abe looked the knife over, and then he stuck a jeweler's loop into his eye and held the knife up to his face. It took him only a few seconds to answer our question.

"Yes, I see," Abe said. "Fine, fine. Yes, these are real diamonds all right. Very nice ones. Yes, these are very nice. You don't often find them quite this nice."

"What does that mean?" I asked.

"They have great clarity, and a minimum of flaws. In fact, I can't see a single flaw in any of them."

"Are they worth a lot?" Robert asked.

"Yes, they're worth quite a bit."

"Like how much?" Robert asked.

"Off the top of my head?"

"Yes," I said. "Give us a ballpark number."

Abe looked them over again, giving us a number, and Robert gasped. I probably did too. The diamonds were worth a heck of a lot more than we thought. "Are you looking to sell this?" Abe asked.

"I don't know," I said.

"We can't sell it," Robert said to me. "The knife doesn't belong to us."

"Whose is it?" Abe asked.

"We don't know," I said. "My son found it in the gutter near our house."

"I see," Abe said.

"We need to find the owner," Robert said. "He's probably looking all over for it."

And that meeting with the jeweler marked the beginning of our search for the owner of the mysterious knife. Robert was bound and determined to find the guy. The first thing we did when we got home was to make a stack of paper fliers describing the knife and giving out our phone number. We didn't mention the initials since we figured the real owner of the knife would be able to confirm the initials to us over the phone, thus proving that the knife was his. Robert took off with the fliers and proceeded to poke them into all the mailboxes on our street. Robert was sure this would work, but we waited for two days, and no one called. No one at all.

"I guess if no one claims it, it's yours," I said to Robert, and he shook his head.

"We'll find him," he said.

"We've already tried."

"We can put an ad in the paper, can't we?"

"I suppose we could."

"How much would that cost?"

"I have no idea," I said, but the next thing I knew, I was calling the newspaper, providing my credit card information, and listing the knife in its classified lost-and-found section. I tried to warn Robert. As soon as people learned about the five diamonds, dishonest idiots from all over town were all going to be calling us, trying to claim the item. But this wouldn't be a problem, right? We had the three initials etched on the blade to verify the true owner. No, Robert was sure we were doing the right thing.

Well, we received eight phone calls from the ad over the following week, and none of the callers could recite the initials. In fact, as soon as we asked them about the initials, they hung up. I told Robert, "It looks like you've done everything you could. We handed out fliers. We put an ad in the paper. I think the knife is now yours. So, do you want to keep it or sell it?"

"Neither," said Robert. "There's still one more thing we can do."

"And what would that be?"

"We can check with all the jewelers in the area to see if one of them recognizes the knife. Maybe one of them originally sold it to the owner. Or maybe they put the diamonds in it for him."

"That's kind of a long shot," I said.

"But we have to do it," Robert insisted. "I have a feeling this knife is very important to somebody and that they would be very happy to have it back."

"Well, you're right about that," I said, thinking about what the diamonds were worth.

So, to the phone book's yellow pages we went. Robert wrote down the names and addresses of every confounded jeweler in the area. There were a lot more than I thought. We left the next day at ten in the morning, and by one in the afternoon we found who we were looking for. A jeweler named Henry Best recognized the knife right away. In fact, he claimed to be the jeweler who had installed the diamonds in the handle in the first place. He said he'd done the work for a woman named Abigail Rothchild, who had the knife customized for her husband, and Henry gave us her phone number.

Robert and I went home, and the first thing Robert did was call Mrs. Rothchild and tell her he had her husband's knife. She was elated, of course. They lived around the block from us, and it turned out her husband had been riding his bike down our street when the knife fell from a hole in his pocket. She said he'd been sick about it. He'd been looking all over town for the thing. So she and her husband came over to our house that evening, and Robert handed the man his long-lost knife.

"Jesus, kid," he said. "You're a lifesaver. I thought it was gone for good."

"Does it mean a lot to you?" Robert asked.

"Does it ever," Mr. Rothchild said. "Mrs. Rothchild had it made especially for our fifth wedding anniversary. So, yes, it means a lot."

Robert smiled. I then said to the couple, "My son wasn't going to rest until he found its owner."

"We looked high and low for you," Robert said. "We were about to give up."

"No, this is wonderful," Mr. Rothchild said.

"Give the boy his reward," Mrs. Rothchild said, nudging her husband in the ribs with her elbow.

"Of course," Mr. Rothchild said, and he reached to his back pocket for his wallet. He opened up the wallet and removed a crisp hundred-dollar bill, handing the bill to Robert.

Robert smiled again and said, "Thank you."

"No, thank *you*," Mr. Rothchild said.

And everyone lived happily ever after. Isn't that the way these kinds of memories go? When the Rothchilds left our house that night, I told Robert I was proud of him. That was Robert. That was my son at age seven. Or was that my son at all? Like I said, the wine Plato had poured for me was going to my head a bit. Suddenly, I wasn't sure whether this was a true-to-life memory or an optimistic fiction. Or both? Or neither? I just didn't know.

"So," Plato said, "what happened?"

"I just told you," I said. "The Rothchilds left our house, and Robert was happy with himself."

"No, I mean what *happened*?"

"What happened to what?"

"What happened to Robert?"

Suddenly, I knew what Plato was driving at. He wanted to know what had happened to Robert that turned him from an honest and thoughtful boy into a coin-filching teenager. I said, "I don't know what happened."

"More wine?"

"No thanks," I said. The last thing I needed was another glass of wine.

"It was knowledge," Plato said. "But the question is, what morsel of knowledge found its way onto Robert's plate that made him do such an about-face?

"I don't know," I said.

"Of course, there is also the very likely possibility that you're remembering this story all wrong, that you're recalling the events as you would like them to have occurred and not as they actually happened."

"Is that really possible?"

"Sure, it is. Our memories fail us all the time. The very last thing I would ever depend on when seeking the truth is a human memory."

"What else could have happened? Do you think there was no knife? No diamonds? No Rothchilds? Do you think I'm making up the entire story?"

"No, I think there definitely was a pocketknife your son found in the gutter, just as you said. And I think it was Mr. Rothchild's knife, and I think you gave it back to him. I even think he gave Robert a reward. Yes, all of these things probably happened exactly as you said."

"Then how can the story be wrong?"

"Maybe things happened a little differently. Maybe, like you said, when he found the knife, you both suspected it might be very valuable, so you went to the jeweler where you confirmed that the diamonds were real. And, yes, the knife was worth more than either of you imagined, but as you drove home, Robert was playing with the knife and said, 'I guess that makes me rich. Finders keepers, right?' And maybe you said, 'Not quite yet, Son. We need to make an honest effort to find the knife's owner.' So when the two of you got home, you and Robert made all the fliers, and Robert stuck them in all the mailboxes on your street. Then you waited a couple of days, but no one called to claim the knife. Robert was now truly excited, and he said, 'So, now it's mine, right?' But you say no, that you wanted to place an ad in the paper, so you called and placed the ad. Yes, you got a few calls, but no, you didn't hear anything from the actual owner. Robert asked, 'So, *now* is it mine? We've done everything we can.' But you said, 'There's one more thing we can do,' and you saw the disappointment in his eyes as soon as you said this. 'It's a long shot,' you went on to say. 'But we can take the knife to all the jewelers in the area and see if one of them recognizes it.' Robert said, 'Well, you can drive all around town if you want, but I'm not coming.' Robert was now angry at your apparent zeal to have the knife taken from him. It seemed you were taking this do-gooder thing way too far. Anyway, you went to the jewelers in the area on your own, and you found the jeweler who set the diamonds. He gave you the phone number of the Rothchilds."

"So, I called the Rothchilds?"

"First, you asked Robert to call them, since he was the one who found the knife. You wanted him to experience for himself what it was like to do the right thing. But Robert was furious, and he refused to make the call. 'You're the one who can't wait to give the knife away,' he said. "So you can go ahead and call them.' So you called the Rothchilds, and you explained how Robert found the knife, and they told you they'd come over to your house to get it. They were thrilled that the knife was found, but when they arrived at your house, Robert refused to come out of his room to meet with them. He stayed in his room, fuming and pouting. So you gave Mr. Rothchild his pocketknife without Robert, explaining that Robert was coming down with a cold or something, not feeling well. The man then gave you a hundred-dollar bill. He told you to give the money to Robert, and then they left. You went up to Robert's room to give him the cash, and he snatched it from your hand. But then he said, 'What a sucker you are, Dad. It's no wonder you make so little money.'"

I stared at Plato for a moment and said, "Well, I would certainly have remembered Robert saying something like that to me."

"Would you?"

"I think I would."

"Sometimes people hear only what they want to hear. Often they will completely misconstrue what's being said to them. It happens all the time. And there are also times things happen a certain way, but we remember them wrongly. You'd be surprised at how often this happens, even to the most rational, reliable people on earth. You'd be amazed by just how inept we are when it comes to remembering. There is nothing more astonishingly unreliable and shaky than a human memory."

"So, which is it?"

"Which is what?"

"Which story about the knife is true?"

"How should I know? It was your story. I wasn't even there."

"Maybe there was no knife at all," I said.

"That's a definite possibility."

"So maybe our conversation about the knife has been a complete waste of time."

"Oh, no, I wouldn't say that."

"Why not?"

"All inquiries are worthwhile, whether they're made into the fantastic, wrong, or real. It's what sets man apart from the animal world. It is what makes man so outrageously unique. It is what makes us so admirable. Any giraffe, coyote, beetle, or bird can go through life without ever thinking, questioning, probing, comparing, wondering, or doubting, yet what are they in the long run? They are robots. They may as well be constructed of electrical wires, circuit boards, spinning gears, camshafts, pistons, pulleys, and cables. They eat, defecate, and copulate. They sing a few stupid songs, howl at the moon, do battle with their enemies, run from their predators, and sleep in the bushes when they're tired. They carry out this routine over and over ad infinitum. No, man is truly one of a kind, and you should never doubt or question the great significance of your doubts and questions."

"Even if I'm doubting and questioning a totally invented fantasy?"

189

"Especially then. For what are fantasies but our deepest and most sincere revelations?"

"Revelations?"

"I'll leave you with that thought."

"You're leaving?" I asked. Where did this guy think he was going? Was he really going away?

"I have students to teach."

"I thought you were teaching me."

"I *have* been teaching you. I've given you quite a lesson. There's much for you to think about."

And with that, Plato was gone. I don't know whether he walked away or just disappeared. It had stopped raining, and the sun was now out. The little robot birds were chirping on the wet tree branches.

I set my wine glass down and stepped out of the gazebo. I walked along a muddy trail that meandered through the tall grass of the meadow until I saw where it led into the woods. When I arrived at the thicket of trees, I held my breath for a moment. Then I stepped into the shadows. The birds were especially loud in the woods, and I wondered what the heck they were saying to each other. Maybe they were talking about me, the new intruder, or maybe they weren't saying anything at all. It was then that I saw him.

He was in one of the trees, as red as a boiled lobster. He was perched like a joker-in-the-deck fool on a branch that could barely hold his weight. The branch was bending over so that it looked like it was about to snap in half. Steam rose from the tops of his head and shoulders, and there was a soft sizzling, spitting sound, like bacon cooking. "Tweet, tweet," he said in a low voice.

"Pardon me?" I said.

"Tweet, tweet," he said again.

CHAPTER 19

BEELZEBUB

———————•❖•———————

"Who are you supposed to be?"

"I'm a bird, you idiot. Didn't you hear me? Tweet, tweet, tweet."

I laughed and said, "You're no bird. Birds don't weigh two hundred pounds."

"I'm a very large bird."

"Let's see you fly."

"Not all birds can fly. I'm the non-flying variety."

"Then how'd you get up in the tree?"

"I climbed up."

"A tree-climbing bird?" I said. "I don't think so. And what's that in your hand?" It appeared the man was holding a garden tool.

"It's my pitchfork."

"A bird with a pitchfork?"

The man sighed. "Very well, you're right. I'm not a bird at all."

"I thought so," I said, shaking my head.

"So, what do you *want* from me?"

"What do I want?"

"Everyone wants something from me. I mean everybody and their brother. You people are always pestering me for favors. Like I'm some kind of a Santa Claus with a sack full of gifts. Get me this, or make me into that. I'm telling you, there's no end to it."

"I don't want anything. First, there's nothing I really need, and second, I don't even know who you are or what you're capable of giving me. So, I'll ask you again. Who the heck *are* you?"

"I almost believe you."

"Almost believe what?"

"That you don't know who I am."

"Listen," I said. "As far as I'm concerned, you could be Marvin the Robot or Long John Silver."

"Ha," the man laughed. "Marvin the Robot? Good one. I could be happy being an unhappy robot."

"Do you have a name?"

"I actually have many names."

"Throw one my way. Maybe I'll recognize it."

"Does Satan ring a bell?"

"Satan?"

"Or the devil? Or Abaddon or Apollyon or the Beast or Lucifer or my all-time favorite, Beelzebub? Do any of these names ring a bell? Now do you understand why I'm hiding up in this confounded tree?"

"I get who you're supposed to be, but I still don't get why you're hiding."

Satan looked at me with one suspicious eye and said, "You don't want any favors from me?"

"None at all," I said.

"Well, that's very good. Very good indeed. So, I'll come right down." I watched as Satan carefully climbed down through the wet branches, somehow maintaining his grip on his pitchfork at the same time. When he dropped from the bottom branch, the damp earth sizzled beneath his hooved feet. "Ah, this is much better. I really don't care for climbing trees. Heights make me dizzy. So, what's your name, my friend."

"My name is Robinson," I said.

"Like Robinson Crusoe?"

"Exactly."

"You don't seem very surprised to see me."

"I'm dreaming. Apparently, I can run into about anyone I can imagine, and at this point, no one surprises me. I just got done talking to Plato, if you can believe that."

"Plato? The ancient Greek fellow?"

"Yes," I said, laughing. "The Greek fellow."

"He can be confusing."

"I noticed that."

"Well, I'm not confusing. You'll find that I deal strictly in realities."

"That will be refreshing."

"Listen, I like you right off the bat," Satan said. "You seem like an honest and guileless fellow, so I'm going to help you out. I'm going to answer all of your questions. Ask me any question at all. Pose it to me, and I'll give you a forthright answer. How many times in your life do you think you'll have an opportunity like this, to interrogate Satan? So, go ahead and ask away. Anything at all."

"Okay," I said.

"Well?"

"Okay, why my son?"

"Ah, you're talking about Robert?"

"Of course. He's the only son I have."

"Yes, yes, Robert. The teenage thief. Well, Robert is an interesting case. He was a very good kid. Just for the record, I went to him. He didn't come to me, if that's what's bothering you."

"Why did you go to him?"

"Why do I go to anyone?"

I thought about this and said, "I don't know. Maybe that's my question."

"People have a gross misconception about what I do. They think what I do is devious and awful. They think immorality is innately bad. They shun thievery, greed, lust, hatred, crime, violence, illnesses, pain, and destruction like they're somehow harmful things, like these things must be avoided at all costs, and they're constantly working to undo my efforts. They want to fight me tooth and nail."

"And why wouldn't they fight you?"

"Because what I do is necessary."

"Necessary?"

"I bring joy to their lives. I make the mediocre things in life shine as though they're stupendous. I make a good day much better than it is. I make people chuckle and laugh, and I bring heartfelt smiles to their otherwise-humdrum faces. By being so dark and nefarious, I make life worth living. Without me and my efforts, humanity is doomed."

"That makes no sense."

"No?" Satan said.

"No, it makes no sense at all."

"On the contrary, it makes perfect sense. Even God would agree with the logic. You must be aware that God knows I exist, and yet he does nothing to stop me. God knows I *must* exist in order for any of his actions to have any meaning. We may not exactly be chums, but we work hand in hand. Always have and always will."

"I don't get it," I said.

"I'll explain with a very simple example."

"That would be helpful."

"Let's talk about pain. I love pain. You've felt pain in your life, no?"

"I have," I said.

"How about the time you were building that wood deck in the backyard of your house? Do you remember that? Ha, your one and only carpentry project."

"Yes, I remember."

"Do you recall what you did?"

"Yes, I built the deck."

"With a saw, hammer, and nails?"

"Yes," I said.

"And what did you do on the second day?"

"I don't know."

"You hit your thumb with the hammer."

"Yes, you're right."

"And it hurt like hell, didn't it?"

I thought back, and then I said, "Yes, it was terrible. I whacked it hard. I was trying to hit a nail I was holding, and I hit my thumb instead."

"And you cussed?"

"Yes," I said, laughing. "I cussed up a storm."

"And it throbbed for the rest of the day?"

"It swelled up and throbbed, and half my thumbnail turned purple. And yes, it hurt all day. Like I said, I had hit it pretty hard."

"So, it's safe to say you experienced pain?"

"Yes, but so what?"

"The next day it was sore, but it was no longer throbbing like it was before. And eventually after a few days, it was as good as new. And how did you feel then?"

"I felt good. It was a good feeling, and I was grateful that the pain went away."

"Well, I submit to you that without the initial pain, you wouldn't have felt grateful at all. In fact, you would've felt nothing. Before you hit your thumb, you didn't even appreciate how fortunate you were to be pain free. It was the pain that made you glean joy from your comfort. It was the pain in your thumb that gave your comfort meaning. It was the pain that made you grateful for what you had to begin with, namely a pain-free thumb."

"And your point is?"

"That pain gives comfort meaning. Without the experience of pain, comfort means nothing."

"So, you conclude that pain is a good thing?"

"Yes, that's my conclusion."

"I see," I said. I was thinking about what Satan had just said, and I said, "I get it, and I can see how this might make sense to you."

"But does it make sense to *you?*"

"I don't know," I said. "I have a hard time placing pain in the good column."

"Listen," Satan said. "It isn't just pain. It's the whole spectrum of quote, unquote bad things that can befall a person in life. Bad is good. That's the lesson here, that bad is good. If you had cut off your finger with your saw while building the deck, you would certainly have gained a whole new appreciation for your remaining nine digits. If you had slipped and broken your leg, you would've had a whole new appreciation for having two working legs. And if some thief had stolen your tools from your backyard, you would certainly have appreciated having had the right tools to work with. And if you wrecked your car, you would appreciate an undamaged car. And if you came down with the flu, you'd appreciate being well. And if your house burned down, you'd have a whole new appreciation for having a roof over your head. Do you see what I'm trying to say? Let's take this even further. Recessions make us appreciate the good economic times, and cold-blooded murders make us appreciate life, and wars make us appreciate peace, and famines make us appreciate feasts, and freezing-cold weather makes us appreciate summers, and miserably hot summers make us appreciate winters. And most importantly, hatred and bigotry make us appreciate love. And that is the ultimate goal, isn't it? We all want love, sweet love. I submit that love means nothing without a lot of good old-fashioned hatred to back it up."

"Amazing," I said.

"Isn't it?"

"I actually think I understand."

Satan nodded and said, "Most people don't get it. They don't get it at all. It's as if they *want* to despise me. But I'm probably the most misunderstood man on earth. I am in reality the very backbone and spinal column of all that's good in the world."

"You know what I think?" I asked.

"What?" Satan said.

I smiled at him and said, "I think when I wake up from this dream, nothing you've said is going to make any sense."

"That could happen."

"I won't remember what you've just told me, and I won't understand."

"You might not."

"For example, what good could possibly come from Robert's propensity to steal? I'm not sure I even understand this right now."

"Ah, now that's the big question, isn't it?"

"Yes," I said.

"Let me tell you about your son. Actually, first let me talk a little about gestalt theory. Have you heard of it? Do you know what I'm talking about?"

"I've heard of it."

"Do you understand it?"

"I have to admit that while I read about it when I was younger, I've forgotten what it involves."

"Someone who's an expert may say I'm oversimplifying the theory, but I'll provide you with my own interpretation. I think you'll at least get the gist of it, at least so far as your son is concerned."

"Fine," I said.

"As is relevant to our conversation, the theory states that if units are similar in nature—and I'm using the word *units* to describe just about anything—then the human mind will group them all together. The focal point of the overall picture are those units which are dissimilar. The mind then tends to create two things. It creates both an image and a background. Are you following me? While the background is not the focal point, it is the background that creates the shape of the image. There are other aspects of this theory, but they don't really apply to Robert's circumstance. What I've given you is a quick-and-easy lesson on what you need to know. Hopefully, you understand what I'm trying to say."

"I get it," I said. "It's pretty simple."

"Then let's look at Robert this way. He is a whole person. He is the whole picture."

"Got it," I said.

"He is made of many different units. There are many varied aspects to his self and his personality. When you look at your son, your mind groups his similar traits together. And I know Robert well. His similar traits are good traits. He is a kind boy. He is thoughtful, understanding, and polite. He cares about people, and he loves his family. He is, when all is said and done, what one would call a good kid. Yet there are also some incongruities in the picture. This thievery thing is what I'm now talking about. The kid has a problem with it, largely thanks to me. So, what does your mind do? It groups all of his good traits together and turns them into a background. And you focus on what? You focus on his very worst traits, and then you wrongly conclude that your boy is just a thief. And you're so disappointed in him. I hope this is making sense to you. Your mind is playing tricks on you, and what you should be saying to yourself is, 'My son is a great young man, and his kleptomania is the exception that proves the rule.'"

"Yes, I can see that," I said.

"You should pay closer attention to the background. Tell me, have you ever been interested in optical illusions?"

"Maybe a little."

"But you're familiar with them?"

"Yes, to a degree."

"Do you recall the illusion of the two faces and the vase? It's a silhouette drawing of two people facing each other that can be interpreted as either two people facing each other or a vase. The vase is the shape made by the space between the faces. Or maybe it's actually a picture of a vase, where two faces can be seen in *its* background. You're able to take your pick, and now I'm telling you that you can take your pick with Robert. Are you going to see the incongruous focal point of his thieving, or are you going to visualize the good Robert who lives in the background? Are you going to see the vase or the faces? Or can you see them both and live with the whole?"

Satan was done talking, and I stared at him for nearly a minute. I knew he was a liar, so what was preventing him from lying to me now? "What you're saying makes a lot of sense," I finally said. "But I have to consider the source of what I've just heard."

"Yes, I was aware that could be a problem for you."

"So, what am I supposed to do?"

"How about a fable?"

I thought a moment and asked, "Why does everyone in this dream suddenly want to tell me fables?"

Satan laughed and said, "How about one from Aesop?"

"I suppose you're going to claim he was a friend of yours?" I asked.

"Actually, he was."

"I figured you'd say that." I rolled my eyes, but Satan ignored me.

"Do you want to hear the fable or not?"

"Go ahead," I said.

"This is a story about an old spider and a young fly. The old spider had built his web in a garden between two branches of a tree. The spider's web was just a short flight from a young fly's home. The fly lived in his fly home with his fly mother and fly father. His father was a professor at a fly university, while Mom was a housekeeper. They lived happily in their little home, and they all loved each other dearly. The young fly's mom and dad were always careful to advise him and warn him about the dangers in the garden. Of special concern to these parents was the old spider's web. They let the young fly enjoy the garden on his own during the daytime, but they did go out of their way to warn him about the old spider and his web. 'Stay clear of that old spider,' his father said. 'He's dangerous, and he's a liar. You can't believe a single thing he says.'

"The young fly promised his parents that he would stay away from the spider, but as young people are inclined to do, he let his curiosity get the best of him. One day the young fly flew up to the web, and he saw the old spider sunning himself. The old spider spied the young fly, and he called him over. 'Don't be afraid of me,' he said. 'I mean you no harm. Come and have a little lunch with me. My table is set for two.' The young fly replied, 'My mom and dad warned me about you and your lies.' And the old spider said, 'I'll make a deal with you, and you can decide if I'm a liar or not. I'll tell you something I know, and you can go to your parents and ask them if it's true, or if it's a lie. Then you'll know if I'm a liar.' The young fly thought about it, and he figured there'd be no harm in doing this. 'Go ahead,' the young fly said. 'Tell me something other than a lie if you can.' The spider scratched his bald head and proclaimed, 'The square root of four is two.' Well, the young spider knew nothing about square roots, but he was sure his father did. So he flew home and asked his dad, 'What is the square roof of four?' His father said, 'That's an easy question. The answer is two.' The young spider was astonished. The spider had told him the truth!

"The next day the young fly flew past the spiderweb again, and again the old spider was out in the sun. 'Tell me something more,' the young fly said. 'Let's see if you're really telling me the truth or if your first effort was just a lucky fluke.' The spider said, 'Fine. Your taste buds are in your feet.' The young fly laughed. 'That's got to be about the silliest thing I've ever heard.' But he flew home and asked his father, 'Where are our taste buds?' His father said, 'Believe it or not, they're in our feet.' The young fly was astonished again. The old spider had told him the truth.

"The next day the young fly flew back to the spider's web, and again the spider was outside. 'I have a question for *you*,' the young fly said. 'Let's hear it,' the old spider said. 'My dad tells me to steer clear of the frogs in the garden because they can grab me with their long, sticky tongues. Is that really true? Just how long is a frog's tongue?' The old spider smiled and said, 'Yes, your dad is right. A frog's tongue is about as long as a third of the length of its body. If a human had such a tongue, it would hang down to its belly button.' The young fly laughed aloud and said, 'That's ridiculous.' But when the young fly came home for dinner that night, he asked his father the same question, and his father confirmed what the old spider had said. Again, the old spider was telling the truth.

"So the next day the fly flew over to the spider's web. The old spider said, 'Come join me for lunch. There is still a place for you here at my table. I was hoping you would finally join me. I get lonely hanging around all day by myself on this big empty web.' The young fly thought for a moment and then said, 'You've been telling me the truth for the past three days, so I honestly don't have a reason to doubt you now. You're not a liar after all. So, yes I'll join you.' The fly flew into the web, and he immediately found himself stuck to the webbing. The old spider approached him. Then he bared his fangs and bit the helpless fly in the head, and his venom paralyzed the young fly so he would be easier for the old spider to eat. The spider then wrapped the young fly with webbing and set him aside for his dinner."

"That's the end?" I asked.

"That's it," Satan said.

"That was awful long."

"It's a long fable."

"I doubt that was from Aesop."

"Well, you're right about that. I made it up. But you do get the moral, right?"

"I don't know. What is it?"

"That even liars can tell you the truth."

"Jesus," I said.

"I guess the trick is knowing when they're lying to you and when they're on the level."

"You know what I think?" I said.

"What do you think?"

"I think it's time for me to go."

"And where are you going?"

"Definitely away from you."

"It was the fable, wasn't it? No one ever likes that fable. I should come up with another one."

"The fable was fine."

"Then you're afraid of me?"

"No, I just remembered there is somewhere I need to be. I made a promise to someone. Where's the hospital?"

"The hospital?"

"I'm going to miss everything."

"Miss everything what?"

"Huh?" I said. Someone was shaking my arm. I had fallen asleep, and someone was trying to wake me up.

"Wake up, sir," a nurse said. "We're ready for you."

"Ready for me?" I asked. I looked around, and now I knew where I was. "Of course," I said. "Sorry, I must have dozed off. How is Martha doing?"

"She's doing fine. She's waiting for you."

"So, it *is* time?"

"Yes, sir. You can follow me."

CHAPTER 20

AH, MADAME IVORY

———•◆•———

The nurse led me along one of the hospital hallways to a broad pair of doors and then into another hall. Finally, we reached the room. She pushed the room door open and stepped aside so I could walk in. In the middle were a hospital bed and a lot of blinking and beeping medical equipment, and Martha was in the bed on her back. Her knees were up high, and her feet were set in the stirrups. A big, white sheet was draped like a circus tent over her knees, thighs, and shins; and sitting on a stool so he could face Martha's open legs was Dr. Winslow, his head buried deep in the tent so he could monitor Martha's progress.

"Yes, I can now see the top of its head," the doctor said. He sounded like he'd seen this condition a thousand times before. "Now would be a good time for you people to start up the music."

Music? Sure enough, I looked across the room and saw a classical string quartet, the musicians seated in the fold-up chairs that had been set up against the far wall. At the doctor's prompting, they began to play, performing a piece by Antonio Vivaldi. I wasn't sure which piece it was, but it was definitely Vivaldi. It was a little stodgy and frenetic for my taste, but I figured the doctor knew what he was doing. Don't we all figure that our doctors know what they're doing? And I recalled learning in our Lamaze classes that the sound of music was helpful during labor. Yes, some soothing, classical music was just what the doctor ordered, literally. It would help Martha cope with the pain. So the violins, viola, and cello sang out their squeaky notes in unison, and the nurse told Martha to push as hard as she could.

"Push it out," she said.

"Push harder," the doctor said.

"I'm pushing as hard as I can."

"Keep it up."

"Someone, turn up the air," the doctor said. "It's hot as hell in here."

"It's up as high as it will go."

"Ouch!" Martha exclaimed.

"Push harder!"

"Crank up the IV drip," the doctor said.

"Doesn't she need to be breathing?" I asked.

"She *is* breathing," the doctor said. "What the hell do you think she's doing?"

"I mean, you know, like they taught us in Lamaze."

The doctor's hands were now on the baby's head. "I'm trying to deliver a baby, and he's talking about Lamaze?"

"The IV drip is up as high as I can get it," the nurse said.

"Good, good," the doctor said.

"Is there anything I can do to help?" I asked.

"No," the doctor said. "Just keep clear."

"Ouch!" Martha cried.

"Push harder," the nurse said. "You've got to push a little harder."

"That's what you can do," the doctor said to me. "You can tell you wife to push harder. She isn't pushing hard enough. She has to give it her all."

"Push harder," I said.

"I am, I am."

"It's not coming forward," the doctor said. "We're going to be here all day."

"God, this hurts so much!"

"Play the music louder," the doctor said to the musicians. "I can barely hear you. Don't be so bashful." The musicians kicked it up a notch, and the doctor said, "Nurse, wipe my forehead, please. My sweat is getting into my eyes, and I can't see a Goddamn thing."

"Yes, doctor."

"Ouch!" Martha cried.

"Shouldn't it be coming out?" I asked.

"Bring in the juggler."

"The juggler?"

The nurse opened the door and brought in a man dressed like a clown with juggling bowling pins. I wasn't quite sure what the point of this was.

"Watch the juggler," the doctor said to Martha. "It will keep your mind off the pain. Then give us another good push."

"I'm watching," Martha said.

"And push!"

"I am, I am."

"Jesus," the doctor said. "I can't do this for you."

"I'm trying."

"Bring in the stand-up comic," the doctor said.

The what? Yes, I'd heard him right.

The nurse opened the door again, and in walked a guy with a microphone. I recognized him right away. I couldn't remember his name, but I'd seen him on TV. I think he was on *America's Got Talent*. Wasn't he the runner-up in the finals? He said to us, "So, a woman goes to her doctor, and she verifies that she's pregnant. This is her first pregnancy, and the doctor asks if she has any questions for him."

I thought I may have heard this one before, but I didn't interrupt. Instead, I let the comic continue.

He was still holding the microphone to his mouth. "The woman tells the doctor, 'I'm a little nervous about all the pain I'll feel. How much is it going to hurt? Can you describe it for me?' The doctor tells her it's difficult to put into words, but to give her an idea, he tells her to grab her upper lip and pull on it. She pulls on her lip, and then the doctor tells her to pull it harder. She does as he says, and then he tells her to pull even harder. Finally, he asks if it is hurting. 'Yes, I can feel the pain,' she says. The doctor says, 'Now stretch it over your head.'"

"Ha, ha, drumroll," the doctor said.

"Good God," Martha said.

"Let's hear another one."

"Are you sure this is such a good idea?" I asked. "My wife is in a lot of discomfort."

"Laughter is the best painkiller on the market. Your wife needs this. Where's that damn juggler?"

"I'm over here."

"You've moved. Who the heck told you to move all the way over there? Come closer to the patient. She can't see you." Then to Martha he said, "Are you still pushing? You've got to keep pushing."

"I'm pushing."

"One more joke, please."

The comic brought the microphone up to his mouth and said, "A man calls his doctor frantically on the phone. He shouts, 'You've got to help me! My wife is about to have a baby!' The doctor calmly asks, 'Is this her first child?' The man says, 'No, you idiot, this is her husband!'"

"Ha ha. Another drumroll."

"Can't you give me something besides this music and comedy for the pain?" Martha asked.

"We've given you everything we can," the nurse said.

"And then some," the doctor said.

"Ma'am, you're really going to have to push."

"This damn kid hasn't budged an inch," the doctor said, his hands still up between Martha's legs.

"Ouch!"

"Push harder."

"It's no use," the doctor said. "The birth canal is way too narrow. We're going to have to do a C-section. Everyone needs to move to the OR. And I mean everyone. This includes you," he said to me. "We're all in this together."

"Scat," the nurse said, motioning for us to get out of the room.

"Wheel her out," the doctor said.

For a couple of minutes, everything was pandemonium. Then we were all standing in the operating room. The string quartet started to play Vivaldi again, and the doctor said, "Don't you people know anything more modern? Something with some pep to it? You know, like 'Flight of the Bumblebee'? That's what I'd like to hear, just like Al Hirt used to play, except play it with your strings."

The musicians looked at each other curiously and shrugged. Then they played the doctor's song. It was so bizarre, this crazy bumblebee music, the juggler, the comic, the nurses, and the doctor, who was now cutting into Martha's belly with a large steel knife like he was carving up a turkey for a Thanksgiving dinner.

"Jesus," I said.

"It's best you don't watch this," the doctor said. Just as he said that, a stream of blood squirted up from Martha's belly and into his eyes. "Nurse, wipe me off," he said, and the nurse ran over and wiped the blood from his face with a sponge. "I must've hit a little artery," he said, looking at me. "Nothing for you to worry about."

"How does it look?" Martha asked me. She was unable to see because they had hung a sheet to block what they were doing. If she'd seen what they were doing to her body, she probably would've freaked and fainted.

"It looks fine," I said, but honestly, I felt like *I* was going to freak and faint. It looked like my wife had been in a terrible automobile accident. Lots of blood and guts, and somewhere in this gory mess was our baby.

"Look what I found," the doctor said. He pulled something out of Martha and held it up. "A set of keys."

"I'll be damned," I said. "Those are mine. I lost them last year. I wondered where they went. We looked all over the place for them."

"Well, now you have them back," the doctor said. Then he handed the keys to the nurse and said, "Rinse these off and give them to the dad."

"Anything else in there?" I asked.

"Not yet, but you never know what we'll find when we do one of these C-sections. Last week we found a girl's Barbie doll in the patient's intestines. Can you imagine that? Can I have another joke, please?"

The comic stood up. "You mean me?" he asked.

"Go on, go on," the doctor said.

The comic brought the microphone to his lips and asked us all, "How did the baby know it was ready to be born? Give up? It was running out of womb."

I laughed at this one. It was a pretty stupid joke, but I was now so nervous that I think I would've laughed at anything. I wanted to laugh in the worst way.

Then the comic said, "Here's another one. There was a dad who tried to keep his wife happy through labor by telling a few jokes, but she didn't laugh once. Do you know why?"

"Why?" I said.

"It was the delivery."

This time Martha laughed. Then I looked down at her bloody belly, at the mess the doctor was making. I could be wrong, but I swear I saw half of her internal organs sitting on her stomach just above the incision. Then the doctor reached abruptly into the cavity with both hands, pulling out our baby. They cut the cord, and the doctor raised the purple child up into the air, holding it by its feet.

"It's a boy," he said, and everyone in the room cheered.

One of the musicians asked, "What's going to be his name?"

"Robert," I said.

"Okay, the show is over," the doctor said.

"Everyone out," the nurse said.

"That's it?" I asked.

"Scat," the nurse said, waving her hands. Everyone piled out the door, and the next thing I knew, Martha and I were in a small room for her recovery. Martha was tucked neatly into the hospital bed with the back of the bed raised so she was in a near-sitting position, and she was holding little Robert in her arms.

"Jesus," I said to her. "We did it. We have a son."

"I couldn't have done it without the juggler," Martha said. "He was a godsend."

"Sure, he was."

"And the comic wasn't bad."

"They think of everything here, don't they? This is a good hospital."

"Only the best for our boy," Martha said.

"I told you it would be a boy. Didn't I call it? Didn't I tell you it would be a boy?"

"You did."

"It's so hard to believe. We came here, just as the two of us, and now we're going to go home as three." Martha smiled, and I leaned over to kiss her forehead.

Just then the door to the room flew open, and there were the grandparents, all four of them, grinning from ear to ear like they'd all just won the lottery. It was my mom and dad and Martha's parents.

"Too big to come out of the old birth canal, eh?" my dad said. "A big kid. He's a football player for sure."

"Behave yourself," my mom said.

"An attorney," Martha's dad said. "A modern-day Clarence Darrow."

"Or a writer like his father," Martha's mom said, but everyone in the room ignored her.

"He *could* be a writer," I said, and this time everyone ignored me.

There was a knock on the door, and my mother went to answer it. She opened the door and turned to the rest of us. "She's here!" she exclaimed.

"Wonderful," Martha's dad said.

"Show her in," Martha's mom said. "I can't wait to meet her."

"Who's here?" I asked.

"Madame Ivory," Martha's mom said.

"We all chipped in."

"It's our present to you and Martha."

"You're going to love her."

"I don't understand," I said.

"She's a palm reader," my dad explained. "She's a genuine bell-jingling, fortune-telling gypsy of a palm reader. You're going to love the hell out of her."

"I am?"

"We asked her to tell Robert's fortune. You know, reading his little palm. No sense in not knowing when you *can* know. We may as well find out what's in store for your little bundle of joy."

"Isn't palm reading a scam?" I asked.

"Oh, not at all," my mom said. "Madame Ivory knows exactly what she's doing. She read my palm five years ago, and she was right on the money. I was once a skeptic too but not now. No way. Not me."

"She predicted your mom's tumor," my dad said.

"You had a tumor?"

"It's gone now. The doctor's removed it, and I'm as fit as a fiddle, all thanks to Madame Ivory. We would never have even known about the tumor if she hadn't seen it in my palm. Nipped the little rascal in the bud, so to speak. And it isn't just Robert's health she'll predict. She can see everything. It's uncanny."

"That's right," Martha's dad said.

"You won't regret this," Martha's mom said.

"I wish we'd done this when you were just an infant," my dad said. "God knows what we could've prevented."

"Prevented?"

"You know, options we may have had."

"Are you saying you don't like the way I turned out?"

"I'm just talking about options, Robinson. Nothing for you to worry about. We all love you anyway."

Everyone laughed at this.

"Where is the new bambino?" Madame Ivory asked. I looked her over. God knows how old the gypsy woman was, maybe eighty or ninety. She was quite short, and she was hunched over as though there was something wrong with her spine. She was dressed like a typical gypsy and had big, golden hoop-dee-do earrings and long, crooked fingers. I pointed over to Robert, who was still in Martha's arms, and she walked slowly over to them.

"Do you need to hold him?" Martha asked.

"No, dear," Madame Ivory said. "You can hold him. I just need to see his little palms."

"This is so exciting," my mom said.

"Now we're going to get down to brass tacks," Martha's dad said, jutting his chin forward. Sometimes her dad could really be annoying.

"You people have to be kidding," I said. "Are we really going through with this?"

"Hush, hush," Madame Ivory said to me, putting her crooked finger over her lips. "This is a fragile procedure. I need silence from all of you."

"Yes, keep quiet," my mom said.

"She has to be able to concentrate."

"Not another word."

I watched as Madame Ivory took Robert's hand in hers. She turned his hand over so his palm was facing up. She then put on a pair of reading glasses and proceeded to examine my son's hand. "Ah," she said. Then she said it again. Then she said it a third time.

"What do you see?" my mom asked.

"A football player?" my dad said.

"I see a lot of feet," Madame Ivory said. "Yes, I can see feet. This boy is definitely going to have something to do with feet. Yes, feet play a very dominant role in his life. I see lots of feet."

"He's going to be a running back," my dad said. "Or a wide receiver. They use their feet."

"Or a podiatrist," my mom said. "I've always pictured him becoming a doctor."

"Or a personal injury attorney specializing in injuries to people's feet," Martha's dad said.

"Is there such a thing?" I asked.

"Well, there should be."

"Maybe he'll be in the shoe business," Martha's mom said. "As in athletic shoes. There's big money these days in athletic shoes."

We all looked at Madame Ivory.

"I also see a redhead," Madame Ivory said in a very low voice.

"A redhead?"

"Like a girlfriend?"

"Or a wife?"

"Not exactly sure. Just beware of the redhead," Madame Ivory said. "She will be bad news. Very bad news. He must stay away."

"We need to make a note of that."

"No damn redheads," Martha's dad said.

"Yes, avoid the redheads like the plague," Madame Ivory said. "Otherwise, I see horrible consequences."

"What else do you see?" my dad asked.

"I see some large hospital bills," the gypsy said.

"For what?"

"It isn't clear."

"That could be for a lot of things."

"That could be for this week," I said. "The juggler, the musicians, the comic, and the surgery. And this room. How much are they charging for the room? This little Cecil B. DeMille production of ours is surely going to cost us a small fortune."

"You can't put a price on good medical care," my dad said. "Only the best for our little Robert."

"Yes, only the best."

"Maybe he's going to get sick one day," my mom said. "I mean, when he's an adult. Does it say if he's going to be sick?"

"No, I just see the hospital bills."

"That's so vague."

"That's part of the scam," I said, but no one paid attention to me.

"Maybe he gets seriously injured playing football," my mom said. Then to my dad she said, "You're the one who wants him to be in sports. Do you see what you've done?"

"He's going to be an attorney," Martha's dad said. "Don't get all worked up. Maybe the hospital bills Madame is talking about belong to one of his clients, and maybe he wins a great big judgment to pay them off."

"Do you see anything about thievery?" I asked.

"Thievery?" my dad said to me. "What are you even talking about?"

"You say the queerest things," my mom said.

"I'm talking about stealing things. Like coin collections. Tell us about the coin collection."

"Bah," my dad said.

"Here's what I'd like to know," Martha's dad said. "Is he going to be the breadwinner in his family? Or is he going to be like his father, writing novels no one buys and living off the brains and hard work of his wife?"

"Oh, stop it," Martha's mom said.

"I was just kidding."

"Well, it wasn't funny."

"I thought it was funny," my dad said.

"We haven't heard anything from Martha," my mom said. Then to Martha she said, "What do you want to know, dear?"

"Yes," her dad said. "Speak up, girl."

Martha smiled sweetly. "I just want Robert to be happy," she said. "Is he going to be happy?"

Madame Ivory looked at Robert's palm again. "If he stays away from that redhead, I see many years of joy and happiness," she said. "He'll lead a good life. A happy life."

"You know, I'm getting the distinct impression that this redhead sounds pretty serious," Martha's dad said. "I say we all join forces and keep this girl away from our boy. You know, I never have trusted redheads. They're like black cats. Nothing but bad luck."

"I second that motion," my dad said.

"This is ridiculous," I said. "This is a joke. All this nonsense about redheads and feet and hospital bills. Are you guys crazy? I think you're all nuts."

"Robinson, please," Martha said. She obviously didn't want me rocking the boat.

"I'm just calling a spade a spade."

"They're only trying to help."

"Robinson obviously hasn't done his homework," my dad said sternly. "He always had a problem with that."

"He's never been very responsible," Martha's dad said.

"And he's ungrateful."

"Think of everything we've done."

"Books, tuition, and living expenses."

"What are you guys even talking about?" I asked.

"If you don't get on the ball, you're going to miss another class," my dad said. He was glaring at me. But he was right, of course. What the heck had I been thinking? I suddenly ran out of the room and into the hallway, grabbing a stray nurse by her elbow.

"Do you know where room 102 is?" I asked her.

"You're going to be late," she said.

"I know, I know. Just point toward the room."

"It's over there," the nurse said, and she pointed to our left. I took off running. I was suddenly carrying a stack of books and a heavy three-ring binder under my arm. How could I have been so stupid? I ran as fast as I could, looking right and left for the room. What hall was I in? It all looked so familiar, and yet it wasn't familiar at all.

When I arrived, all the students were seated, and the professor was standing before them in front of a big chalkboard. I looked for a vacant seat and plopped into an empty chair. I got dirty looks from several of the students. The messy-haired professor ignored my tardiness and continued with his lecture.

"Open your books to page sixty-three," he said. But which book was he talking about? Like I said, I had a whole stack of them. "We're going to discuss last night's reading assignment. Can I assume you all did your reading?"

Reading? I was supposed to read? Heck, I didn't even know what class this was, let alone which book I was supposed to be reading. And how old was I? And what the heck was happening to me? I raised my hand.

The professor noticed my hand, but he didn't seem at all interested. When I refused to lower my arm, he finally stopped lecturing and called on me.

"Yes," he said. "Do you have a question the class would be interested in?"

"I do," I said. "Well, I don't know about the rest of the class, but I'm kind of lost here. Maybe this is going to sound stupid, but what book are we reading?"

CHAPTER 21

UNDERWOOD & SON

———————•◦•———————

O kay, it *was* a dumb question. The professor cleared his throat angrily, and several of the girls giggled. It looked like he wasn't going to call on me, so the kid sitting next to me helped me out and whispered, "We're reading Vonnegut."

"Which one?" I asked.

"*Underwood & Son.* You have it right there. It's under your geography textbook."

"So it is," I said, pulling the book out. "Which page did he say to turn to?"

"Page sixty-three."

"Thanks," I whispered. "I'm a big fan of Vonnegut, but I've never heard of this book."

"It was just published."

"Just published?"

"Posthumously."

"No kidding?"

"His family found in among his unpublished writings. It hasn't really caught on big yet, but it's gradually becoming a cult favorite."

"I see. Are you a Vonnegut fan?"

"I can take him or leave him. But then I feel that way about most writers. I'm not a big reader." The kid smiled at me and said, "We should probably shut up and pay attention to the teacher. He doesn't like students whispering while he's lecturing."

"Of course," I said.

Then I noticed something that caused the hairs on my arms to stand on end. There was something extraordinary about this boy. He looked just like my son, Robert. No kidding, he was the spitting image. In fact, he *was* Robert, and I found myself staring at him. I could tell he knew I was staring at him, so I averted my eyes and looked at the professor. This was so weird! I knew he was Robert, but he had no idea who I was. As far as he was concerned, I was just some kid who had come rushing in late to class.

"Anyone care to explain what Vonnegut meant?" the professor asked the class.

No one raised his or her hand.

"How about you?" The professor looked directly at me. This was just great.

"I'm sorry," I said. "What sentence on the page were you reading?"

"Third paragraph, first sentence."

"Yes, of course," I said. I opened the book to page sixty-three and looked for the sentence.

"Can you read it aloud for us? It wouldn't hurt if we all heard it again."

"Sure," I said. I found the sentence and I read it to the class. It said, "I suddenly came to the realization that when it came to my mother and father, if they were turning left, I had them turning right, and if they shouted the word *black*, I had them shouting white." I looked up from my book and asked, "Was that the right sentence?"

"It was," the professor said. "What did that sentence mean to you when you read it?"

"Well," I said. "Vonnegut's main character seems to have a difficult time relating to the actions of his parents."

"Obviously, but why?"

I thought about this a moment and then like an idiot said, "I'm not exactly sure."

"Do you think this is a common problem?"

"It could be."

"What about you? What has been your experience? Do you understand the actions of your parents?"

"I don't know," I said, and that was an honest answer. My parents and many of the things they did had always been kind of a mystery to me.

"How is it that we have so much difficulty understanding our own ancestral flesh and blood, the people we've lived within an arm's reach of for our entire lives? What is it with parents? Shouldn't we know and understand them much better than we know and understand anyone? Shouldn't we know and understand them like the backs of our hands?"

"One would think so," I said.

The professor stared at me for a moment, and then he turned and grabbed a stick of chalk, writing on the chalkboard. It was our homework assignment. He wrote, "In approximately 500 words, describe your parents. Then write another 500 words describing why your description is wrong." When he was done writing on the board, the professor looked at the class and said, "You'll have to take a step back from your personal perceptions and feelings to come up with the second part of this assignment. It will require you to be objective. You'll need to put your feet in your parents' shoes. It will require honesty, and it may even require some creativity. It will also require that you try to be unselfish. Most children are naturally selfish, but believe it or not, you're all considered adults now. Let's see if you can think like adults."

One kid raised his hand, and the professor called on him. The kid asked, "If *you* don't know our parents—and I'm guessing you don't—how will you know if our papers are complete or accurate? And how will you grade them?"

"This assignment is for you and not for me," the professor said. "That should answer your question."

There were a couple of moans from the students. It was one of *those* kinds of assignments. A girl in the back raised her hand, and the professor called on her. She said, "I haven't seen my father since I was five."

"Then write about your mom," the professor said.

"And what about some of the other kids in this class? For example, maybe some kids grew up in foster homes. Who should they write about?"

"They can write about their foster parents. If they were raised by their grandparents, then they can write about their grandparents. If they were raised by an aunt, they can write about the aunt. Have I made myself clear?"

The girl nodded.

Robert turned to me. "What a weird assignment," he whispered.

"Could be interesting," I said.

"Could be."

When the class was over, everyone stood up to leave. I was ready to leave, but I wanted to stick with Robert. So I walked out of the class with him and asked, "Have you eaten any lunch yet?"

"Not yet," he said.

"Do you want to join me?"

Robert looked at me and said, "Sure, why not. Where did you plan on eating?"

"I thought I'd grab a sandwich at Jack's Place." Jack's was a small soup and sandwich restaurant a couple of blocks from the school.

"Sounds good to me."

"My name is Eric, by the way," I said. "What's your name?" I used a phony name so Robert wouldn't catch on to the fact that I was his father.

"It's Robert."

"Thanks for helping me with the book, Robert."

"It was no problem. You looked confused. Did you miss the last class?"

"I guess I did." In fact, I couldn't remember coming to any of the classes, but I didn't tell Robert that. Then we were suddenly at the restaurant, seated at a table with our open menus, trying to decide what to order for lunch. "What are you going to get?" I asked.

"The same thing I always get. Bologna and cheese and a bowl of tomato. How about you?"

"I feel like a Reuben."

"That sounds good too."

"Can I ask you a question?" I said.

"Sure," Robert said.

"Do you get along with your dad? What are you going to say when you write about him?"

"You mean for the assignment?"

"Yes," I said.

"I don't know."

"How would you describe your dad in just a few words? Not necessarily a sentence. Just a few words."

Robert thought for a moment. Then he said, "Intelligent, aloof, self-centered, self-absorbed, and selfish. And maybe a little weird."

Jeez, that was me? This answer surprised me, and I wanted to hear more. I wanted more than anything to know what Robert actually thought of me. "Why would you describe him as being selfish?" I asked. "Does he do selfish things? Do you honestly think he doesn't care about you?"

"Oh, he cares about me, and he cares about my mom. But the guy is definitely selfish. My dad is a writer. Maybe it just comes with the territory, but my dad is the most selfish person I know. It's all about what he cares about, and all he cares about is his writing. It's in his head twenty-four hours a day and eight days a week. Do you want to know what it's like being the son of a writer? It's like being served wax food for dinner when you're starving to death. It all looks great. It looks just like real food. But when you take a big bite, it's nothing. It's there, but it isn't there at all. That's my dad. He has two arms, two legs, a torso, a neck, and a head. But who is he? He says he loves me, and he recites platitudes, and he tells me a story now and again, and he issues warnings, and he pats me on the head when I do things he likes, but he doesn't know me. And he makes no effort to know me any better than he knows the old illegal immigrant who does our yardwork or the kid who delivers our newspaper or the lady who cuts his hair every month. Where has he been all my life? He's been at his computer, typing on his keyboard, staring in a daze at his monitor.

"Oh, once and a while he'll come up for air. Then you know what we do? Things *he* wants to do. We'll go to a boring museum or to a classical music concert or maybe to a bookstore so we can browse through his competition's latest offerings. But how about mixing in a football game here and there? I love football. I always wanted him to take me to a football game. Is that really asking too much? You know who takes me to see football games? I go with my grandfather. Dad shakes his head and says football is just a lot of pushing and shoving. Well, if you ask me, literature is just a lot of words. And he wonders why I don't like to read. He can be so exceedingly smart and so incredibly dumb at the same time."

"I had no idea," I said.

"Do you want to know what really makes me laugh?" Robert asked. "Ever since I was a dopey little kid, I've been trying to get my dad's attention. And do you want to know the one thing that actually gets him to look at me? I mean, it really gets him excited. It's not getting an A on a school paper or exam. It's not hitting a home run in a baseball game. It's not being told by a neighbor what a good kid I am. It's not doing a great job at washing his car. No, no, what really gets my dad's attention is when

I get caught stealing. He'll drop everything. I mean, he'll suddenly care about me like he's never cared about me before. I can see the love in his eyes. Do you know what I mean by that? I can see the hurt. And love is all about being hurt, right? Do you know my dad actually took me in to see a shrink? I kid you not. Dad was totally freaking out. He was beside himself. He thought I was headed to wind up on the FBI's Ten Most Wanted list. He thought I was going to murder someone and be strapped to the electric chair. Like I said, I could see it in his eyes. And you know what? I liked what I saw. He was finally paying attention to me rather than his stupid computer. It was our father-and-son moment."

"That's awful," I said.

Our waitress showed up. She held a little notepad and pen, and her hair was a mess. She looked like she was having a terrible day. "So, what'll it be, boys?" she asked.

"Bologna and cheese and a bowl of tomato soup," Robert said. "And a cup of coffee."

"I'll have a Reuben," I said. "And a coffee too."

"That's it?"

"Yes," I said.

"Bring us separate checks," Robert said.

"Got it," the waitress said. Then she added, "We're busy as hell today, and only one cook showed up this morning. So, don't get all bent out of shape if it takes a while for me to bring your food."

"It's no problem," Robert said, and the waitress hurried away. Then he said, "I probably told you a lot more about my dad than you wanted to hear."

"No, not at all," I said.

"I could talk about my dad for hours."

"He sounds like an interesting man."

"Not exactly the word I'd use."

"My dad always hated his job. I think it would be nice to have a father who was so passionate about his work."

"If you can call it work."

"You don't think writing is work?"

"When I think of work, I think of something a person does in exchange for money. Considering how much he gets paid for writing his books, he'd be better off running a cash register at a fast-food restaurant. I'm not kidding. Do you know who really works in our family? Do you know whose labor pays the bills and keeps the lights on? It's my mother's. Mom's an attorney and a good one, from what I understand. She works her tail off, and they pay her a ton of money. She's the parent with her nose to the grindstone, the worker bee, the spouse who brings home the loot. I told you my dad was selfish, and what could be more selfish? He gets to play around with his heroes, villains, settings, and idiotic plots while my mom is swinging her sledgehammer on the rock pile. Not that Mom doesn't like what she does for a living, but wouldn't you think she'd like to know she's at work because she *wants* to work and not because she *has* to? Big difference, I think."

"I can see that," I said. "But maybe your mom and dad have an understanding."

"An understanding?"

"Can I play the devil's advocate with you?"

"You want to defend my father?"

"I don't want to defend him. I would just like to provide you what may be his side of the circumstance. You know, another way of looking at things. Obviously, I don't know your dad, so I'll only be guessing. But still, you might find what I have to say helpful."

"Go ahead," Robert said.

The waitress brought our coffee.

"Thanks," I said.

"No problem," the waitress said. "Here's some creamer and sweetener. And sugar, if you want sugar." The poor gal still seemed rushed. What a thankless job.

I looked at Robert and said, "I'm thinking that maybe your dad's a better man than you've described. Maybe he does have an understanding with your mom, one they both agreed to before you were even born. Could it be that years ago your dad woke up one morning and realized he only had one life to live? Could it be that he realized also that he only had one true passion in life, his burning desire to write? For your dad, it was now or never. No, this wasn't a profit-and-loss business decision. It was an artist's dream, the same sort of noble dream that has motivated artists for centuries. Then one day your father met your mom and shared his vision with her. She was as loopy about his writing as he was. So she willingly became a part of the dream. She wasn't hoodwinked into anything. She was not an artist; instead, she found fulfillment in her legal work, and they came up with a perfect plan. He would be the artist in the family, and she would earn the cash they needed to pay all the bills. This was teamwork, Robert, not one lazy spouse sponging off the sweat and toil of the other. Neither party was taking advantage of the other. What you now had were two people in love striving toward the same glorious goal. Neither has had to give up a single thing, and they are both getting exactly what they want out of life."

Robert stared at me. I had no idea what he was thinking. Then he asked, "So where do I fit in?"

"A perfectly appropriate question," I said. "Where do you fit in? Where does any child fit in? I have to be honest. It sounds like your father has let you down. But maybe there is hope for him. Maybe he now realizes what he's done by putting so much of himself first and pushing so much of you off to the sidelines. You know that people are not perfect, Robert. I'm sure that isn't news to you. We all have our flaws, and we all do things we are not proud of. Have you ever sat down with your father and told him how you feel? I think you should do this. I think he will listen to you. In fact, I know he will listen. In fact, perhaps he's already heard you. Do you actually doubt that your father loves you?"

"He says he loves me."

"Then take his hand and guide him. I think he'll follow your lead without resistance. Honestly, I can feel this in my bones."

"You talk as though you know him."

"No," I said. "I obviously don't know him."

"Then what makes you so confident?"

I didn't know quite how to answer this, so I said, "It's just a feeling."

"Did you have something similar happen with your own father?"

"No," I said.

"Do you get along with him?"

"As best as one can expect," I said. Of course, I didn't tell Robert, but my dad was dead and cremated. My old man was over and done with. But ah, the things I *should* have done! Hindsight is exactly as they say.

Just then, my cell phone rang, and I looked at it. "Do you mind if I take this?" I asked Robert.

"Go ahead," he said.

I took the call. It was Dr. Bell, my crying psychiatrist. "Hello," I said.

"Robinson, is that you?"

"It is," I said.

"Are you busy?"

"Actually, I'm about to have lunch."

"Can we fit in a short session?"

I looked at Robert. "Do you mind if I take this outside?" I asked. "It's personal."

"No problem," Robert said. "If the food gets here while you're out, I'll come get you."

"Thanks," I said. I walked outside to the sidewalk and leaned against a building, out of the way of pedestrians. "So, what's on your mind?" I asked the doctor.

"We didn't get to finish our last session."

"I remember that," I said.

"I wanted to continue our word association exercise. I'd like to pick up where we left off."

"Okay," I said.

"Remember that I gave you the word *father*? You immediately said it made you think of a *New York Times* crossword puzzle, but after talking to your son today, I'd like to know if your answer is different. That's what I'd like to know. What now comes to mind?"

I thought for a moment about my conversation with Robert, and then I said, "Baseball comes to mind."

"Baseball?"

"Yes," I said. "Swinging your wooden bat and missing the ball. Swinging and hitting it. Home runs, triples, doubles, singles, double plays, strikeouts, and walks. You know, the whole ball of wax."

CHAPTER 22

TICKTOCK

———— •◦• ————

"Being a father is like hitting a baseball," I said. "Think of it this way. How many years have we been swinging our bats at baseballs? The Abner Doubleday mythology aside, they say this sport goes back to the eighteenth century, maybe earlier. This is how long boys, girls, and adults have been trying to knock the skin off the ball. That's a lot of swings. Surely, after all this time, you'd expect professional ballplayers to bat a thousand each season or near to it. Yet they're still hitting as they always have. And why is this? Why aren't they getting better? I'll tell you why. It's the same reason why fathers, after thousands of years and billions of attempts to raise their children, are all still just bumbling, imperfect, shortsighted, and inept nitwits. Humans are human. They are not perfect or even close to it, and they never will be. It's a law of nature. So long as there are clouds in the sky and flowers blooming in the spring, men will be making a riotous fiasco of fatherhood. You can bet your bottom dollar on it. Fashions will change, new fads will come and go, and years will speed on one after the other, but the game will always remain the same. Getting called out is an immutable fact of life."

"I like how you've put that."

"Thanks," I said. "I'd like to think I have a way with words. I am, after all, a writer."

"I have so many parent patients who don't understand how or why they can't be perfect. To you it is obvious, but you might be surprised by how many parents these days can't swallow the fact that they have shortcomings."

"When I was a little boy, my dad used to tell me, 'You may think I'm Superman today, but as you get older, you're going to realize I'm only another Clark Kent.' I never had any idea what he was talking about, so

I forgot the words. But when I became a father, the words came back to me. And as the years passed, I began to understand exactly what he was saying. You can be a best-selling author or a genius scientist or a famous painter or a marvelously talented musician or a successful businessman or a life-rescuing medical doctor or a hotshot attorney, but you can only be an average father. That just happens to be the way the world works. Men who don't get this are only fooling themselves."

"Words of wisdom."

"I like to think so."

"Shall we try another word?"

"Why not?" I said.

The doctor looked up at the clock on her wall. The clock? How did I know she was looking at her clock? Where exactly was I? No, I was no longer on the sidewalk outside of Jack's Place. Instead, I was *in* the doctor's office. Her clock was an antique oak-and-pendulum contraption, but it kept perfect time. I knew this because the last time I had been there, I compared the time on the clock with the time on my wristwatch.

"*Time*," the doctor said.

"Time to what?" I asked.

"*Time* is our next word. What comes to your mind when I say the word *time*?"

I thought for a moment. Actually, I thought about the word for quite a while. Then I said, "When you say *time*, quite a few things come to my mind."

"Go ahead."

"Well, first of all. Are you charging me for this time? I don't think I need a session today, and you're the one who asked for me. I didn't call you. Maybe this session is more for you than it is for me. Can we agree on that?"

"Yes," the doctor said. "We can agree on that. I won't be charging you."

"Good," I said. "In that case, the second thing that came to my mind when you said *time* was the way time feels. I think time has a feeling. When I was younger, time felt as huge as a planet and as slow as molasses. A day took forever. There was a morning, noon, afternoon, dinnertime, and evening. It seemed like I could pack so many activities into a day. Then I don't know what happened, if it occurred all of a sudden or just one step at a time. I wasn't really paying attention, but time suddenly sped up. It made my mornings, noons, afternoons, et cetera all meld together into one monolithic strike, and now the day was minuscule. Now my days are literally whizzing by both sides of my head, and a year, which used to feel like an eternity, feels like only a week. I'd been warned that this would happen, but I still didn't expect it to feel so profound. Time is no longer my friend."

"What do you mean, no longer your friend?"

"I'm now racing against time instead of jogging along with it. It scares the heck out of me. Honestly, I feel like I'm going to open my eyes one of these mornings and find that I'm an old man. Then I'll open my eyes the next day and be saying all my goodbyes. I'll be alive and breathing on a Monday and leaving on Tuesday, just like that. No, time isn't my friend at all."

"What else came to mind when I said the word?"

"I thought of it as a treasure. Time is the treasure God gives to us at birth, the one great thing other than our minds and bodies that he hands over to us. Your time is all yours, and my time is all mine. And we get to use it as we wish. God leaves the decision up to us. We can use it wisely or squander it or sell it or kill it or rush through it or try to extend it. Most people? What do they do with their time? They work and play. They watch a lot of TV. They sleep like hibernating bears. They eat like pigs. Some people spend a lot of their time worrying, and some people spend it being fearful. You can hoard your time, or you can give your time to others. You can lose your time by going to jail or prison, or you can free up your time by being careful.

"So how does time compare to other treasures? Gold is gold, silver is silver, rubies are rubies, and diamonds are diamonds, but I'd take a pirate's chest full of time over any of them in a heartbeat. It's the treasure of all treasures, and you only get so much of it. In my opinion, it's more valuable than anything. You can't touch it or wear it around your neck or put it on display or deposit it in a bank. But it's priceless."

"Ticktock."

"Yes," I said, and the doctor laughed. She then asked me, "What else comes to your mind?"

"Remorse," I said.

"Time makes you feel bad?"

"It makes me feel both guilty and foolish. I feel guilty for not spending more time with Robert when he was a boy, and I feel foolish for not having been more aware of how important it was."

"You know what they say about hindsight?"

"Sure, but that doesn't make me feel any better about it. And I really don't want to excuse my behavior by taking solace in a cliché."

The doctor was staring at me. I think she realized I had said all I had to say about time. She asked, "Shall we move on to the next word?"

"Please, let's move on."

"How about the word *nun*?"

"Nun?"

"Yes, a nun. A lot of people have strong feelings about nuns. Deep-rooted and emotional feelings."

"I know a nun joke."

The doctor gave me a slightly disapproving look. Then she said, "Okay, let's hear your joke."

"You'll like it."

"Maybe I will."

I said, "A cabbie picks up a nun early in the evening. As she gets into the cab, the nun notices that the cab driver won't stop staring at her. Finally, she asks him why he's staring, and he says, 'I have a question to ask, but I don't want to offend you.' The nun says, 'Son, you cannot offend me. When you've been a nun as long as me, you've heard just about everything. Go ahead and ask your question.' The cab driver says, 'Well, to tell you the truth, I've always had a fantasy about having a nun kiss me. Will you kiss me?' The nun laughs and says, 'I may be able to help you. But you have to meet two conditions. First, you have to be single, and second, you must be Catholic.' The cab driver is very excited, and he says, 'I'm single, and I'm Catholic!' The nun smiles and tells the driver to pull into the next alley. She leans forward and fulfills the man's fantasy, giving him a long, wet, and passionate smooch. She wipes her mouth, and the cab driver starts sobbing. 'My dear child,' the nun says, 'why are you crying?" The driver says, 'You must forgive me, for I have sinned something awful. I lied to you. For not only am I married, but I also happen to be Jewish!' The nun says, 'That's okay. Don't worry about it. My name happens to be Kevin, and I'm going to a Halloween costume party.'"

I watched the doctor's face. She didn't laugh aloud, but she was smiling. Then she said, "Let's move on to another word."

"Fine," I said.

"How about *cat*?"

"Like the animal?"

"Yes," the doctor said.

"We had a cat," I said. "This was many years ago. Martha decided we had to have a pet, and by a pet, she meant that she wanted a cat. She knew I didn't care much for cats. I mean, I had nothing against them. They just didn't light my fire like they did with some people. Maybe it was because they were so aloof and independent, unlike dogs, who are in tune with your every desire and mood. Anyway, Martha came home with a little black-and-white kitten she named Cookie because of the cookie-shaped spot on her side. Martha adored this little cat, and I'll have to admit the cat began to grow on me. I became very fond of the little creature, and she grew very fond of me. I couldn't sit down anywhere without this cat jumping up into my lap. She would purr and rub her head against my chest like I was its mother. Eventually, I took over all the chores, changing and cleaning the litter box, filling the food dish, and making sure she had water. She would talk to me, looking me right in the eyes and meowing her cat words. It got ridiculous. I mean, here I was, this guy who never really wanted a cat in the first place, now this kitty's object of love and infatuation. Martha said, 'Cookie has adopted you,' and she was a hundred percent right. But thanks to that cat, I'll never get a cat again. Not ever."

"Why not?" the doctor asked.

"She lived a good, long life for a cat. And that was just fine with me. But around the time that she turned seventeen, I noticed something strange about her. I saw it in her eyes. I told you how she would look at me. Well, now I saw something I'd never noticed before. It was sadness. I swear to God, my cat was sad. And do you want to know why she was sad? It was because she was dying. Her time was coming soon, and she knew it instinctively. She didn't want to say goodbye to me, and I didn't want to say goodbye to her. But her body began to give out. She couldn't jump up into my lap without assistance, and her hind legs grew weaker and weaker. I would pick her up and hold her, and I think she liked that. But those sad eyes were almost more than I could bear. Finally, she couldn't walk. Her hind legs refused to cooperate, and she couldn't even get up to walk to the litter box to take care of her business. Martha said, 'It's time, you know. We're going to have to take her to the vet. We're going to have to put her to sleep.' But guess what? I couldn't do it."

"So, what'd you do?"

"I had Martha and Robert take her. I couldn't go. I was too upset. When they left with Cookie, I broke down and cried my eyes out for an hour. It was murder. I'd never felt such pure sadness and heartbreak. You know, my mom died, and my dad died, and the sadness I felt when they passed away didn't even come close to how I felt when Cookie left us. Why is that? Was there something wrong with me? You'd think a person would feel more grief about his parents than a black-and-white house cat, but it was the cat that made me cry. And still, when I think of those sad cat eyes, knowing she was about to die, I still feel the awful pain. Damn that cat. Damn that cat and the horse she rode in on. No, never in a million years. I'll never go through that again. So, no more cats. No cat in the yard, on the couch, or in my lap. Jeez, just talking about it now makes me get all choked up."

"It's tough losing pets."

"It's worse than losing humans. I don't know why, but it's true for me."

"At least she lived a full life."

"There's that."

"And she was loved."

I suddenly thought of something. I looked the doctor in the eye and said, "Everything I tell you during our sessions is confidential, right?"

"Of course," the doctor said.

"That's good. You can keep all this to yourself. I don't want anyone to know about it."

"Why not?"

"I just don't. I don't want the word to get out that I'm some kind of cat lover. So let's move on. See if you can think of a happier word."

"My next word was going to be *house*. Is that okay?"

"*House* is fine."

"Tell me then what comes into your mind?"

I thought for a moment, then said, "The first thing I think of is the first house Martha and I bought shortly after we were married. What a pile of junk that place was. What a dump. But it was our first house, and we loved it. I set my writing aside during the first few months, and I did nothing but home improvement projects. I put on a new roof. I laid new tile in the bathrooms. I installed a new dishwasher and kitchen sink. I became quite the handyman, and to tell you the truth, it was kind of fun.

"I wouldn't touch that sort of work these days with a ten-foot pole, but back then, I really got a kick out of it all. These days I hire other people to do everything. I hire them to mow the lawn, plant new flowers, trim the shrubs, paint the house, repair leaks, and even change some of the light bulbs. I can get the lower bulbs myself, but the higher ones requiring a ladder I leave to others. Once and a while I'll take on a small project but not very often. It's not that I'm lazy. It's just that I figure my time is better spent writing than it is doing repair and improvement work on a house. Seriously, you can book every hour of the day doing all this fix-it and improvement work. Some of my friends who are retired do just that eight hours a day."

The doctor laughed, then said, "So, you're talking about retirement now?"

"Not for me."

"But you're at that age?"

"I guess I am. Yes, I'm getting older. All of us are. Even you are, right? So it goes. There's nothing we can do about it." I was getting sleepy, and I could feel myself nodding off.

"But maybe there is something you *can* do."

"Like what?" I asked. I was now dreaming. I had fallen asleep in the doctor's office.

"Do you watch *Jeopardy* on TV?"

"I've been known to watch it."

"The host is a good friend of mine."

"You're friends with Alex Trebek?"

"No, no, not that guy. He's an idiot. I mean the original host. The real host of *Jeopardy*. You remember him? Do you recall his name?"

"I can't remember."

"Think, man. Think hard."

"I can recall his face, but I don't remember his name. He looked like a door-to-door Bible salesman."

"Yes, that's him."

"I can't remember his name."

"Try putting it in the form of a question."

I thought about this, and then it came to me. "Who is Art Fleming?" I asked.

"Right, and the announcer? You've got to remember who he was."

"Who was Don Pardo?"

"Right again."

"So, are you ready to play?"

"Play what?"

"Play *Jeopardy*. Where have you been? Aren't you paying attention to me?"

I stared at the doctor for a moment. Then I said, "I thought we were doing the word association thing."

"I ran out of words."

"Out of all the words in the English language, you ran out of words?" I asked, laughing.

"And your last little blurb was boring."

"You mean, about the house?"

"Yes, ho hum. Your first house. So you did some repair work. Honestly, who cares?"

"Okay," I said. I felt a little embarrassed.

"Okay what?"

"Okay, yes, I'll play *Jeopardy* with you."

"So, let's make it interesting."

"Interesting, how?" I asked.

"Let say you win a year for each correct question you come up with."

"Win a year?"

"We add a year to your life."

"Is that possible?"

"Of course it is. I wouldn't say it was if it wasn't. And for each incorrect question you come up with, you lose a year of your life."

"Lose a year?"

"Fair is fair, right?"

"I guess so."

"So, are you ready?"

This was all a little strange, but I said, "As ready as I'll ever be."

"I'll play the roles of Pardo and Fleming, and you can play yourself."

"Got it," I said.

"Then let's play *Jeopardy!*" the doctor exclaimed. She was now trying to reproduce the enthusiastic voice of Don Pardo, and it made me chuckle. She looked at me and said, "So, you don't like my Don Pardo voice?"

"No, it's fine," I said.

Then, trying to imitate the host, Art Fleming, she said in a slightly lower voice, "Welcome to *Jeopardy*, Mr. Robinson Cahill! Are you ready to play the game?"

"I'm ready," I said. I laughed. I was beginning to get a kick out of this.

"Don't forget to phrase your answers as questions."

"Yes, I understand that."

"Very good then. Pick a category."

"I'll take Animal Letters."

"Okay then, it's Animal Letters. Your first answer is the letter *a*."

"The letter *a*?"

"Is that your question?"

"No, let me think a minute."

"Ticktock, Mr. Cahill. Time is running out."

"I don't know what to say."

"Not even a wild guess?"

"Not even," I said.

"The correct question is, 'What is the second letter in the word *cat*?'"

"That's it?"

"That just cost you a year. Are you ready to move on?"

"Give me the next one, in the same category."

"The answer is the letter *o*."

"Ha," I said. "That's easy. The question is, 'What is the second letter in word *dog*?'"

"No, sorry. The correct question is 'what is the second letter in the word *fox*.'"

"But *dog* works," I said.

"But that wasn't the question. You have to state the exact question. That just cost you another year."

"Let's try one more."

"Same category?"

"Yes," I said.

"The answer is the letter *i*."

I thought for a moment, then said, "The question is, 'What's the second letter in the word *pig*?' Am I right?"

"Sorry, Mr. Cahill. It's the second letter in the word *hippopotamus*."

"That ridiculous," I said.

"Sorry. I really am. You're three years down now. Maybe you'd like to try a different category?"

"I would," I said. "How about Famous Clowns?"

"Okay, Famous Clowns is your category. Here is a beloved American clown you're likely to recall. The answer is, 'I'm a twice-elected president of the United States who, despite his schooling and many years in public office, never learned to pronounce the word *nuclear*.'"

"Who is George Bush?" I said.

"You are correct! Now we'll add a year. Now you're only down two years. Do you want to keep going?"

"Yes," I said. "This is more like it. Give me the next answer."

"Here it is. 'I am famous for holding public office and cheating on my wife with a woman most men in their right minds wouldn't touch if you held a gun to their heads.'"

"That's easy," I said. "Who is Bill Clinton?"

"Good try, but that's not the question we were looking for. The correct question is, 'Who is Arnold Schwarzenegger?'"

"Of course," I said.

"You're back down to negative three years."

"Let's try another Famous Clown."

"Okay, the answer to this third one is, 'I'd like to take myself seriously, but when I look at my face in the mirror, I can't help but laugh out loud. All the way to the bank, that is!'"

"Who is Donald Trump?" I said.

"Good question, but that's not the clown we had in mind. You're down four years now. The correct question is, 'Who is Phil McGraw?'"

"Of course," I said. "Dr. Phil."

"One of the all-time greats."

"Agreed," I said.

"This isn't my first rodeo, ha ha. Very funny stuff. Who said bald men couldn't be sex symbols?"

I suddenly felt someone shaking my arm. Who in the world would be shaking me? "Wake up, Mr. Cahill. Wake up for us. You have visitors."

CHAPTER 23

WAKE UP!

———— •●• ————

"Wake up," she said again.

I opened my eyes. I was on my back in a beige-walled room with a large picture window that looked out over a nicely kept garden. A landscape painting hung from the wall, and there was a kitchenette barely big enough to move in. There was a TV big enough for an entire family and some medical equipment off to the side of my hospital bed. What was this place? It took me a moment to get my bearings. The nurse was an overweight gal with short blonde hair and a bulbous nose, and she was still shaking my arm.

"I'm awake," I said, and she let go of me. She then went to open the door to my room to let in my visitors, and I could hear their voices. They were speaking quietly at first, in a sort of a hush, as though they were afraid of disturbing me, but when they saw I was awake, their voices perked up, and they circled around me.

"How's my man doing this morning?" Martha asked.

"I think I'm doing okay," I said.

"The doctor told all of us to come. He said this might be our last visit."

"Your last visit?"

"Before you kick the bucket," Robert said.

"Please, Robert," Martha said.

"He looks confused," someone said. It sounded a lot like Martha's father.

"I am a little confused."

"The doctor said you would've lived another four years if you hadn't played that game."

"Game?"

"With Dr. Bell."

234

"Oh, yes," I said.

"You should've stuck with word association."

"She said she ran out of words."

Martha laughed and said, "There are a million words in the English language."

"That's what *I* thought," I said.

Martha shrugged and said, "But what's done is done."

"Yes," I said.

"Are you hungry? Or thirsty? Is there anything we can get for you?"

"I'm fine."

"How about a lawyer joke?" Robert said.

"A lawyer joke?"

"We all know how much you love lawyer jokes," Martha said. "It'll cheer you up."

"Listen, Pop," Robert said. "You've really got to hear this. It's a good one."

"So long as your mom isn't offended."

"You know I like lawyer jokes."

"You do?"

"Listen to your son."

"There's a truck driver," Robert said. "He's driving down a highway. This guy likes to amuse himself by running over lawyers. Every time he sees a lawyer walking down the road, he swerves his truck to run him over. Anyway, one day he's driving down the highway, and he sees a priest who is hitchhiking. He pulls over and asks the priest where he's going, and the priest tells him he's headed for the church a couple of miles up the road. 'Hop in,' the truck driver says. 'The church is on my way, and I'll drop you off.' The priest gets in the truck, and the men drive off. Then they come upon a lawyer who's walking down the road. Instinctively, the truck driver swerves to run him over, but he suddenly remembers that the priest is in the truck with him. So he jerks the truck back into his lane. But as they pass the lawyer, the driver hears a loud thud, and, unsure of where the noise came from, he glances in his mirrors. As he is looking in his mirrors, he says to the priest, 'Please forgive me, Father. I almost ran over that poor lawyer.' The priest laughs and says, 'Don't worry about it, son. I got him with my door.'"

I laughed, and so did Martha.

And what about everyone else? The rest of my visitors were all talking to each other, not paying any attention to the joke. There were ten or fifteen of them. Mom and Dad were there, and so were both of Martha's parents. There were a couple of students I knew back from college and a few from high school. And there were other friends, acquaintances, and some people I didn't know too well. I recognized them from where? From my life? One of them was the guy with the red hair and freckles who had worked the cash register at the gas station I used to go to, and one was the gal with long fingernails who had worked at the florist shop I went to when I bought Martha anniversary flowers. Why were *they* there? I had no idea.

"Am I dying?" I asked Martha. "Is this it?"

"We think so," Martha said.

"Art Fleming," I said. "It was Art Fleming."

"What's he talking about," Martha's mom asked.

"He's probably delirious," her dad said.

"They've got him full of painkillers and God knows what else," Martha said.

"Poor guy."

"Maybe we shouldn't be here."

"No, no, the doctor said it's important," Martha said.

"What's important?" I asked.

"That you're allowed to say goodbye."

"Oh, yes, of course."

"Is there anything you'd like to say?" Martha asked.

"Now is the time," my dad said. "Time to put your cards on the table, Son."

"There is one thing I'd like to get off my chest," I said. I looked specifically at Martha. "It's a secret I've been keeping for years."

"I love secrets," Martha's mom said.

"Let's hear it," Martha said.

"It happened about twenty years ago. Do you remember how we used to go to Maxwell's for dinner?"

"Every Sunday night," Martha said.

"And do you remember that waitress? The one who usually served us. The cute blonde?"

"Natalie?"

"Yes," I said. "Well, do you remember when you had to go out of town for that client your firm worked for in Detroit? I don't remember the name of the company."

"Able Exhaust Systems?"

"Yes, that's the one."

"What about them?"

"You went to Detroit around Halloween that year. This was before Robert was born. You were gone for a couple of nights."

"Yes, I remember."

"Well, on the night before Halloween, I went to Maxwell's for dinner. There wasn't anything to cook in the house, and I didn't feel like going to the grocery store. So, I went to Maxwell's and ordered my usual Caesar salad and prime rib, and guess who my waitress was?"

"Natalie?"

"Yes," I said.

"So what?"

"Well, we got to talking, and she asked me why I was alone that night, and I told her you were out of town. You know, I always had kind of a thing for this girl. I don't know if you knew that. I don't think I ever told you, but I found her very attractive. There was something about her. You know how some people just rub you the right way? Natalie felt right to me. I don't know how else to explain it.

"Anyway, there I was, and one thing led to another, and I asked her if she wanted to come over to our house after work to watch TV with me. I told her I was lonely with you being gone and that I wasn't trying to seduce her or do anything devious. I said I just thought it would be nice to watch a movie with her. Then I couldn't believe it, but she actually said yes. I guess I really didn't expect her to go along with this, but she said yes, and she seemed excited about it. I was glad she said yes."

"You asked her to our house?" Martha said.

"I did, and after she got off work, she came right over to our house. I had her park down the street so that the neighbors wouldn't have anything to gossip about. I knew how odd it might appear with her car in our driveway while you were out of town, and I didn't want to embarrass you. It was innocent, but you know how people like to talk. Anyway, I made a bowl of popcorn, and we sat on the sofa together. I found an old Vincent Price movie they were showing on TV because it was the night before Halloween. It was *The House of Usher*. I think I watched that with you once, and I think we both liked it. It was corny, but a fun movie. You know, I don't think Vincent Price ever made a movie that didn't have a mansion or castle in it, did he?

"The two of us then talked while we watched the movie, and somehow we got on the subject of men who cheated on their wives. I told Natalie that I had never cheated on you. And that happened to be the truth, and she said she respected me for my loyalty to you. This made what happened next all the more surprising and out of character for me."

"Why? What happened next?"

"I don't know what came over me, or should I say what came over us? Somehow—and I don't have any idea how this happened—the two of us moved in closer together, and we were holding hands. Isn't that kind of weird? I mean, who holds hands? It was such a silly thing to do, but that's exactly how it began. The next thing I knew I had placed the bowl of popcorn on the coffee table, and Natalie and I were kissing."

"You kissed her?"

"I know, this sounds hard to believe. I don't know what came over me. Maybe it was her perfume? Or maybe it was her long blonde hair? Or maybe it was the clothes she was wearing, but she was—how do I put this?—yes, she was irresistible. And suddenly I didn't have the slightest clue what was going on in the movie. All I wanted to do was kiss and embrace this girl, and apparently, she felt the same way about me. She certainly wasn't pushing me away or telling me to think twice about what I was doing. You want to know how I really felt? I felt like I loved her. I felt like I had always loved her, and I felt like what we were doing was the right thing after all. It was the only thing that made any sense. I know this sounds horrible, but we belonged together."

"Did you think about me at all?" Martha asked.

"At this point, it was like I was under a spell. I'm not sure *what* I was thinking. But, no, I guess I didn't think of you. In fact, you weren't even in the picture. I was so bedeviled by this girl that I had forgotten about you completely. I know how bad this sounds, a man embracing and kissing another woman and forgetting about his own wife. I hate myself for it now.

And it has bothered me for years. But like I said, it didn't bother me that night, and after about fifteen minutes, we went even further.

"We began to take off each other's clothes, and the next thing I knew we were making love on the sofa, stark naked, and right in front of Vincent Price. I can't even put into words how wonderful it was. It was only after we were done with the act that I realized what a terrible thing we'd done. I came crashing back down to earth, and so did Natalie. She said, 'I think I better go home,' and I said, yes, that would probably be the best thing for her to do. So, we put our clothes on, and we acted like nothing had happened. Off she went without even a goodbye kiss, and that was the end of it."

"I can't believe this," Martha said. Her voice cracked, and there were tears welling in her eyes.

"I'm so sorry," I said.

"All these years."

"I had to tell you."

"What I jerk," Martha's dad said. "Didn't I always tell you the guy was a jerk?"

"I loved you," Martha said.

"I've always loved you," I said.

As I looked at Martha, I could see the terrible hurt I'd caused. It was dreadful. I had betrayed her in the worst way possible, and now everyone in the room knew about it. Then I got to thinking, and I wondered if the night with Natalie ever actually happened. Hopefully I had just made the whole thing up. Maybe it was the plot from one of my stories that I got confused with the events of my real life, and maybe Martha had nothing to be upset about after all. Or maybe it had nothing to do with a story at all. Maybe it was just a lame male fantasy. Yes, maybe I had thought about it but only in the way people sometimes think about doing wrong things they'll never actually do. And was that really so bad? Was thinking of something the same as doing it?

"Just die, you bastard," Martha said.

"Leave us all alone," Robert said.

"Didn't I warn you all?" Martha's dad said.

"Go, and never come back."

"Wake up," Martha said. Wake up? What was she now talking about? I thought I *was* awake. I opened my eyes.

God, what a relief. I was on our sofa, and Martha was shaking my arm. "If you sleep during the day, you're not going to be able to fall asleep tonight."

"I'm awake," I said.

"Do you want me to get you a cup of coffee?"

"That would be great."

"How late were you up last night?"

"Late," I said. I rubbed my eyes. "I was just having the strangest dream."

"What about?"

"I dreamed I was dying."

"That sounds horrible."

"It wasn't much fun," I said. "I learned that honesty and goodbyes do not make good partners."

Martha smiled. She was used to not always understanding what I was saying. "Whatever that means," she said.

"I have a question for you," I said. "What do you think happens to us after we die? Do you really think we live on, or is death the end of it all?"

"Of course we live on."

"What makes you think that?"

"My mom and dad are both dead, yet I can feel them looking over me every day."

"You feel that literally?"

"I do. Don't you feel your parents looking over you?"

"I don't know. Maybe."

"You want to know what I really think?"

"What do you think?"

"I think you're way too concerned with what you can prove and not concerned enough with what you feel. Just because you can't hold something in your hands or weigh it or measure it or photograph it or smell it or taste it or eat it or bathe it or dress it, that doesn't mean it doesn't exist. This doesn't mean it doesn't happen. Maybe it's just as real as the sky or the clouds or the mountains below. I say it *is* real, Robinson. We can feel it, and we can know it. Can you weigh love? Can you taste it? Can you measure it with a yardstick? No, you certainly can't. But you know in your heart that love is as real as anything else in the universe. Maybe it's even more real than anything else, right? Often it's a whole lot more powerful and more influential and more brilliant and more in your face than even the most rock solid and provable of anything."

"I suppose you believe in heaven and hell?"

"Not hell."

"No?" I said.

"Only heaven, Robinson. I only believe in heaven. I'll leave hell to all the fanatics. They have no idea what they're talking about. They don't get God. Sure, they read the Bible, but the Bible is nonsense. The Bible is just fiction. It's written by men for fools. The Bible is a comic book without all the pictures."

"If there's no hell, then where do all the wicked people go?"

"There are no wicked people."

"Sure, there are."

"We were all made in God's image. *That* part of creation the Bible has right. Tell me, why would God punish beings who were made in his image?"

"I don't know."

"We all go astray during our time on earth to one degree or the other. Then we die, and we all go to heaven, where we meet and talk and tell our stories about what life was like on the great planet. We talk to each other free and unfettered by the loveless and evil-instigating influences of all corporal things mucking up the works. We are free of all the crap, so to speak. We have no reason to dislike or distrust or hate or envy or lust each other. We are free and pure spirits. And the more we learn from each other in heaven, the more it all makes sense. We finally get it. We understand. Our lives now have meaning, and we are one. Even the very worst men and women from earth see the brilliant light of love and knowledge because they too can finally think clearly. And we all learn to do what God has always known how to do. We learn to forgive. And we laugh at what we used to be."

I thought for a moment and said, "I never knew you felt this way."

"You never asked me how I felt."

"We must've talked before."

"Never, Robinson."

"But why not?"

"Ask yourself. Don't ask me. And while you're at it, ask yourself what you know of your son's thoughts. He's your own flesh and blood. He was made by you and raised by you, and you have no more of an idea about what makes him tick than you have an understanding of quantum physics or string theory. You're in the dark. You're utterly clueless. You always have been, and you always will be."

"I don't think that's fair to say."

"He's a mystery to you."

"He's my son."

"Which makes it all the more tragic."

"Tragic?"

"As in a classic tragedy. Your story? It could have been written by Sophocles."

"That isn't fair to say."

"No?"

"I'm close to Robert."

"You're light-years away from him."

"That just isn't true."

"Let's ask Robert, shall we?"

"Ask him?"

"Summon him forth!" Martha suddenly exclaimed. Her formal speech and enthusiasm startled me.

Robert appeared in the room. He had a can of Coke in one hand and a sandwich in the other. "Can't a guy eat lunch around here?" he asked.

"We have a question for you," Martha said. "Your dad says he's close to you. He thinks he knows you. He thinks he understands you."

"Okay," Robert said. He took a bite from his sandwich and began to chew.

"What say *you*?"

"Hang on a second," Robert said. He wanted to finish with his mouthful of sandwich before he spoke. He chewed and then finally swallowed. He drank a few gulps of Coke to wash the food down, and then he set his things down on an end table and spoke. He said, "I've got a good one. I don't think you've heard it before. Stop me if you've heard it. Have you heard the one about the Bulgarian train driver?"

"No," I said.

"I haven't heard it either," Martha said.

"It goes like this. There was a man in Bulgaria who wanted to drive trains ever since he was a small child. Finally, when he grew up, his dream came true, and he was hired to drive one of the country's major trains. There was one problem. He liked to go fast, and one day he went too fast and wrecked the train, killing six of the passengers. He was taken to court, tried for murder, and found guilty and sentenced to death. On the day of his execution, he was given the last meal of his choice. He asked for one banana, and that was all. This surprised the men in charge, but they gave him what he asked for. He then ate the banana, and several hours later, he was strapped into an electric chair. They flipped the switch, and sparks and smoke filled the room, but to everyone's surprise, the man wouldn't die. They decided it had to be divine intervention, and it was the law in Bulgaria that if God intervened with an execution, the accused was to be set free. So the man was freed, and the first thing he did was to get his old job back. Then two months later, he wrecked another train, this time killing eight passengers. He was tried and convicted of murder again. This time before being executed he asked for two bananas. He ate the bananas, and lo and behold, when they tried to electrocute the man, he survived again. So once again he was freed, and again he got his job back, driving the train. Sure enough, just a few months later, he wrecked the train again, this time killing twelve passengers. He was convicted of murder a third time and sent to be executed in the electric chair. This time he requested three bananas, and the official said, 'Enough with these damn bananas already. This time you're going to die.'

"With no bananas to eat, they strapped the man in the chair and threw the switch. Sparks and smoke filled the room, but believe it or not, the man was still alive when they turned the power off. The officials couldn't believe their eyes, and they asked the man how he was able to live without eating the bananas. 'It's got nothing at all to do with eating the bananas,' the man said. 'I'm just a terrible conductor.'"

The audience laughed. They liked this dumb joke, and they seemed to like Robert. Martha and I were no longer at home. We were seated up toward the stage at a small round table. There were two drinks on the table, a Scotch for me and a strawberry margarita for Martha. It was very dark in the club except for the lights aimed at Robert. "They seem to like him," I said to Martha.

"He's getting to be so popular," Martha said.

"That was a pretty corny joke."

"It was," Martha agreed.

"We have some special guests with us here tonight," Robert said to the audience. "Let's have a round of applause. My parents are here tonight."

"Jesus," I said to Martha.

"Let's hear it for my mom and dad."

"Bravo!" someone in the audience yelled. The rest of the audience applauded, and for a moment the spotlight shone on us. The light was very bright, and I had to squint. I was knee-knocking nervous, and I could feel my heart beat accelerate and perspiration running down my sides.

"Stand up," Robert said to us. Martha and I stood. Then to the audience, Robert said, "If you don't like tonight's show, these are the people to blame. Everything I am today I learned and inherited from them."

CHAPTER 24

THE MASKED MAN

———•———

"**M**y dad," Robert said, rolling his eyes. "He's a writer, you know. He's always had his eye on bringing home the big bucks. Listen, it was either he became a writer or one of those uber- rich entrepreneurs, who holds a SLOW versus STOP sign for cars where they're doing road construction."

The audience laughed at this. "I guess I deserved that," I said to Martha.

"We all have dads, right?" Robert said. "Here are several things you'll never hear my dad say." Robert imitated my voice and said, "'Can you please turn up that music?' 'Here's the TV remote.' 'Here are the keys to my brand-new car and some cash for gas. Have a great time tonight.'"

The audience was still laughing. "I think he's making fun of me," I whispered to Martha.

"Hush," she said.

"And since when did Robert become a comic?"

"He's always wanted to do this."

"I thought he wanted to open a restaurant in Las Vegas. It was The Outlaw's something or other. Yes, he was going to call it The Outlaw's Hideout. That's what it was."

"Will you please stop talking?"

"My father is getting up there in years," Robert said. "He likes to pretend he's still young, but he's so old that even his fingernails have wrinkles. My dad is so old that when God said, 'Let there be light,' he was the guy who hit the switch. Hell, let's face it, he's so old that when he was a boy, the Dead Sea was only sick."

Martha was laughing. "Wait until he gets to you," I said. "It's funny now."

"He *is* funny," Martha said.

"I see that my time here is about up," Robert finally said, glancing at his watch. "But I have one more story to tell about my dear, old dad. You know, my wife and I just had a baby, and we asked my parents to babysit. We were gone about an hour when my parents realized we were out of diapers, so my dad drove to the drugstore to pick some up. There was a girl working there, and my dad said, 'Excuse me, miss. What aisle are the diapers in?' She looked at him, totally serious, and asked him, 'For adults or for babies?'"

Everyone in the place roared. Obviously, it was a young crowd, and adult diapers were funny. "I didn't know we had a grandchild," I said to Martha.

"Where have you been?" Martha asked.

"I don't know."

"You need to pay closer attention."

"No kidding," I said, and Robert walked off the stage. His show at the club was over, and the house lights came on. "Let's go backstage and see him," I said.

"Should we bother him?"

"Why not?" I asked.

"We might embarrass him."

"Let him be embarrassed," I said. "We have every right to embarrass the kid. We're his parents, aren't we? Isn't that our purpose on this planet?"

I stood up, and Martha followed me through the lobby to the old door that opened to the backstage. The sign on the door said the entrance was for employees only, but I figured it would be okay for us to go in. I pushed on the door, and it swung open. And there was Robert.

He was standing about twenty feet from us, up against a wall. There was a man arguing with him, and he held onto Robert's shirt collar, as if trying to provoke a fight. Martha and I stopped and stared at the scene. We weren't sure what to do. The man was giving Robert a lot of grief about something important to him, and our son was shaking his head and saying, "You need to just leave me alone."

Then the man pushed Robert backward so that Robert's head thumped against the wall, and the man said, "Next time I'll kick your thieving ass. Do you understand what I'm saying?" Robert nodded but didn't reply.

The man stormed away, and we approached our son. "What was that all about?" I asked.

"Just an angry guy," Robert said.

"Why was he angry?"

"He thinks I stole something."

"Like what?"

"A couple of his jokes."

"He's a comedian?"

"Well, he thinks he is."

"Is he, or isn't he?"

"I guess he is. But he isn't very funny."

"He didn't seem very funny," Martha said.

"I'm glad you guys came tonight," Robert said, changing the subject. "I didn't think you were going to make it. It was a good show, right?"

"You were funny," I said.

"How long until your next show?"

"A couple of hours."

"Do you want to grab some dinner with us?"

"That would be great," Robert said. "Let's go to Carl's. It's a great little restaurant down the street."

Martha and I agreed to go, and the three of us walked out of the club and onto the outside sidewalk. We followed Robert, since he knew where we were going. We came to a quaint, little place and took our seats at an outside table. A young tattooed waitress immediately handed us our menus, and we opened them up and read through the offerings.

"Tell me the truth," I said to Robert. "Did you steal that man's jokes?"

"Steal?" Robert said.

"Yes, you know what I mean."

"What is stealing really?"

"The man seemed very angry," Martha said.

"People don't just get that angry for no reason," I said. "You must have done something to get under his skin."

"I may have borrowed a couple of gags."

"Borrowed?"

"Okay, so I stole them. But it's okay. Everyone steals from everyone around here."

"Everyone?"

"In fact, everyone steals, period. That is, if they ever want to get anywhere."

"Where did you ever get such an idea?"

"Just look around, Pop. Are you really so naïve that you can't see what's going on?"

"He's right," Martha said.

"What do you mean, he's right?"

"You *are* kind of naïve," Martha said.

"Hardly," I said.

"Look at this café we're eating at," Robert said. "Do you see a single original idea here? The outdoor tables and white tablecloths, the paper napkins, the silverware, the cream and sugar packets, the bottle of ketchup, the little candles in the middle of each table. Each feature is an idea blatantly stolen from another restaurant, who stole the idea from another restaurant, who stole their ideas from yet another restaurant. And do you see anything original listed on your menu? It's just a rundown of main courses, beverages, and desserts stolen from other chefs, all stolen from other restaurants. It's like I said. Everyone steals from everyone. I can't believe I have to explain this to you."

"Have you folks made up your minds?" the waitress asked. She was now standing before us, poised stiff like a mannequin, ready to take our orders. Martha ordered her meal first and then Robert. I didn't hear what they were ordering, because I wasn't paying attention to them. I was still lost in thought, thinking about what Robert had said about the restaurant, and I was trying to come up with an argument that would make Robert think more rationally about what he was saying. Why? Because he was wrong, and obviously these restaurants were not stealing ideas from each other. Or were they? "I'll have the fettuccini Alfredo," I said. I heard myself talking. I sounded just like a robot. The tattooed waitress walked away with her notepad and ballpoint pen, also like a robot.

Robots? Copycats? Is that what we all were? Fettuccini Alfredo? How many servings were cooked up each day around the world? In this town alone?

Martha asked Robert how Cynthia was doing. So who in the heck was Cynthia? Robert's wife? Why didn't I know about her? She was doing fine, according to Robert. She was working at the same place. She worked at an insurance company, where she helped process claims, which meant what? I knew exactly what it meant. She came up with fine-print reasons why money shouldn't be paid out to policyholders. Charge the suckers for the policies and deny the claims. Isn't that what the insurance racket was all about? Every one of them, doing the same thing. There ought to have been a law against it, but there wasn't. Once not long ago, I had planned to cancel all my insurance policies, at least those that seemed superfluous, the lame ones I wasn't required by law to have. But I chickened out, because what if? In other words, what if a volcano erupted in my front yard? Or what if all four wheels fell off my car? Or what if I came down with a rare case of a tropical flu? I'd be wiped out if I didn't have the right insurance.

Suddenly I heard two gunshots. They could have been a car backfiring, but I was pretty sure they were gunshots. I looked to my left, and there was a man wearing a Donald Trump Halloween mask, holding a handgun, and pointing it at our waitress. She was crying and was obviously frightened. I know she was scared to death because yellow urine was now dribbling down the insides of her legs toward her feet.

"Open up the cash register for me," the man said.

"Hey!" a bald man next to us said, as if he were going to stop the robbery with a word. The masked man shot the candle off the man's table.

"Shut up," the masked man said. "This has nothing to do with you." He aimed the gun back at the waitress, and she took him to the cash register. "Open it up," he said, and she opened it.

"You don't want to do this," I said loudly. For some reason I now had it in my head that I was going to get the man to stop what he was doing by being rational with him.

"Who the fuck asked you for an opinion?" the man said.

"You're making a big mistake."

"We'll see about that."

"Stealing is wrong," I said. I don't know why I said this. It seemed so childishly trite, and yet that's what I said to a man who obviously couldn't have cared less about what I thought. What the heck was wrong with me? Why did I have to open my big, idiotic mouth?

The man grabbed all the money from the cash register, and then he came to our table. I thought he was coming after me, but he came after

Martha. He grabbed Martha by the hair, and Martha shut her eyes. "How about if I steal your girlfriend?" the masked man said.

"She's my wife, not my girlfriend."

"Okay, your wife. She's coming with me."

"You can't do that."

"But I can," the man said, yanking Martha up to her feet and pointing his gun at her head. Her eyes were still shut, as if by keeping them closed the man would go away. "She's coming with me. She'll be my insurance policy."

"Against what?"

"Against any of you well-behaved citizens calling the police."

"We won't call the cops."

"You'll call them the first chance you get. As soon as I leave this place, all you idiots will be holding your cell phones and calling 9-1-1."

"No one will call," I said.

"You're right," the man said. "No one will call, because if you do, I'll blow your wife's brains out."

"Please don't do this."

"Fuck off."

"I'm begging you. Please?"

The man laughed like an evil spirit, and then he dragged Martha with him out of the restaurant and down the sidewalk. In a second they disappeared. I had a knot in my stomach the size of a prize watermelon. "What do we do now?" Robert asked me.

"I don't know."

"We wait," the bald man said. "We give him fifteen minutes to get away, and then we call the cops. I don't think he'll hurt your wife if we give him fifteen minutes. That should be enough time for him to get away."

"You know about these things?" I asked.

"No, I'm just guessing."

"Jesus," I said.

"Fifteen minutes sounds reasonable to me," a woman at another table said.

"That gives us a little time," Robert said.

"Time for what?"

"I can keep everyone entertained while we're waiting. I'm good at this. I can rattle off a few jokes. I know some good ones about robbers."

"I'm game," the bald man said.

"Let's hear them," the woman said.

"But Martha?" I said.

"She'll be okay," Robert said.

"Don't worry so much," the bald man said.

"Have you heard about the bank robber who got caught in the act of stealing a quarter of a million dollars?" Robert asked, now determined to tell a joke. "When the cops handcuffed him and walked him to the patrol car, one of the cops asked him why he tried to rob the money, and the man said he needed the cash to pay for his daughter's college tuition. The cop, who also had a kid in college, said, 'I understand that, but I have one question. Where'd you plan to get the rest of the money?'"

Everyone in the restaurant laughed. "That's a pretty good one," the bald man said.

"Do you know any more?" the woman asked.

"I know a ton of them," Robert said. "Have you heard the one about the man who was convicted of armed robbery? The angry judge sentenced him to ten years in prison, and the man asked if he could say something in response. The judge agreed to let the man talk, and the man asked the judge, 'Would it be okay if I called you a dick?' The judge, growing even angrier, said, 'Absolutely not! If you call me a dick, I'll add another five years to your sentence.' The man asked, 'What if I just thought you were a dick? Would that be okay?' The judge said there was no way he could control what the man happened to be thinking, so yes, the man could think whatever he wanted. Upon hearing this, the man jutted out his chin and said, 'Fine, in that case, I think you're a dick.'"

"That's terrible," the woman said, but she was laughing when she said it.

"Another good one," the bald man said. "You should do this for a living."

"I kind of do," Robert said. "You should catch one of my shows. Have you heard the one about the parrot and the burglar? This ought to tickle your funny bone. My dad told me this one when I was in high school."

"I did?" I said.

251

Robert ignored me and said, "There's a burglar in a home at night while the owners are away at a party. He is going through the house with his flashlight, looking for things worth taking. Suddenly, he hears an ominous voice coming from another room, and the voice startles him. The voice says, 'Jesus is watching you.' This kind of freaks the guy out, but he doesn't stop his search for valuables. Then five minutes later, he hears the same voice saying, 'Jesus is watching you.' This time he walks toward the voice to find out who's talking. He soon comes upon a parrot, and he shines his flashlight on the bird. 'Are you the one talking to me?' he asks the bird, and the bird says yes. 'My name happens to be Moses,' the parrot says to the man. 'And you can take my word for it. Jesus *is* watching you.' The man laughs and says, 'This is ridiculous. What kind of idiots would name their parrot Moses?' The parrot says, 'I guess it would be the same kind of idiots who would name their rottweiler Jesus.'"

Everyone laughed at this. Everyone except for me, because I wasn't paying attention.

"I've got to do something," I said.

"About what?" Robert asked.

"About your mother."

"What are you going to do?"

"I need to go after her."

"That's not a wise idea," the bald man said.

"I can't just sit here, listening to jokes."

"You could endanger her life."

"I doubt it. Besides, her life is already endangered. If I do nothing and she is hurt or killed, I'll never be able to forgive myself."

Robert seemed to agree with me. He said, "You go, Pop. I'll stay here and keep everyone entertained."

"And you'll call the police soon?"

"Yes, we'll call them. Let me tell one more joke, and then we'll call 9-1-1."

"Good," I said, and I stood up from the table. I hurried to the sidewalk, and I looked in the direction my wife and the robber had gone. They were nowhere in sight.

"Do you see them?" Robert asked.

"No," I said.

"Well, what are you waiting for?" the bald man said. "Go find them."

"I will," I said, and I took off down the sidewalk. After about half a block, I grabbed a woman's arm. I could tell I had startled her. "Ma'am, did you see a man wearing a Donald Trump mask pass by here?" I asked her. "He would have had a woman with him."

"No," the woman said.

"I saw them," a kid on a bicycle said. "When I saw them, they were down there, to the right, around the corner from that mailbox." The kid pointed in their direction.

I thanked the kid and took off running toward the mailbox. When I got there, I turned right on the cross street. I kept running, but I still couldn't see them. They had to be somewhere. I came upon a man walking the opposite direction, and I stopped to ask him, "Have you seen a man in a Trump mask with a woman?" I said. I was now out of breath, and I barely got the words out of my mouth.

"I saw them," the man said. "They went into that grocery store." The man pointed to a grocery store about a half block away.

"Thanks," I said, and I took off running. When I got to the store, I stepped inside through the automatic glass doors. I then looked up and down at the cash register stations, but neither the robber nor Martha was in any line. They had to be down one of the aisles. So I started at one end of the store, and I walked toward the other, peering carefully down each aisle.

I finally spotted Martha. She was pushing a shopping cart full of groceries. She stopped to reach for a big jar of mayonnaise. "Martha!" I exclaimed, and I ran to her. "What the heck are you doing?"

"I'm shopping," she said.

"Shopping? Where's Donald Trump?"

"He ditched the mask and ran out of the store ten minutes ago. He left me in the snack and cookie aisle, so I figured I may as well get some shopping done while I'm here. It'll save me a trip to the store tomorrow."

"Mayonnaise, seriously?"

"Don't we need it?"

"There's a full jar in the pantry."

"I couldn't remember. I figured better safe than sorry. But if you say we have some, I'll put this back."

"What we need is mustard."

"Do we?"

"We used the last of it last weekend when you cooked hot dogs for dinner."

"I remember something about that."

"We're also out of potato chips."

"Is that all?" my mother's voice asked.

Yes, it was now my mother. She was not dead but quite alive. And you can forget about the grocery store. I was no longer with Martha. Instead, I was at my parents' house, sitting at the kitchen table with my mother. We were having coffee and cake. The cake was left over from my cousin's birthday party. It was a chocolate cake with chocolate icing. I'm not sure what the leftover cake was doing in our refrigerator, but never mind. I wasn't sure of a lot of things, but I was sure of the dream. I remembered every bit of it: Robert's jokes, the man with the Donald Trump mask, and then Martha in the grocery store.

Mom reached over and put her hand on mine. She said, "Dreams can be exhausting. You've been through a lot."

"I have," I said.

"And your dream makes sense to me."

"I'm glad it makes sense to someone."

"You're worried about Robert."

"I am," I said.

"All children eventually color outside the lines."

"Outside the lines?"

"Love is always the answer."

"I'm not sure what you mean by that."

"I mean that love is the answer."

"Obviously, I heard you the first time. I'm just not sure what you mean. Do you think I don't love my son?"

"No, all fathers love their sons."

"Then what *do* you mean?"

"I mean that it's one thing to feel love and another thing to show it. It's one thing to know all your lines and another to deliver them. You're a writer, aren't you? You should know it's one thing to dream up a story and another thing to sit at your desk and write it."

CHAPTER 25

THE INVISIBLE MOM

---•---

It was my mother all right, but there were a few things different about her. First, there was the lipstick. I didn't remember my mom ever wearing such bright red lipstick. And there was her hair. Mom always wore her straight hair short and simple, but now she was wearing the sort of blonde wig a Las Vegas cocktail waitress would wear. It looked so stiff, wavy, and fake. And I guess her synthetic hair went along with her false eyelashes and dark penciled eyebrows. But the most different thing I noticed about my mom was the cigarette that smoldered from between her fingers and the ashtray on the kitchen table, overflowing with butts.

Smoking? No, my mom never smoked. She took a long drag from her cigarette and blew the gray smoke out from her nostrils like she had just gotten done breathing a big throat full of fire and needed to clear her sinuses.

"It's tough when your children misbehave," she said.

"It is," I said.

"I know exactly what it's like. I remember you well. You were such a handful."

"You mean when I was a kid? How so? I remember being very well behaved."

"You're kidding, right?"

"No, why? What do you recall?"

"Do you remember Timothy Cosgrove?"

"Vaguely."

"Do you remember when he spent time at our house?"

"No," I said.

"He slept over at our house. You boys were in the eighth grade. His mom was a friend of mine. He was a nice boy, very polite. I thought you liked him."

"I barely remember him, but I recall that I did kind of like him."

"Then why'd you do it?"

"Why did I do what?" I asked.

"I can't believe you don't remember," Mom said. "You let him use your bed while you slept on the floor in your sleeping bag. You let him sleep in your bed because he was your guest. You said he would be more comfortable in the bed, and it was such a good thing for you to do. You were nice to him, and I was proud of you."

"If you say so."

"Timothy got out of bed in the middle of the night, and he came to get me. He knocked on our bedroom door, and I answered. The poor kid. His pajama bottoms were sopping wet, and he was terribly upset. He wasn't crying, but there were tears welled in his eyes. He had peed himself in your bed, and he didn't know what to do. I took him back to your bedroom, and we tried not to wake you. But you heard us moving around and whispering, and you woke up. 'What's going on?' you asked. I told you to just go back to sleep, but you were too curious to close your eyes. I didn't want you to know, but you knew."

"I knew what?"

"That Timothy had peed in your bed. And it was a lot more than just a little dribble. He had all-out peed, and the sheets and blanket on the bed were soaked with urine. I had Timothy take off his pajama bottoms and dry himself in the bathroom. I gave him a pair of your pajama bottoms to wear, and I took his to the laundry room along with the sheets and blanket. Then I stuffed them into the washing machine and returned to your room, where I put clean sheets and a fresh blanket on your bed. You remained in your sleeping bag the entire time. You weren't sure what to do or say. I thought you were embarrassed for the boy, and I could understand that. I tucked Timothy into the bed and turned off your light so the two of you could go back to sleep. That poor kid. I had no idea he was a bed-wetter. His mother should've warned us."

"I thought she was your friend."

"She *was* a good friend. I guess she was just hoping Timothy wouldn't have an accident."

"I don't remember any of this. I'll have to take your word for it. But you also said I did something wrong. What did I do that was so bad?"

"The incident occurred on Saturday night. The next Monday at school you decided to blab to all your friends about it. It was such a cruel thing to do. The next thing we knew, the whole school knew Timothy was a bed-wetter. Timothy's mom called me to tell me what had happened at school, and she was sniffing and sobbing the entire time. Her sweet child had been betrayed and humiliated by a boy he thought was his friend, namely you. For a week or so, the teasing at school was relentless. It did eventually die down, but still everyone in the school knew Timothy had peed in your bed, thanks to you. Your callousness was alarming."

"My callousness?"

"You couldn't have cared less about his feelings. Do you want to know what your main concern was? You didn't care at all about what you'd done to hurt Timothy. You only wanted to know what we planned to do about the bed. You wouldn't sleep in it, no matter what. You said it smelled like wet urine, even though I'd scrubbed the mattress totally clean. You insisted that we buy you a brand-new bed, and so we did. I was so angry with you. You did eventually apologize to Timothy but only because Dad and I made you do it."

"I feel like you're talking about someone else. I don't remember any of this."

"So now you're calling me a liar?"

"I'm just saying I don't remember," I said.

"Then you *are* calling me a liar."

"Maybe I am."

Mom looked into my eyes and said, "Maybe I'm a liar, but what are you?"

"Well, I'm not a liar. I'm trying to be honest."

"I mean, what *are* you?"

"What does that even mean?"

"What do you do for a living? Day and night until you get carpel tunnel syndrome? What do you spend all of your working hours doing?"

"I'm a writer."

"You make stories up?"

"I do," I said.

"From your imagination?"

"You could say that."

"You're a peddler of fiction, right?"

"Yes, I guess I am."

"And what do you expect your readers to gain by reading your made-up stories?"

"Insight, I hope."

"Insight into what?"

"Insight into the truth," I said.

"Ah, then there you have it."

I thought for a moment and said, "But you're claiming that your story is true. I don't claim to write true stories for anyone."

"Yes, you do. If your readers didn't accept them as truth, there'd be nothing for them to gain from them. If your stories were totally unreal, they'd be totally worthless. You claimed just a few seconds ago that you wanted to present your readers with insight into the truth, but can truth be distilled from lies? I don't think so. Yes, you write fiction, but you also write the truth. Or at least you try to."

Mom was confusing me a little, but I said, "I guess that makes sense."

"So, you're not really a fiction writer."

"But I am."

My mom laughed and said, "You *think* you're a fiction writer, but like my supposedly made-up story about you and your friend, you are writing nonfiction. If people didn't see the truth in what you were writing, there'd be no point to it. No point at all."

"You're giving me a headache," I said, rubbing my temples with my fingertips. I felt like a computer that had just been fed an unsolvable conundrum.

We sat silent for a moment. Then my mom asked, "Can I continue with Timothy's story?"

"There's more?"

"Yes, there is more."

"Go on," I said.

"You won't call me a liar?"

"I'll try not to," I said.

"Well, like I said, Timothy's eighth grade in school was a nightmare, largely thanks to you. But over the next two years, things began to change. For one thing, Timothy began to mature physically, and as he matured, not only did his bed-wetting subside, but he also turned into a rather handsome young man. He no longer looked like an awkward, little prepubescent child who peed the bed, and the kids at school gradually forgot about the bed-wetting story, as kids are inclined to do. Kids are cruel, yes. But they are also forgiving of each other's prior immaturities while they are growing up. They tend to cut each other slack, hoping the same slack will be cut for them. Girls who were homely can be suddenly pretty, and boys who were at one time weaklings can be strong and athletic. Anyway, the bed-wetting was all but forgotten, and while he certainly wasn't the most popular boy in school, Timothy did gain many friends. And there were now girls who liked him. He was smart as a whip, and when his senior year rolled around, his academic record got him into a first-rate college."

"Which college was that?" I asked.

"I don't remember which one," my mom said. "I just recall that it was one of the better schools. And Timothy shined like a brilliant star. He did well in college. He dated nice girls and made lots of friends. Two years after he graduated, he got married, and three years after that, they had their first child. Then the next year, there was a second child, and then the year after that, a third child. It was then that he started up his own computer software company. Within the decade, Timothy was a millionaire ten times over, and not to say money is everything, but Timothy had it made. He had a happy family, a healthy life, and to his great delight, none of his children ever wet the bed. Now I'm not going to exaggerate and say that Timothy's life was perfect, but it was a good life. Who would've guessed Timothy would do so well? Who would've figured he'd survive what you did to him? In fact, he didn't just survive. He achieved and thrived."

I looked at my mom. I looked at her with disbelief and said, "What a load of crap."

"What's a load of crap?"

"Your whole story. You just made the entire thing up to teach me a stupid lesson, didn't you?"

"Do you *know* it's false?"

"I can guess that it is."

"But do you *know*? I mean, for sure?"

"I guess not."

"That's the beauty of fiction. Good fiction, anyway. *If it could happen, it may as well have happened.*"

These words stopped me dead in my tracks. Words of wisdom from my mother? Honestly? I didn't think she had it in her. I had always imagined my mother as a mother, never as a teacher. She was always the woman wearing the apron, who cooked the meals in our kitchen, vacuumed the carpets, swept the floors, cleaned the smudges off the windows, did the laundry, changed out the plants in the flower beds, and did all the shopping for Dad and me. And perhaps, even more importantly, she was the one who loved. She loved my dad, and she loved me—not just a little but unconditionally. There wasn't a thing my father or I could do or say that would ever weaken this love. So she had love to offer in spades. But profound thoughts on subjects such as truth versus fiction in literature were never what I expected from her. Yet there she was, with her bright-red lipstick and cocktail waitress wig, cutting into the fatty meat of my chosen profession with a sharp philosophical knife. And *this* caused me to think I must be dreaming, so I decided to put her to the test. I would ask her a series of well-targeted questions that would reveal whether she was truly my mom or a figment of my sleeping imagination.

"What do you get when you mix yellow and red?" I asked. A wrong answer would indicate this was a dream.

"You get orange," Mom said.

"And blue and red?"

"Purple."

"And the square root of sixteen is?"

"Four," Mom said.

"Okay then," I said. "Let me make the questions a little tougher. What's brown and has a human head and a tail but no arms or legs?"

"A penny?"

"You must have heard that one before. Okay, then try this one on for size. What city did Dad's parents live in before they got married?"

"St. Louis."

"What was the name of Grandma and Grandpa's dog."

"My parents or Dad's parents?"

"Your parents."

"They never had a dog. They were cat people. They went through more cats than Ernest Hemingway."

I chuckled and said, "Okay, then what's the name of the girl I had a crush on in high school?"

"Which one?"

"The one I still dream about."

"That's easy. Her name is Gabriela Sachs." Mom snuffed her cigarette out in the ashtray. She knew a lot. Maybe too much.

"Here's a question for you. Here it is, the sixty-four-thousand-dollar question. What am I going to do about Robert? What am I going to do about my son?"

"Regarding?"

"The coins, of course."

"Ah, the coins."

"What would *you* do?"

Mom lit a new cigarette. She blew the gray smoke down on the table and said, "You are due for another fable."

"Another fable?"

"Did I ever tell you the story about the lovesick zebra?"

"Not that I recall," I said. To be honest, I didn't want to hear another fable. But I listened.

"Once upon a time in the wilderness of Africa, there lived a young zebra boy, who fell head over heels in love with a beautiful zebra girl. More than anything in the world, he wanted to be the girl's sweetheart. He thought that if he could write the perfect love poem to her, he would be able to win her heart. The problem was that he was not any good at writing poetry. In fact, he was terrible at it, so he sought help. The first animal he went to was a giraffe who lived nearby and had a reputation for writing fine poetry. He said to the giraffe, 'I hear you're a talented poet, and I'm trying to win the heart of a girl I love. Would you be so kind as to write a love poem for me? I would like to give it to her so that I can prove how much I love her.'"

"And I suppose the giraffe said yes," I said.

"Yes, the giraffe agreed to write the poem. And two days later, the poem was complete. The giraffe gave the poem to the boy zebra, and the boy gave the poem to the girl. She read it, and, handing it back to him, said, 'This is a very nice little poem, and it would be terrific if I were a giraffe, but I'm not a giraffe. I am a zebra.' Disappointed, the young zebra threw the poem away, but this didn't mean he was giving up on his idea. He went to a cheetah, who had a good reputation for writing even better poetry. The cheetah agreed to write the young zebra's love poem, and when it was done, the zebra handed the new poem to the girl. She read it and said, 'This is even better than the last poem, and it would be terrific if I were a cheetah. But I am not a cheetah. I'm a zebra.' She handed the poem back to the young zebra, and he threw it away. Then he asked around and learned to his surprise that there was an old hippopotamus who wrote even better poetry. He went to the hippo and asked him to write the poem. The hippo agreed and wrote a wonderful poem. It was the most amazing poem the zebra had ever read. The young zebra took the poem to the girl zebra, and she read it."

"So, did she like this one?"

"Well, she said, 'Oh my, this is even better than the last two poems you gave me, and it would be terrific if I happened to be a hippopotamus. But alas, I am a zebra.' The poor zebra was beside himself. Finally, he went to the wisest animal of all, a very old owl who lived nearby in a tree. He asked the old owl to write a poem for him, and the owl said, 'I can write your poem, and it will be the best poem of them all. But it won't do you any good. You see, you need to write the poem yourself if you want to have a chance at winning this girl's heart. The poem cannot come from a giraffe, a cheetah, a hippo, or even a wise old owl like me. The poem must come from you, from your own beating heart. So, my advice? Go and write your own poem.' The zebra was not happy with the owl's advice, but he decided to take it. He sat down and wrote a love poem to the girl zebra, pouring his heart into every word and verse. And how did it turn out? It was awful! It was clumsy, the words were all wrong, and most of them didn't even rhyme. But the young zebra had no choice in the matter. The owl was his last shot, and he had to follow the old sage's advice. So, he took his awful poem to the girl zebra, and she read every word of it."

"And what did the girl zebra say?"

"She smiled and said, 'I love this poem. I can tell this came from your heart, and I will be your sweetheart.' The boy zebra breathed a big sigh of relief. And then the two zebras kissed and became lovers, and they went on to live happily ever after."

"That's it?" I said.

"Don't you like it?" my mom asked.

"I guess it's okay, but what does it have to do with Robert and me?"

"Everything," Mom said. She took a long drag from her cigarette again, curling her lips and blowing the smoke over her head.

"But you've told me a fable about romantic lovers," I said.

"Do you love Robert?"

"I do," I said.

"Then write your own poem to him. Don't expect me to write the poem for you."

"You want me to write a poem?"

"I'm speaking figuratively, of course."

"Okay. But still, your fable is about lovers. You know, as in a boy loving a girl."

"Ah, love. That's it, isn't it? Isn't it *all* about love? It's always one kind of love or the other, whether it be between couples like the boy and girl zebra, between a father and his son, between a mother and her daughter, or between aunts and cousins—it's always about love. It's all different, yet it's all the same. Love is where all good things begin. I thought you knew this."

I thought about what Mom had just said to me. I was about to reply to her, and then I thought about it more. Then it was like a light bulb turned on over my head. What she was saying made perfect sense.

"Where *were* you?" I asked.

"Where was I?"

"When I was younger. Where were you?"

"I was right at your side."

"But you were invisible."

"Only because you were too young to see. Only because you were too young to hear. Do you want another slice of cake? We have plenty here."

"No thanks," I said.

"Coffee?"

"No more coffee."

"Let me ask. Are you and Martha sure that Robert stole the coins?"

"Yes, we're sure."

"Then show him your love. Start with love, then work your way forward."

"Mom?" I said.

She was suddenly fading. I mean to say that her image was disappearing. She flickered, and the sound of her maternal voice cracked and sputtered until there was nothing left but her bright-red lips, saying nothing. Then the lips popped like a champagne cork, and she was gone. Her cigarette consequently fell out of midair and was smoldering on the table. I picked up the lit cigarette and snuffed it out in the ashtray.

"Damn," I said.

Then I was no longer in the kitchen. So, where was I? I was in the middle of nowhere. There was nothing but blackness and the twinkling pinpricks of distant stars, and the earth was floating in space far behind. It was *way* back there.

I looked at the instrument panel, and I realized I was in trouble. No one back home could hear or see me. No one could help. Mars was my destination, but I was far off course, hurtling through the vacuum of space at twenty-five thousand miles per hour. Who knew where I'd wind up?

It was a science fiction dream. God, how I loved science fiction dreams. They were pretty cool. When I was a kid, I used to read Ray Bradbury stories right before I went to bed, hoping to relive the stories in my dreams. This never actually worked, but that didn't stop me from trying again and again. And now? Is this what was happening? No, I read nothing that night that would have prompted it. In fact, I hadn't read a science fiction story for years.

CHAPTER 26

TWO KINDS OF PEOPLE

———————•◦•———————

It was hard to believe that I had volunteered for such an insane and dangerous mission. No one else wanted to do it. I had been warned of all the fatal possibilities and told I might never, ever see Martha or Robert again. Listen, I thought they were just trying to scare me, trying to see whether I was really made of the right stuff. Well, I passed their test, but now? I had this sinking feeling that I was about to die. And why? It was because I *was* about to die. I would run out of oxygen. I would suffocate, and that would be that. It would soon be the end of Robinson Cahill, the end of the idiot who had enthusiastically agreed to let NASA shoot him into outer space like a ball from a giant cannon toward the planet Mars.

There was a clock on the instrument panel, but clocks mean nothing, and calendars even less when you're away from earth, never to return. Do you think some bug-eyed alien from the far reaches of the galaxy is really going to give a rat's behind about how many times the earth has revolved around the sun since Jesus bought the farm? He won't even know who Jesus is, let alone care. He'll probably pity the living hell out of me. He'll probably see me the same way we see a lost dog on a busy freeway, dodging the cosmic traffic, panicked, trying to stay alive. Or perhaps this alien, upon discovering me in my ship, would feel threatened and blow me to smithereens before I would have a chance to say a single friendly word to him. And why? It was possible that the propagation of sound waves by a saliva-drenched eating orifice was considered by his species to be an overt act of aggression.

I was amusing myself with these annoying thoughts because at first I couldn't think of anything better to do with my free time. I still had some time. I still had light and power, and it occurred to me that the onboard computer *was* working. A game of chess sounded good. Of all the things I

265

could do with this crazy computer, that's what came to my mind. I would play a game of chess against it. Back on earth, it had been programmed to play but not to win every game. It was designed to let me win now and again. It had been programmed with weaknesses and lapses in judgment I could exploit. The eminent psychologists at NASA determined that it wouldn't be rewarding or any fun for me to play against an unbeatable opponent.

So I said to the computer, "How about a game of chess before we run out of oxygen?" An instant response. On the instrument panel, a chessboard flickered to life on the touch screen, and below the board were the words "Your move, Robinson." A nice touch, adding my first name. In addition to the chinks in its game, the computer was also programmed to be personable. Mildly personable, mind you, and not obsequious. This made me chuckle. I reached over to the screen and moved a pawn forward.

"Your move, Grandpa," I said. No, I wasn't losing my mind. Not yet. I just figured it would be a lot more entertaining for me to pretend I was playing chess against my grandpa rather than against a soulless collection of circuit boards, electrons, and codes. And I pretended Grandpa spoke back to me.

"You always move the same pawn forward to start the game," he said. "You sure you want to make that move?"

"I'm sure," I said.

"Okay, it's your funeral."

"Speaking of funerals," I said, "I have a question for you."

"Yes?" Grandpa said.

"Can you tell me something?"

"I'll tell you what I can. What's on your mind? It's your move, by the way."

"I'd like to know what it's like to die."

"As in really die? As in die like at the end of your life? As in the end of the long and winding road?"

"Yes," I said.

"Well, yes, I can tell you exactly what it's like. But why the sudden interest?"

"Because I'm about to die."

"So you are," Grandpa said. "So you are." He was looking at the instrument panel, and the oxygen gauge said it all.

"I'll be running out soon."

"Yes, I can see that."

"This mission was a complete failure."

"You won't be landing on Mars?"

"God knows how far off course I am."

"Yes, God knows."

"So, what's it like?"

"I wouldn't worry much about it. It's not near as bad as everyone imagines."

"But what happens?"

"Well, at first you'll feel light headed, and your limbs and heart will heat up and tingle. It's like downing a great, big glass of good whiskey, except much more potent. It's a very pleasant feeling. I take that back. It's a wonderful feeling. From head to toe you'll feel all weightless and euphoric, and suddenly you'll have the sensation that you're ready to learn. I don't know how else to describe it. You'll be ready to learn. You'll have an open mind, and you'll *want* to learn."

"Learn what?"

"You'll want to learn about everything, all things good and evil, hot and cold, dark and light, high and low, to and fro, in and out, dull and sharp. You'll be so ready that it'll surprise you. You'll feel like an empty glass vessel about to be filled by the gods with their finest wine, like a blank notebook about to be loaded with Einstein's notes, like an empty theater stage about to be brought to life with howling thespians and the lines and scenes of every play ever written and every play yet to be written. My words don't do the feeling justice. Until you've felt it for yourself, you can't imagine what it's like to want to learn like this. You'll feel like with one breath you could inhale and exhale the entire solar system and understand every cubic inch of it. You were going to Mars? Hell, you're going so far beyond Mars when you die that it will astonish you. No, the word *astonish* doesn't do it justice. There is no verb both profound and intense enough to describe this burning desire and capacity to learn."

"And then?" I asked.

"And then it will all come to you, slowly at first. You'll experience images, lots and lots of brilliant images, and then sounds, smells, and flavors. And you'll experience the texture of time. It will be the oddest sensation. It will bend, turn, propagate, and pulsate in ways you never thought possible. And everything will suddenly twist up as one and will suddenly make sense. All questions will be answered. All the puzzles will be solved. And all the *t*'s will be crossed, and the small *i*'s will be dotted. Good and evil will be one, greed and generosity will marry, and lust and repulsion will meld and bubble, like in a pot of a witch's brew.

"And lo and behold, your opinions will fall from your psyche like dead leaves from an autumn deciduous tree. You will now have faith in one thing and one thing only, faith that everything in the universe is correct, balanced, and precisely as it should be. And in this process, your ego will dissolve like sugar into a cup of hot tea. You will no longer be you. You will be the air, billowy clouds, earth, fire, and splashing, running, and trickling water. You'll cry for just a second, and then you'll forget your name."

"It sounds frightening," I said.

"Frightening? No, not at all. You'll feel as safe as an infant cradled in its mother's arms. And finally, you will see why it's important that you do die. You'll understand that no one and nothing lives forever, not even God. Without death, the whole plan falls flat on its face. God bless death, Robinson. Without death, life means nothing. In fact, you will now know for sure that death *is* life."

"And after that?"

"Nothing. What else can there be but the quiet absence of everything? You'll know a glorious silence, peace, and an unending world of solitude. There is not even the slightest hint of an amoeba's whisper. In one final flash of black brilliance, all is gone."

I thought about all my grandpa had just said. "It seems so pointless," I said.

"It will make good sense when you get there."

"Can you promise me that?"

"That's the one thing I *can* promise."

"Wake up!" a woman's voice said.

"Wake up?" I asked.

"You fell asleep. We're not done yet."

I opened my eyes. I was not in space, and I was not on my failed mission to Mars. I was not playing chess or talking to my grandpa. Instead, leaning and shaking my shoulder was Dr. Bell, my psychiatrist. How long had I been sleeping? It seemed like I'd been dreaming for hours. It was very confusing. "How long have I been asleep?" I asked.

"Less than a minute. You were recounting your house, and then *boom*; the next thing I knew, you were out of it, snoring up a storm."

"I was talking about my house?"

"That was my word."

"Yes, of course," I said. "I remember now. We were doing that word association thing. House, house—I was talking about my house. Was I done?"

"We were about to move on to my next word."

"Yes, I remember that."

"Are you sure you're okay?"

"I'm fine," I said. "I'm just a little disoriented." The doctor walked back to her chair and sat down. She picked up my file so she could continue to take notes.

"Are you ready for a new word?"

"I'm ready," I said.

"The next word is *table*."

"Table?"

"What comes to mind? What is the word making you think about?"

"When I think of *table*, I think of a card table. I think of our card table, turning it upside down and trying to figure out how to fold up the damn legs. For some reason—only God knows why—this always makes me a little crazy. I also think of our coffee table and the coasters Martha buys for it. Every six months or so, she comes home with a new set of coasters, I suppose, because for some reason she's never content with the coasters she already has. I always ask her, 'If you don't like the coasters you have, then why did you buy them in the first place?' This always makes her a little angry, and she says I just don't understand. And she's right. I don't.

"The word *table* also makes me think about our dining room table. It's an antique, a nice piece of furniture. We only sit at it during special occasions, like for a Thanksgiving dinner. I remember when we had our entire family over to celebrate the holiday some years ago. There was

Martha, me, and Robert. My dad was there with us, and so were Martha's mom and dad. There was Martha's sister, Ida, and her husband, Ed, along with their twenty-year-old daughter, Courtney. Joining us that day was also Courtney's good friend, Jenna. I will never forget that dinner. It began okay. We all looked like that famous Norman Rockwell painting. Martha and her sister brought out the food for us. There was a big turkey, mashed potatoes, yams, cranberries, crescent rolls, green beans, and a bowl of stuffing. You know, it was the whole nine yards. Then we all got to talking, and Courtney decided to light the Norman Rockwell painting on fire. It all went up in flames."

"What'd she do?" the doctor asked.

"She decided this was an appropriate time to announce that she was gay and that Jenna was her lover. She said Jenna was going to move in with her that month. Well, if that wasn't a mood changer. All the laughter stopped, and everyone suddenly became serious and quiet. She may as well just have informed us that she was a serial killer or a porn star. It was pretty bad. I think Ed took it the worst. The poor clown just sat at the table, staring at Courtney incredulously. Ida acted like the news was no big deal, but she was just as flabbergasted as her husband. I don't think Martha was surprised, and I think she'd suspected Courtney was gay for some time. Robert didn't seem to care one way or the other. He just asked for someone to pass him the mashed potatoes. And me? I guess I was like Martha in a way. I had also had my suspicions about Courtney being gay for some time."

"Did Courtney's parents eventually accept the fact that she was gay?"

"That's a good question. I mean, they put on a pretty good show. They said it was all okay with them, and they didn't make a big fuss about it during the months that followed. And they treated Jenna like they would've treated any other good friend of their daughter. But there was something Ed said to me a year or so later that caught my attention, and maybe it revealed more about his feelings than he was letting on."

"What'd he say?"

"The two of us were alone in the front room of his house, and he was pouring me a Scotch. He said, 'Children, Robinson. No one tells you when you first decide to have them, but they will break your fucking heart.'"

"Oh my," the doctor said.

"I felt for the guy."

"But he still loved Courtney?"

"He did. I guess that was the problem. If he didn't love her, she wouldn't be able to hurt him."

The doctor thought about this for a moment, staring at me. Then she asked, "How about *night*?"

"Night?"

"For your next word."

"Yes, *night*," I said. "I guess for most people night is a nice and quiet resting time. It's a time to recharge the old batteries. But you know what? Night for me is busier and more frantic than any day. Night is when I dream. Night is when it all happens. Night is when my mind runs amok, when my thoughts go a little wild. It's a period of time when I'm no longer restrained by the shackles of the real world. It's colorful, frenzied, and as hot as the sun. It's fast paced and often all but completely out of control. Night is when I feel, when I laugh, when I cry, when I scream, when I cringe, and when I shiver in fear. When I wake up in the morning, I'm often exhausted, and I'm so relieved that the dreams are over. Yes, my days are a relief. I know that most people will tell you that it's just the opposite, but I think we experience reality to gain strength and to prepare ourselves for our nights, not the other way around. I'm not sure I would've said this to you when I was younger. When I was younger, my dreams prepared me for my days, but now I feel like my days are a calm sojourn from my dreams. Not always but most of the time, if that makes any sense. Does that make sense to you?"

"I think I understand."

"Also, I think you can learn ten times as much about a man if you can live with him in his dreams than you will ever learn by living with him in his reality. Night is where you'll find the soul of men. Night is the essence of society. Night is the throbbing, blood-pumping heart of civilization. Daylight is for all the chrome and machinery, while night illuminates the true spirit and marrow of men. When the sun drops out of sight, life begins. When we dream, we are as whole, unequivocal, and true blue as we'll ever be. We are stark naked. We all stand at attention, unclothed and exposed."

The doctor was writing all this down. She then set down her pen and looked at me. "What about bed?"

"Bed?"

"For your next word."

"Ah, *bed*. Well, I'll tell you what this immediately makes me think of. It's kind of weird. I mean, you'd think I would think of my bed at home. Maybe of Martha? Maybe of our sex life? But, no that's not what I first think of. The first thing that comes to mind for me is my father and the hospital bed he was confined to during his last days. You know, I dream of Dad dying many different ways. I don't know why, but I don't ever seem to be able to put my finger on his ultimate cause of death. But the most popular cause seems to be cancer. This is how I most often see the old man dying. In any event he spent at least a week in that hospital room, boxed in by those four beige walls, confined to that awful bed. That bed! He always complained about how uncomfortable it was, but there was nothing we could do. Hospital beds are hospital beds, and that's life. That's what I told him. We did bring in his pillow from home, and I think that helped a little. But I look back now and think maybe we should've just let him die at his home, in his own bed. I remember Robert. Robert was there during those last days. I mean, he was *there*."

"I don't think I understand."

"Martha and I would visit for a while each day, but Robert was there for hours. From the time he got out of school to the time he had to come home to sleep, he was in that hospital room, keeping my father company. And I've always wondered what they talked about during all those hours. Robert never really told us, and we didn't pry. Martha and I talked about it and decided that Robert's talks with his grandpa were personal and private, that if he wanted to share any details, he would do so at his own pace. I was a little jealous of how close the two of them became. Robert had a special bond with my father that I never had, and Robert was such a good grandson. I'm sure the time he spent there meant the world to Dad."

"Did Robert ever finally tell you what the two of them talked about?"

"He did reveal a couple of stories my dad shared with him, one being my about my experience playing flag football in the eighth grade for Coach Backlund. Did I tell you that story? I have a lot of regret."

"Regret?"

"Did I tell you the story?"

"You did, in one of our prior sessions. Your father signed you up for football, and at the first play of the game you were bashed in the face so that you got a bloody nose. Your mom ran out and took you off the field, and ultimately she took you off the team."

"Yes," I said. "I should've stuck with it."

"You said you hated it."

"I didn't hate it. I was afraid of it. I should've faced my fears. I've always regretted that. And I let my dad down. I felt terrible about that. My dad was just trying to help me become a man. He was right, and I was wrong. And I hate to say it, but my mom was wrong too. I should've got up off the grass and got back into the game. On the next play, I should've hit that kid in *his* nose."

"What else did Robert say your father told him? You said there were two stories."

"The second story my dad told Robert about me concerned the first piece of writing I had published. I have no idea how my father even remembered this. It was a short story about a kid who starts up his own car-detailing company. It was purchased by a local magazine that paid me a pittance for it. It was the first time I'd ever been paid to write anything, and while it was hardly worth the effort financially, I was very happy that someone actually thought one of my stories was worth publishing and paying for.

"Anyway, Dad told Robert about the story, and he told Robert it was the best short story he'd ever read. He said I had a real gift for writing, and while I had never become a best-selling author, my work was worthwhile. Then he explained to Robert that there were two kinds of people in the world. He said there were businessmen, and there were artists. He told Robert that businessmen were people who were capable of getting paid for what they did, enough money to live on. Artists, on the other hand, were people like me who toiled and labored for nothing. My dad said some so-called artists were really just businessmen, but a few artists—the true artists—were artists because they loved what they did. My dad told Robert there was no one purer of heart and more admirable than a true artist, and he said our society needed artists. He told Robert not to look down on me for making so little money. He said he should look up to me.

He told Robert that artists are the real heroes in this day and age. He said they were the men and women future historians would look at when it came time to judge the value of our era. 'Who do you know more about?' he asked Robert. 'The men and women who fattened their bank accounts by sheltering, defending, doctoring, feeding, supplying, and clothing all the Renaissance's unwashed masses? Or Michelangelo? We know about Mike, of course. Mike and his fellow artists.'"

"This *is* surprising."

"Isn't it?"

"How did it make you feel?"

"Angry at first."

"Why angry?"

"Because my dad never told me any of this to my face. Not once did he say anything even remotely resembling it."

"It's not unusual for people who are about to die to have sudden insights."

"I guess," I said. "Of course, I know I'm no Michelangelo, but I understand what my dad was trying to say."

The doctor wrote something into my file. Then she looked up at me and said, "It was nice of Robert to tell you about this; of course, it's possible that your father never said it. Robert could've made the whole story up."

"Made it up? Why?"

"To please you."

"That is possible."

The doctor set my file on her desk and her pen down beside it. She said, "There are two men in the waiting room I would like you to meet."

"Two men?"

"They contacted me yesterday, and I told them about our appointment today. I said it would be okay for them to join us. I hope you don't mind."

"I guess I don't."

"Let me get them then," the doctor said, and she stood up. She walked to the door and opened it. She motioned for the men to enter, and into the room they came. I couldn't believe my eyes. It turned out that they were the two annoying detectives from the police department, Rudy and Eddie. "These men would like to ask you a few questions," the doctor said.

"I bet they would."

"We have your son in custody," Rudy said. "Now we just need to get your side of the story."

"You have Robert?"

"He's safe with us," Eddie said.

"How could he be safe with you? You're the ones trying to persecute him."

"He's in good hands," the doctor said. "I've known these two men for years. They've handled many of my patients."

"They have?"

"This isn't my first rodeo," the doctor said, and everyone except me laughed.

I started to stand so I could leave, but Rudy said, "Please stay seated, Mr. Cahill. Be patient with us. This won't take too long."

I reluctantly remained in my chair. Rudy and Eddie sat down on a sofa, and the doctor took her seat back behind her desk. Would I lie to the men, or would I tell the truth? I wasn't sure yet. I let them speak first.

CHAPTER 27

BEEP, BEEP, BEEP

———————•◦•———————

"We have some questions for you," Rudy said. "Can we rely on you to answer them honestly?"

"It shouldn't be a problem," I said.

"Shouldn't be or won't be?"

I thought about this and replied, "It won't be." Of course, it was going to depend on the questions. Surely these two jokers knew that if they backed me into a corner, I might be less than honest. That was just the name of the game when it came to talking to cops.

"What is your favorite color?" Rudy asked me.

"My favorite color?"

"Yes," Rudy said.

"I don't know. Blue, I guess."

"Do you have a dog?"

"No dog and no cat."

"No pets at all?"

"None," I said. "Not even a canary."

"What kind of car do you drive?"

"A Toyota."

"Do you have a nickname for your car?"

"No nickname."

"I see," Rudy said. He then looked at Eddie and said, "No pets and no nickname for his car."

"Interesting," Eddie said, rubbing his chin.

Rudy looked at me again and asked, "Have you been to Hawaii?"

"Yes," I said.

"How many times?"

"Four, I think."

"Do you have a favorite island?"

"We're partial to the Big Island."

"Ah, the Big Island."

"My wife also likes Maui."

"Did I ask about your wife?" Rudy asked, now a little perturbed. "I was asking specifically about you."

"Okay," I said.

"Let's keep our ducks in a row. Your wife is in just as deep into this mess as you, but her culpability is an entirely different issue. A whole different ball of wax."

"If you say so."

"What's your favorite candy bar?"

"My favorite candy bar?"

"You heard me."

"I like Milky Ways. But I also like Hershey bars."

"But which is your favorite?"

"I guess I'd have to say a Milky Way."

"Very interesting."

"Interesting, how?" I said. "What in the world do favorite colors and candy bars have to do with your investigation of my son?"

"We'll ask the questions," Rudy said. "We'll do all the asking, and you just give us answers."

"But your questions aren't making any sense."

"To a layman, perhaps they aren't."

"We've been doing this a long time," Eddie said. "We know exactly what we're doing."

I looked at the doctor, who had been sitting quietly. She nodded, indicating that I should continue.

"Okay," I said to Rudy. "Keep going."

Rudy said, "Here's a little riddle for you. What do you throw out when you want to use it but take in when you don't want to use it?"

"You're asking me a riddle?"

"Do you know the answer?"

I thought for a moment about this and said, "How about a Frisbee?"

"No, no, no," Rudy said.

I thought a little longer and said, "How about a fishing line?"

"Not exactly."

"No?" I said.

"The correct answer is a ship's anchor," Eddie said. "That's the answer we were looking for."

"But a Frisbee and a fishing line also work."

"Those aren't the responses we wanted," Rudy said, shaking his head. "You should give your answers more thought. You should be putting yourself in our shoes. You should be paying closer attention."

"Fine," I said.

"See if you can get this one. Every man has one, and some are longer than others. The pope doesn't use his, and most men like to give theirs to their wives. What thing am I talking about?"

"I don't know," I said. "I mean, I can give the obvious answer, but it's probably not what you're looking for."

"The answer is a last name," Eddie said. The detectives laughed, and so did the doctor.

"That's kind of dumb," I said.

"Cop humor," Rudy said.

"What does being a cop have to do with anything?"

"Everything," Rudy said.

Eddie then screwed up his face and asked, "Why are you such a lousy father?"

"Am I a lousy father?"

"Isn't it obvious?"

"What have I done to make you think I'm a lousy father?"

"Lousy son, lousy father," Eddie said.

"We've seen a lot of fathers," Rudy said. "And we've seen a lot of sons."

"We've seen it all," Eddie said.

"From the worst to the best."

"And you are definitely not one of the best," Eddie said, and again, everyone except me laughed.

"What exactly is your problem with me?" I asked. I heard my voice, and I was coming across a little angrier than I had planned.

"Don't get your hackles up."

"Yeah, watch the hackles, pal."

"Seriously," I said. "You guys seem to have it in for me. You've been on my case ever since you first came into my house. I've tried to cooperate, but rather than say thank you, you now choose to insult me. Maybe I should just hire an attorney. Is that what you want me to do?"

"It might not be a bad idea," Rudy said.

"Yes, all things being considered," Eddie said.

"All *what* things being considered?"

"You know, your guilt and all."

"My guilt over what?"

Rudy leaned back and sighed. He said, "I think what you need is a fable."

"The last thing I need is another fable," I said. "I need another fable like I need a hole in my head."

"Just listen."

"Yeah," Eddie said. "Sit still and listen."

"If I must," I said.

"This is about a king," Rudy said. "The king was visited by a learned man named Shridutt who taught the king many things about the ins and outs of life, thus making the king a much better ruler. When it came time for Shridutt to leave, the king wanted to express his gratitude, so he gave Shridutt a precious gold and ruby necklace to commemorate their time together. On his way back to his village, Shridutt was held up by a robber, who killed him and made off with the necklace. Upon hearing of this, the king sent his men after the robber, and they brought him back to the palace. The king took the necklace back and had the robber hanged.

"But the hanging didn't satisfy the king. He felt terribly guilty about Shridutt's death, for, as he saw it, if he hadn't given the man the necklace, he would never have been killed by the robber. He cursed himself daily for his bad judgment, and he became very ill, refusing to eat or drink, punishing himself over his guilt. The royal doctors were not able to cure him no matter what they tried, and then one day the queen heard of a shaman who said he had the power to bring Shridutt back to life. It seemed like this shaman had the perfect solution to the king's dilemma, so the queen summoned him to the palace. The king asked this shaman if he could also bring the robber back to life, and the shaman said no, that he could only bring back one person. 'Well, in that case,' the king said, "we will not bring Shridutt back to life.' Shocked at the king's sudden refusal to bring back Shridutt, the shaman and the queen asked him why this was his decision. The king said if they brought Shridutt back to life, the robber would no longer be guilty of murder, and thus he should not have been hanged for it. 'You are absolutely right,' the shaman said, and he left the palace. For the rest of his life the king lived in misery with his guilt."

"And?" I said.

"That's the end of the fable," Rudy said.

"I don't get it. What does any of that fable have to do with me?"

"Nothing."

"Nothing? Then why did you waste my time with it?"

"Because it's a good fable," Rudy said.

"Didn't you like it?" Eddie asked.

"Honestly? I thought it was stupid."

"No wonder you've been such a lousy father. And a lousy son. And for that matter, probably not a very good husband either."

Everyone started laughing again, and I blinked. It was hard to believe what I was now seeing. I was no longer in the doctor's office. Rudy, Eddie, and the doctor had vanished. Had I been hallucinating? Had I made the whole thing up in my mind?

I was in my space capsule. I was still hurtling through the blackness of space. "I take it we're done playing chess," my grandpa said.

"I'm finding it difficult to concentrate," I said. "The fable definitely didn't help."

"No soap, radio."

"Yes, something like that."

"It isn't pleasant, being judged," a voice said. It was a familiar voice. Yes, I knew who it was. He was now sitting to my left, strapped into his seat. It was Plato.

"What are you doing here?" I asked.

"The same thing you're doing. I'm flying through space at twenty-five thousand miles per hour, heading nowhere."

"This is awful."

"I know this is going to sound obvious, but have you tried turning the ship around?"

"There are no manual controls. Everything is done from the ground. I lost contact with all of them a couple of hours ago. It appears there's nothing they can do."

"That's tough."

"I don't know what to do."

"Maybe you can count your blessings."

"Count my blessings?"

"Whenever things are difficult for me, I find it useful to count my blessings."

"I'm about to suffocate to death."

"Well, there's that."

"What's this going to do to Martha and Robert?"

"It's going to leave them without a husband and a father. They're going to miss you something awful."

"What was I even thinking, agreeing to fly to Mars in this defective hunk-of-junk tin can?"

"You probably anticipated things going off a little better. You probably thought they'd be proud of you, being the first man to land on Mars."

"Maybe."

"And maybe they *are* proud of you, despite everything. Then again, maybe they're just terribly disappointed."

"Or maybe both or maybe neither. Who the hell knows? It was dumb of me. That's a fact. What crazy wires got crossed in my brain that made me think I had to be a hero? I'm no hero. That's obviously not who I am. Why couldn't I just have been Robinson Cahill, a husband and father who went to work each day and brought home his paychecks, who mowed the lawn and cleaned the cars on weekends, who took Robert to football games on Sundays, and who didn't spend all hours of the day and night locked up in his study with his confounded computer, playing make-believe and shooting for the stars? Always shooting for the stars. God, what a fool I've been."

"You had it all in the palm of your hand."

"I did, didn't I?"

"And you just tossed it all away," Plato said, and I looked at him.

"You don't have to agree with me."

"You know what they say," Plato said. "When you're right, you're right."

"Jesus," I said. Now I was staring at the oxygen gauge. We were so close to zero.

"I know a good fable," Plato said. "Now might be a good time for me to tell it."

"Please, no more fables. I've had it up to here with fables."

"Very well. I was just trying to help."

"I have something to say," a woman's voice said. I turned and looked. Plato was no longer seated beside me. Instead it was Gabriela. At least I thought it was her. Yes, it was her, but she looked so different. She was no longer the young and vibrant girl in my dreams. Instead, she was a sixty-something-year-old woman with wrinkles all over her face, gray hair, and yellow, coffee-stained teeth.

She laughed when I looked at her and said, "Not exactly what you were expecting?"

"You're older," I said.

"So are you."

"I guess I am. What are you doing here?"

"I've come to ask you a favor."

"Which is?"

"Stop dreaming about me."

This embarrassed me. I wondered how she knew. "I'm so sorry," I said. "I didn't know you knew anything about my dreams."

"Of course I knew about them. This has been going on since we were in high school."

"And it bothers you?"

"How would you feel? What if some person you didn't know from Adam was always dreaming about you? What if he or she had you doing things you knew you'd never do? What if they had you intimately loving a person you didn't even know?"

"Maybe I'd be flattered," I said. I didn't really mean to say this, but I said it. It was a dumb thing to say.

"Flattered?" Gabriela said. "Is that how you think I feel? You must have a very high opinion of yourself."

"Not really."

"For years you have been having your way with me, and I'm here to tell you enough is enough."

"You've made your point."

"And lay off your kid."

"Lay off Robert?"

"What he did when he stole those coins was nothing compared to what you've been doing to me over the past forty years. Do you think there's even any comparison? A few cases full of old coins compared to a human life? My life! Sure, you're a fine one to talk. You're a fine one to be passing judgment. You and your despicable dreams. Violating a person you don't even know just because you once happened to think she was pretty, just because she made you squirm in your seat when you were a dumb high school student. Tell me, what did I ever do to you?"

"Nothing really."

"Then why?"

"I don't know."

"I'm not going to tell you a fable, but I have three words for you. Knock it off."

"Okay," I said.

I didn't think it was possible for me to feel more foolish, and then Gabriela disappeared. "She seemed to mean business," my grandpa said.

"She did, didn't she?"

"We should've stuck with the chess game."

"You're probably right," I said.

"I don't know how he turned out that way," my mom's voice said. She was talking to Gabriela, but Gabriela was gone. "We did everything we could to raise him right."

"Mom?" I said.

"We're both here," my dad said.

"It certainly wasn't anything I did," Mom said.

"Don't look at me," Dad said. "My biggest crime was asking him to play football. So, throw me in jail."

"That awful sport," Mom said.

"It wasn't so bad," I said to my mom.

"Wasn't so bad? That mean kid on the other team could have broken your nose."

"It was no big deal," Dad said. "Noses are a dime a dozen."

I thought to myself, *Was it really possible for a person to buy twelve noses for ten cents? Probably not. Anyway, who in the heck sells noses?* I said, "Dad was right about football. I should've stuck with it."

"You could've written a few good books about it," Dad said. "People pay money to read stories about football. Now there's a subject a guy can really sink his teeth into."

"I guess," I said.

"You could've written a best seller."

Martha's dad joined in. "Better than that, you could've written a series of crime dramas. They always sell like hot cakes. There's a huge market for them, and they never get old. People continue reading them over and over. They love trying to figure the crimes out. They love seeing the bad guys get their due. All you have to do is come up with a lovable, charismatic detective or inspector. That's the secret. That's the key. The rest of it will be so easy to write that you can do it with your eyes closed."

"Just what I've always wanted to do," I said. "Write with my eyes closed."

"Don't knock it until you've tried it."

"Yeah," Martha's mom said. "Don't knock it until you've tried it."

So I didn't knock it. I thought, as repulsive as the idea was to me, it *would* be nice to sell a few hundred thousand or so books and have a few hundred thousand or so readers.

"I'm not knocking it," I said.

Now came Martha's voice, joining in with the others. "I've been telling him for years," she said. "I keep telling him to write a story about a dog. You know, as in life from the dog's point of view. People love those stories, and they're always a big success. The books sell well, and they make great movies. Wouldn't it be great to see one of your stories turned into a movie? To see your name up there on the screen? It would say, 'Based on a novel by Robinson Cahill.'"

"I'll admit it would be a boost to my ego, but that's not why I'm writing."

"Then why the hell *are* you writing?" Martha's dad asked. The man was such a concrete thinker. I really didn't like him much, and I was liking him less and less.

"I'd also like to hear the answer to his question," Coach Backlund said. Remember, he was the coach of my eighth-grade flag football team. The Swede with the crew cut.

Then my trailer park God chimed in, and so did a hooved Satan. Together they said, almost in harmony, "We'd both like to know."

Then there was Natalie, and she also wanted to know. Remember, she was the waitress I'd snuggled up with on our sofa while we watched an old Vincent Price movie while Martha was out of town. And then Vincent Price spoke, and his distinctive voice was loud and clear. "Tell me too, Robinson," he said. God, what a creepy voice the famous actor had. Then there was Jeremy Whitehouse, *the idiot who owned the coins*; and Robert, my son the thief; and Mr. Green and Mr. Caldwell, my former employers; and Gabriela's husband, Chet; and a whole slew of other people from my past, all asking the same questions.

"Why the heck are you writing?"

"Tell us now."

"Answer the question."

I felt like I was going to go crazy. "Everyone, just *shut up!*" I shouted. "All of you, stop talking *now!*"

And then there was silence. It was a dreadful, vacant, and lonely silence that could mean only one thing. It meant I was about to die. The oxygen was all but gone. The gauge on the instrument panel couldn't plummet any lower, and I suddenly began to gasp for air. What had my grandpa told me about dying earlier? He said dying would be something like downing a glass of strong whiskey, right? My body would tingle and turn warm. Didn't he say something about feeling weightless and euphoric? Well, no such luck, folks. I simply coughed, choked, and gasped like I was being throttled. It felt like someone had thrust a knife into my chest. There was no burning desire to learn about anything. No, I couldn't have cared less. All I wanted was some decent and oxygen-rich air. That was all. That was the only thing I could think about.

Then there was the beeping. Some genius engineers at NASA had decided that when the oxygen in the capsule was gone, an alarm should sound, as if whoever was trapped in the capsule needed to be reminded with an annoying alarm that he or she couldn't breathe.

Beep, beep, beep!

If you die in your dream, do you die in real life? I had heard that idea somewhere, but I had absolutely no intention of finding out firsthand.

Beep, beep, beep!

Wake up, you idiot. Wake up!

CHAPTER 28

THE FABULOUS URN

———•◦•———

My cell phone was on the nightstand, and the alarm was going off. It was six in the morning.

Beep, beep, beep.

I reached over and turned the thing off. Then I sat up in bed, looking around at the room, and I recognized all of it: the pictures hanging on the walls, the drapes at each side of the window, the chair in the corner of the room, and the antique dresser. On top of the dresser was an old China dish, and in the dish were my keys and wallet.

I took a deep breath. There was plenty of healthy oxygen in the air, and I inhaled again. It felt so good to breathe, but why? I didn't know for sure. It had something to do with a spaceship, something I'd been dreaming about. Martha was still asleep beside me, and the sun was coming up. The stars in the outside sky were fading into the pale twilight, the violet sky turning blue.

I climbed out of my covers and walked to the bathroom to pee. I flushed the toilet and looked at myself in the mirror over the sink. There I was, Robinson Cahill, me looking back at me. When I moved, he moved. When I blinked, so did he. There was nothing queer about my image in the mirror. I opened a cabinet drawer to remove my hairbrush, and I brushed my hair, still looking at the mirror. My hair was so confoundedly thin these days. It had been thinning because I was getting older, like everyone I knew, like everyone on the planet. One more night down, and all of us were another day older.

In the kitchen I made a pot of coffee. Everything in the kitchen was as it should have been, all things in their proper places. I wasn't dreaming. I was wide awake, finally. How did I know for sure? You just know, right?

When you're dreaming, you're not sure about anything, but when you're awake, you're sure of one thing. You do know you're awake.

I turned on the kitchen TV to the morning news show, and I proceeded to make breakfast. I broke a couple of eggs on the edge of a pan, and the lady on the TV talked about a traffic accident that had occurred the previous night. It had been a horrific, gory mess. Three people were killed, two of them children. They said the cops had arrested a man for drunk driving. Apparently, he wasn't injured in the wreck, and they took him straight to a jail cell.

I stirred up the eggs to scramble them, and I put a couple of slices of bread in the toaster. Eggs and toast for breakfast. And a hot cup of coffee. And the awful, stomach-churning news stories on the color TV.

Martha came into the kitchen while I was eating, and she made herself a bowl of cereal with milk. She also had half of a grapefruit. She sprinkled sweetener on top of the grapefruit and brought her breakfast to the table. The lady on the TV was now describing the weather for the day. It would be mild, no rain, and we would have partly cloudy skies. Robert was still in his room, sleeping. Since it was a Saturday, he wouldn't be out of bed until around eleven. The kid loved to sleep in. I remembered that I used to sleep like that when I was his age but no longer. I hadn't let myself sleep past six for at least thirty years.

"How did you sleep last night?" Martha asked me. She was eating her cereal.

"Good," I said.

"Not me. I slept like crap. I was tossing and turning all night."

"Were you? I didn't notice."

"I don't know how you could sleep."

"I had a lot of dreams," I said. "At least I feel like I had a lot of dreams."

"About what?"

"I don't remember."

"You don't remember anything?"

"Just bits and pieces. I remember something about being in Peru. And I remember being in Vietnam. And I remember being in a spaceship."

"A spaceship?"

"Flying to Mars, I think. But something went wrong. It turned into a nightmare."

"So," Martha said abruptly, "what are we going to do? Any bright ideas?"

She wasn't wasting any time. She was, of course, talking about Robert and the stolen coins. We had both decided the evening before to sleep on the matter, and now we had slept. It was time for us to make a decision. It was time. "How do you feel about it?" I asked.

"You first."

"I think we have to return the coins."

"Agreed, but how?"

"That's the big question, isn't it? Now we just need an answer. The right answer."

I had the strangest sensation while talking to Martha. I felt an answer had been handed over to me but that I had lost it. It had been given in my dreams, and I had lost the darn thing when I woke up. So I tried to think. I tried to recall the twisted montage of scenarios and scenes I'd been living with for the past eight hours. Somewhere, somehow, in the jumbled maze of these dreams, was the life-saving master key. Somewhere but untouchable. This key was just out of my reach, barely beyond my fingertips. It was within sight yet out of sight. I could hear the voices, but I couldn't make out what they were saying. There was a mood, and yet there was no mood at all. There were images, colorful and important images, but they were distorted and out of focus. Trying to remember my dreams was, in and of itself, resembling its own kind of dream. It was impossible, frustrating, and oddly irrational. Why was I unable to access memories in my own head? It didn't make any sense.

"I don't think we should let him off easy," I said.

"I agree," Martha said.

"And we have to come to terms with the fact that our son has a problem. He steals."

"He does."

"He's a good kid otherwise."

"I like to think so. I really do."

"He has a big heart."

"He does," Martha said. "He's a good boy."

"And he's a hard worker. And except for the stealing, he's very responsible."

"Agreed, but what do you propose we do?"

"I think we have to make him take responsibility for what he's done."

"You want to call the police?"

"No, no, that's the last thing I want to do."

"Then what?"

"I say we return the coins to your boss and tell him about Robert. We leave it up to him. We let him decide what he wants to do about it. And if he does get the police involved, we do everything we can to defend Robert, to protect him. We'll hire an attorney. We'll try to talk to Jeremy, but Robert has to learn that there are repercussions for bad behavior. He has to understand that."

"Yes," Martha said.

"So I say we tell Robert that we're going to return the coins, and we give him the option of coming along with us when we hand the coins over. Hopefully he will decide to come. I'd like to see him apologize in person to Jeremy. He needs to do that. And maybe his apology will be enough to satisfy Jeremy and calm him down. Hopefully Jeremy will see that Robert is just a good kid who made a bad decision."

"Yes," Martha said.

"Then we agree on this?"

"Yes," Martha said. "We agree."

Somehow, I felt we were missing something. Perhaps a lot. There were other things we should tell him, other things that needed to be said.

It seemed like there should be much more. It's funny how much we learn in life and how little we have to teach when the time comes for us to pass our knowledge on to our children. We have so much to offer, and we give them so little. It seems like most of our time is spent on what? On so many irrelevant things. I don't know if that's been your experience as a parent or a child, but it's been mine. If only I could take Robert's hand and lead him along that path running through the forest of my dreams so he could see all that I was seeing and all that I had seen.

I have a new fable for you. Sure, maybe you were under the impression that I didn't like fables. Well, I do like this one. It's the story of a poor man named Bhiku and a shopkeeper named Bansi Lai. The way I heard it, poor Bhiku went to Bansi Lai's shop and stood outside the front door, waiting. He stood there for hours on end until finally Bansi Lai came out of the shop and asked him, "Why are you standing outside of my shop? Are you waiting for someone?"

Poor Bhiku smiled and said, "I had a wonderful dream last night." Bansi Lai asked Bhiku what this dream was about, and Bhiku replied, "I dreamed that if I stood outside your shop long enough, a terrific fortune of gold would fall into my lap."

Bansi Lai laughed at this and patted poor Bhiku on the head. He said, "Sure, and I had a dream too. I dreamed that there was a great fortune in gold buried in your courtyard. What do you think of that?" Bansi Lai went back into his shop, laughing, and poor Bhiku took off running.

He ran home, grabbed a shovel, and began digging in his courtyard. Soon he hit a hard object, and he dug it up. It was an urn filled to its top with gold coins. He took the fabulous urn into his house and said to his amused cat, "Thank you, thank you! Thanks to Bansi Lai teasing me about my dream, I am no longer a poor man."

Robert finally climbed out of bed at a little after eleven, and he came to the kitchen for a cup of coffee. We gave him a chance to drink his coffee, and then I told him we wanted to sit down and talk.

"About what?" he asked.

"About you," I said.

"What about me?"

"Your mom and I are worried about you."

"Why?" Robert asked. He obviously had no idea we knew about the stolen coins.

"Let's just all sit down at the table," I said, and Robert sat. The three of us were now at the table, and Robert was on his second cup of coffee. "I want to start by saying we're not mad at you," I said.

"Why would you be mad at me?"

"Because we know about the stolen coin collection."

You should've seen Robert's face. It said it all. He was truly surprised. "Coin collection?" he said.

"My boss's coins," Martha said.

Robert said nothing. He was realizing it was pointless to pretend he was innocent. He was realizing, like they say in the old movies, that "the jig was up."

291

We all stared at each other for several long seconds, and finally Robert said, "How the heck did you find out?"

"I discovered the coins in your closet," Martha said.

"What were you doing in my closet?"

"Does it matter?"

"No, not now it doesn't."

"The question isn't why mom was in your closet," I said. "The question is, why did you steal the coins?"

"You're asking me?"

"Who else would I ask?"

Robert thought for a moment. Then he shook his head and looked into his coffee cup, saying, "I don't know. I honestly don't know."

It was an honest answer. The truth was, I didn't think he did know. Then I said to him, "Listen, Son, I'm going to speak to you from my heart. It's not that often that I've done this, but it's high time. You need to know a few things about me, and you need to know a few things about yourself. As for me? You need to know that I love you. And I'm sure I speak for your mom when I say she loves you too. You are our son, and we love you more than anything or anyone on this planet. You simply mean everything to us. So, are we mad at you? No, we're not even a little bit angry. Are we disappointed? No, that also isn't an accurate description of how we feel. What we feel is empathy, love, and forgiveness from the bottoms of our hearts. You are a fine young man. You are *our* young man. There isn't anything we wouldn't do to help you, and we both feel that right now you need help, not our outrage, ire, or distrust.

"No one in this world is perfect, not even close, despite what they want you to believe. We all have our own flaws and imperfections to contend with, one way or the other. It's what makes us human, but human is good. Don't ever let anyone tell you that you're less of a man for having a fault or two or three, or too many to count. It's our faults and deformities that define each and every one of us and make us who we are. They are simply colors from the rainbow. They are grains of sand. They are snowflakes. They are like clouds, always changing, always moving. The wonderful thing about being a human being is that there are few things we are that can't be changed for the better if we want to change. We are malleable. So, will you live to have regrets? Well, of course you will. We all have regrets, but regrets have a real purpose. They make our victories and successes all the sweeter.

"In any event, I'm asking you if you want our help. There isn't anything we wouldn't do for you. There is no price too steep to pay for your happiness and well-being. This isn't a gift that we're giving to you. It's something we owe you. We have owed it to you since the day our doctor removed you from Mom's belly, since the day we first decided to have a child. It is our debt, so let us pay it off. All you have to do is ask, and we will be there for you."

Well, I hadn't planned on speaking for so long, and Robert just stared at me. Honestly, I don't know what came over me. It was like I was speaking from someone else's heart, and yet it was *my* heart. A complicated heart. A tragic heart. A hilarious heart. A loving heart. I saw this heart, and I knew it in my dreams.

"I'd like your help," Robert said.

Four little words. That's all he had to say. And what did these words mean to me? They were my urn full of golden coins, that fabulous urn, unearthed from *my* courtyard, all thanks to a dream all soon to be forgotten. Presto! Now you see it, and now you don't.

CPSIA information can be obtained
at www.ICGtesting.com
Printed in the USA
BVHW031013130420
577136BV00006B/3